PARTY AT THE WORLD'S END

BOOK ONE: The Fallen Cycle

This edition published by
Mythos Media

www.PartyAtTheWorldsEnd.com

Based on FALLEN NATION:
BABYLON BURNING a screenplay by
James Curcio and Jason Stackhouse.

Cover Design:
James Curcio

Photo:
Jeff Cohn

Models:
Key
Tamar Levine
Genna Bee
Adrianne Anderson

Internal art:
Christopher DiSalvatore and James Curcio

Collaboration and Thanks:
To those that have helped inspire and develop this work, Anna Young Kelland and the rest of the Fas Ferox team; Nate Sampsel for assisting in writing the Bradley the Buyer arc; Beta, Sarah Iyer, Scott Landes and Rahul Iyer from "Babalon"; Joseph Matheny, Jason Wyse, and all the friends, family, and lovers who've helped along the way; and most of all Jazmin, my wife and best friend.

First early-release edition published as
"Fallen Nation: Party At The World's End" in 2010.
This full second edition, 2014

ISBN-13: 978-0692239070
ISBN-10: 0692239073

Contents

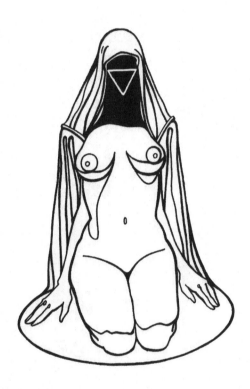

Fallen! Babylon the Great has fallen!
She has become a home for demons.
She is a prison for every evil spirit, every unclean bird,
and every unclean and hated beast.
—Revelations 18:2

0. Rome Wasn't Burnt In A Day

2021

Lola Rose Parsons. But she was always Lilith.

I still try to envision her face. It's like trying to draw blindfolded.

Of course, I could just look at a poster—she went and got famous, while I stayed in this same, slowly-bloating suburban town—but I wanted to remember not what she had become, but instead how she had been. I wanted every detail, like the force of my will could peel back time if I gave it a little attention every day. I would get the arch of her eyebrow—just an eyebrow could telegraph such mischief and vulnerability—but which was the act? And then I'd move on to her eyes and get lost, or I would second-guess the eyebrow.

It never came out quite right, so I had to start all over again.

Memory is no great artist. Or maybe it is a far greater artist than I know. How could I be sure that I hadn't invented her, or constructed that month we spent together like I did her face, trying to turn these jigsaw pieces into a coherent image? And where was she in all this? Absent.

She must have known she was trapped on the other side of the sob stories of so many ex-lovers, the one who changed everything and got away, giving that enigmatic Mona Lisa smile, except when the façade broke at that practiced moment. I can't imagine how lonely she must have been. I know now that there was a method behind it all—well, you'll see, if I do my part and get that eyebrow and eye right and can move on to the lips.

I was a sophomore back then. A virgin, which meant less to me than it seemed to for others. I had never taken a drug stronger than amoxicillin, never committed a crime, and most definitely had never been in love. It was August. The month before planes started flying into buildings.

By late September, I had been party to a car jacking. Subcutaneous ketamine injection. That's a long story. I'd seen a shooting, felt true rage—just punching and punching until you may as well be pounding sirloin. By October, and for the first time, I'd had my heart broken.

It was all a lot for a month—or was it two? And this is the only excuse I can give for the fact that I'm still obsessed with a girl I haven't seen in over a decade.

I'm honestly a little embarrassed to say how it began. I was living in an apartment complex with my parents, and in the middle of the complex was a playground, a tennis court, and a pool—which, by this time of year, was full of baby urine. Every day I walked by the swings on the way to and from the bus, and on that day, for whatever reason, I happened to climb atop the slide. I sat there, my head in one hand, and found myself thinking. I don't remember what about, only that it was a dark thought, a lonely one, a very typical thing for a teenager to think.

"You live here?" a voice asked, and I turned toward it. I had to shield the sun from my eyes and saw the outline of a girl. No face, just trails of red hair whipping around in the wind, like spun copper. A nose ring glittered in the late-day sun, a plaid skirt and punk T, backpack festooned with pins and patches. Hunting gear.

She was on the swing, kicking up her legs. "Yeah," I said. I slid down and hopped up, getting a better look at her in the process. Anyone who has surfed the Internet knows what she looks like, now. A chameleon, but the red hair never changed. I later wondered if her makeup had been tattooed on. Even a downpour never disturbed it.

"My family just moved in." She stopped, staring at something in my eyes for a split-second. I think it was my soul. (All nascent and atrophied, a suburban white-boy hiding beyond the projected swagger of Ghostface Killa.)

"Apartment 156. I'm going swimming though. Do you want to go swimming?" she asked.

"The water's full of, uh, baby urine," I said.

"Then don't drink it," she said.

8

I hadn't brought swim trunks with me, so I jumped into the water in the shorts I was wearing. She sidled up beside me and slid past. Her breasts pressed into my back, her hand grazing my stomach.

It dawns on me now, how weak most hetero men are to the wiles of women. If you're just hitting puberty? Forget about it. You are a moody cock with legs. Find a girl who knows how to wield her sexual energy like a weapon and you're done for. Most men counter this insecurity by trying to make women think they're powerless. 'You're stupid. You're ugly. You're weak'.

I had no idea about any of that, back then. I thought, 'What was special about me?' Nothing. But her attention spoke to that inner vanity, the same emotion that somehow wrapped itself like a cloak around something else— that we're not special, that we don't deserve anything, so we have to put on a front to trick other people into believing we are.

I'm stuck on this because the truth is, I can't remember what I said in response, but I'm sure it was perfectly idiotic. I've blanked out my memory, it was that embarrassing. I was anxious and aroused and confused and who the fuck was this girl anyway?

A gust of wind whipped across the water, sending an abrupt chill through me. The sky was changing suddenly. One of those freak thunderstorms that comes from nowhere. I made an 'oh well' kind of shrug and pulled myself out of the water, semi-consciously sucking in my gut as I did so, wondering what angle would present a better view for her. She watched me get out with an expression of bemusement.

I started toward the gate, expecting I'd make for home and probably feel a little regretful later, and secretly a little relieved that I wouldn't need to deal with the anxiety. The truth is, I wanted to run from this dangerous creature, with every cell in my body.

"Thunder! I bet you were going to go home and play video games or something," she said.

"I had...considered it." I stopped walking. Fuck. She still had me in her tractor beam.

"Well, how about this. Take me for a drive in the thunderstorm."

"I'm fourteen," I said, like it was a final concession. I turned back to her. "What are you, eighteen?"

"Meh. Numbers. Sixteen. Sixteen thousand," she said. "Come on."

I followed behind her to a cherry red Camaro. "You like this car?" she asked.

"Yeah."

"Me too." She ripped off her shirt faster than I could say anything and wrapped her fist in it. CRASH. Put it right through the driver's side window. She got in.

My mouth wouldn't close. I looked from side to side. Strangely, no one seemed to have noticed.

"Get in."

By the time I'd rationalized this course of action, she already had the engine growling. The first splashes of rain were pinging on the hood.

We tore off into the storm. She drove exactly the way you would imagine. Terror blotted out any joy I might otherwise have felt. My hands were cramped to uselessness by the time we were out of the complex. Pretty soon the storm hit in earnest, bending trees as it picked up.

"Getting really serious," I said, watching streams form beside us.

"And predictably enough, I don't care. Let's try this. You drive."

"What? NO!"

Let it be testament to what a fucking tool I am, that my indignation was swayed by a mere look. "It's not stealing, it's borrowing," she said. It wasn't much harder to coax me into topping out the engine on a straight away, 120 miles an hour down back roads.

"You mean you actually—" I started. I never got a chance to finish. We hit a wall of water and the car lifted clean into the air, tumbled, and slammed right side up again in four feet of water. Luck, or I don't know what, but we were completely unharmed. "FUCK!" I yelled. "Fuck. Fuck."

She surveyed the situation for a second. We were mired in the valley between two tree-lined hills. "Damnit. OK. Roll down your window," she said. "The doors will never open. Let's go."

When we got out, she climbed on the hood and stood, her arms outstretched. Lightning arced across the sky like electric effects at a Nikola Tesla event. She grabbed my hand and held it against her heart, pounding in her chest. Then she put it against mine. "Do you feel that?"

Of course I did.

She looked me in the eyes. I think this was the first time she had paid me real attention.

"You do this kind of thing often?" I asked.

"Sssssshhh," she said, suddenly serious. "Feel it. Breathe with me." The wind whistled through the grass, trees cracked, tires squealed in the distance. The music of Right Now.

I tried. My heart was still pounding in my ears. I was worried about how we could get in trouble. About where we were, and how we would possibly get home. I was cold and getting wet. I could get sick. I looked at her again. Improbably, we were standing on top of a Camaro in a rainstorm, submerged, begging to be hit by lightning. And I was spending it worrying about being cold and thinking about my mother.

"Alright, try this," she said. She turned away from me, untying her bathing suit top slowly. She turned toward me and cupped my hands on her breasts. Her nipples were hard, pleasantly cold from the rain.

All of those anxieties washed away. I felt her breath striking my breath, the engine ticking beneath us, felt the lightning arc and the leaves struggle in the wind and water, everything around us breathing out and up that long hill, the fish-eyed lens of NOW, expanding like a bubble everywhich-way in space and time.

The two of us huddled in the rain. She let the illusion permeate out of her, for that moment, that we were completely in love. It was a defining moment in my life. I would never admit it, but I've gone back to this memory almost every day since.

As I watched the torrent of water rushing down the hill, I had an unusual thought, clear as a droplet of rain before it hits the mud. We live our lives always swimming against the current. When you're as alive as I felt right then, you could swim upstream forever. What progress we're making! But...

There's always a 'but'.

Either all at once, or gradually, the current overtakes us. We are swept out to sea.

That's beautiful or terrible, depending on how you feel about what was left behind, on how attached you are to... Well, to you. But this is all we know—we came from that sea, and we return. It is inevitable. And I thought, it'd all be worth it, if I got to spend my life with a creature like this one.

She put on her top as she hopped off the car. The quiet moment where we pretended to have a life together was over, and there were other, more interesting adventures to be had. "Come on. The sky is falling."

Its rage renewed, the rainstorm bore down on the hill as we charged upward and directly into its force. This quickly became a slog against the flood. Half-submerged cars swelled past, like the prows of desolate boats. Their headlights shone eerily through murky water, and lit a group of men further up the hill. They were swaddled in jackets and scarves, which struck me as odd, because the chill of autumn hadn't really reached us yet. "Hey!" one bellowed, but they weren't looking at us. They headed toward the light, and punched the windshield of a car which wouldn't slow down for them.

"FUCKING ASSHOLE!" one screamed, another pointlessly punching out the tail light as it struggled past.

The driver stopped, even rolling down his window in the downpour.

"Are you nuts?!" he yelled. "Who the fuck are you people?" Then he laid on his horn, slamming it again and again. I wondered if he was the crazy one. Someone had just punched his car, and he was trying to talk to them? And then yeah, the horn. That'll scare them off.

"Get the fuck out!" I yelled, trying to be helpful.

One of the men laughed. "Hey, this guy has the right idea," he said, inspecting the blood trickling between his fingers. He grabbed the driver, and with one motion unbuckled him and slammed his head into the steer-ing wheel.

Another grabbed the door, yanked it open and dragged the stunned driver to the road. They piled in and drifted off into the early evening gloom.

The remaining tail light disappeared. There was a squeal, the sound of a loud splash and then a solid WHOMP as the car hit something in the darkness. Lilith laughed so hard she could barely keep on her feet, though it passed quickly.

"Second car jacking today," I said to her. This time, at least we weren't the perpetrators.

"Bet you money they slammed into that Camaro," Lilith said. The driver groaned loudly and flopped around in the water, like someone was flaying him alive.

She sighed and then put out her hand at him coquettishly. He was wearing a nice suit that was pretty much destroyed. "You lost a car, gained your life." She kissed him on the cheek. This did seem to calm him down a little.

"Close your eyes and open your mouth," she suddenly said.

He looked at me, as if my judgment should for some reason matter. "I'd do what the girl says, sir," I said, mostly curious to see what the fuck she was up to.

He closed his eyes forcefully. Rain splashed his tongue. In this light he looked like Frankenstein, blue-skinned, lightning-lit, but a childish laugh bubbled out of him, an escaping, hidden memory. Maybe he was recalling being three and having his first ice cream? I really don't know. She produced a dropper and a vial which read 'Europharm AG'.

"To laughter and forgetting," she said cryptically. One drop on the tongue.

His eyes opened, he smacked his lips. "Minty?"

"Yeah, your mouth is going to taste minty for about twenty minutes. Then you're not going to understand taste in quite the same way ever again."

She pressed a token into his hand. "The bus stop is up that hill and to the left," she said, pointing. "We're going somewhere else. Follow us, and I will snap your neck. Do you understand?"

The driver and I both looked at her in shock. She didn't wait for us to get our bearings, instead cutting off the road and into pine trees that clung to the hill. This was rain like I had never seen.

"Where are we going?" I called ahead. Track team and I still couldn't keep up with her.

"Out of the flood and into darkness," she said matter-of-factually.

Sure enough, she led me to an enormous tree which had been felled, probably minutes before, by lightning. It created a sort of lean-to space underneath. "Spend the night with me," she said.

"My parents will be worried sick," I said feebly.

"Tell them you were trapped in the rain, or tell them—look, trust me. I'm really good at lying. You'll be fine. I'll make them so glad you're still alive, they'll buy you a new bike." She bit her lip. "You really are adorable. You're a virgin, aren't you?"

My silence was answer enough. She slid under the tree effortlessly, somehow already naked.

I wasn't sure how I felt about her plan, I thought, as I climbed under the tree with her.

—

Disney movies have a strange connotation for me, thanks to Lola. Her mother would be clinking glasses in the kitchen, making her fourth martini too many, or even in the room with us. In the background Ariel would be singing with whimsical crabs or Beauty would be dancing through the ballroom, and my fingers would be buried inside Lola's cunt, working to find just the right rhythm to bring her to the edge and keep her there until she couldn't resist it any longer and was swept up in the sensation; an eyelid flutter, a sentence which trailed off to nothing but a guttural sigh.

To this day, I can't see a Disney film without being filled with a cyclone of ambivalence. It takes real skill to transform such a seemingly-innocuous piece of Americana into a national sex cult deprogramming regime. I couldn't have been the only one. How many are haunted by her taste, whenever they see a shot of Ariel, or her smell, when they hear the soundtrack from the Lion King?

I loved her smell. Everything about her was like a musk, almost overpowering but in such a delicious way. Marketing says girls should smell like hyacinths or baby-soft breezes or peach cuddles. No one wants that 'not-so-fresh feeling'. But Lola, she smelled good, you know, but she had this girl-stink like whiskey and leather mini-skirt and pussy. I crave it constantly. I'm getting distracted. I'm sorry.

The first time this happened—and it was not the only time, I was over there every fucking day and we worked our way through the entire Disney back catalog—her mother was playing cards with the two of us and her eleven-year-old sister Evelyn.

Her mother had the glassy look old alcoholics get, especially those who weren't that bright in the first place. Even then, it was a real feat keeping the pillow on her lap from jumping around like a balloon full of crickets. Her sister suspected, I think, because she would roll her eyes when we took just a second longer than normal to say "hit me" when playing jackpot. (Plus, who always has a pillow over their lap?) I discovered that I was a pretty good poker player, though. Poker face is no challenge when you're used to covertly finger fucking a nubile goddess in front of her family day after day.

Lola told me later that day the "dry old bag" wasn't really her mother. She'd been adopted. Her sister too. I really didn't get much out of her about the past. Her real mother was some kind of gypsy. Some blind bureaucracy tore them apart. That was all she told me. She didn't want to talk about why they were hiding from her sister's father, why she jumped when a door would slam. I tried, but it would just piss her off.

I thought she was just terrified of intimacy, but looking back, I think she realized she'd have to fuck-initiate half the nation if she was going to have a successful band by age twenty six, when all the rest of the world was listening to dance music. She was the main attraction and that meant living as Lilith 24-7.

No time to be a human being. No time for relationships not played on fast-forward, three years of insanity burned through in a week, over and over and over again. Babylon seemed to explode from out of nowhere, an overnight sensation. The party at the world's end. But I knew better.

One day, she said, "Before I die, everyone will know who I am."

"Why?" I asked.

"Because," she said. And she shut up and moved on to something else. Whatever she gave you is all you got. That's just how it was.

It's a little funny, and a little sad. I really wanted to be her friend. Yeah. A fourteen-year-old boy. I'm not trying to fool anyone, I couldn't be near her and not be overwhelmed with the need to fuck her. But fucking doesn't have to be a zero-sum game. It doesn't have to be a game at all.

I desperately wanted to see under her mask. I harbored this sentimentality quietly at first. But toward the end—day twenty-eight or was it nine?—I realized that I loved her, somehow. Or that I wanted to love her.

That was that.

—

It's been a long time since that week. Twenty years. Twenty years to wonder why I'd given such a shitty speech. Completely out of nowhere, too. We had just been sitting on her porch having a cigarette and it just burbled out of me.

"Fuck Lola. I love you, please let me be there for you. Any way. You want to push the envelope, let's do it. You want to... I'll drop out of school, I'll go anywhere. Do anything. When I'm with you it's like we're invincible. Run away with me. You hate your Mom. Your sister... she could come with, if that's, I mean if that's..." And that's about where my speech ended. No conclusion. Just trailing off into silence, looking for a sign that I wasn't, in fact, measuring out the rope she was going to hang me with.

She heard me, I mean she listened and seemed to understand all the words, but when it came time to respond she just giggled. Like you might giggle when your cat hops into a box and then can't find its way out. Her hand shoved past my jeans and underwear and wrapped around my balls. She squeezed them lightly. She didn't say a word.

For a second, I misread this as a good sign, and gave a giant, goofy grin. Right before she put a gun to my heart and blew my chest out the back of my rib cage.

Figuratively speaking, of course.

In fact, she never spoke to me again. She kissed me hard and then slammed the door in my face.

I stood out there in the cold, crying for an hour. My balls felt like they had shriveled up and crawled inside my body. Like I should cut an incision along the side of my thigh and shove them inside there and sew it shut, cut holes in my chest and sew my arms inside, then my legs, my whole miserable body stitched into a quivering, quadriplegic abortion. I called her a hundred times. I banged on the door, howling senselessly.

The door eventually opened a crack. Evelyn peered out at me, a half-lit cigarette dangling from her lip. For the first time, I realized she looked far more wise than her years. Eleven? I had this crazy thought that she wasn't human, that neither of them were human.

"Listen," she said.

"Oh. Alright," I said, suddenly deflated.

She seemed to struggle a moment, and then exploded. "Do you have any idea how many times I've had to deliver this speech for my sister? She's in there, right now, laughing her ass off. I don't know how to put this. She's a slut, okay? She's been one for as long as I can fucking remember, which is at least several thousand years. She is the Queen of the Sluts, the very reincarnation of the Whore of Babylon. My adopted mom's a martini glass. My step-dad is a fuck up of an ex-Marine who thinks the way to be a real man is to beat women. And I run this place. Me. I don't get a fucking childhood. I pay the bills with Mom's welfare money and read fantasy novels. That's my life. And you're standing out on my porch, at two in the morning making a scene, and I'm supposed to feel something? Please! Pull it together. Welcome to the rest of your life. Have it elsewhere."

I stopped crying. I had never heard an eleven-year-old say something like that in my entire life. I was too stunned to cry. Either something in me snapped, or my entire perspective shifted.

I can't explain it, but I went from being heartbroken to just fucking confused. And that feeling lasted a long time afterward.

In fact, I don't think it ever left.

—

I never got a chance to find out what their story really was, of course. The next day, the apartment was empty, like I had built her out of wet dreams and nebulous fantasy. Bare. Not a hair or speck of dust.

I was afraid to ask the apartment maintenance if there had been someone living there. I mean, what if they said no?

This left me with no option. I had to move on. But how?

—

My life before her was a monotonous haze. My life since has been that of a junkie, chasing the rush of that first, perfect hit. For years, I compared girls to Lola in my mind. From some of them, I even got the thing she would never do. I could actually be their friend. We were merely human.

Lilith was on some other plane of existence I touched for a mere moment because it suited her, I guess. Every time, a girlfriend would open up and it'd hit me hard. They weren't the right flavor of psychopath. I'd fuck them one last time, imagining that I was offering them to her, somehow. Like a ritual. I knew it was twisted, but that just made it more appealing.

She completely scrambled my expectations. If I called Lola a slut, she would grin ear to ear. If I had punched her in the face, I bet she would've punched right back without hesitation. That would've been foreplay, and tame at that.

One time, we broke into someone's condo. She smashed a bottle of expensive stolen tequila over the bedpost, and shoved me so hard my body punctured the drywall like a bullet through fabric. We fucked bloody in the broken glass, inside that wall, on the floor, on their kitchen table, leaving a trail of sex and crimson right out their door.

She was an artist and her art was breaking people. Cracking us like glass with her body, with her music. With our dreams. At first one at a time, and then she went mass-market with it, blazing a path across the nation.

It wasn't until years later, when I saw her perform with Babylon as Lilith, that I was certain I hadn't invented the whole thing. Sometimes, surfing Babylon's livefeed late at night, I'd catch my exes riding on her arm —like she had some kind of homing beacon in her crotch, something with the wattage to rip the heart out of your chest from a thousand miles away.

It made me happy. I hoped some small part of what Lilith—Lola—had given me was for them, too. I wasn't some kind of monster.

When I heard she was probably dead, I wrote something. More like it was written through me. It hangs on the wall now, surrounded by all these half completed sketches, an altar to this stranger who haunts my life.

She rubbed the skin off your headstone of a sternum, and painted a sad picture of herself in your eyes. We fell in love with that little peep-show projection on the inside of an iris, pictures which amount to nothing more than the thirsty moon over a spot of bloody ground. Those weren't the nothings we restless sleepwalkers knew, no place, no home, no song. So we heard her and we followed, until she went where we couldn't follow.

She went down beyond the mountains and disappeared between the crease of sky and land, like a great eyelid folding shut. No one knows what happened out in the Black Hills, but I imagine she lies buried in a rusty coffin under the stars. She had Marilyn's enchanting gaze, Hendrix's cool, Morrison's smoldering insanity, but the grave was still surely bare. Not that it mattered. Her face was burned into all our minds, forever young, the mantra of every generation's counter-culture. And on nights when the desert crickets sing her tune, they say she will rise again. On that day, there is no telling the kind of vengeance she'll demand of us. Fair is fair.

They say, when she fell from Heaven she wore a crown of seven jagged stars that slit the sky's throat. They say she loved us all, in the secret corners of our shallow sleep. They say a lot of things. They're all lies. Everything is already written.

I'm just some forgotten ex, one fan out of millions. You'll never hear from me again. But of this I'm quite certain: she will be coming back. Maybe not tomorrow. Maybe not for a thousand years. And when she does...

I turn away. Close my eyes. In my mind I draw her eyebrow, the mouth, the nose. I lose it again. But I'm getting closer.

JAMES CURCIO

I. Some Still Despair In A Prozac Nation

2012

Nothing on the face of this earth—and I do mean nothing—is half so dangerous as a children's story that happens to be real, and you and I are wandering blindfolded through a myth devised by a maniac.
— **Master Li Kao (T'ang Dynasty)**

The day nurse put on her jacket. She scrawled the final lines onto her daily report. Date: March 15th, 2012. Signature: Stephanie Anne Heickle. Her veiny hands looked fat. She was getting old, and there wasn't a damn thing to be done about it.

She explained the events of the day to her replacement, handing her a clipboard in the process.

It had been an uneventful day, she explained. No orderlies with oozing compound fractures. No flailing and howling. The worst was trying to get

'Dionysus' to take his meds, which was more like arguing with a pedantic philosophy major than dealing with a schizophrenic. He was tedious, but not usually dangerous.

Eventful days provided distraction. Home was a furnished apartment with a stained rug, an ungrateful bitch of a house cat who liked to urinate on furniture just because she could, and the obvious absence of a significant other to share it with. The invalids drooling on her at work were as close as she got to hot and heavy these days.

Dionysus was one of three patients brought in after some stunt at a mall which turned ugly. The others, Johny, a maladjusted paranoid—most paranoids were maladjusted, right?—and a gender-dysphoric turnip with a genius IQ, that referred to herself on good days as Jesus. It had never been entirely clear why they were dumped here. So many years spent working in the system and its machinations remained opaque. But it stood to reason they had to be put somewhere, after all.

Supposedly, Dionysus was the head of a cabal of domestic terrorists. She doubted it. It seemed to her that he was just as bored as she was, spinning imaginative yarns for the sake of juvenile entertainment. The only sign to the contrary was that anyone who spent too much time with him had a habit of going insane.

After signing in and waving goodbye, the night shift nurse started walking down the hallway to fourth ward, where she would check on the patients, as if they were eggs coming off the factory line. Her shoes squeaked loudly on the yellow linoleum, making her task—confirming they were asleep and hadn't cracked overnight—slightly counter-productive.

She clicked her tongue at herself, trying to walk more carefully.

—

Scritch, scritch, scritch. The night nurse waddles through the hallways on those god-awful rubber-soled shoes. Back and forth. I can't rationally blame her pacing for my insomnia, but I do it all the same.

I feel the walls leering in at me each night, as I roll around in my lice-infested bed, my eyelids clenched shut. They will probably look like two desiccated grapes by morning—swollen, sticky, and purple-veined—as I toss back the meds with bitter-tasting water. I just finished counting the blocks again. (There are 551 cinder blocks, 104 and a half floor tiles, and 25 asbestos-dusted ceiling tiles in my room.)

I've gone by Dionysus for a long time now. Good a name as any. But what's really in a name? I think about this often. Was it thanks to my namesake that a sentence of no sex or music and terrible food was such an unimaginable hell? Bored is bad. Bad for me, and even worse for the staff. I get creative when I get bored. Maybe those who tend the mental health machine are as much slaves as we are. I wouldn't know, stuck as I am on the inside of the metal-insulated plate glass.

It's 'depressive ideation', the doctors say, to think about the poisonous PCBs, polluting our bodies' water by proxy. It is an 'obsessive fixation' to mention the soil, leached of its vital nutrients, leaving us all as hollow as dried gourds. Granting dreams equal reality with waking was 'magical thinking'. They had a name for everything. A real obsession with sickness. They saw it everywhere.

The lie is grinning talk show hosts, Prozac, Reality TV, the American Dream of normalcy, homogeneity, safety. The natural state of the human animal in troubling times is not happiness. Show me a man grinning in the trenches as the bombs fall, and I will show you a lunatic.

They say that you can remain conscious for four minutes after your head is severed from your body. This entire nation is just like that head, desperately trying to tell itself that it was all a bad dream.

The first couple of months in this place, I was sure the story wouldn't end here. I held out hope. I was, after all, just an overeager, idealistic kid. I thought I could break the cultural brainwash by hopping on a table with a toy gun and scream "You're free!" Apparently, that gets you incarcerated these days.

The terrorists didn't just fly planes into buildings. After the World Trade center was blasted to the ground, many in the States, certainly many in New York, witnessed an interesting transformation. In the weeks that followed, we looked at one another with new eyes. We were snapped awake, startled as if from a dream, and though frightening, there was also a sense of possibility, even hope, in those new eyes. We all operate under the mandates of a myth—until we are shown, in a stark way, that the previous illusion cannot hold.

If you brave that passageway with eyes open, you spy just a fleeting glimpse at the naked truth, before she is again wrapped in new cloth. Collectively, we couldn't face our nakedness. Instead of hope, we got fear. A solemn, reverent fear that feared laughter most of all. Somewhere in that twisted rubble lies the shattered remains of this country's sense of humor. (I admit that the Shahada flag flying behind us in our propaganda video may have been a shade too far.)

Bottom line: ideas don't count for a whole lot in this world, but on their own, they're mostly benign. Ideals, on the other hand, get you a special jacket with one sleeve. Ideals get you shot.

I lost that idealism as months turned into a year. Our guerrilla street teams of lunatics—whole lot of good they were to the two of us who weren't supposed to get caught.

Jesus was lost to us all, wandering endlessly in an inner world of possibility. She would rather bask in an inner Eden than live in a world that deifies the flat-line of an EKG, a world without moods or personality, a place where stability only equals stagnation and where genocide and rape in the name of national interest is fine, so long as you choke down the meds and ride the neon escalator to zombie-land. Who could blame her?

And Johny. Well. We're all a bit worried about Johny.

Socrates said, "An unexamined life isn't worth living," didn't he? Well, an examined life inside a black box isn't a life at all. Each day atrophies my soul. I want to be drumming my hands to pieces deep in the woods. And with this goddamned three foot tall Venusian goddess squatting just behind my shoulder? Cow teats jangling and flapping wetly, her breath sweet like honey and milk with the copper tang of blood—I mean, how can anyone expect to get any rest with that? It's just not right.

Fuck is it ever hard to get to sleep around here.

—

The next day, I was in the rec room. The drugs were just starting to wear off, and there was some awful cartoon playing on a beat up TV hanging above us.

"What's on the toob today?" Johny mumbled.

"I don't know, man. You're the one that's been watching," I said, trying not to make eye-contact. I think I still felt guilty about how he got locked in this place, though the blame for that really lay at Bradley the Buyer's feet.

Johny shrunk like a hermit crab into his scrubs. Then he rolled his eyes at me, and did a complete one-eighty in affect. Pointing at the television, he yelled, "I played your games, bought your albums and wore your fucking t-shirts! I was a pawn in your shit-show! The only solution to a circle is a straight line, a straight beeline out, over, beyond! The Mother Hive Brain syndicate must be the line, beeline! Hit them where it counts. I...*triangle!*" he exclaimed, leaning back, his eyes bugging out.

"Listen. You don't want to clue them into our plot," I said conspiratorially.

"Triangle! Beep! A beep it goes!" He looked around suspiciously as he linked three paper clips together in a triangle, dipped it in nearby table syrup, and stuck it to his forehead. Regally, as if it were a crown. "This is how I contact them. Jam the signal! Ha..."

"Oh hey, that's great," I said, wondering what kind of Alchemical formula might turn me invisible.

Suddenly hopeful, he chewed on a nail, and then asked me, "Will you pass it up the chain? You know. Get a message to Bradley... or—or Gabriel?"

He handed me a crumpled paper.

—

White walls are here forever, because they caught me Working. Bombed the Hive building. The imaginary flames danced and sang about me. Millions of souls were freed from slavery to the Great Eye, Novus Ordo Seclorum, Eye

of Shiva, Blaster of Towers. Of course the gatekeepers
called me 'terrorist'! Through the powers of sympath-
etic magick, the entire structure will topple in due
time. This is high ritual, and the ultimate sacrifice
for the survival and evolution of my species. Even my
friends and teachers have disowned me. Horus, the Bull
of your Father will be avenged. We can now return to
our Mother, whole. The dove resides within the blasted
tower, and within that destruction, that madness, we
lay the seed of the purest aspects of life.
     The whole structure erupted in a final, defiant
exhalation, invisible but to the most subtle eyes. The
machine sputters, Leviathan chokes. With ruthless hand
you have destroyed this fair edifice! We children of
Dionysus lock hands together and sing: In the temple of
the temple of the temple of the Holy sits a woman who
is waiting who is waiting for the sun in the temple of
the temple in the temple of the Holy creeping shadows
falling darkness she is waiting for the sun for the
people of the people by the people making people in the
temple of the temple of the temple of the Holy she is
weeping for the people of the people making people in
the temple of the temple in the temple of the sun...

I honestly couldn't tell if he was fucking with me or not. He was never
this crazy before the meds.
     I walked past him, giving up on TV.

—

Time is different when you're locked up. The building takes on a life of
its own. You are just a parasite in its metal and concrete bowels. Clocks dictate your movements. When drugs are administered. When it is time to eat,
when it is time for walkies. Saturn rules us. This is the underworld. But the
empty routine is what saves and breaks you in this place.
     Please understand, this is coming from someone who might find talking
to a Goddess while the world burns an entertaining, but not otherwise
abnormal experience. Maybe serpents writhe out from under her skirt.
Maybe your nose is overwhelmed with the smell of sandalwood and you
discover that she has a head like a rooster. Maybe you're both Egyptian
Gods. She has a screaming orgasm, and only then do you realize you both
ate a ten-strip a few aeons ago. Et cetera, et cetera. My point is, I can
handle that. That's normal, but this routine... it's like a snake coiled round
my lungs.
     The routine nearly won. The story very well could have ended here; an
endless procession of days lost in these hallways, living on anti-psychotics,

industrial food, coffee, and nicotine, and nights peering through cracked windows at starless skies.

Routine said today was Wednesday—one-on-one time with Doctor Fein at noon. I took a quick glance at our ticking overlord. It was eleven forty-five.

At eleven forty-seven, the first glimmer of hope arrived in an unexpected place. A package from FedEx. I was scrawling another page in the journal Doctor Fein had asked me to keep for him. (Instead, he got a jaunt through my head. Poor guy.)

As I looked up and paused to chew on my crayon, I locked gazes with a familiar, mischievous face. Loki. John Waters-Peter Lorre looking mother-fucker.

He gave me one of those 'don't blow my cover, asshole' stares. That is how he usually looks at me, though.

He's brought me a present. I lean back and take in a deep breath. The first full, down-to-the-stomach breath I've taken in months. Birds flutter outside the barred windows of the commons, the first signs I've seen of spring. Suddenly, time was on my side.

The orderlies walk up to me—two shambling Golems with brains rendered little better than off-brand Jell-o by years of American Idol and a strict diet of high fructose corn syrup. They drop a sorry-looking teddy bear. It stares back at me from the ground with button eyes. I'm not sure how buttons can look simultaneously cute and forlorn, but these do. Just a little lost Mr. Teddy.

"This came in the mail today, it was from your family," one of them said.

I pick it up.

"Mr. Teddy! You've come back to me!"

I amble back towards my room and try to look like I'm having a conversation with little men in the ceiling. My fingers run a pattern across threadbare fur. They come to something solid, deep inside its fuzzy little belly. Oh, Loki. If these are as good as the last batch of capsules, then the staff of this ward are in for an interesting evening.

I'm sorry Mr. Teddy. It looks like it's time for exploratory surgery... and I'm no doctor.

II. Just One More Op

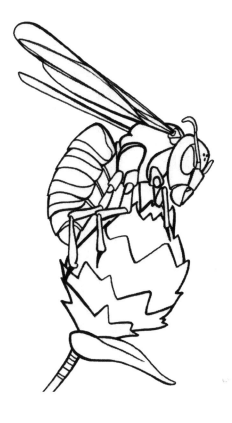

2011

We don't die, it's much worse: we vanish.
In other words, we never were. There is no reality.
—Petr Krahl

November 11, 2011. Johny Jones (aka 'Agent 888'), age thirty-two, was charged with terrorism offenses after being arrested as part of a investigation linked to a new organization operating within the United States. He is accused of participating in a conspiracy to disrupt trade and commerce, and is claiming insanity...

My 'friend' Bradley the Buyer once said to me, "If you want to get press attention, don't write a good book. Blow up a mall."

He was right. Not that I blew up that mall. I wouldn't have a clue how to do that kind of thing. I was always zoning out in science class, staring at the dingy floor, thinking instead about the broken thermostat in our culture. There was clearly no self regulation. Or maybe that's where The Buyer comes in.

I'm getting off topic, right? Because you probably want to know more about this mall/bomb scare thing which made the news, and less about the systemic dynamics of a culture. But that's just how my mind works.

If you really want to understand what happened. Well. Say you're wearing a plaid shirt. And you notice I can't pay attention to a word you're saying. That's not because I'm addle-minded, though a lot of people think so. It's because I'm thinking about the mathematical topology of the patches on your shirt, their surface area, the possible relation of numerological and linguistic categorization systems and those crumpled surfaces. Your plaid shirt can teach you the theory of relativity, see? But you're not thinking about that. You're thinking about the news stories, the broken glass, the wall of shrieking housewives.

We live in different worlds.

It wasn't about politics. It was about physics and fate. This is my account of a bombing which never occurred, and the way it ruined my life. Maybe it's a cautionary tale and maybe not, but I assure you at least this much—this is the truth, so far as I recall it.

—

I guess it all started about a year ago, when I received a phone call from The Buyer. My first response was to hit 'ignore' when I saw his name come up—not least of all because I knew taking a call from him was like inviting the NSA to fondle my teeth through my asshole. And if I didn't listen to that response, I should have listened to Stella. She never trusted Bradley. She complained about him so much, I think it made me want to hang out with him more.

I picked up after the fifth ring and feigned civility. "Hey Brad, it's been a minute. What's on your mind?"

"I have an Op which may interest you. If you're still active in the field, that is."

I took a deep breath, exhaled and sighed. Fished for a mentholated cigarette from my shirt pocket and lit it. Closed my eyes, rubbed my temples.

"Bradley, I don't know how many times I have to tell you. This...the 'mother hive brain', 'agency', 'syndicate', whatever you insist on calling it, depending on what drug you've stuck up your ass in the last three hours... it's all a ruse, man. Yeah, we all know you're ironic and glib with that post- modern electro- music you churn out, and you don't like faceless corporate entities raping the planet. Incidentally, how was your breakfast at Taco Bell this morning?"

"Listen, pigfucker," he snapped back. "I don't know if you realized this, but a young starving artist can't survive on Ramen and Nyquil alone. I can't cook. I have far more important things to do with my time. I never claimed to be immune to cultural brainwash, and understand that after we disassemble Leviathan, there will be plenty of time to grow our own produce. Hell, maybe we can even start our own commune, Manson family style. Tell me you never considered what a pretty little acid-crazed Squeaky Fromme type could do to you in the sack..."

This was really how we talked to one another. I'm not embellishing. Mini-monologues, back and forth. Rat-a-tat showers of words which even bleach couldn't remove. Though they were blunted by the transparency of our motives. At the end of the conversation, he always got what he wanted, and even if I made him look like a slime-ball in the process, it really didn't matter, since it was just the two of us on the line.

Well, us and the NSA.

"Get to the point," I said.

"As you wish," he replied, with mock subservience. "Agency or no agency, we both know the power of ideas in influencing primate behavior. Once an idea gets into someone, it ceases to be just an idea, yeah? So, I wanted to talk to you about the 404 Attacks... virally outsourced, cultural denial of service attack. File not found."

"Man... please do not talk to me on a cellular device about this. As I have mentioned to you repeatedly, there are emphatically no '404 Attacks'. You are taking a fictional literary device from a book you read somewhere, and attempting to impose this structure on real life. I am telling you, I'm done with this. I'm finally stable. I'm in a better place and I don't have time to play games. I've been down the rabbit hole man, and I'm telling you..."

I lost my thought, and then grabbed it again. "There is nothing there. There is no conspiracy, there is no agency, and you suffer from apophenia. You are a very sick individual. And even if I were to help you with this, I don't have much to offer anymore. No financial backing. I cut ties with all of the old operatives. Do you know why? Because they were over-privileged college kids like yourself, playing Don Quixote, taking on ideological constructs with petty DDoS attacks and crudely made 'zines. Shitty noise music. Poorly made propaganda that'd make Mao Tse-tung blush. What do you want from me?"

Silence on the other end. For a moment, I thought he might actually be pondering what I had said, that he might back down, or heaven forbid, apologize, but then I heard the telltale sound of a lighter clicking, and the slick inhale which follows. "One more Op. I promise. And then you're done. I will let you be. Your last Op. I swear to baby Santa Jesus on a cross."

"And if I don't?"

"Well, I suppose you can go back to living the lie... By the way, how's your girl? Sheila, right? She's a sweetheart, that one... She ever do ATM, like those freak bitches in pornos? You two make a great couple, you know, I've always thought. And I'm sure you could just go back to your happy life as a domesticated primate and forget this conversation ever happened and you would sleep quite well at night... Although, I'd have to tell you, it sure would be a crying shame if you were publicly outed for nearly every Op you ever participated in. I'm sure there's a room full of men in black dress suits with ball-gags, blowtorches and pliers out there, in one of those nice FEMA camps.

He paused, waiting for that to sink in. "I don't have to do any of this, anyway, you know. You got it set in your head that I have to do things physically. I don't. I THINK IT!"

I winced. Never should have answered the call. I reached for another cigarette and monkey-fucked it with the cherry of my last smoke, now burnt down to the filter. If I lived to be thirty-four, I'd surely be stricken with cancer, liver disease or any number of incurable terminal diseases. Occupational hazards of the 'counterculture'.

"Bradley, I want you to listen very carefully to me. Your Manson routine doesn't cut it. I'm not afraid of you. You were the one who got me into this in the first place and there is no blood on my hands. Sure, I participated in a few Ops here and there. But you... What the hell makes you think you're immune if they caught me? Like I wouldn't tell them anything and everything about your personal history? I know everything about you. And I know that if I went down, you would go down right alongside me. What gives you the cojones to threaten my wellbeing?" I asked.

"Firstly," he continued as if I'd said nothing at all, "I do not know any Johny Jones. I once had a contact within the agency that went by the moniker '888'. Why yes, I seem to recall an 'Agent 888', however, I never met with him personally, nor is there any conclusive evidence that I ever did. How many 'Agent 888's' have there been before him? Three? Four? How should I know? I barely knew the assholes. Furthermore, do you think that I haven't already resolved myself to a slow, painful death? The hammer *will* come down on me. When the time comes, I'm prepared. Are you? You can kill a man, friend. You can't kill an idea."

Perhaps for the first time, with a sort of dreadful finality reserved only for the condemned man, I realized what I was dealing with. He was a walking caricature of popular culture. Every single Gen X cliché, from Alan Moore to Tarantino, from the Doom Generation to Doom, from Chaz Manson emulation, to would-be revolutionary posturing, was present in the external mask he referred to as his personality.

To make matters worse, people listened to him and respected him. I no longer doubted that what once had started as a joke had transformed from hilarious to hideously ironic to... something I didn't have words to describe. A monster.

"Bradley... I never know with you, whether you actually believe you're a character in a book or a movie, or a cult leader, or a revolutionary, or a culture jammer, or any number of other clichés you grokked from your stupid futurist friends on drugs. But I am here to tell you that you are not. And fuck you for threatening me. You're a coward in a Guy Fawkes mask."

Bradley laughed. "With all due respect to my Brothers, Guy Fawkes masks went out of style when Anonymous became a T-shirt slogan for mall rats. Useful for influencing those who are easily swept away by jingles and logos, but not much more. I am going to refer to you as 'Agent 888'. That is your only identity to me. So this is what I am going to tell you, and this is the final word: You have your opportunity, Agent, to go down in history as one of the catalysts. Together we'll break the established order of Western Civilization."

"And you don't think we're being listened to right now?"

He chuckled and then shouted into the receiver. "CRYSTAL METH LABS! CHINESE BOMB PLANS COCKTAILS LIVE ROOSTER SHOWS PCP RECIPE! QUICHE ATTACK IMMINENT! DIVERT PLACENTAL PRESIDENT DEATH! ENGORGED WEAPONS! TASTY VIRUS!"

I had to hold the phone away from my ear.

"What?" he continued. "No Secret agents busting down your door? Calm down, man. You'll have the opportunity to go down in history as a man who helped to trigger a domino effect, enabling the mutants and the freaks to regain the power to which they are lawfully entitled. This is not blackmail. This is a promise. I am prepared to die a free man and take you down with me as collateral damage. I'd rather not resort to this, as I have always considered you to be a compatriot and a friend."

Far-fucking-out. This drugged out, paranoid schizophrenic with a vendetta against society had insulted my intelligence, threatened my physical and emotional well-being, and referred to me as his 'friend' in the course of a five minute dialogue.

Deep down, I was seething with indignity and revulsion. I once considered the Buyer to be a friend and a comrade. I grew up, and now he wanted to take me on the Hindenburg with him.

Instead of speaking my heart, or just hanging up on him, I responded. "Alright Bradley, entertaining this hypothetical... *if* I were to help you, and I want to emphasize here that it would be to get you to finally leave me alone and mostly because I pity you and the hollow shell of a human being you have become... why me? Why do you need me?"

He wheezed asthmatically and coughed. I could sense the gears spinning in his brain in the uncomfortable silence which followed my query.

"I don't need you. You are convenient. I've been waiting for this opportunity, the opportunity to make a real difference for years. You poseur would-be activists, jerking off onto diagrams of Molotov cocktails and imagining yourselves to be making a difference... you bail at the first possible sign of danger. You got yourself a nice little house and a nice woman now? You think to yourself, 'Well, those days are behind me. Might as well get a nice five-figure income job... maybe invest in the stock market, try my luck'. I don't play that game... but I keep plenty in my bank, Agent. And do you know what my bank is? The underworld. It has never let me down yet. Yes, I am an entrepreneur. You can call me a hypocrite if you'd like, but I did it on my own terms and I play by no one's rules but my own. And I did it all for the greater good. Long live the Syndicate."

I chuckled at the irony. "So do the fascists you are fighting your imaginary war against, Bradley." I realized he was just wearing me down. I was just a game fish, my stamina slowly ground away by the steely-eyed angler above. If I had any chance of real escape, I'd have to cut now.

I don't know why, to this day, but I stayed on the line. I chose to stay on the line. I said earlier it was fate, and I do believe that. But there are moments when we have the opportunity to break out of the orbit we're on and get to a new one. Most of the rest of our lives, it's just inertia at work, and no amount of struggle will amount to much of anything.

III. The Impeccable Doctor Fein

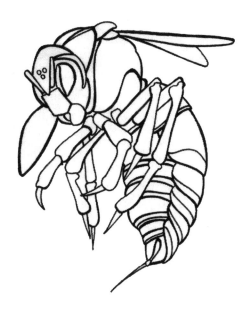

2012

As history teaches, a name may be given, but not taken away.
—Pavle Gantar

Doctor Fein sat at his desk, rigid as a statue. Final rays of sunlight filtered into his room through the slats of the blinds behind him, revealing all the dust and detritus freely dancing in the air. Filth. He ran his hand across his desk, leaving a trail behind it. Filth.

A thin veil of fog and indecisive storm clouds seemed to envelop the asylum grounds, and with a grumble like an empty stomach, the deluge began. The yard, a small spot of verdant green in a grim bulwark of stone and concrete, struggled to drink in the soupy run off. He could hear the rain falling, the gurgle of the drains beneath his window. The echoing report of a nurse's footfalls in the hallway, leading some patient through their meaningless routines. It would be a rainy Wednesday afternoon, just like the last, and the one before that.

The building followed the Kirkbride model, save minor eccentricities like the enclosed courtyard. The outside was ornate, almost Second Empire architecture, but, with the exception of the administrative offices, the internal structure showed how tired this building truly was. Exhausted, weighted down by long years and poor company. His office was in the westernmost point of the central administration building, flanked by symmetrical pavilions housing patients, swept back like a flock of birds in flight. That's how all Kirkbrides were built.

He laughed to himself, 'What am I, an architect?' and turned his attention to his secret journal, reading it repeatedly, looking for signs of mental illness. Certain irregularities had appeared in his behavior. It was a rational precaution.

03/15/12 11:39:31 AM. The Journal of Dr. Fein, M.D., Ph. D. Here is the life I have chosen for myself: I arrive at the hospital every morning at seven. I'm not expected until eight, but I use the time to digest the reports from the evening staff and have a cup of coffee in my office. Pink, blue, yellow pages, I match checked boxes and phrases of jargon with known faces and emotions. 'Unusual or excessive emotional reaction' dryly encapsulates bloody shrieks and hoarse-voiced prayers for death. 'Weapons prevention violation' neatly condenses hours spent patiently honing a length of table leg, visualizing my face slit to ribbons.

This new patient—he has a gift for lessening the self. I have been sorting for references to him. The reports indicate that he has quickly gained rapport with the other patients in the ward. They shuffle into a loose circle to hear him rant, whether his glazed eyes focus on them or not. He draws diagrams on his body and shares self-coherent madness with paranoid schizophrenics. I've even seen them pass around his little journal manifesto, 'Join My Cult!' Aptly named. An incoherent mess of half-truth and philosophical musing. But it holds some peculiar fascination.

I imagine their thin hospital robes, transformed into vestments. They become agitated when staff act to redirect them, protect them. Shared Psychotic Disorder or Folie á deux. It is unstable, contagious; like a virus. The carrier, the new patient, is calm. I believe he plots.

Lately I have not felt entirely present. Another
world is opening up beneath me. My sense of self and
other is disintegrating. I shouldn't think of this.
    I open my desk, pop out a sample of Wellbutrin, and
drink it down. Wellbutrin is indicated. Clearly.

Twenty minutes had passed since the clock on his desk showed twelve
o'clock.

The next patient arrives soon. Dr. Fein pulled out the patient's manila
file and opened it. He rearranged his features to be pleasantly interested
and engaging.

This one was yet another Doe, though she had been using 'Meredith' in
recent evaluations. Caucasian intersexed; height six feet, four-and-one-half
inches tall; age unknown but estimated to be late-twenties. Expected to
present with a depressive affect, possibly catatonic throughout our session.

*Guiltily, I love the catatonics. I gaze, and sit with them in silence. Sometimes I
use them as a blank-affected analyst and babble for the few minutes we have
together each week. This frees me for a time, yet leaves a thin patina of shame.*

He flipped through her file without reading any of it. His brow furrowed,
posture enrapt.

I present deeply in thought, concerned, silently strong. I wait for Ms. Smith.

Another minute and a knock. She shuffled in, braced by orderlies, and
sat.

She matched type, initially. Slumped, immobile across the desk. The
desk is a metal barrier. It is too heavy to move easily, and long enough to
provide him with something to run around until orderlies can restrain an
agitated patient. Her hair was straggling, long—it was unbelievably long
because she attacked anyone who came near it. Her robe, constantly worn
open, in mockery of the mockery our system makes of her. Clothing
wrinkled and stained. Staff insisted she stained them deliberately, smearing little impressionist doodles with ketchup and crayon and occasionally
blood. None have ever seen it happen.

*I make my face still and welcoming. I smile with a cautious degree of warmth,
enough to seem friendly but not intrusively so.*

"Good morning, Meredith. I've been looking forward to our meeting."
She slumped regally; sternly loose and uncaring. What would bring me that
detached, rigid pose of comfort?

"You haven't been with us very long," he continued after a polite inter-
val. "My name is Dr. Fein. Do you remember me?"

She showed no response. The orderlies made 'she's-all-yours' gestures
and departed. Grateful, he took his coffee out of the drawer and proceeded
to ignore her. It was still warm.

I catch my reflection in its opaque, glossy surface.

"What you're looking at is the cessation of falsehood," she said, and he spat coffee all over her file. "Entropic. The surface whirls and turns. The double of your own image shatters in the liquid mirror. You are a fleet of shards."

She nods slowly. Only her head has moved.

Regaining control, I smile precisely. She caught me by surprise again. Shallow, existential problems melt to the demands of skill. I may be sick, but I'm a damn fine psychiatrist.

"Thank you for that observation, Meredith."

"I'm not Meredith. I'm Jesus," she said placidly. But her lip curled into a smile.

"We hear that a lot around here," he said.

"Figures," she said, "Jesus would be intersexed this time around, locked up in a mental asylum."

She remained silent the rest of the session.

—

The next patient slouched in the door frame. Orderlies flanked him, but despite their hulking menace, he seemed to strike a casual pose somewhere mid-way between Shaolin monk and Hunter S. Thompson in his prime. His head shaved, now growing in. A last act of defiance. The orderlies glanced at Doctor Fein in concern, but he waved them off.

"Won't you come in?" Doctor Fein asked. He nodded and sat. "What is your name?"

"Same as yesterday. Dionysus. Well, Dionysus Katachtonios, but we don't need to be so formal."

"What day is today?" the Doctor asked next.

"Et tu, Brute?" Dionysus quipped in reply.

"Excuse me?"

The corners of his mouth darted downward. "It's the Ides of March. That line is apocryphal, anyway. Can I ask you a question?"

"I don't see why not." On the surface Dionysus was often all wit and humor. Even self-deprecating. But something dark lurked under that surface. Anyone could sense it. A restless hunger. Fein knew he couldn't drop his guard.

"What experience gives you the right to be my shaman?" Dionysus asked.

Doctor Fein blinked for several moments before replying. "I'm sorry? I'm a psychiatrist. And I'm here to help you, but only if you want it."

"Alright. Try to follow along with me here. I've been driving myself nuts, trying to figure out why my stomach was in knots last night. Could be repressed childhood trauma, right? Could be the awful 'food.' The meds. It could be the displaced, angry spirit of an Ibo tribesman, who, for reasons passing understanding, feels the need to take out his vengeance on my bowels." Dionysus was gesturing rapidly with his hands as he spoke, his enthusiasm building. Plunk, plunk. Doctor Fein, in his distraction, didn't notice the ripples on the surface of his now hallucinogenic coffee.

"This is the problem with diagnosis. Attribution of cause. So many cognitive biases at work. Tell me, what can either of us *know*?"

"What are you feeling right now?" Doctor Fein asked, trying for rapport. But it had a forced, rictus quality.

"Well, disappointment, mostly. I had a lot of questions about my identity as a kid. Thought I was maybe an alien. I had an imaginary friend who lived in the woods; she was like a nightshade that lived on blood. You know how it is. Normal, kid stuff. And I met a man who helped me find myself—find my name. When something has a name, it is real. Without a name, without a real name, we are always uncertain. *He* was a shaman. So I ask you—" Dionysus said, standing up.

Doctor Fein jumped.

"You seem tense today, Doctor. Now, if you don't know what is giving me heartburn, then how the fuck are you supposed to be my shaman?"

Doctor Fein shook his head and made some quick notes in the file. *Dionysus' delusions are getting worse. The patient-doctor relationship is clearly breaking down in a fundamental way.*

Dionysus stared at him. The Doctor stared back, his pupils' twin black holes. Dionysus shrugged. "Scale. See? Scale is the key. Nothing in the limited span of a human life amounts to anything... if it wasn't for the secret that eternity hides in the smallest spaces between each moment."

A fly buzzed on the wall. Filth, Doctor Fein thought, swatting at it. Entropy and filth. He took another slurp of cold coffee.

"Think of raindrops falling from the sky. Splash! They hit a windshield, grip on, slide down slowly, mingling with dirt and grit. Things behave differently at different scales. Sub-atomic, atomic, molecular... this room here. The fluid and sedimentary dynamics of a riverbed. An ecosystem. A fucking solar system. Galaxies! Scale is a frame of reference, an idea, much like molecules themselves. The matter that composes this desk is mostly empty space. This is just basic physics. They didn't teach this to you in school?"

The fly was rubbing its legs together, and it was cacophonous. Like steel wool on a rusted pan played through the speakers at an AC/DC concert. Its eyes were huge, a fractal rainbow of fruit flavors. Synesthesia, a new symptom. Time is passing, but how much?

"I can help you," Dionysus said.

Without thinking, Dr. Fein blurted out, "How?"

"Find it, Doctor Fein. Find eternity," Dionysus said, tapping on the desk.

The tapping snapped Doctor Fein back into time and Euclidean space. His hands bit down on themselves, curling into tight balls, as if his fingers desired escape from servitude to the almighty Hand. Fingernails parted flesh.

"NOW!" Dionysus screamed, slamming his fist on the table. Files flew into the air, containers full of pens and the Doctor's remaining coffee toppled end-over-end, crashing to the floor.

Dionysus paused, his arms in the air, waiting for the great reveal. There was none. The Doctor stared dully at the droplets of coffee on the ground.

"I'm sorry, Doc. You missed it. Maybe next time around. Just pray the Buddhists are right about that. Sorry about the coffee. Oh, have you heard of the Zen stick of encouragement?"

"No."

"See the way you attain Satori, that's what they call enlightenment, is by sitting. Just fucking sitting. But you need to be constantly jolted into the present, so that you can grasp it. Grasp eternity now. It is here, or it is nowhere. So the Roshi, the teacher, walks around and whacks students with a stick. The stick of encouragement."

They locked gazes. A rivulet of sweat dripped down Doctor Fein's nose.

"There is only one way to really show you." Dionysus grabbed a pen and drove it into Doctor Fein's forearm. It stuck out like a mini-erection, a Bic Priapus, spurting blood instead of semen. The Doctor screamed and flailed, ripping it free.

"Breathe, Doctor Fein. You are alive!"

"HELP! GET IN HERE!" Doctor Fein gasped.

"Oh, calm down. You'll be fine. Now take this opportunity–"

Two orderlies burst into the room and grabbed Dionysus so forcefully that the chair beneath him spun and crashed to the floor.

He offered no resistance, but looked at Doctor Fein with concern. "You tell me I need to be cured, but you've got issues, my friend. I think you should talk to somebody."

The orderlies slammed a syringe into Dionysus' neck. The world, an Aristotelian universe of clockwork, slowed down and unspooled itself. Gears and glass clattered and crashed around him. His eyes fluttered closed as he was carried through the door.

A last thought stuck in his mind, before darkness: Janus was the God of doorways. Janus, two-faced, the ambivalent hermaphrodite.

A passageway... to dream.

—

He was carried unceremoniously to his shared cell. His roommate, Cody, sat in his own bunk, strumming on an imaginary guitar.

"Trouble again?" Cody asked, not looking up.

The orderlies grunted as they shackled Dionysus to the bed.

"That's not code, you know," Cody said.

They glared at him, as if to ask if he wanted to be tied down, too. Cody shrugged and went back to transmuting the melody of Seal's 'Kiss From A Rose' through the key changes in John Coltrane's 'Giant Steps'.

—

Doctor Fein was rushed through corridors, strapped to a gurney. Cables dangled and flapped against him. *They were filling me with their fluids!*

"Catatonia," one of the nurses said. "Damn shame," said another.

He knew he would be fine. He was the one in control. Everything in his manner, voice, his surface thoughts all screamed: "this man knows." He was integrated, wise, with a sturdy grasp on the here-and-now. He understood everything, standing on the shoulders of rational giants and the scientific method born from the great Enlightenment. He knew. He knew who he was, where he was, when he was, and why. He knew when yesterday was, when tomorrow will be. Things fall down, but the center holds.

The center holds.

The center holds.

The feeling lasted until he opened his mouth to speak the truth, to let the nurses know that everything was okay. Instead, he gagged; jackknife vomiting in a steep, sour arc.

He knew he'd been there before. He'll be there tomorrow. Be here be here. Oh God. No escape from eternity. No escape from uncertainty.

Anything, anything, anything but this.

"Wouldn't you feel less incurably mad after a nice, long nap?" he thought he heard a nurse say.

He tasted vomit and smiled at her. Tried to make a joke and bear down on his gorge. But all the words had turned to grease and coated his tongue black.

"Go to sleep, Doctor. Rock-a-bye, Fein, on the wave front..." The nurse leaned in and opened her mouth. Wide. Stretch marks formed at the hinges of her jaw before the skin tore with a running, wet zzzzziiiipppp! And she was growing, looming over the table, rows of sharp teeth sprouting with muted pops from a gummy pink palate. She grabbed his bed as if it was a dinner plate and tilted it up, the hospital machinery sliding into her wet maw with cracks and crashes.

"You're not real!" he shrieked. "None of this is real!"

"Then there's nothing to lose. Hop in!" She smiled.

Nothing. Nothing except dying, alone and quite mad.

—

Dionysus tossed in his bunk, his hands latched in place.

Sharp, tawny blades of wheat parted and gave way to a stone path, which wound its way through picturesque hills. The sound of creaking chains rolled towards him with the fog. Atop the hills stood the outline of dangling figures, swaying in the wind like marionettes. Beyond the macabre forms laid a village.

Those who watched over the village must have seen it fit to hang deviants from iron chains on a stone gallows. Tongues cut out meant watch your own. Eyes gouged out meant mind your business. Hands removed with a splitting maul meant no begging, idling or street busking.

The village itself couldn't be placed in time, or by culture—each house varied too widely in construction, placement, and class, though overall it was a pastiche of peasantry throughout time. In these buildings, he believed he could see an untold history of the rise and fall of civilizations, of the sleepy forgetfulness that greets the passage of all ages. A stone maze, which seemed the handiwork of some long lost people, receded into a whirling fog. The immensity of its whirls and turns was beyond calculation, but even at this distance it appeared crumbling, at places having lost its structure altogether.

He stumbled through the field, not yet aware of himself. The familiar sound of a girl's laughter danced on the wind. Then he saw her. Eyes sparkled and shifted colors, as he gawked and fell in love. Each of her gestures had the slow motion, natural grace of a high quality shampoo ad.

It was her eyes he kept returning to—impossibly huge, self-contained worlds. Dream eyes. Every longing he'd ever had was distilled in the form of her face, framed by thick braids of crimson hair. He wanted to clutch them with both hands as they made endless love in the field, distracted by nothing, serenaded by the whispering of wind through the wheat and the crickets.

She wore a summer dress of red cotton that fit her like a nightgown, and as she laughed a strap worked free from her shoulder, stopping his heart.

"Do you think we can fly?" she asked.

He grinned and took a step. "It seems reasonable. I'm dreaming, right? We're dreaming?"

"Are we?"

"Isn't it obvious? Fields of wheat, a cobblestone maze, an eternally receding village that exists outside of time. And you."

"Me?" she asked, resetting the strap on her shoulder. "Where do you think I fit in?"

He racked his brain for poetry to steal, but found nothing. "You're the dream."

She swayed minutely towards him and smiled. His heart came in his ribs.

"You're almost right."

"Almost?"

She glided up and around him, breathing so close to his ear that he felt himself fainting. "I'm bait," she whispered, ducking his encircling arms. She sprinted, naked, into the wheat.

He stood frozen, holding her red dress in his hands.

Without so much as a thought, Dionysus followed. The wheat blotted out the sky. Broad, brittle leaves cut him as he dove through rows of it, chasing a giggle, a flash of her taut calf, a breath of musk. He ran to the drums of the blood behind his eyes, panting with a mixture of horny abandon, supplication, and elation that formed a nameless emotion somewhere behind his navel. He tore his clothes as he thudded through the stalks, toppling them. Their stems popped gunshots under his feet.

He remembered her question. "Do you think we can fly," she had asked. Can we?

He jumped, hoping to see over the heads of the stalks. He floated above them, defying the laws of gravity, defying the laws of anything save will-power. Airborne, he swiveled and watched her disappear into the alleys of the village with a toss of her braids.

The ground was so very far beneath him. Fear surged through his veins. He had always been afraid of heights. The vast empty space would make his head swim. Sometimes, as a child, he had lost consciousness entirely.

Gravity wrapped its fingers around him and dragged him to the ground. The world rolled end-over-end. He tasted dirt, and was sure she was gone.

—

He shook his head and got to his feet. When he stood, he was in a corridor. The walls lined with filing cabinets that seemed to go on forever. Ahead he saw a desk in the middle of the hallway.

With a mere thought, he was standing in front of a gnomish old man on the other side of the desk. The name tag on his ill-fitting suit read 'FILE CLERK A743G1'. All caps, black type, probably Helvetica. The clerk's arms were unnaturally long and spindly. His eyebrows were cloud-like wisps. A girl in an 'Alice in Wonderland' dress sat on the corner, bouncing her legs back and forth as she hummed to herself.

"Young man, do you have an appointment?"

"Appointment?"

"You must have an appointment."

"No. I was following someone. Did a woman run this way?"

"There is nothing here but words."

The girl looked askance at Dionysus. "She went that way."

Dionysus turned to pursue.

"Or, no. Was it that way?" She giggled.

"Are you messing with me?"

"I haven't even started."

The File Clerk leaned forward, motioning for Dionysus to come closer. "Listen to me, and listen carefully. You don't belong here, and bad things happen to those who don't belong. The walls taste your breathing. The floor ponders your warmth. This is not a where, at all," he whispered.

Indeed, the walls breathed with a regular rhythm, bulging and hissing like a living thing. Machines dwelled in that sound too, behind the filing cabinets. A living world of clanking cogs and wheels, whistles and steam bellows.

"You mustn't tell him such horrible things," the child said.

"You are in the belly of a sleeping whale," the File Clerk said. A cabinet flew open of its own accord, extending the entire distance to the desk. A single piece of paper shot out and danced down before him.

"Now you've done it!" The girl clapped playfully.

"Your appointment has been confirmed."

"My appointment?"

The File Clerk shrugged.

The lights went out, one at a time. Dionysus was left in darkness.

—

Light returned in the form of the sun dancing out from behind the clouds. His shadow grew long and thin as he crossed a school yard—past a broken merry-go-round that tilted off its axis, a skeletal jungle gym, an empty swing set. The scent of opium flooded his nostrils as he approached a sheet-metal slide.

A girl was perched atop, hands clasped around her knees. She peered down at him with an eerie intensity. They were the eyes of an adult. No. Something ageless and incalculably cunning. A slight shudder passed through his spine as the odor became more pronounced, and it dawned on him: this was the girl he was chasing, though she was younger now.

She wordlessly extended her hand toward him, and he stretched his arm to clasp it. As she slid down, her red locks and sun dress billowed behind her, revealing pink cotton panties.

"Pick me up," she demanded, brushing sand off her bottom.

He felt uncomfortable, but found himself strangely compelled to do what she asked.

"Over there," she said, motioning towards a gulag-like school building, reminiscent of the high school he had attended.

Foreboding followed him as he cut a path across the lawn, cradling her in his arms. Something was very wrong.

The door creaked open, and he walked cautiously down the hallway. "This room, over there. Room 49."

As he approached the door, her lips found his earlobe, delicately sucking, nibbling, and biting. *No!* He let go and spun. She was gone. Her laughter echoed around him.

He stood alone in an old classroom. There was a dust-coated chalkboard in the front of the room.

"I am always here," her voice said. It was the voice of the girl he had seen in the field, matured.

"Hello?" he asked, looking behind desks.

"I hide in the gaps between your breaths," she replied.

The door to the classroom opened and three women entered. Three distinct moments in a life. One was younger, a student. Maybe nineteen, with spiked hair. A striped skirt clung to her hips and a sticker-and-patch plastered bag slung over one shoulder. Another came behind her, this one in her late twenties and dressed like a rock star, on her way down the red carpet at an event. That shampoo-ad hair. And there was another: mature, naked and utterly terrifying. All wore the same vicious indifference, the same intensity on a face not so much pretty as savage.

"Who are you?" he managed to ask.

The elder one spoke first. "We've met."

"And parted," spoke another.

"And met again," the third.

"We have?"

They seemed to regard him with amusement.

The eldest grabbed him, as the student dropped to her knees in front of him. Her book-bag slipped off her shoulder. She gave him a long look before yanking down his pants with a tug.

He stammered a bunch of gibberish.

The girl at his fly bit her lip impatiently. She glanced back at the other two.

"By all means..."

His body reacted despite his fear, as she locked gazes with him, her mouth opening expectantly. The others tittered and circled slowly, watching... herself? He heard the familiar sound of chalk scraping against the blackboard, but he was too distracted to look.

"This one seems different than the others," her voice drifted to him as he watched her head bob, back and forth, beneath.

She ripped off his shirt, planted her hands on his chest and shoved. She smiled wickedly as his head slammed against the linoleum tile. They were all over him, sucking on every finger, lapping at every crease and crevice and bulge of his body.

Her mouth tasted of berries and loamy wine. The taste flowed into him as the youngest of the three rode him ferociously.

Meanwhile, they whispered high weirdness in his ears, though he was scarcely paying attention to the words.

"You don't remember us?"

"Best wake soon."

"—Oh, but not too soon."

"The hydra-headed creature stirs—"

"Lilith," another moaned. "Lilith."

"Eyes like seer's globes—"

"Gazing in this world—"

"And the next."

He felt the sting of fingernails ripping into his flesh with each slick thrust as he moaned into the ruby-lipped mouth of another.

She wrapped her hands around the throat of her younger self astride him, staring into his eyes all the while. She grinned, before wrenching that

41

head to the side, snapping the spine with a wet pop. The body reflexively convulsed and flexed around him as he screamed in shock.

But then the strangest thing happened. The dead form turned to vapor. At the same time, silver strands began drooping from the mouths of the other two, and they quickly weaved this liquid moonlight about themselves like spiders building a nest.

And he was lying alone on the floor of an abandoned school, his pants around his ankles, surrounded by milky, fibrous eggs about the size of a girl curled in fetal position.

He read what she had written on the board:

'The dreamer is still asleep. WAKE UP!'

—

The air was full of smoke and brick dust.

"Wake up Dionysus. Wake the fuck up!" Loki was dressed in maintenance coveralls. He cut the restraints quickly with a box-cutter. "Hell. Wake the fuck up, and get that stupid look off your face. What were you dreaming about anyway?"

Dionysus sat upright. "Already?" He looked over to see that the window had blown open. The alarms buzzed painfully in his ears. Cody huddled in the corner, his eyes wide with terror.

"Hey, Cody... pssht. It's fine. This is... a friend of mine. Get out, if you can," Dionysus said.

Dionysus shook his head a final time, trying to dislodge the cobwebbed traces of dream, which stuck to his thoughts. Other voices joined the din of the alarm, panicked patients, and the clamor of administrative staff.

"Up and go, let's climb," Loki said. They grabbed hold of the rope and scaled up to the roof. Dionysus grunted and faltered.

Loki hauled him over the edge and detached the rope ladder. It was still anchored next to the window and swung down, coming to rest near a twisted grate at the perimeter grounds.

"Problem?" Loki asked, in a whisper.

Dionysus shook his head. "No, no. We just don't get much... exercise around here."

"Don't like fucking the orderlies?"

"There's a ladder! He went down!" they heard from below.

"Is it really this easy?" Dionysus asked.

Loki shook his head. "Don't tempt fate, okay? Just follow me. We have to get Jesus."

"What about that kid... Johny?"

"The patsy? He's safer in here." 'And', Loki thought, 'if the two of you had followed the plan he'd be the only one in here, too'.

They approached a security access door with a black duffel bag propped against it. Dionysus was grinning like a kid on Christmas. Loki's face was a perfect blank.

Loki reached into the bag and threw a security uniform at Dionysus, before stripping off his coveralls and replacing them with his own uniform.

Loki looked him up and down. "You still a 32/36?"

"Fuck, no. I've been taking benzos and coloring for ten months."

"Huh. How do I look?" Loki asked, adjusting his security badge and nameplate.

"A pig among men."

Loki spent a moment fussing with Dionysus' collar, and then opened the door behind them with a key card. They entered, Loki carrying the duffel over his shoulder.

Alarms and running feet echoed throughout the building. Dionysus and Loki approached the door, Loki with a small mirror in hand. He angled to look through the window in the door, glancing back at Dionysus. He frowned.

"What?" Dionysus asked.

"You're grinning like a mental patient."

Dionysus grinned wider, showing his teeth. "How's this?"

Loki sighed. "Okay. Rent-a-cop, right? In over your head and trying to take charge of that." He waved in the general direction of the alarms. "You want commanding, confused and a little hostile."

Dionysus pursed his lips. "All at once, huh?"

"Yeah." Loki's expression and posture shifted, somehow perfectly nailing his description.

"That's...creepy."

Loki shook his head and swiped the key-card in the door. They entered.

—

They moved purposefully down a hallway lined with high-security doors, shining flashlights through the windows of each door in passing, as though checking on patients. Two rent-a-cops trotted past them, exiting through the stairwell. Dionysus and Loki dropped the act as soon as the cops passed.

Loki opened a door. "She's in here, come on."

—

Standing in the middle of a padded cell, arms outstretched, was a tall, broad-shouldered androgyne with a mane of purple hair.

"Jesus! Time to go!"

Loki tossed the duffel across the room at her. It hit her chest, bounced off and fell to the floor.

"This bag contains uniforms like those, right?" Jesus said slowly. It had been months since she'd bothered to speak.

"Yeah."

"No."

"The hell do you mean, no?"

Jesus nudged the bag dourly. "No. I'm not doing it in drag."

Loki rolled his eyes. "You're fucking kidding me."

"No," Jesus said again.

"You're going to blow this plan over..." Loki was at a loss for words.

"If we argue much longer, yeah," Dionysus said.

"Look, just..." Loki paused, calculating something in his head. "Fuck it."

He grabbed Jesus from behind and manhandled her out the door. Dionysus joined in. They made their way towards a stairwell, which disgorged two staff.

Loki shoved her against the wall. "We got this one. Go to East Second to assist." Jesus spit at Loki and faked a struggle.

The staff looked at each other blankly.

"Go. Now."

When they were out of earshot, Loki looked at Jesus. "Was the spitting really necessary?"

Jesus' head bobbed from side to side. "No, but when will I get to do that again?"

—

A janitor stood outside the motor pool parking lot, back to the wall, kicking back and smoking his second cigarette in a row. The door slammed open. His cigarette hung precariously on his lip as three crazed faces regarded him with confusion.

As he would tell the News reporter later, "Then a freak faggot with purple hair punched the living Christ out of me, jumped into the nearest van and drove away."

—

As Loki drove, the other two shined flashlights out the windows, as though looking for escapees.

"We'll do a loop, then head for the gate. You two duck and I'll–"

"Stop!" Dionysus yelled.

Loki slammed on the brakes. Standing in the glare of the headlights was Cody, his curly hair pulled back in a ponytail, his few belongings wrapped up in a blanket.

"Friend of yours?"

"Roomie, remember?" Dionysus said, nodding.

"Destiny," Jesus said.

Loki scrutinized their faces. "No use arguing, is it? Fine."

They pulled alongside, and he jumped in.

"Stay low, okay?" Loki said.

—

They halted at the exterior gate. A security guard nervously squinted up at them. Loki opened the driver's window.

"There's a breach in the East fence, I'm gonna check it out. You have a radio?"

The security guard patted the walkie-talkie on his belt. "Just this one."

"Mine's dead. Shit. Call it in and have someone follow me out."

"Got it," the security guard said, waving them out. They drove into the darkness of night. The moon hung in the sky, nearly invisible. She sent her borrowed sunlight off into space instead, perhaps jealous of her big blue brother.

JAMES CURCIO

IV. The Three Suits Contained Separate Bodies

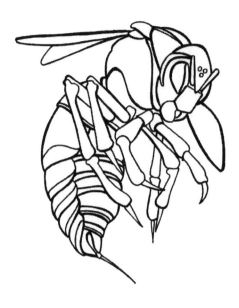

2012

We are on the side of man, of life and of the individual.
Therefore, we are against religion, morality, and government.
Therefore, our name is Lucifer.
We are on the side of freedom, of love, of joy and laughter and divine
drunkenness. Therefore, our name is Babalon.
Sometimes we move openly, sometimes in silence and in secret.
Night and day are one to us, calm and storm, seasons and the cycles
of man, all these things are one, for we are at the roots. Supplicant
we stand before the Powers of Life and Death, and are heard of these
powers and avail. Our way is the secret way, the unknown direction.
—**Jack Parsons**

A white Crown Victoria, unmarked, pulled up in front of a brick apartment building. The engine hitched and knocked a moment before stopping. The door kicked open, and Adam Trevino heaved a sigh for no apparent reason.

He plodded up the stairs to his apartment, brooding at the way his sidearm thumped his ribs as he climbed. Might as well fret about the gun; its weight, suddenly uncomfortable, the vast legal machinery dedicated to keeping it in the holster. Better that than to contemplate the empty pocket in his overcoat, where his credentials used to be. His suspension was in its third day. It wouldn't be reviewed for two more, and in all likelihood, he would be stripped of rank. Orphaned. Better to sit at home and watch the news.

At the door, he reached into his pocket and removed a key-less entry fob. Pushing it once shut down the motion and pressure sensors, pushing it twice unlocked the door. Trevino's front door featured a typical urban dweller's fetish of deadbolts, though vestigial. Inserting a key or a tension bar would only set off the alarm.

Upon entering one's apartment, one hung up one's coat. One locked the door, and pushed play on the answering machine. One removed shoes and turned on the television against the backdrop of coffee brewing.

His eyes caught on the citations hanging on his otherwise bare walls: bravery, marksmanship, and forensics. None of it mattered; it seemed, after one mistake.

He hit play on an old-fashioned answering machine and continued through the apartment towards his coffee machine.

"Adam, hi. It's Sheila. Look, I heard about that suspect vanishing into thin air... it's bullshit, you're damn fine police. It'll blow over, I just know it..."

Having poured himself a cup—black, no sugar—Trevino flopped onto a worn leather couch. He started flipping through the channels, though he couldn't manage to ignore the damn answering machine.

"I just wanted to say, we're all here for you, you know? Anything we can do to get you back out there, just... call me, okay?"

"Christ, Sheila. Adopt a dog," Trevino grunted. The machine beeped. "Next message..." There was a long pause.

"Good evening, Adam. We understand PA SBI unit no longer requires your services. Subject to 28 U.S.C. 561 (d), you are hereby informed of appointment as Special Deputy US Marshal Adam Trevino." This voice sounded somehow more robotic, more cold, than the automated voice of the answering machine.

Trevino almost dropped his coffee.

"You report for duty tomorrow, 7 AM, in Room 101 of the Federal Building. Congratulations, Deputy."

Trevino stared at the answering machine, waiting for the other shoe to drop. He entertained the thought that his old buddies were playing a practical joke. But no. They knew there were things an officer did not joke about. Certainly, not now. He looked up at the citations on his walls. Finally, he smiled to himself. "Beats the shit out of the Pinkertons, doesn't it?"

He settled into the news, still unable to wipe the smile from his face. A blond news reporter stood in front of a fence with a sign that read 'Pennhurst Psychiatric Hospital'. Her perfect little face was creased with solemnity and her eyes were perfectly blank.

"Can you tell us more about that, Amy?" the voice-over asked.

Trevino's attention wandered as he wondered why he was planning to drink a pot of coffee at this hour.

"... for ten months, involuntarily committed in the wake of a series of bizarre attacks on twenty four-hour eateries and places of worship in Montgomery county, concluding with a bomb threat in the King of Prussia Mall."

Amy was replaced with grainy surveillance footage of the mall, devoid of audio. A grim psychopath stood on a counter, dressed like a South American guerrilla, wearing what appeared to be an explosive vest. He was preaching wildly while waving a detonator. A purple-haired freak ran around the food court, throwing money at hostages. Terrified looking protesters stood in the background, holding up a black banner with white Arabic writing. In front of the banner stood a row of giant paper mache penises, spray-painted with pink swastikas and the words 'GAY FOR ISLAM'. Protesters and fake SWAT agents clamored in the background. Then someone dressed in a Santa suit was raised above the throng, tied to a cross with a giant bow on top.

Trevino shook his head in disbelief. Those kids were obviously not real terrorists, but you simply do not fuck around like that. They ought to be locked up.

Amy's voice over continued, "...while staff report the two were responding well to therapy and medication, it is now clear their recovery was anything but genuine."

There was a close up cut of the psycho's stubbled jaw, mouthing the words 'Lip reading is dead sexy. Call me'.

Trevino blinked. The smile was gone. He'd worked this case two years back. Dionysus. The purple-haired one, Jesus. They were caught fleeing the mall. Dumb luck. And Johny—a mild, middle aged adolescent—was implicated in every possible way. Trevino had argued he was innocent of everything save being a clown, but the DA wanted the press. They were written off as head cases, and eventually it was brushed aside.

Amy continued, standing in front of Pennhurst's barren gates. "In a daring, late-night escape, the two have vanished, taking with them a hostage:

49

twenty-nine-year-old Cody Kilroy. Hospital staff are unwilling to comment on their pending investigation…" There was a close up of the rope ladder, dangling from the blown-out window, fluttering in the breeze.

Trevino frowned.

"…but Action News has learned that explosive devices were triggered in the course of their escape, before the three fled, apparently on foot."

Trevino shook his head. "My ass. That ladder's upside down. Loki and Dionysus hit the roof…" He turned off the TV. "…then grabbed Jesus while everyone ran off into the woods. Steal a van, join the pursuit, split off." He shook his head and stared at the ceiling. "I'm glad you shit-canned me, Major. Twelve more hours and this could've been my ass."

He frowned again, and looked around his empty apartment. "I really need to adopt a damn dog. All this talking to myself is getting creepy."

—

Trevino arrived at 7 A.M. sharp, wearing a new suit and with a spring in his shamble. Grim-looking people bustled through cryptic errands. After passing a security checkpoint, Trevino crossed towards a bulletproof glass gate, manned by a receptionist.

"Morning, I'm—"

Without making eye contact, the receptionist replied. "Elevator to B1, make a left, second door on the right."

The gate buzzed and slid open.

—

The three suits contained separate bodies. They sat in separate chairs along the polished walnut table, and carried separate briefcases. None of that meant anything.

There came a discrete tap on the door, and the suit paired with a blue tie called, "Yes?"

A dour, Eastern European woman leaned in. "Mr. Trevino is here for his interview. Shall I send him in?"

"Thank you, Ms. Bejta. Have him wait, please."

She nodded and slipped out.

—

The three drained of animation and turned their attention elsewhere. Folders opened, pens went into motion, and knuckles thoughtfully cracked.

"Ms. Bejta?"

With post-Soviet efficiency, Trevino was bullied through the door. He appeared pale, intimidated. The suits relaxed as he took in the Seal on the wall behind them.

They sat on one side of the table, each one equal parts salesman and bureaucrat. Between them were a badge and a thick file, bearing the 'CLASSIFIED' stamp. Like hungry cats, all three sets of eyes latched onto Trevino as he sat stiffly and tried to appear competent.

"Special Deputy Trevino. Adam. Welcome."

He shook each of their hands in turn, unable to tell them apart. They may as well have been triplets.

"SBI's loss is our gain. Glad to have you."

"Sit."

One of them pushed the badge across to Trevino, while the others passed him the file. Trevino put the badge in his pocket and patted it. "Let's hope it stays there." He gestured towards the folder. "May I?"

"Your clearance was updated this morning."

"That's the spirit."

"We approve."

Trevino raised an eyebrow, feeling a vague twinge of memory, something about a scene from Macbeth. He pushed it away and opened the file. He was immediately confronted with the close-up of Dionysus from the previous night's news footage.

"You worked the Mother Hive Brain case in early 2011, is that correct? Remanded these two and a third? Two went by monikers. Dionysus, Jesus, and Johny Jones. What is that, some kind of a joke?"

"Sir..." Trevino started.

"You don't look happy, Adam."

He continued turning the pages in the folder. "Happy doesn't enter into it, sir. Though that name never meant anything. It was just something for the news. 'Mother Hive Brain, agents everywhere, alien brain terrorists, be afraid.' Four madmen and an insanity defense."

"There were three."

"That we made," Trevino said. "This one–" he tapped a photo of Loki and several other terrified patrons being escorted from the mall by solicitous fire-fighters, "stayed out of the file. He remained at large, and I believe he broke the other two out last night."

"This theory wasn't well-received at SBI, I take it."

Trevino laughed bitterly. "It wasn't like that. We just had nothing and said nothing. With these two in custody, we closed the file. Good guys win."

"Film at eleven."

"Yeah. Something like that. So, why DoJ? They're just a bunch of punks."

"We have reason to believe these... individuals are, or will be, instrumental in a widespread terrorist conspiracy to manufacture domestic insurrection in advance of a series of attacks."

"We want them, Deputy."

Trevino closed the file and tried very hard not to laugh. "I don't see that, here. What am I missing?"

"Nothing."

"That's why you're here, Adam."

"Your mission is to gather human intelligence on these subjects, liaise with our office to correlate your reports and build a domestic terrorism case. Once you've gathered sufficient information about all their associates, only then do you take them down."

The three looked queasy. Nothing in their vocabulary enabled them to tell Trevino the simple truth: that those three had to be stopped. They could barely think it, let alone express it in human language. Their only answer was a deep, blind howl in themselves, a primal negation of those in that folder who could not be allowed to live.

Trevino blinked, finally taking their awkward silence as a kick under the table. "Ah. So, let me see if I understand you. I locate and observe the subjects, determine if they have co-conspirators, investigating them as well, if they do. Then, once I have sufficient information and evidence... I am to ask them to accompany me to the nearest, duly constituted authority for whatever reason seems most convenient. And when they resist with deadly force, I am to prevent civilian casualties by dropping them all in their tracks. Am I correct?"

The suits deflated. "Precisely, Agent."

"You start now."

"Emphasis on now."

"Good luck, Deputy. We'll be in touch."

The door closed behind him, and the three slumped in their seats like discarded dolls. They had another meeting in an hour with the military people, and bodies need their sleep.

V. Nothing To See Here

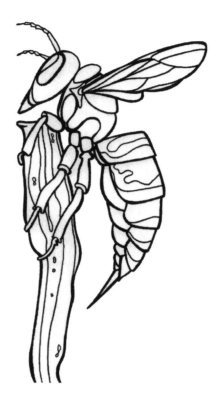

2011

The best lies are also true.
—Gabriel De Leon

It was a year before my imprisonment, almost to the day. 2011. A day seemingly like any other. The alarm dragged me out of sleep. Not so much kicking and screaming as a pathetic sort of shamble in bunny slippers. There was no need to rush anything. I had my routine down to an exact science. I intuitively knew how long I had to half-read the headlines on my iPad as the TV blathered in the background and the coffee gurgled like a pimp with his throat cut. I wasn't thinking about Bradley. I wasn't thinking about anything.

Stella was performing her own ritual, which at this time amounted to about fifteen minutes standing in a steaming hot shower. Some mornings I would break the monotony by joining her in there. Just the opportunity to see her pleasing shape all wet and smooth was enough to make my day. But at the same time, we didn't have much to say to one another.

This morning I didn't join her. I ate my waffle and waited for her to finish, so she could drop me off at the office before going about her day.

My mind kept wandering back to Bradley and his Op. I had agreed, by the end of our long talk last night. Now it was a waiting game. Eventually I'd get a message from him or one of the other Agents. That's just how it always worked. Eventually Stella was dressed, and we were out the door.

Sure enough, I got an email from Agent 156 later that day. It was equal parts cryptic and amusing. Or was that irritating? I'm not even sure anymore. Still, I knew more of the lingo than I liked to admit. Truth is, the moment I finished reading the email, I felt like I had a purpose again. As an Agent, the daily grind became just a front. You can keep your dignity. The suburban dream looks nice from the outside, but that's all it is. A shell wrapped around nothing.

DATE: 3-8-2011
TO: Agent 888
FROM: Agent 156
Subject: Briefing for Op. Mem-Nun-Aleph.
I am working on developing a questionnaire, which will be used to determine an applicant's 'placement' into one of six cells. (Part of the questionnaire will be a release form. We can't take responsibility for what these crazy kids are doing...)
True or false:
I often cry after masturbating.
I sometimes dream about having sex with my mother/father.
I have an interest in theater.
I consider myself comfortable speaking openly to others. I have a psychological case file, which is currently open, or have received psychiatric treatment in the past two years.
I have faced significant legal problems in my life. I often find myself daydreaming about violent acts...
Pretty basic stuff, psychological profiling and such.
B.B. O.H.O. has provided cell diagrams. These cells will continue to be provided with missions, projects, etc. relevant to their placement. If successful, this would provide for memetic infection, and good times for all. (Additionally it would allow us to provide cultural nudges. Part of the beauty of the cell concept

is, of course, that no one involved at any level knows who else is involved, or where information is coming from. We are all moles. I will say that I am not the one running the show, nor is the Mother Hive Brain syndicate the only dis-organization involved-this connected with other similarly intentioned orgs.)

So what I want to know... is ? Are you ready? Meet us in front of the KOP mall in a week. We will have supplies.

In closing, consider this aphorism:

Our sages say, 'the kidneys give advice'. In particular, the right kidney relates to spiritual advice or introspection. The kidneys act similarly to the 'conscience', as is said, 'by night my kidneys chastise me'.

This refers to the 'chesbon nefesh' (introspection) of the month of Iyar. Mind your dreams, Agent 888. Mind your dreams.

It was only when I finished that I realized one of my coworkers had been reading it over my shoulder.

"What is that all about, man?" he asked, trying to be chummy. You'd have to meet the guy, but trust me. He has no friends for a reason.

"It's... online role-playing."

"Oh," he said. "Is that some kind of sex thing?"

"What? No. It's... you know, swords. Castles. Demons. Like D&D."

"Right. Dork." He had lost interest, and wandered out of the cubicle like a drunken rhinoceros.

Keeping the two worlds separate wasn't that difficult. The 'Real World' was an autopilot routine that I followed, so I could eat without having to hunt game with a spear, and sleep without foraging for branches in the forest. Idle hands.

—

A week later, I found myself staring at one of the many entrances to the King of Prussia mall from inside a gas mask. For those who haven't had the pleasure, let me just say KOP is like the Platonic ideal of 'shopping mall', which is to say that it is placid Hell on Earth, with elevator music. The 7th circle, fake marble, and all the people are display mannequins come to life.

It was a warm day in early fall, and I was a great deal more warm because the hazmat suit was less than breezy. I looked down at myself and shook my head. Was the giant bumblebee screen print going too far?

Beside me stood Agent777, Agent117, and Agent113. Agent156 had called out at the last minute, because he said he had to babysit his friend's pet spider monkey. I had met some of them before, but knew none of them particularly well.

All of us were wearing these obnoxious hazmat suits, and holding devices that Agent036 had designed in a garage, choked with second-hand electronics and pot smoke. He'd scored the suits too, or so I was told. Suburban patrons whipped past, coming and going like ants, casting hasty and uncomfortable glances in our direction.

The devices were covered with flashing lights, dials, and weird analog visual displays. They looked a lot like something from Ghostbusters. Very scary to the proles, but absolutely useless.

As I looked us all up and down, it dawned on me that with the gas masks and suits on, we could have been anyone. I mean, I'd communicated with many of them online before. I had met someone going by 'Agent777' at a cafe a few months ago. But anyone could go by 'Agent777'. This was the veil of anonymity that we all hid behind, like our suits.

Hm, strike that from this brain-wave transcribed record. It sounded better in my head. Or I guess this is my head. At any rate, our mission was simple: go into the mall, walk up to patrons, and run these devices up and down their bodies.

Meanwhile, one of the other Agents checked down meaningless notes on a clipboard, and another repeated the mantra repeatedly:

"Nothing to worry about, ma'am (or sir)."

"Nothing to see here, carry on."

"This is just a routine inspection."

"Enjoy your shopping, sir."

And so on. Of course, when people hear "nothing to worry about," they worry a lot. When they hear, "nothing to see here," they look around with new eyes.

I imagined that was the purpose of this reality pranking: to snap people out of their daily habits. In the past, that had always been the M.O., when you got down to it. Even after my conversation with the Buyer, I had no way to know if he had actually, finally, gone completely over the edge. And he'd dragged us all with him.

Inside the mall, I glanced over my shoulder to see 777 bantering with a bleached blonde with pigtails and a tramp stamp at the food court.

He spoke: "I see you are a student of medicine or the hermetic arts... Agent 777, pleased to 'meat' you." He emphasized the word with the sort of a relish which made his lecherous double entendre explicitly audible.

She stared back blankly, with a glazed-over expression. I couldn't tell if this was because she had no idea what he was getting at, or if she was simply—like any other normal human being would be—shocked at the sight of a man in a hazmat suit with a device looking like the PKE meter from Ghostbusters, casually hitting on her in the middle of the food court as she ate her Mu Gu Gai Pan. "Excuse me?"

"What, did I sneeze?" he asked.

"No... I mean, I don't think so. I'm not a nurse... and I don't know anything about your hermit studies."

"Hermetic," he corrected gently with a chuckle. "Your tattoo... those are the twin serpents of Hermes, entwined around the staff of caduceus. The serpents represent, alternately, the double-helix coil of human DNA, and the ida and pingala currents of the Kundalini, the male and female principles of energy which are polarities that constantly seek reconciliation through union..." He licked his lips.

To the detached observer—and I'd say I qualified as both—this conversation could have been happening anywhere, between any two people. The mammalian mating script is the same, and it might not even matter if the people involved understand what the other is saying. Like watching a bad sex ed video with a head full of blotter acid. Let me cut to the end: teenage pregnancy isn't pretty.

And holy fucking Christ, he was still going at it—

"... and the polarities and 'check and balance' masculine or feminine qualities inherent in the sephira on the tree of life. The duality of these principles are only apparent below the abyss, however... Above the abyss, the two become one. Could be inaccurate to say they 'become' one, as they always were... Three in One, if you will. And the one is none, or Nun, a fish, which is to say Death, according to traditional correspondences... As it was written by the Ancients, 'By My Smell Shall Ye Know Me, And By My Smell I Shall Be Known. As Above, So Below, Sim Salabim bim ba Saladoo Saladin'. This is all exceedingly technical and scientific, mind you. I am a scientist. I work for the government."

Predictably, she stared back at him, mouth agape. "Ohhh kay? The tattoo... I saw it at the display counter of Sacred Art Designs. That place is great, they do very cool spiritual designs, you know? I'm very spiritual..."

Jackpot, I could plainly read from his expression.

She frowned. "This doesn't have anything to do with any... terrorism or anything, does it?" The word was whispered, barely audible.

"All I can say is we are investigating a claim of some sort, which I can neither confirm nor deny at this point."

"Just what Agency are you working for, anyway?" she asked.

He ignored her question. "We suspect this is just a routine sort of prank. But our Agency would be negligent if we didn't take the time to investigate. So far, we've found nothing and I suspect that will be that."

Meanwhile, Agent 117 was giving a woman hell. She flapped her piglet arms up and down in a comical expression of frustration, stomping her foot as she screamed, "I KNOW MY RIGHTS, YOU GODDAMNED SONUVABITCH. DO I LOOK LIKE A GODDAMNED SANDNIGGER TO YOU? I AIN'T NO GODDAMNED TERRORIST!"

"Ma'am," he began. "I'm afraid our meters are reading some sort of paleoanametamystikal interference coming from your shopping bags or purse. Now, if you would just cooperate with my questioning I will be happy to let you go on shopping but if you give me trouble I'm going to have to bring you in for a full body cavity search."

Her eyes were like two beets, rupturing out of their fleshy sockets. "I TOLD YOUR ASS ALREADY! TAKE A LOOK AT ME, I AIN'T NO TERRORIST! WHO'S YOUR GODDAMNED SUPERVISOR? I WANT YOUR BADGE NUMBER AND I WANNA SPEAK TO YOUR SUPERVISOR."

Agent 117 smiled. "Ma'am, the Agency I represent is sanctioned by the U.S. National Defense Authorization Act, and by this act I am entitled to detain you, indefinitely and without trial, if you continue to obstruct justice and interfere with my investigations here. You don't like it? Take it up with your government."

Her face had turned the same color as her eyes. He smiled, and paused to crack his knuckles for dramatic effect.

Agent 113 strolled leisurely through the entrance to Feverish Trend. He moseyed up behind a young teenage boy shopping for 'Rage Against the Machine' T-shirts and tapped him nonchalantly on the back. The young boy whirled around. His expression changed quickly from surprise to terror.

"Son, do you realize you are supporting dissident materials, and as such, you are encouraging domestic terrorism and unlawful enemy combatants? I hope you realize this is grounds for a search. Show me your ID. Now."

The kid looked ready to piss himself, and for a moment, Agent 113 felt a slight pang of sympathy. But the ends justified the means. Or, he was just a sadist. "Son... we can do this two ways. The easy way, or my way. Your ID, if you please."

The boy began to puff up his chest. "Hey man, I know my rights. You can't just search me for no reason. You pull that shit on me and I'll sue your ass and whatever NWO fascists you are working for."

"When a man in a hazmat suit asks you very politely to show your ID to him, you'd best comply before you get your skull cracked open. Now please, your ID, and you can be back on your way to listening to Avril Lavigne in no time..."

—

In a similar way, all of us were having a Grand Old Time playing dress up in our Mother Hive Brain issue hazmat suits, when—as if out of nowhere—sirens and loudspeakers blared through the acoustically reflective mall:

"STAY WHERE YOU ARE."

Everything froze and then broke into chaos, like a giant pane of glass, which shudders for a moment and then—POOF!—explodes in a great huff of shards. Down the hallway, we could see a group of mall cops pointing in our general direction, throngs of white suburban mannequin people pushing and shoving in all directions, and behind them stood real cops in SWAT gear. We took one look at each other and tore off in the opposite direction.

We scattered down side corridors and into random stores, depositing pieces of our costumes in trash bins and clothing racks as we went.

I was feeling pretty superior as I made a turn around the bend behind Baskin Robbins, when I plowed full speed into a blur of black. Skidding backward on the floor with a squeal, I looked up to see a scowling face and a nightstick.

As if in slow motion, the stick raised another few inches, and then came down on my shin. Hard. I wailed uncontrollably, and curled into a ball. He grabbed me by my neck and somehow managed to lift me to my feet, in one fluid motion slapping cuffs on my hands and dragging me down the corridor.

He certainly outperformed the stereotypes I knew of donut eating cops.

"Look," I managed to get out, "we were just—it was just a fucking joke, OK?"

"You really don't want to talk right now," he said, still dragging me, my toes barely kissing the ground.

"Wait. How did you know where we'd be?" I asked. "You got here real fast."

"We got a tip, telling us exactly what you planned to do."

"What?"

He elbowed me in the ribs as a reply. "I said shut up."

"You're not going to read me my rights?" I momentarily felt like the kid in the record store must have felt.

He stopped and stared right through me. His eyes were made of chiseled ivory. "You have no rights." He dropped me on the floor. I could hear boots clacking, the hushed whispers of onlookers, my stomach growling in agitation. Then everything went black as a bag went over my head.

—

The interrogation room was nothing special. An office conference room. The man seated opposite me was husky, forty going on seven-hundred, and world-weary. I could tell this from the lines under his eyes, like the rings on the inside of a hewn tree.

"I'm Trevino," he said, the tone of his voice doing nothing to dispel my narrative.

"Agent 888, err, Johny Jones," I replied, a little more cheery than one might expect. "Oppositional-defiant, I guess," I said aloud, accidentally.

"Christ, you kids," the man muttered, leaning back in his chair. "Alright, I'm going to ask you some questions, and you're going to answer them, you know. In a way that makes some kind of fucking sense."

I nodded.

"What was that stunt you pulled today?"

"It was a prank."

"A prank?"

"Yeah."

"To start, it's illegal to go into a public place as a group with your face covered. Did you know that?" he asked.

"No, I didn't actually."

"Oh, so you didn't hear about those kids on Wall Street, getting bagged and tagged for wearing those Guy Fawkes masks at their little sit in?"

Silence. He tapped a finger on the table. "I'm going to cut to it. There was an anonymous tip of a terrorist attack on the mall. So the hammer came down pretty hard. If you can answer a few things for me, we'll overlook the criminal charges and you can overlook the splint on your shin, yeah?"

I looked down, only then realizing what had happened. I had a vague recollection of being in a hospital and getting a morphine injection. The pieces suddenly clicked into place. Not oppositional-defiance. I was high as a fucking kite on acid, holding another kite on ketamine 20,000 leagues under a sea of tits. Hold on. A *tip*? Fucking Bradley. I wanted to be angry, but I couldn't find that emotion. There was just a warm gooey blob where anger was supposed to be.

"What do you know about Mother Hive Brain?" Trevino asked. Hard to say that and sound imposing.

"That some kind of club?"

He scrutinized my face. "Yeah."

"Are you asking me out on a date?"

He frowned. "Stop trying to be cute. They're wanted for starting an insurrection. Sleeper agents popping up all over the place, it's like playing whack-a-mole."

"Ah." My eyes narrowed. Why would he tell me that? Was he testing me? "I wouldn't know anything about that, sir. I'll be honest with you too, okay? A friend of mine put us up to this stunt. I mean he suggested it and we thought it would be funny. And I bet you all the donuts in the world that he was the one who gave that anonymous tip. I am so going to kick his ass." The best cover story is often the truth.

"Donuts? Was that supposed to be a cop joke?"

"Hm. Sorry."

"No, it was pretty funny. It's not like we can't take a fucking joke from a twenty-something role-playing nerd playing dress up."

"I'm just a hair past thirty," I said.

Trevino sighed. "Mm, right. Whatever. Look. You're free to go."

The surveillance must have started then. Or had Bradley handed my scent to their dogs from the beginning?

—

I should have expected it, but the following day I was fired. I sat down on my desk, opened up my work email, and there was a letter in my box. The salient details ended with "...please clean out your desk by the end of the day."

I had been outed as a 'terrorist'. Now everyone who knew, would treat me like something between a rabid dog and the creepy uncle who gets too touchy-feely when he gets drunk. I tried to look on the bright side. After all, I hated the fucking place. I didn't like anyone there, and nothing I did in any way contributed to anyone's life in any meaningful way. Except for the whole money thing.

I rode home in our Nissan. I put on the jazz music that tends to cheer me up at the end of the workday. Stella normally tolerated it quietly. I think this evening it was Thelonius Monk, live with Coltrane at the Carnegie Hall. My mind raced on about how I would start the conversation upon returning home. I envisioned a mortifying interaction:

"Hey, hon... so, uh. You know how I had that job which secured our financial situation, letting us eat and afford the custom furniture and high-end wine we like so much? Well, I kind of fucked that up because I was arrested in connection with a faked bomb threat... I'm sure McDonalds won't mind, I'll just apply there."

I knew she loved me, but maybe in the way someone would love an orphaned puppy... a scruffy, socially awkward puppy. And everyone has their limit. I could only get away with being uncompromisingly myself, while being fired from every job I had, for so long.

And I loved her. Maybe more than any of the others, not because she represented the unattainable goal but because she represented the ideal made flesh. The real, the imminent, and the immediate woman I had always hoped I would someday have at my side. She always grounded me when I needed it throughout all of my ups and downs, and the worst of my anxiety had to do with the fear of her abandoning me when I needed her to lean on. All that said, I'm not sure I entirely knew her.

The Nissan pulled into the driveway. There was a pregnant silence.

"I have to tell you something, Stella."

She breathed in deeply and let out a barely audible sigh.

I attempted to cushion the blow. "I love you, you know that?"

More silence. She sized me up, and gave a wry smile.

"You lost your job again, didn't you?" she said blandly. There was only a hint of detectable emotion—that of an exasperated mother trying to deal with a stubborn and insubordinate child.

"Look, before you start in on me like I know you're going to do, just let me explain... this time it's different, it really wasn't my fault. I mean, it's not my responsibility. I didn't make this happen to myself. And Bradley..."

"I don't like that creep. And I know he was the reason you got it into your head to do that bullshit... I think you're out of your mind. This isn't a game."

I was getting dry mouth and my palms were starting to sweat. "Bradley told me it was just going to be a little prank. We'd have a bit of a laugh and that'd be it. I had no idea any of the bomb threat stuff was going to happen."

"Jesus Christ, Johny, are you fifteen? Most adults... they... they just don't do that kind of thing, and I think you must be bored with me, or something, because you are really reaching... I don't think this is who you are. And now, this little piece of concept art or geek fest role-play thing, or whatever it is, has cost you your job."

"I was a suspect!" I shot back, feeling dejected.

"It doesn't matter, Johny. Anyone they even 'suspect' of farting and coughing the wrong way, they'll come and lock them away now, and you're playing at this with your twisted fuck of a friend? This is serious, people could get hurt."

I was reaching for the right words. They wouldn't come. "Stella," I began. "I love you. I had no idea it would happen like this. You don't understand. I've known Bradley for years and he just... always has this way of coming back into my life. I can't help it. He's just an old friend, and we thought this would be a funny prank to do to help wake people up..." I was trembling.

"What the hell do you think you're waking them up to, anyway?" she asked. She looked into me without a trace of any recognizable emotion. I searched for something human in her eyes, but found them strangely blank. She smiled again, briefly, and taking another deep breath, she opened the door and walked briskly into the house.

—

I remember Bradley taking me aside once, and confiding in me in one of his rare moments of near-humanity. He seemed perturbed, anxious.

"You are familiar with some of the black ops the CIA ran on unsuspecting test subjects concerning mind control, right?"

I nodded. We were in my basement at the time, converted into a make-shift recording studio. He was making me uncomfortable, but didn't seem to notice or care.

"Yeah, sure. What are you getting at?"

"Well, I'm sure you've heard of Operation Monarch, alternately Operation Mockingbird. They call it 'Monarch' or 'Butterfly Programming' because the butterfly always returns to its point of origin again... it's a way of controlling chaos. Zero-point, end game, dig? Commonly referred to in Discordian circles as Operation Mindfuck, or just 'O.M.'..."

"Bradley, you look like a tool when you attempt to make connections between the CIA mind control and Discordian propaganda." And probably reading it to me straight off the Internet, I thought to myself.

"Am I?" he replied ambiguously. "I will tell you this: Kerry Thornley, who helped bring Discordianism to the forefront of the 'new age' hodge podge of metaphysical wankery, knew Lee Harvey personally. His public story regarding this matter was that he was originally an unwitting test subject of MK Ultra or Operation Monarch, depending on what you'd like to call it. The bottom line is that Thornley knew something most people don't. And that became Discordianism. Doesn't it strike you as odd that Operation Mindfuck would bear the same initials as a legit CIA mind control op like Operation Monarch? Do you know how many people have now been conditioned with Monarch mind control cues, via pop culture and media? Teachers? Friends? Family?" he asked.

"No, Brad. Not exactly." I wasn't really paying attention. Maybe that's my trouble: I never pay attention to the right things. Didn't pay attention to Stella, never even paid attention to the Buyer until long after he had played me like a pawn.

"I'll tell you how many, Agent. A lot. A whole lot, that's how many. A fucking majority. That's how many."

I finally looked his way. "How does that tie in to what we're doing, Bradley?"

"I've discovered the OMEGA self-destruct button. IT is a fail-safe level of programming for human automatons, which ensures a timely death for all of those in whom the response has been triggered. I've learned how to trigger it. I'm building it into all MHB sleeper agents."

"Uh huh," I mumbled absent-mindedly, zoning out again. "You got into my Adderall again, didn't you?"

"Uh huh. Listen, you ever hear of the .'.B.B.'.?" He eyed me in a really strange way. "The Blue Brotherhood," he continued. "They're a mystical recruiting organization in theory, but in practice, they're a front for the Brotherhood of the Sacerdotal Knights of National Security or the N.'.S.'.A.'., which is to say, the only real occult lodge operating behind the scenes with any real political clout these days other than the C.'.I.'.A.'.."

"Whatever you say, Bradley." I spoke softly, shrugging it off. I continued with my work and he left silently.

That's the last thing I remembered for a while, because Benzodiazavision kicked in and the next moment was, by the clocks, almost a day later. Benzos are like some kind of time-travel device, if you take enough of them. Pop! Suddenly you're in the future. (And you have no pants).

I awoke to find a 'field report' I'd written, I guess.

```
FIELD REPORT: AGENT 888
OPERATION MONARCH MIND CONTROL CONTEL
Be forewarned: we are entering dangerously weird
territory here. The cover-up I'm reporting on was
allegedly responsible for the death of at least
three individuals, all ostensibly suicides. All
were artists and writers attempting to deal with
the material I am now piecing together. I feel as
though I may be following footprints directly into
```

quicksand, but I feel the risk is always worth it,
when the Truth is at stake...

I buried my head in my hands. This was getting out of control.

VI. Getting the Band Back Together

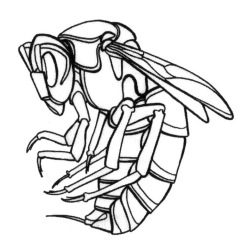

2012

The mask you happen to wear is just a role, but the name whispered to you in dreams, that's another story. Every action from the smallest to the largest is directed at advancing the evolution of the species, taking whatever risks are necessary to attain that peak of pressure that results in genius or insanity.
I am not speaking strictly scientifically. I mean the unfolding of the potentialities contained within each of us, like a rosebud gradually opening into a flower, the secrets encoded in our DNA spirals which only the right sequence of events can unlock...
Like us, each of these "locks" is unique, and so we must find equally unique keys. —**Gabriel De Leon**

Jesus rubbed her eyes. The lights of passing cars streaked by, like trails during an acid trip. It was raining. Soothing patter of droplets on the glass. A slate blue, gloomy evening. She blinked, tried to sit up, but something was holding her in place. Seat belt.

She heard voices in the front seat, chattering like two squirrels. Though she could only make out part of the conversation, she knew the speakers well: Dionysus and Loki.

Her eyes closed again. She took another drag off a cigarette, only then realizing she had lit one. Being comatose was so much more pleasant.

"That was brilliant. I prefer a plan with more mescaline, but..." That would be Dionysus.

"All your plans start with getting high. You ever notice that?" Loki asked.

"Ah, but there wouldn't be a ward to escape from. We'd just slip between the dancing molecules," Dionysus said.

"It really amazes me that you can tie your own shoes."

Jesus cracked open her eye. She was still dressed in inmate chic. A cigarette dangled from her lips, half ash. The ash finally fell all over her chest.

"What. The. Fuck," she said, brushing the ashes away with three curt motions.

Loki looked back at her, driving casually with one hand. "Oh, she speaks. Have a nice nap, did we?"

Jesus groaned. "Ugh. Had to wait almost a year to break us out of that hell-hole, did we?"

Snorting, Loki said, "I can turn around. Come back for your anniversary?"

Cody shook his head. "No way, man. No fucking way. I'll get out and walk." He craned his head, looking out the window. "Really, the corner up ahead looks just fine..."

"How'd you spend ten months locked up with this guy, if you can't take a joke?" Loki asked.

Dionysus laughed. "He's from So Cal, They don't have sarcasm out there. Maybe we can import it for them, along with irony and a healthy dose of Eastern indifference. What's the conversion rate on that?"

Cody crossed his arms. "We do indifference just fine."

"Terrific. Now that we have that sorted, where exactly are we going?" Jesus asked.

Loki shrugged. "Well, I broke you guys out. I thought maybe you could come up with step two of this plan."

Silence fell in the van for several moments.

"Alright, so... I bunked with Dionysus here. And I recognize Jesus from the halls of the asylum... but who are you?" Cody asked.

"Loki."

Cody pondered that a moment. "Huh. You guys a cult or something?"

66

"Well, since you put it that way, I suppose we are," Dionysus said.

"Or were," Jesus said.

"They kind of got themselves mistaken for terrorists. It put a little crimp in the Wednesday potluck," Loki said.

"Since I put it what way?" Cody asked.

Dionysus shrugged. "Well, you could put it a lot of other ways. Like... we are a disorganization, a chaote order of the highest disorder, a mythological manifestation of—"

Cody put up his hands. "Now you're just freaking me out."

"I'd think you would be used to that by now, too," Jesus said.

"You'd think that, but no. For my part, there's not much to say. I'm Cody. I play guitar."

"They put you in Pennhurst for playing guitar?" Jesus asked.

"Music wasn't how I lost my mind. It's how I got it back," Cody said.

"Er. Right," Jesus said.

Cody sighed. "It all started with my wife, Margarite. We met at a small coffeehouse in Santa Cruz. I remember... the place was heavy with the tangy smell of lemon, dill and shrimp that night. I'll never forget the smell. I matched gazes with Margarite's chocolate brown eyes after I started the second set. My hands fumbled, the notes came out all wrong. Then I ripped loose. It was a message for only one set of ears. I was asking—are you Her? The tears in her eyes said yes. The awkward sensation felt by the rest of the audience was the result of their unwitting voyeurism."

"I think I know how they felt," Jesus said.

Cody didn't seem to notice the not-so-subtle nudge. "The two of us spent that night drinking margaritas, salty as sweat, first in a nearby bar, then in a hotel room. It could've been tawdry, but it was our Eden. The next month in Vegas was painfully sweet, mostly spent looking into her eyes as the two of us lay moistly entwined..."

"Whoa, whoa, whoa, man. I was trying to be polite, but stop." Jesus broke into laughter.

"—She let out a faint gasp, and then suddenly, she wasn't there at all. Her softness was still all around me. Rose petals everywhere, drifting away coyly in the spring breeze." Cody looked out the window with ghostly eyes.

"See? There's a reason he was in the bin with us. Though I think that's more than he said the whole time we roomed together," Dionysus said.

Jesus kept laughing.

Dionysus continued, "But this much I can vouch for: he can play better than you or I, Jesus. And I know you're no slouch."

Jesus' hysterical laughter wouldn't subside. She was crying. "We've got an over-sharing idiot savant, a transsexual, and two assholes. Sounds like a rock band to me!"

"Count me out. More of an audio book guy," Loki said.

"What do you do, then?" Cody asked.

"Paint-by-numbers. Prison breaks."

Jesus' laughing fit subsided very suddenly. "Ahem. Since we have no better plans, do you guys want to find a place to eat? I'm fucking starving."

—

They pulled up in front of a pub in the outskirts of the Philadelphia suburbs, right in the spot where the Venn diagram of WASP, redneck, and Amish country overlapped. The sky looked like cracked charcoal.

"This place work?" Loki asked.

Jesus noticed there was a tractor in the parking lot. That wasn't a good sign. "You have cash?"

"Yes." Loki sighed.

It was a busy night. From the look and sound of it, half the place was half lit, and the rest were about ready to make sweet love to a toilet seat. There was a small stage and the setup for a band, but the band was nowhere in sight.

Jesus headed straight for the bar.

"I thought you were hungry," Dionysus said.

"Liquid bread!" Jesus exclaimed, grabbing the last free bar stool. The rest of them clustered uncomfortably behind.

"When we go on, man?" Someone to their left asked. Jesus turned towards the voice. It was a group of three would-be cock-rockers two decades past their prime. Her favorite sort of assholes.

"I don't know. Where's Rich?" another asked.

"Rich?" Jesus asked.

"Rich! You know, the guy that runs the place. He disappeared with that girl with the..." He made the universal 'large breasts' hand gesture.

"Fuck if I know. Not here?"

Jesus turned to the bartender, a sadly energetic woman who looked like she had taken one too many 'falls down the stairs'.

"DRINKS ALL AROUND!" Jesus exclaimed.

Loki rolled his eyes. "Sure. Why not?"

"What'll ya have?" the bartender asked.

"Stouts and whiskey," Jesus said.

A redhead leaned towards Jesus. "Can you count me in on that, babe?"

Dionysus stared at her, slack-jawed. She had been listening in since they entered the bar, but that isn't what caught his attention. Nor was it those eyes and teeth, glistening like beetles.

Loki elbowed him. But she either didn't seem to notice, or didn't care, and he remained lost in thought.

"Drinks for the musicians, too. You're the entertainment, right?" Jesus asked.

With a grin, one of them nodded. "Yeah. Thanks."

—

The three of them carried their drinks to a nearby table, leaving Jesus to her peculiar carousing.

"I swear I've seen that woman before," Dionysus said.

"Who?" Loki asked.

"The smokin' redhead at the bar, I'm guessing," Cody said.

"Eh," Loki said.

"I'm not kidding. It's on the tip of my tongue..." Dionysus said.

"I'll bet it is," Cody said. He lit a smoke. "Nice to be somewhere civilized, where you can kick back, light up a smoke–"

"You're not listening to me," Dionysus said, refusing to let it drop.

"I'm just saying, you've been locked up for a year..."

"Right, which makes this all the stranger. I'm sure I've seen her. Recently," Dionysus said. She radiated a hungry confidence that seemed to coil around his chest like a python. This presence rubbed against buried memories more than any detail of appearance. But the headstone was worn blank.

A waitress approached them. "What'll it be?"

—

Jesus passed yet another drink to the band. Just 'one of the guys'. Har-har. She made exaggerated manly gestures and gave them a wide smile. Anyone who knew her would recognize the smile as bitingly insincere, but it was already too late for this lot.

"No, no, no. What I'm saying is—" One of them started, but he was over-run by a series of guffaws.

"Liquididated bread!" his friend screamed, still laughing. The laughter turned into a gurgle as a stream of alcoholic vomit lurched out of his stom-ach. Waitresses scrambled to the site of the incident as the band rolled and slipped on their regurgitated fluids. The ensuing series of events would surely haunt their dreams for the rest of their lives.

"Why are you—wait, we're the band! Where's Rich?" one of them yelled.

His friend mewled and wheezed like a newborn, muttering "ma... ma... ma..." with each desperate breath.

The bouncers went into motion, escorting them rather impolitely out the door.

"Don't you remember? You guys already played! Awesome show. No, really fantastic. Now out you go..." Jesus said, sitting back down on the barstool.

"Ah, I love doing that," she said, sipping her stout. "It's like the tortoise and the hare. Slow and steady wins the race."

"Nice performance," the redhead said.

"Oh. We haven't gotten started yet," Jesus said.

She gave a crooked grin. "Is that right?"

"Jesus. Pleased to meet you." She bowed and did a sarcastic, Renn-faire hand-gesture.

"Lilith. Likewise."

"Lilith... really?" Jesus asked.

"You go by 'Jesus' and you want to give me a hard time?"

Jesus laughed. "Touche."

"It's Lola Rose Parsons. But that's a fucking mouthful. Who are your friends?"

Jesus led her over to the table. "This is Loki, Dionysus, and... Cody."

They looked at one another awkwardly. Dionysus scrutinized her, and made a decision. "So, yeah. This is going to sound like the oldest line in the book. And it's not a good line, or book, but... do I know you from somewhere?"

Lilith smiled. "Sure. We fucked like crazed alley cats."

"We did?"

"Maybe in a past incarnation," she said. They stared at one another, until Lilith smiled. "Can I have a seat, or..."

Dionysus moved over in the booth to make room. "You're a Buddhist? The idea of karma-as-ethical-imperative seems really childish to me. No offense. Under whose authority am I forced to be reincarnated as a shrew, based on my actions in this life? And how can a particular ant be such a 'good' ant that one day it gets to be—joy of joys—a human?"

Lilith watched him talk, amused. "Is this how you hit on all the women?"

Loki snorted. "And it works. Go figure."

"Listen," Jesus said. "I just sent the band out the door, full of enough alcohol to kill Leonard Cohen three times over. You want to steal the stage, or argue about reincarnation?"

"Finally, one of you says something I can understand!" Cody exclaimed, leaping out of his seat.

They approached the stage. No one seemed to notice, or care. Cody, Dionysus and Jesus began tinkering with the gear. Loki went off to find the mythical 'Rich' character. Lilith sat on the side of the stage, kicking her legs back and forth. She quickly sketched out a series of chord progressions with her lipstick on a notepad.

They nodded at each other. She took a deep breath, then stood up and grabbed the mic, a bottle of tequila in her other hand.

"You ready?" she asked.

Jesus and Cody nodded. Dionysus just looked stunned.

Lilith began chanting. "...In the temple of the temple of the temple of the Holy sits a woman who is waiting who is waiting for the sun in the temple of the temple in the temple of the Holy creeping..." Dionysus recognized the words from somewhere, but didn't have time to think about it. He tapped out the time and started building a rhythm atop it. Cody followed right along with something modal, like a Moravian village musician had been handed a telecaster and distortion pedal. Jesus joined with a steady, loping baseline. And here, leading the service, was a sleazy Joan of Arc, telegraphing the virgin-whore affectation like the costume it is. Wanting to show everyone God so they could piss in his eye.

It took the audience several minutes to realize that music was playing, but by the time they figured it out, an unusual thing happened. Casual nodding became whiplash-inducing head banging. Dancers started peeling off their clothes, which in several cases was a less than good thing. A kissing couple fell on a table, rolled off and went right on to fucking on the bar-room floor. Drunks circle-danced around the pair, scream-singing along with the chorus to some song, a song that had nothing to do with the music which was playing. The bartender poured liquor from bottles straight into open mouths.

And that was when things got really crazy.

—

Eventually, the white trash hurricane ran out of fuel and dispersed to the four corners of the Earth. Bouncers carried those who couldn't carry themselves, leaving bodies strewn across the field behind the parking lot, all bloated and moaning like civil war ghosts who refused to leave York. The bar was a disaster. Several tables were splintered. Bottles and glasses smashed. Quite a few laws broken. But, surprisingly, no one was seriously injured, and most of the damage was superficial.

During the show, Loki had found Rich. He was sauntering out of what could have been his office, or a closet, dressed like a hair-metal version of Robin Hood. From the looks of it, he'd just finished a whole lot of coke with his 'female companion'. She was hanging on his arm and had makeup smeared nearly down to her over-abundant cleavage. The smile on her face said she wasn't minding her job at the moment.

Loki figured things could go either way. There was a full-scale mob in his bar, and a band was playing whom he hadn't scheduled for the night. He braced himself for the worst.

As it turned out, Rich was in a benevolent mood. So, rather than working on an escape plan, Loki casually introduced them all after the show.

—

"I don't know who the hell you are. But that was great," Rich said.

"We're Babylon," Lilith announced casually.

Loki eyed her. Dionysus and Jesus shrugged simultaneously.

"Don't think I've heard of you. Anyhow, I've got to take damages out... but I've got somethin'," Rich said. He held out a wad of bills that insisted on re-rolling themselves into little cylinders when left alone.

"Sorry about the mess," Loki reiterated.

"Are you kidding?" Rich laughed. His face was redder than Santa Claus. "Our bar is cleaned out. Maybe some of it was on the house, but I've never seen anything like that. And I was at the original Woodstock. Fuck man! What a fucking party!" he clapped his hands together, and then wiped them on his leopard-print spandex pants.

"I tend to have that kind of effect on people," Lilith said.

"Yes. Well. Yes." He fumbled for something witty to say but found nothing, so he just moved on. "We'll be closing soon, though. I'd offer you drinks, but..."

"No worries," Lilith said.

"I was wondering, you wanna do this every week?" Rich asked unexpectedly.

They eyed one another. Lilith shrugged. "You guys want to go pro?"

"Guys?" Jesus asked sharply.

"Bipeds," Lilith said. "Sorry."

"What do you mean, 'go pro'?" Loki asked.

"I mean cracking open life's ribcage and crawling out like the tendrils of a sprout. I mean eating goat cheese in the sun and fucking her anywhichway possible. Obviously," she said.

"Hey now," Cody said. Loki merely sighed.

"Sure. Pro." Jesus looked around the room, frowning. "I'm hungry."

Loki sighed again and handed over some of the cash.

If anyone asked later, Lilith would say they'd gotten their start in some shit bar, before they went on a national rampage. "It was always easiest," she'd say, "making myth out of the truth. Though a lie will do in a pinch."

—

Trevino was signing paperwork for a clerk. The clerk was staring over his shoulder, his mouth half-hanging open to reveal a set of buckteeth.

A children's chorus stood in front of the motel, singing an off-key version of Annie's 'Tomorrow'.

"Length of stay?" the clerk finally asked.

"Two days. When's checkout?" Trevino answered. The clerk didn't respond. "Hey. When's checkout?"

"Eleven. ...Is that what they mean by mongoloid?"

Trevino finally looked over his shoulder at the procession outside. "Mongol...?"

The children's chorus was set up on temporary bleachers. They were developmentally disabled to various degrees, but all of them were unquestionably the happiest children to butcher 'Tomorrow'. Behind them, a banner read 'The Holding Hands Chorus! WE LOVE YOU!' A small crowd of parents and onlookers clustered around the children, waving miniature American flags. Trevino also noticed a mobile broadcast HQ and the expected entourage of press, cameramen, and interns who came along with such a media travesty.

"Downs. Not mongoloid," Trevino said.

"So what's mongoloid mean?"

"Downs. But it's insulting."

A technician in overalls walked up to the mobile broadcast HQ from behind, opened the driver's door, and hopped in.

The clerk furrowed his brow in thought. "So 'mongoloid' is like 'nigger', but for retards."

Trevino fixed the clerk with a level stare. Behind them, the mobile broadcast HQ rumbled to a start. With looks of horror, the reporter and cameraman put down their equipment and ran towards it, but were forced to dive to the ground to avoid being crushed. Trevino barreled out of the door, surveyed the scene, and stopped in his tracks.

The mobile broadcast HQ did a tire-squealing turn around the bleachers, honking wildly. A horde of children scattered, cried, and applauded. Straightening out, it ran over the camera equipment and accelerated to escape.

Trevino drew his weapon, but struggled to get a clear shot. There were just too many waffling, wailing mongoloids. "IIIICE CWWWEAM TWUCK!" one of them screamed, pathetically trying to give chase.

Jesus clung to the rear door, waving a scimitar and bellowing incoherently as they drove off.

"Cunt," Trevino growled. The clerk raised his eyebrow at him.

Trevino sighed as he re-holstered his gun. "Sorry about that. Cancel the room. I've got to go."

—

Stonesifer Autobody was located in an old shipping warehouse, just outside of Grand Junction, Colorado, amidst a thick tangle of trees, brambles and the rusted hulls of cars and vans, strewn about like boats after a tsunami.

From the outside, the structure looked abandoned. Indeed, it was a rare night when the thin tendrils of headlights would slither down the nearby street. However, walk up through the brush and put your ear to the sliding doors on the backside of the building, and you might hear the whirring sound of pneumatic winches, or the huffing of hydraulics. Inside was a sprawling complex of automotive gear, bunks built out of wood from flats, and rusted barrels full of everything from gasoline to ether.

Beside this garage was a small office done up like any other red-blooded American mechanic's reception area: potted plastic plants, various muscle car and pin-up magazines, a coffee pot which gurgled sludge and a fake, conspicuously-stained leather sofa. 'My Way Or The Highway' was written on a giant placard, lashed, for no apparent reason, to a bunch of steer horns and some empty bottles of Southern Comfort.

The owner and sole proprietor was surrounded by an array of electrical equipment and half-read sci-fi novels.

The phone rang. His secretary didn't seem to know what the noise was. It had obviously been a while since their last paying gig.

"It's the phone Courtney," Gregor said, chuckling to himself as his lazy eye drifted in her direction and caressed her young frame. He whipped out a Camel Wide and lit it with his Zippo in the same practiced motion. "Answer it, hon."

"Stonesifer Autobody: My Way Or The Highway, how can I help you? Yes... yes... okay, one moment. Phone call for you, sir..." Courtney said, resting the receiver on her shoulder as she pressed on the hold button with an artificial pink fingernail. "Sounds like he might be drunk," she whispered.

Gregor took the phone. "Yo," he said gruffly.

She pursed her lips at him, winked, and walked away. Nodding his head, he pulled off his baseball cap and ran the back of his hand over his fore-head, leaving a sweaty smear in its wake.

"Fuck," he said. Then, "What? Oh, no, not you. Go on. I just soiled my purdy self. Yep, yep. All right, well, let me know the budget and when you'll need'r by and I'll fix it up real special... Someplace to lie low while I'm working on it? Fine. Fuck."

He pulled out a notepad and frantically took notes. When the list was complete, he said, "Don't dare tell me how a bunch of good-fer-nothings like yerselves got out of the loony bin. And in return, I won't tell you what I done with my sexretary last night," he grinned and hung up.

He wiped his hands with the oil-spattered rag meditatively, as if the action helped him think. It certainly didn't make his hands any cleaner. The smear on his forehead remained, forgotten. After a couple of minutes of contemplation, he looked up and started rummaging around piles of equipment in the garage.

—

The call came at four o'clock in the morning. Gregor flipped open his phone, still singing in a falsetto along with his Journey ring-tone.

"*Don't. Stop... believin'! Hold on to the feeeeelin'!* Uh huh. Look. It's four in the morning and this is my personal line. I'll sing whatever the fuck I want to sing. You almost here with your 'legally acquired' mobile broadcast... Uh. You want to call it 'The Behemoth' and paint it like a bumblebee? You're high, aren't you? Yeah, I can do that." He closed the phone.

"Put on the coffee, Courtney," he yelled. "It's gonna be a long night."

—

They all stood under the fluorescent lights in his office for a minute before anyone spoke.

Dionysus broke into a grin and hugged Gregor, clapping him on the back. "Agent 140! You smell like you've been fucking chimpanzees for a week. As usual." Though he was tall, his forehead still knocked against Gregor's chin.

"You too. So, let's see what you've got."

Gregor whistled when they walked into the garage. "This is like one of those C-40-X2's... though I guess it's a newer model. My thing is muscle cars, you know." He walked around it. "This vehicle is the fucking tits. Bumblebee pattern, you said?"

Dionysus and Jesus nodded eagerly. Loki sighed and shook his head.

Gregor laughed. "Talk about hiding in plain sight, huh? Bunks for how many?"

"Eight, more if we're getting cozy," Lilith said.

"Weapons?"

"Subtle," Loki said. "If we have to use them, it's probably too late."

Gregor looked slightly disappointed. He pushed play on a nearby boom box, which dangled from a chord on the wall. The theme from 'The A-Team' blared from the speakers. "Inspiration music. Let's go."

He handed a pair of welding goggles to Dionysus.

"Are you kidding me?" Loki asked.

"Oh, we're gonna have a shit-ton of fun!" Gregor took a pull from a bottle of Southern Comfort. "Let's start with the armor."

—

Almost a week to the day, they stood in the room, marveling at what they'd done.

"We turned an instrument of the devil into a bohemian's paradise," Dionysus said.

"Let's hope it doesn't end like Bohemian Rhapsody," Loki said.

"You've been a grump this whole damn time," Lilith said.

"I just... I have a deep phobia of imprisonment." Loki scowled.

"I dub thee Behemoth!" Lilith cracked a tequila bottle on the armored side of the vehicle.

Dionysus sadly watched its contents drip to the floor.

—

They were out of Colorado in a matter of hours, brazenly taking Route 70 straight out of Grand Junction, into the red bluffs and dusty plains of Utah. After several hours of stifling humidity, the water broke and unleashed a torrential downpour. Loki grumbled something about Noah's Ark as he cut speed. Uncommon weather was now common. He frowned. Did that make it common, or uncommon? Either way, he was sure that if he turned on the radio, there would be flash flood warnings on every AM station which wasn't presently preaching fire and brimstone damnation and $19.95 salvation.

Dionysus gazed through one of the windows by his bunk as he spoke into his hand-held recorder. This would be the first of many missives tossed out to lonely satellites and a sea of anonymous listeners, bobbing along in the night. He spoke quietly, but with gravity, like a coke addict after a long night out.

"...that's in the past now," he was saying. "The myth of the American dream. The great American novel. Even the word American now evokes a shudder. We all know something our parents didn't in the 60s: we've been had. All the myths we'd been sold, painted atop crushing brutality. Freedom a mask for its opposite. Maybe each generation has to awake to the lies of the previous, I don't know. Either way, once you see it, you can't unsee it. Now, it's like a snowball rolling down a hill, gathering momentum and power. Even gentle footfalls can start an avalanche, given the proper conditions. Once it gains enough velocity, anything in its path will be crushed. Crushed by the weight of a myth. An idea."

"What are you rambling about?" Loki asked over the intercom, somehow able to make out his spitfire monologue over the rumble of the engine. "Reality isn't up for grabs. It's *real*."

Dionysus got up and sat in the passenger seat. "That was really creepy, man. How did you hear me?"

"I'm half German Shepherd. But seriously, explain yourself."

"You think war comes from innate biology? Or a conflict over resources?" Dionysus asked.

"I suppose," Loki said. "I don't know if I'd be so pretentious about it..."

"The hell you wouldn't. What I'm saying is that it's a war of ideology. People could go their own ways, let well enough alone. But many people aren't content with that. They identify with an idea so strongly, that it's as if the idea *possesses* them. God's chosen are victorious. So long as it's all for something. And if that certainty demanded the possibility—even probability—of delivering pain or death... all the better. Once a myth has a body count, it's real enough. There's no war of attrition when every fatality lends further conviction. Death is the price of certainty. The bond between two people is never stronger than when they die to prove their point. It doesn't even matter if it's true or not. You die with that certainty, the world and made-up Gods be damned. And let there be no mistake: this is war."

Loki narrowed his eyes at Dionysus. "I've got to think. This idea makes me really uncomfortable. But I'll pretend for a minute that you're not just, you know..."

"Nuts?" Dionysus asked, smirking.

"Yeah, that. Well, our brains don't discriminate between reality and fiction. I get that. They simply create and act. But that's how people are manipulated with fairy tales." His eyes lit up suddenly. "You're on a crusade, aren't you? You think we're going to change the fucking world!"

Dionysus nodded. "You're halfway there. Memes are how the evolved wage war. Ontological terrorism, where have you been, man?"

"Keeping your ass out of prison. Reality doesn't give a shit about our ideas."

"You're talking about natural law. I'm talking about... personal myth. We are how we represent ourselves. The stories we tell ourselves and each other replace whatever dim reality that lurks behind it. Don't you see? I'm not trying to plumb the dark recesses of Plato's cave. I'm trying to unchain

Prometheus." Dionysus turned off his recorder and tapped it with a smile. "And this is how I'm going to do it."

"With an MP3 recorder?" Loki asked.

"It actually records in WMV," Dionysus said with a frown.

"Ugh," Loki said, lighting a smoke and waving him away. "Stop talking to me."

VII. Monarch

2011

My original Fall is the birth of the Other.
—Jean-Paul Sartre

Memories flash back to me, layers of skin carefully peeled off, revealing pink machinery beneath. Was this work related stress? The missions, the drugs, a genuine pre-existing mental condition unmasked by these factors... or something else entirely?

"You're on Substance D, man. You are spun the fuck out," Bradley said.

What were we talking about? Two journalists suicided by scientologists? Nothing is remembered. All is lost.

"The Blue Brotherhood doesn't exist. These journalists weren't onto anything, the Monarch Mind Control lead is a dead end. And of course, the

Scientologists wanted to fuck over these dead journalists... the Scientologists want to destroy anyone who isn't a part of their fruity little club. You need to sleep. How many days has it been now?" He looked at his watch. The hands twitched their way around the face, little shivering cockroach legs.

Agent 888 pushed aside empty bottles of Dos Equix and various piles of debris, coughed asthmatically and fished for another mentholated cigarette from his shirt pocket. *Holy shit! That was me. I was seeing inside the hole in my memory made by the Benzos. Or was I just telling myself it was the drugs? Maybe something else was at work here.*

"Oh yeah?" Agent 888 replied. "I thought Substance D was a fictional name for 'speed' from a Philip K. Dick book."

"No. It is who you are in general, man. Specifically you. Any drug. Any mind altering substance. Your life, living out investigations into things which don't exist, and searching for answers, suspecting friend in enemy and enemy in friend.

"Your brain has detached and split into two different polarities: the left and right hemispheres, fighting for dominion over each other. What you need is balance. There is a schism in your brain and you are fragmented. That is 'Substance D'. It's not a drug; it is a state of mind.

"Did I happen to mention that I'm your handler and that you are actually working for the CIA? Do you know I used to work for Europharm AG? Did you know some of their meds were started as part of MK-ULTRA? That's right, buddy. You still think 'Mother Hive Brain' is bullshit? You have potential if you stick with it. You have made it past at least three disinfo shells already, you're hacking your way to the core of the syndicate and we are aware of who you are.... just kidding man, I think you're a fucking nut job and I like to watch you grind your geeeears... or am I?" the Buyer asked.

—

I woke up in a cold sweat. Heart beating rapidly, sweaty palms, ache in jaw, swallow down. Better soon. Who am I now? Endless corridors, twisted sheets, uneasy alliances, labyrinths, rat race, drinking scotch, playing ball with the men at the top... the top of... what? What was IT?

I feel IT, that means IT is there-there, there is a there there there... (And so on and so on, perhaps forever)... IT reproduced ITself in the mind of the young, and fed from our nocturnal emissions and tears.

Most would discredit IT. In fact, IT did not exist materially. IT existed as a living myth. There is no There, There. Floating in the mythspace. Something about a vortex... Like Schrodinger's cat, but more... like it. Somehow. I curled up inside these uncertainties, and slept there a while.

—

I was sitting with Stella at the crap diner we frequented. The food was terrible, but there was something comforting in how constantly underachieving the place was. She absent-mindedly pushed her deep fried cod through a trough of mayonnaise and relish. There was a drawn out and uncomfortable silence, something which seemed to be happening a lot lately.

Silences like that have always been the death of me. I'll say anything to make it stop. Usually it is harmless, some random detritus floating at the top of my mind like a cluster of oil-soaked pelicans. But sometimes it isn't.

"I think I'm losing my mind," I said.

She stopped chewing for a moment, but then nodded as if she had already known that. "Yeah?"

"Yeah."

We kept chewing in silence.

I guess this wasn't one of those times. But her lack of response was telling: it was already starting to show. Because it was true. I never before thought a mind was something you could lose, but now, I'm just not so sure.

Her eyes were like two porcelain saucers. Beautiful, but empty. I looked down at my food, and suddenly didn't feel very hungry.

That evening I watched some old movies of Stella and myself.

When I watched those videos, I realized that at first, she had been very good to me. I truly did love her, but I couldn't help but take her for granted. It was a game of deflection played out in my own mind, against an invisible judge and jury.

We sometimes become infatuated when we view the other as a means to our ends: an escape from ourselves. When the period of infatuation wears off—the feeling of being so close to someone, you would do anything for them—many run. Maybe my way of doing that was to put everything about her that I didn't care for under a microscope—her taste in music, the way she talked, the things she said, her friends, her ideas. Everything that I didn't like. They were all things I didn't even have a right to judge. But that doesn't keep us from doing it.

Psychological projection is the name of the game.

Are you beginning to see a pattern here? When we see our mirror image, in sharp and uncomfortable detail in an outsider, the 'Other', we begin to see our own faults as if for the first time. You know this about me now. She was the closest thing, and yet I had made our relationship entirely about me. I had alienated her from the conversation. Everything which followed was just the inevitable result of inertia.

Fuck. I have to analyze everything, don't I?

—

Later, the two of us lay intertwined in bed. I was absently tracing the outline of her hips with my finger when I noticed a small tattoo I somehow hadn't seen before, slightly above the small of her back. A tiny black and orange butterfly.

"New tattoo?" I asked.

"No. I got it a while ago, when I turned eighteen."

"Oh." I'd never noticed it. How was that possible?

A monarch.

I closed my eyes, and felt a calm reverie overtake me, but as I nestled on that ledge above the welcome expanse of sleep, something cold and sharp impressed itself on my consciousness. It was like a wedge of sharp static, driven inexorably into my mind. My eye cracked open, and I saw a figure leaning over the bed. It was without any particular features. I can't say that it had a certain kind of face, or eyes, or nose, or hands, though it had all of those things.

It had skin but I couldn't say what color, or if it was rough or smooth. It was just that—a form, a figure, the very shape of a man without any details filled in, as if an artist had started to sketch and then passed out in a drunken stupor instead. I tried to sit up but found that my limbs wouldn't respond.

Only my eyes seemed to work, and they widened in fear as this form leaned in closer to me, peering right through me with its face-that-wasn't-a-face, as it put its hands-that-weren't-hands on my arm, and stepped inside of my body.

I fell then and there into that expanse, but it was no longer welcome. It was an endless free-fall, locked in an invisible embrace with this leaden Other, and my life has never been the same since.

—

As I said, everything was already starting to change for me. These things begin little by little. It seems that all at once, there is an audible snap and your life is wholly different. But when we look back, we can see that it was actually a long time coming.

It seemed to begin with my dreams that night.

—

I was on a giant battleship, which was—I think—steaming toward the US capitol. I'm not sure how, but in some way I understood that our mission was a last ditch effort to save the American Dream. Crew were carrying missiles back and forth through the hull. Screams, smoke, flashing lights.

One of the crew awkwardly dropped one and an auto-door slammed shut on it with a clink.

Everything seemed to stop. The rocking of the boat. The yelling and carrying on of the crew. Even the sloshing of the waves below deck. All our eyes went toward thousands of pounds of munitions, rolling around on the floor as the doors opened and slammed shut again.

And then the gut-wrenching moment. There was a sucking 'oomph' and metal and bodies became high velocity shrapnel themselves, shearing people like they were little more than paper cut-out dolls. I was lying on the ground and I wondered when this was, was this World War 3? Was this the Queen Mary? Was I alive? What the hell was going on?

I thought I was waking up for the first time, at that moment, but of course, I was neither awake nor aware. But it *seemed* that I was. And if things can seem so true and yet be complete lies, then what can we trust, really?

I got up. There was smoke, screaming, chaos, you know, the kinds of noises you would expect... but I was distracted, walking past them in a daze. I was scared of something but couldn't put my finger on it. Not the bomb. Not the war. Something more ephemeral. A lingering something, hiding just outside the bubble of my conscious thoughts. I headed down a deck, and now

now

I'm walking past this cafe. (A cafe on a war ship? I guess even soldiers of the new revolution need lattes). I get that knee jerk hunger for caffeine, and as I'm scanning the scene, I see Stella, sipping a drink, reading a book and holding it in the way only she can, gently as if she's cradling a baby in her arms. I need to bathe in that kind of calm.

I go in to say hi. I remember brushing her hair from her brow, and kissing her, murmuring gently about my dream from the night before, and my brain catches and whirrrrs,

...

I ask her for a hug. An uncomfortable shiver spreads across my skin like ripples on a dark pool, and she's the one thing I can hold onto to avoid slipping into its unknown depths. The mystery, the great mystery, is there, just under the surface. She murmurs something and then gives me a hug with her mind, never taking her eyes off the book.

A conversation ensues, but I don't remember a word of it. I do remember the sensation of being home, for once and only ever-the-still-point, axis-mundi-Foucault's pendulum *home*, and then I was rubbing her back in the way a cat kneads a blanket, somehow my hands were passing through her and onto myself. As the conversation continued, she faded away.

I passed through her shrinking ghost. I was alone.

—

The ship lands. No longer a war ship, she's now a luxury liner. Attractive, naked young men and women are playing tag and water polo, or fucking, right there in the open, heedless of my presence. I'm walking around a patio towards a pool in some sort of upscale compound. Around the bend, there's another pool, and a bunch of people waiting for me.

The Buyer, 139, and 506 are the first three I recognize. They are sitting with someone else, a frenetic man with wild hair and eyes. I had only met 139 and 506 once or twice in person by this point. Bradley, of course, I know all too well. I sit down and turn towards them. Bradley is dressed in army fatigues and smoking a fat, terrible smelling cigar. The other agents are wearing Speedos, I'm sorry to say.

"You taking your pills, son?" Bradley asks me.

"Which pills? Fuck, Bradley. You can't even make sense in my dreams."

"If it is true that alienation has been the principle of all history, it is our task not just to pull the emergency brake, but to bring this history to an end, to clear a way for a new beginning, a new story, illuminated by the dawning of the New," the stranger says, to no one in particular.

At this point Bradley does the most unusual thing. He inspects my hands very closely, and gives me a look. I see the kind of calm, serious, but genuine contemplation that I would never normally attribute to him. Sober.

He says, "See? You're wrong. You've been one of us all along. There are tiny creases, all over your hand..."

I realize we are all lounging on the deck of the Titanic.

—

Then I wake up. His words move around like a scrub-brush, vigorously applied to the inside of my skull, but leave no meaning or realization in their wake. Tiny creases? What the—?

The phone rings, almost right away. If it's Bradley, that is really going to fuck with me.

I pick up the receiver and hear gibberish on the other end.

I assume it's a wrong number. Do I say 'hello'? Do I hang up? That wouldn't be my style. No, I gotta get with the natives, get indigenous. So I parrot back new nonsense words with a similar inflection.

"Woot ginnenah?"

"Sit voo ginneh bah."

"Soo menh hahl bah! kittchee kittchee kittchee joo boo bahhh frennn-wich?"

We go back in forth in a 'conversation' like this for about three minutes, until finally, the voice begins to raise, (is it anger? emphasis?) and then, in clear English, the voice says to me: "THE LIPS OF WISDOM ARE CLOSED, EXCEPT TO THE EARS OF UNDERSTANDING."

Click, the receiver goes dead.

Get out your grapefruit spoons, it's time to dig. Behind the eye sockets, under the cranium. Crack and shuck that husk. The narrative is in there, living inside our bodies.

I drift back to sleep.

—

I am at a feast of some sort, served all these different silver platters by attractive Swedish girls, and the food on the plates are ancient nation states.

Feeling both full and wise after engorging myself on such multi-cultural fare, (Athens was particularly tasty), I take a walk. I am back in southern California now, an endless expanse of overgrown highways and outdoor

84

PARTY AT THE WORLD'S END

malls and shopping centers. Unless you're going back in the mountains, most of the places to walk are parking lots. I've taken many leisurely strolls in them. It's relaxed, because you're absolutely assured of getting absolutely nowhere.

I see a girl standing in the lot. Everything fixates on her, a redhead pulled off the cover of some fashion magazine, a rock star photoshopped in real life.

My perspective moves up and out, blowing up like a balloon, until I am maybe a hundred feet above her. The parking lot is a playing board—like chess, checkers, or Othello, and she is the Red Queen ...Fwooosh! I return back to normal scale, a being of pure perception.

By this point I am flirting with her, which is incomprehensible if you think about it, since I am a point of view with neither mouth nor eyes, but it seems to be going pretty well, because I transform into a bedroom, lined with lace, and strange dangling mobiles and tinkling bells.

She takes her clothes off, inside my walls.

As she undresses inside me, another lily-white clone pops into existence, wearing some kind of nightgown, her hair like a splash of crimson suspended in raw milk. This is quickly becoming a Skinemax 'After Dark' type of production, but condensed and made more tangible as it is squeezes through the churning vortex of a DMT kaleidoscope.

This damsel in a dress narrates up to walls of pressed-wood and plaster that is my body, to the yellow leather chair that is my face, "thanks to the Order of the Hidden Carriage House, I speak in a secret code that will bend all to my Will, which is so Secret that even I, who am but a shadow of my Being within this timeless Company of great Carriage Houses, know it not and lo! if you find yourself performing the most Holy Communion with an ice cream cone, you will know that you are one of the few, True members of this Hidden Interior Order."

She is a simulacra, an ideal sheathed in flesh. I want to slather her in wet plaster.

Yet another peeks behind some kind of boudoir screen and looks up at my ceiling-flesh. She's moving her mouth, but no sound is coming out.

Now all three of them are inside my bedroom body. One is undressed, tied to the bed, struggling against her restraints, the other, in those garters and a dress taut and translucent as a cicada nymph's skin, and this last one is wearing a business suit. The one in the business suit starts making out with the one tied firmly to the bed, though she keeps pulling just out of range, her attention easily switching between playful teasing and intense concentration at the documents in a folder she has splayed across her lap.

She grabs her restrained self by the hair and forces her mouth open. In come all those sweet numbers and words from the spreadsheet, arcane mathematical formula pouring down her consensually non-consenting gullet.

85

I am an ice cream cone, dripping from the ceiling and walls, dairy, sugar, and salt congealing into the approximate shape of a man.

All of the women freeze and turn into play dough. I press one of their perfectly formed bellies and it indents and stays that way. The smell of salty play dough overwhelms me and—

I awake drenched in terrorsweat to a surreal, orange sky, ashes raining down, eyelashes to the red eye of the sun.

The air is still as the day after the apocalypse.

XVIII. Train 'Em Young

2012

Hustlers of the world, there is one mark you cannot beat:
The mark within.
–Bradley the Buyer

Through the 'movie screen' of the porthole windows which lined the sides of the Behemoth, day and night, mountains and plains, sky and forest, all seemed to blur. They were like kids with new toys. Here was a land with no boundaries or rules, a liminal space where creativity ruled

JAMES CURCIO

and reality was what you liked. Rehearsing was the closest anything came
to being a chore or a bore, and sore fingers and aching tendons were nothing compared to the excitement of creating a new language with tribe that
somehow seemed to 'get' you. Not the mask or façade, but you, an identity
captured somehow without irony by the mythic allusion of their nick-
names.

Of course, life on the road wasn't without its snags. It had been raining
hard, maybe a week or two since they had left Grand Junction. As was often
the case, Loki was driving. Lilith was riding shotgun, tapping away on her
netbook. There was a crackle in the air, and conversation ceased a while.
Then she snorted, in delayed response to something he had said minutes
before. "Why is this still a question?"

Loki dragged on his cigarette. "It's posture. Strategy. You can't be fugitives and rock stars. You can't book the Hollywood-fucking-Bowl–"

"But you can drive a giant, armored bumblebee," Lilith said.

"Fair point. Though that was against my strong, and might I say correct,
urging to the contrary. Ahem. But any venue big enough to be worth the
risk is–" Loki drummed his fingers on the steering wheel.

"It's what? If this was about getting clear, you know damn well none of it
—"

"Shut up," Loki said.

"—would be... what did you just say to me?"

"I'm thinking. You like it when I think." He continued drumming his fingers.

Lilith swallowed a retort and continued typing.

"All right. Yes, in theory, you can be both fugitives and rock gods. But in
practice it's impossible."

Lilith shrugged. "Try me."

"Resources first. Who's footing the bill?"

"I am. Give me your vision here, maestro."

"Swarm, concentrate, disperse. Flash mobs, but fucking huge. Decentral-
ization..." Loki thought for a minute.

"Mother Hive Brain!" Dionysus piped in, from his bunk. "The hive acts
without any discernible decision making–"

"—at any level. Yeah, yeah. But that was a joke, compared to what we're
talking about now," Loki said. "Hold on. Let me finish a thought for Christ's
sake."

Lilith finished typing, and turned her netbook to face Loki. He was being
recorded. "Go on."

"You're a part of it. Find your six best friends; determine your level of
commitment. Stay in touch. Take turns listening. Word goes out from
group to group, you pass it around. Call, tweet, and write, lipstick on a mirror, I don't give a fuck. As long as someone else is listening and tells their

six friends. 'You six may get the word that you will help people park, you six deal with renting latrines, you six to–'"

"Latrines?" Lilith asked.

"Six per cell, each cell notifies two others. How many people in six iterations?"

Lilith laughed. "You know, I like how you think I can do that."

"Don't, you. I'm on to your shit," Loki said, waving a finger.

Lilith doodled on a napkin. "Tens of thousands or millions, depending on how you figure it. And you're also assuming... how would you put it? No signal degradation."

"Amateurs study tactics. Professionals study logistics," Loki said, cryptically. "And yeah. Hypothetically. You need the draw of Tupac, or to catch the zeitgeist at some tipping point."

"Have you served yet?" Lilith asked impatiently.

Loki's hands tightened on the steering wheel. The 'big idea' levity had drained from his face.

"No." He took a breath. "Six tell six where and when, six times, and you've got your Hollywood Bowl."

"You missed your calling, you know that?" Lilith asked.

Loki finally smiled. "You'd miss our little talks."

—

About a month later, the Behemoth wound its way along a lonely dirt road running through a densely knit patchwork of forest and open field. The GPS voice spoke in its usual monotone. (John Cleese had gotten old after the first thousand miles). "Make a left 300 yards ahead."

"There is no left 300 yards ahead," Loki said.

"Trust to your machine overlords," Dionysus said.

"I think it means we're supposed to go off-roading," Jesus said. "Look." There was an even smaller dirt road, barely larger than a path, which cut off up ahead.

"You've got to be fucking kidding me," Loki said.

"No," Lilith said. "This looks right to me."

They bumped their way down the smaller dirt path, and it opened up into a field. They were surrounded by other cars, vans, and tents. Strings of electric lights criss-crossed the thickets that covered the hills edging the field, and dew sparkled like starlight in their headlights, but even those bright beams were quickly swamped by clusters of dancing orbs and glowing bodies.

"What are those?" Loki asked, squinting ahead. Then the field broadened and they could see teens running around mostly naked, a mess of glow-paint occult glyphs and LEDs.

They rolled through another patch of trees, and then into another field, with a barn and farmhouse at its furthest corner. The barn was crawling with bodies, a wall of tits and bellies, like the inside of an active bee-hive, all thrumming and quivering, dance-signing the location of nearby pollen to one another.

"Uhhh, Lilith..." Loki said.

She chuckled. "Your plan, pal. I just ran with it."

Loki shook his head. And here were six sweaty kids waiting to help them set up gear on stage. As the speaker walls and drum kit were being assembled, the crowd began changing "BAB-A-LON! BAB-A-LON! BAB-A-LON!"

"You could've made seven figures a year on Madison Avenue, you know that?" Loki asked Lilith.

"I suppose. That wouldn't be nearly as fun."

—

The band waited. Cody peered at the tuner lights twinkling in the near dark, somehow looking like an owl with a beat-up cowboy hat. Dionysus fidgeted with his sticks. Jesus, her bass hanging low between her legs, was inspecting her makeup in a small hand mirror. A wall of compressors, limiters, EQs, and effect units blinked back at them. The PA's were in place, and the sound girl gave thumbs up from her cubby-hole in the corner, her black-light makeup like a kabuki demon, breathing lightning bursts and fury. In the pulses of regular light, her face reverted to human dimensions, a pierced geisha in day-glo kimono.

The drums and bass pounded out a rhythm. Cody's head bobbed along, he would enter with a descending melody halfway through the next bar, and then dig into rhythmic chugging on the one of the next measure.

But the real rush wouldn't come until the vocal unison joined the pack. Lilith waited for her cue, her slender hands resting on her hips, her weight on the balls of her feet, her lips twisted into a victorious smirk, drinking down the howl of the audience as if it was Bordeaux.

Finally, the lights hit, and then the adrenaline. The speakers struggled to keep pace with the wild ululation of the crowd. Terrifying vibrations rocked the barn to its foundations. Strobe and laser-flashes rippled through the darkness. Bodies and light seemed to twine around, between, and through each other.

By the second song, a patch of baseball-cap wearing fans, standing near the front, was bowled over by a group of women. They pushed past the first row and crawled on-stage. Lilith beckoned them as she belted out the last note before Cody's solo. It seemed a part of the performance when they charged her, but her eyes registered surprise as the throng overran her—esurient mouths licking, gnawing, and biting at her curves and soft skin. Dionysus tried to peer through the toms but could only see flailing body parts. He shook his head, sweat shooting off in a spray, and focused on the click track in his earphone. She crawled out of the tangle, catching the pick-up for the next song.

—

Eventually, the performance ended, but the party continued raging as if it had never stopped. Dionysus floated in the post-show void, staring at the drumsticks in his hand.

The roof of the venue drifted away, painted increasingly dark shades of slate blue by strata of smog whirling past. Clouds and silken shadow swallowed both the snakelike peninsula of Baja and the curve of California. The Earth herself was a bobbing speck of dirt, caught in a tide of darkness. Blazing suns, each the size of a thimble in the ocean, hurtled away into blackness. There was a fluttering in the void, like stitches in a sweater.

No, it was a cell. An army of cells. A hand.

My hand.

—

Lilith watched Dionysus stare at his hands. He was clearly deep in the grips of some revelation. Maybe the potent Mescaline she'd slipped into his canteen was having some effect.

"Could I dive back into them and find the Universe?" Dionysus asked her.

"Someday I'll show you. But not now. Now, we play."

He continued to stare at the creases in his hands, murmuring as if in a trance. "The audience is a thousand eyed beast. It is mad and starving for more, and we are just the empty puppet who dances at its pleasure. We feed one another symbiotically, one and yet two, a baby suckling at its mother's ripe breast. All pain, all need, all separation is absolved."

Lilith pulled him close and kissed him. His pupils were saucers that could swallow the moon, should saucers choose to do such a thing. "You're never going to get anywhere with all your talking," she said, flashing a quick smile before wandering off-stage.

Dionysus nodded, and looked over at Jesus. She was unplugging her gear. Loki was talking to a woman with a crossbow. She had curly dark hair; a dancer's build on a full frame, and honey skin.

In a fluid movement, Lilith swept down on the girls who had flocked her during the show, and seemed to propel them past the makeshift stage. "This party's beat," she called after the band. "Let's go!"

Loki was stunned. "With this much energy... can't just leave it lying around. We've gotta do something with it."

Lilith shrugged. "I've had my fill. Come on. I know where we should all go. Four stars, hot tub. Trust me."

Dionysus perked up. "Hot tub?"

Loki gave a nod to the breakdown crew, who jumped to action. The party continued madly, ignorant of the band slipping out the back.

From buses to dorm rooms, across the screens of cell phones, laptops, and flat-panels, the show and ensuing chaos broadcast through the minds of a dormant, desperate populace.

—

"You having fun yet, you dour son-of-a-bitch? There was a time that you weren't so dour," Lilith said to Loki. She was stretched out in the passenger seat, one of the girls sitting on her lap sucking a lollipop, her face an elaborately painted pincushion of piercings.

"It's still sinking in. You have any idea what you've done, here? Fugitives, to guerrilla rock demagogues in what? Several months?" he asked, semi-rhetorically.

"Sounds like fun to me," she said. They kept passing the lollipop back and forth, not breaking eye contact.

"I'm starting to see that, yeah," he said.

"No plan, though. That's your job." She smiled.

Loki nodded, making a mental note to start chain smoking in no more than 30 seconds. The challenge thrilled him, even if it made him anxious as fuck trying to keep this band of nutcases out of jail, or worse.

"What's your name?" the girl on Lilith's lap asked him.

"Loki."

"Amber. I did sound at the sh—"

Lilith interrupted by shoving her tongue down Amber's throat.

OK, then, Loki thought. He felt a rumble in his chest and instinctively swerved into the other lane. A sedan shot past, its sub-woofers rattling the equipment.

"Fucking savages!" he screamed out the window, before accelerating and changing lanes again, the bulk of the Behemoth forcing them onto the shoulder. He thought he heard the sound of guard-rail shrieking against paint-job as he shot away. Now he was having fun.

He caught an image in the rear view, lit vividly, but momentarily by passing headlights. A strip of a disembodied, shapely leg, wreathed in red fishnet. Probably the girl Lilith had introduced as Amanda. She was elfin, even tiny, but well proportioned and far from frail. Mary, another who had joined their group, had long dark hair and skin, charcoal eyes. One of those quiet, watching types. They could be in MENSA or special-ed, for all he knew.

The group in the back was sitting in a circle, passing around a hookah which let out great clouds of hash and opium smoke. Cody was silhouetted behind them as he leaned against the window, clearly drunk, strumming on his guitar. Some experimental Italian film was playing on the large screen monitor with the sound shut off. Loki was catching fragments of conversation but couldn't place it all.

"...what do you mean?"

"Don't play with me. I don't—"

There was a burst of laughter.

"What, I can't make eyes at you and get pretty much everything that I want?"

"Cut it out. I'm not playing."

"Sure you are."

"No, damnit. Answer the question."

"Then ask it to me straight."

"—Semiotic invisibility?" Dionysus was saying, clearly on another tangent. "Really, it's just a matter of misdirection and sorting. What use you are sorting for."

"Sorting?" Jesus asked, letting out a great deal of smoke at the same time.

"Oh, sure. If you're looking for a drink, you go to the guy behind the bar, not the introvert in the corner. It's an old trick. Mismatch. You're not the droids they're looking for. Conform to expectation. When they retell the story, you're not there."

Amanda shook her head at Dionysus disparagingly, her bangs bouncing to and fro, but she leaned her head against his shoulder. When she looked up at him with those too-wide eyes, he knew he was in trouble.

"I can dig it," Jesus said, not really paying attention. Mary was oiling her feet.

Loki tossed cigarette number two out the window.

"It's really–" Dionysus started.

Loki cut in. "–okay, I'm sorry. I gotta ask. You are drowning in pussy back there, and you want to talk about 'invisibility' and 'sorting'?"

"Well. Yeah. Why?"

Amanda scowled. The expression fit strangely on her heart-shaped face. "Excuse me, I'm not 'pussy'."

"Don't take it personally," Dionysus said. "Loki 1.0 runs software programmed in an object-oriented language. It undervalues subjective things like emotions or self-consciousness."

Loki laughed and shook his head. There must be some reason why he liked that bastard so much. But what he said was, "Consciousness is post-hoc."

"Post-hoc ergo propter-hoc!" Dionysus screamed back.

"Oh shut up, you don't even know Latin."

"Sorry to interrupt whatever it is you're talking about, but where are we going, anyway?" Artemis asked. She sat poised as if she thought she was Le Femme Nikita, one hand on her crossbow. That girl was a special sort. Introduced herself as part of 'Lilith's security detail' at the show. When Loki jokingly asked for her credentials, she showed the crossbow. This made her crazy cause she could use it, or crazy cause she couldn't. Either way...

"A hotel," Lilith said, putting Amber's lollipop back in her mouth. "I put it in the GPS already. You're going to love it!"

"How are we paying for this little venture?" Loki asked.

"Paying? Are you joking?"

Loki nodded. "I'm starting to like you, kid."

—

The Behemoth pulled into a gas station, belching out clouds of exhaust. They all stepped into the night air, stretching their legs and blinking in the harsh glow of the lamps set in the overhang. (All except Cody, who had passed out face-down on his guitar after loudly declaring, "Nap time.")

Loki shook his head. "$4.96 a gallon. Jesus Christ."

The rest of them sauntered inside as he fueled the monster. A long line of fashion victims, methed-out truckers, nervous businessmen, and suburban housewives trailed from the counter to the back of the store, where there was a rusted metal box endlessly rotating shriveled meat turds. Jesus sauntered to the fore, seven feet tall in her platforms and wearing a long pleated leather skirt.

"Whew," she said loudly. "After an orgy like that one, I sure could use a hot tub."

The rest of the line went dead silent.

—

The final stop of the evening was an incredibly overpriced hotel.

A valet approached them uncertainly.

"Leave the keys in the... uh... truck?"

"The fuck I will. Just tell me where to park," Loki said.

The side-door opened, and the valet's jaw followed suit.

—

The hotel doors glide, Loki marveled. That was how he knew the place was $500 a night. The lobby was ultra-modern and all the furniture looked like Escher designed it.

"Is that supposed to be a chair?" Loki asked.

Dionysus squinted. "I think it's decorative."

"A decorative *chair*."

"Come on," Dionysus said.

A crowd of attendants, bellhops, and random hotel lobby stragglers stared in bewilderment as their little army approached the concierge. Their boots and heels clicked loudly on the marble floor.

"D-do you have a reservation?" the concierge asked.

"Watch and learn," she said to Loki.

Then, "Hey," to the concierge, all smiles, and breasts.

—

Everything clustered around one focal point, a sublimely tranquil red center surrounded in the black fluttering of the mob.

At first, I can't clearly make out this center. I perch on the tip of my toes despite myself, and then I see what the commotion is about. My God. No, my Goddess.

The rest are a gauché pastiché of whatever they're passing off as punk rock or beatnik these days. One of them may even be a transsexual. Post-op, pre-op, who knows. I'm not about to find out. This goddess shouldn't surround herself with such garbage.

I'm left clutching the table and reeling by the time we're face to face. What is it that you've always craved, that's always pulled you through another day? And what would you do if it suddenly manifested in front of you, clothed in downy skin?

Anything, anything they say. She's talking fast now, and for the first time in my life, the only thing I can think about is myself. That's funny right? I'm hypnotized by the smell of her breath, sweat, and perfume, and all I can think about is me. Climbing an endless ladder, pieces of myself doled out slowly, almost imperceptibly, in exchange for another rung. A grand luxury suite, fourteen hundred square feet, yes, yes. What has this long life of service given me? By all accounts, I had done well, but what had I done for myself? My best instincts reel, but I see my hands floating over the keypad, I see the key card grasped so delicately between her candy-tipped fingers.

Fuck this place. I don't care.

Here is your room card, Miss Parsons.

—

The troupe made their way to the elevator, Lilith in the lead with the key card in her hand.

"That was like some kind of Jedi mind trick you just did there," Mary said.

"And did I hear that right? Miss Parsons? Like Jet-propulsion laboratory occult nut, L Ron stole his cash and started Scientology with it Parsons?" Dionysus asked.

They stopped at the elevator. "I really don't feel like talking about my grandfather," Lilith said with a shrug.

The elevator dinged and the doors closed behind them.

—

It was packed tight: the troupe, a nervous, middle-aged businessman, and his shrew-faced wife. Ding. A momentary wave of nausea passed through all of them. Amber coiled around Lilith like a garment.

Ding. Another floor.

The man scowled, but refused to make eye contact.

"How do you do?" Jesus asked.

"Alright," he said. Ding. More shuffling, and finally he blurted out, "What the hell are you people?"

"We are like nuns," Jesus said. They all giggled.

"Nuns."

"MM-hmm. Whiskey guzzling, gun-toting, pussy-licking nuns. Not quite Mother Theresa, but it still demands absolute commitment of body and soul. The Sisterhood of Lilith. Here to take everything you have and leave you begging for us to take whatever's left." Jesus slid next to the business-man and winked.

The man swallowed, hard.

She put her arm around his shoulder. "I know what you look at when you're up alone in the dead of night. You dirty, dirty boy." His wife looked away, blushing.

Ding. Their floor.

—

They stumbled down the hallway, high on giddiness, lust, and hash. A maid rushed passed, saying Hail Mary's to herself as she went.

They approached the door to Room 777. Lilith turned to Loki before opening the door. "Wait here. We need a guard."

"What? You want me to sleep in the damn hallway?" he asked.

"You've got thinking to do. I like it when you think," she winked at him.

"Look. I'm not like the concierge. It's not like, I see your breasts and sud-denly I'm just a brain-stem attached to a penis."

Lilith shook her head. "It was about catering to his delusions. The breasts only get you in the door. Anyway, listen. If you need something to keep those industrious hands occupied, I could really use the smoke detect-ors in our room shut off. Within about... ten minutes?"

"That's not–"

Artemis patted her crossbow. How the fuck did she get that in here? "I'll help. If you don't mind, that is."

"I don't—Screw it. Why not?" he said.

Lilith let them in and then shut the door with a loud click.

—

The corner suite had the same aesthetic as the rest of the hotel, full of hard lines and stark, incoherent furniture. Amanda whistled. "These are some digs. How much did this cost?" She started putting her hair in pig-tails. Black and red, shaved underneath.

"Don't worry about that," Lilith said, "Girls, there's a hot tub in there, just dying to meet you."

Mary, Amber and Amanda looked at one another uncertainly. Jesus began sauntering towards the bathroom.

"Not you, hon," Lilith said.

Jesus frowned. "What, I'm not a lady?"

"I said girls."

"Point. But I do make bathing an exacting art."

"I bet you do," Lilith said, walking up to her and patting her ass.

"New initiates. Wheat from the chaff," she continued, after the three of them were already in the bathroom. With a silk bag casually flung over her shoulder, Lilith followed, closing the door behind her.

Cody swaggered to a nearby sofa and dropped onto it heavily. He managed to finish the bottle of whiskey he'd been nursing all night before passing out, still sitting up.

Jesus and Dionysus looked at each other. Dionysus sighed, but then smiled wearily. "I was really excited about the hot tub, too."

—

Lilith handed a bundle of candles to Amber and contemplated the layout of the room. Not the bathhouses of Tiberius in Ancient Rome, but it would do. Most importantly, the hot tub could accommodate three.

She made a circular gesture at Amber, who nodded and began placing them around the hot tub. Lilith sat down by the bath and turned the faucet.

"Leave your clothes over there," she said, motioning to the far corner of the room. "Don't be shy. I've seen it all before... not that you aren't fine specimens."

They did as instructed, and stood somewhat awkwardly in the center of the room. Lilith began lighting the candles. "Ardat li li. Lamashtu. Ahi hay lilitu."

She snapped restraints on Mary and Amber's wrists, but when she approached Amanda, she pulled away.

"Now hold on a second. I don't even—"

Lilith grabbed her by the throat. "You bought the ticket, now take the ride."

She let go.

Amanda rubbed her neck for a moment. "Christ you're strong." She felt a strage thrill. Her throat tightened and her cheeks burned.

Lilith smiled, and bound Amanda's hands as well. "I'm not a fan of empty talk. But I'm going to tell you something that Rosencrantz, Guildenstern, Hedwig and MacGyver out there haven't figured out for themselves yet. We are the scions of eternity. My memory goes all the way back to ancient Babylon."

"You're serious?" Amanda asked.

"Women told tales of me... I would steal the men away from them. I would devour their children. I was Lilitu, a demon, an abomination. I lived inside mirrors, to seduce the vanity of nubile girls. Can you imagine? They were afraid of me. I was a demon of the desert, screaming down from the mountains, howling in the winds. The Babylonians heard me and were terrified. They built walls around that city, in part because of their fear of me, though it was when I slipped into the beds of their husbands, of their wives, that their witches and priests were called out to curse me. More worthless gibberish spat my way by day, but as the moon crested the valley, there I was. Smiling. Three, four, or eight girls on my arm, like you. The summer tree, they called me. I know. It's been a long time since I remembered who I was. I don't plan to forget again."

97

Not surprisingly, the other girls had ceased whatever they were doing and stared at this woman as she spoke. "You're probably thinking I'm crazy, and at the same time wondering about all the voices in your head that won't let you sleep at night. I've come to find my sisters. None of you needs to hide anymore. I know just how awful it can be, living in someone else's world. And we don't always remember."

Lilith put her hand under the faucet, testing the temperature. "It can take a real shock to bring it to the surface. First, I've got to draw this bath."

"Now I know why you shackled us before telling us your little story," Amanda said.

"This is some right freaky shit," Amber agreed.

Lilith laughed. "I like you. I hope you make it through in one piece."

"One piece?"

Ignoring the question, Lilith felt the water one last time before turning it off. She got out bronze incense burners, dropped herbs in, and lit them. Thick black smoke filled the room.

"I also hope he got to the alarms, or this is going to be short-lived." She waited, looking up. Nothing. "No? Okay then. It's time. Get in."

The room seemed to distort with the swirling smoke. The girls slipped into the water.

"Breathe in deeply. Let all of it into your lungs. Breathe in and out."

"So you're going to drug us, and then we can attribute the effects of the —wait, what the fuck?" Amanda felt strange. "Nothing like LSD. What's it doing to me?" she felt around the side of the tub before sliding into the water. Her muscles didn't seem to want to respond properly. This wasn't the rubbery limbs or clenched teeth of hallucinogens. Instead, she felt a void opening beneath her in the frothy water. It was a void of time, clouded over with fragments of memory. In that formless void she could nevertheless sense some kind of presence. But how do we know when someone is staring daggers into the back of our heads?

"Ssh. We're clearing out your illusions," Lilith said. She put a hand on Amanda's forehead. "Take your last breath."

Lilith plunged her under the water, and broke into fractals on its surface.

—

Amanda was seventeen again, clad in tight denim and a band T-shirt. Ear-buds dangled like earrings from her ears. Five feet of wristbands, tattoos, and attitude. Riding a bus to 'Anywhere But Here'.

There was no way she could explain to the tear-and-mascara-stained eyes of her sister, why she knew she had to leave. It was more like the pressure before a big storm hits. The leaves turn up, there's a faint smell of petrichor in the air and if you are wise to it, you get the hell out. Most people don't drop everything on a whim like that, but for Amanda, even on a regular day, it was common practice. Winding up like everyone else in that miserable town was worse than any fate she could dream of.

There had been a price, even if she knew it was the right choice, the only choice she could have made. Her sister never called her 'sis' again, never told her she loved her. She became a distant, cold, 'Amanda', delivered on the other end of a phone before she was passed on to their neurotic, equally distant and ever-confused mother.

The bus ride which followed their parting was the longest trip of her life. As she sat stewing in emotional denial, the incredibly flatulent, obese Mexican who sat beside her the whole way from Biloxi to El Paso, leered over at her as if they were sharing some private joke, his eyes surrounded by crinkles like balled aluminum foil. He shot her a disappointed look before he swaggered off at his stop. El Paso spread about her like an oil slick, and she suddenly felt trapped by the world, its expansive blandness, its squat buildings and steel choked skies. In that moment the whole Universe was El Paso, and she was just some piece of trash blowing through on the listless wind. Her head sunk into her hands after she saw his baseball cap disappear into a crowd of weary faces. Maybe the fat bastard expected a blowjob in the bathroom.

—

Lilith pulled Amanda out of the water. She was half-conscious, hyperventilating. Her eyes rolled up into her head. Lilith seemed pleased.

"Is this supposed to happen?" Mary asked. "Should we call 911?"

Lilith stared her down. "This world is ending. There is no getting out." She plunged her under the water again.

Mary turned her racooned eyes toward Amber, who shrugged and deftly cut out a line of ecstasy on a dry part of tile, not in the least restricted by bound hands.

—

Amanda's eyes snapped open.

She tumbled through empty space, landing in a stone labyrinth. Implacable wailing greeted her as she entered light and open air. Squinting, she spun around and saw an old bristlecone pine, heavy with babies suspended by their navels from red, pulsing limbs. At first, all she could hear was her heart, working hard to rush blood through terrified extremities.

Drums beat in the distance. She felt an immediate sense of peril, and got to her feet. Strange murals, gouged with bleeding fingernails, children's paintings and graffiti lined the walls. She followed a length of rope through the maze. The ground was spongy, which made progress slow and exhausting. She heard hooves beating on the stone, drawing nearer. Panic overrode every nerve and she ran, her mouth open in a voiceless scream.

—

Amanda was screaming and thrashing helplessly in the hot tub. Mary and Amber tried to hold her still. Lilith was chanting something guttural.

Neither understood the words, but how would they, when the language hadn't been spoken outside academies in thousands of years?

—

She ran, not knowing what from—only that it was terrible and swift. There wasn't time to think. She fled on shredded feet along a riverbank, through the cold and the wet and the wind. She was underneath the world she knew, retracing her steps along the river and out of the valley. The rope, often knotted, mingled with mud or blood, oil and bones, continued deeper in and she followed it.

Twisted buildings coiled around her as she fled through their remains. The collapsing structures were split through their hearts by trees and vines. The constriction of their limbs twisted basketball hoops in rusted arcs, SUV's toppled and bent, whole buildings crumbled as nature reclaimed it all, chewing it slowly as it recycled the materials once ripped from the Earth.

Silhouettes stood amidst the rubble. Occasionally she would stumble on a root, or a discarded children's toy. Some people stood idly, trying to rebuild homes, as plumes of smoke and fog swirled overhead like peacock feathers. Other hopeless soldiers marched in ordered rows, ants, or Roman centurions.

Police sirens cried out in the distance, startling her. It is a lost cause, she thought.

I don't know why I just thought that.

I just did.

I am her?

I'm looking down at my hands as I walk. If I look away from them, even for a moment, I feel that I might be swept away by an uncontrollable tide. I may become someone else.

I'm still looking at my hands as I glide past, an apparition. But aware now, in some growing premonition of who I am in this endless flow of lonely faces.

I can't help them. These people are already dead.

I climb atop a log, straddling it in the water as if riding a bucking horse. The crowd disappears back into the mist as I float away, apparitions themselves.

Still in a delirium, I look at my reflection in a slender dagger, gently held close to my breast—a silver sliver of lips and eyes. The knife flicked along my neck, bringing a gout of sweet-smelling blood. It rushed down my body in a hot stream, past my breasts and the small oval of my belly to the black water below. Black and polluted. As the blood merges with the water, it runs clear. Soon, I could see the rocks at the bottom of the stream.

I'm dreaming. I'm dreaming, but this is real.

"Wake up, Ariadne," says a voice in my head.

"Who are you?" I ask.

"Wake up," it says again, and I do.

—

Lilith smacked Amanda across the face. Her breathing returned to normal.

"Where am I?"

"Hey, hey," Mary said, stroking her hair. "I was worried—"

"Where am I?" Amanda repeated.

"You're with me. You're safe," Lilith said. She inspected her eyes, as if looking through them. "What did you see?"

"It was a few years ago. And then it was... you know how it is when you're in a dream, and it can be many times at once? No. That doesn't make sense."

Lilith smiled. "It makes perfect sense. An overlapping of many places and times."

She blinked. "I don't know."

"To get there from here you've got to muck through dream," Lilith said. "But the true state, who you are, what you are. It's before birth, after death. What's the future, or the past once you take away the present?"

Amanda scrutinized her face. "I don't know," she said again.

"You will. And when you do, you'll get one of these," Lilith indicated an ouroboros tattoo on her arm, a snake swallowing its tail round its length.

"Maybe? I heard a voice."

"What did it say, dear?"

"It called me Ariadne."

Lilith kissed her on the forehead. "And from now on, so shall we, sister."

Ariadne raised an eyebrow in confusion, but then relaxed into Lilith's embrace.

—

It didn't take Dionysus and Jesus long to find the X-Box. The two of them were presently enmeshed in some horribly complicated space battle.

"You don't think they need our help in there, do you?" Dionysus asked.

"Shut up and die, monkeyman," Jesus said. "Mushrooms?" She held up a bruised blue cap.

Dionysus shook his head. He began mashing on his controller, a crazed look in his eye.

—

Lilith pulled Amber out of the water by her hair with a splash. She gasped and spluttered. "I couldn't breathe!"

After inspecting her for a moment, Lilith chuckled. "Mm-hm. Ariadne, Mary... we're done for now." The smoke in the room was clearing.

The two of them wrapped themselves in thick complimentary bathrobes before slipping out to rejoin the others.

"What about me?" Amber asked suggestively.

"Give me a girl with holes in her eyes, and stars on her garters, oh give me a girl, with scars on her hands, and the heart of a whore," Lilith sang.

—

"Hey guys?" Loki asked through the cracked door. "Did someone order room service?"

"Yes," Jesus said from within the room. "Send them in."

A young bellhop entered with an absurd spread of food and champagne on a cart, and then froze in place at the scene inside. What kind of savages was he dealing with? A flat screen TV lay on its side against the wall for no apparent reason, playing a nature show. The sofa and love seat similarly upturned. Banging and moaning echoed from the bathroom, but there was sign of no one except a blissfully snoring Cody, now relocated to the floor.

"...Hello?"

Dionysus peeked out from under the overturned sofa, like a turtle exploring outside its shell. The sound of Ariadne's giggling followed him.

"Are you sick?" the bellhop asked.

"Oh no. I haven't been in a mental asylum in months. Clean bill of health. Here, let me get your tip." Dionysus started to emerge from his cave. Ariadne looked on from behind. They were both naked.

"No need!" the bellhop said, back-pedaling. He slammed the door behind him. All of them descended into hysterical laughter.

—

Loki and Artemis stood in the hallway like passengers on an elevator. There was a bang and then some loud moaning. Loki tilted his head, listening. Amber, from the sound of it. She would probably have another orgasm in four, three, two,...

"This is just wrong," Artemis said.

"If you'd rather be inside..."

Artemis snorted. "Soldiers never leave their post." She paused. "Might as well call it in. We're getting bagged."

"Good luck with that. State and local cops are jammed," Loki said, grinning proudly.

"How?"

"Hired one of those Indian call centers. They're hitting every line every few seconds with a phony push-poll."

"That's gorgeous," Artemis said. "How?"

"Lilith likes to get things for free, but she seems to be good at supplying resources when they're needed. Frankly, the girl scares me. O brave new war. You want in?"

"I'm not already?" Artemis asked.

"Babylon's ops posture is a synthesis of Anonymous, MEND, Al Qaeda, Hamas, and the Grateful Dead. You need a minute on that?"

"Yes."

"Good. If you said no, you were either a plant or an idiot."

"Al Qaeda and the Grateful Dead... identity. Purpose and movement. Anyone's in who wants in, simply by aligning and educating themselves..."

Loki cocked his head. "Partly."

"No, wait. It's a movement with a thousand centers. They see the broadcasts, they watch your little how-to's..." Artemis said, trying to reason it out.

"Stole the last bit from Hamas. Not so far as setting up an alternate social infrastructure, more like..."

"It becomes a self-fulfilling prophecy," she said. "The illusion of a movement becomes a movement."

"Got it in one."

"And anyone can join, essentially build their own cell. They become the center of their own local franchise."

"Franchise. I like that," Loki said. "You really know how to use that fancy crossbow you got there?"

"Yeah. Always had a thing for bows. Been training ops my whole life, really."

"Military?"

"Fuck no. I'm an artist. Dance. Archery. Martial arts. Acrobatics and circus arts. I was the only Filipino in a rich white neighborhood, adopted. So I had opportunity for extra-curricular activities, I guess."

"Can you get more of those toys?"

"Yeah. But they're not toys."

He cleared his throat. "This is the most I've talked in weeks."

"Yeah," Artemis said, thinking. "D2 to d4."

Loki grinned despite himself, and felt a little thrill when it was returned. Better watch it, he thought, or some uptight gay men might try to revoke his member's card.

—

Dionysus and Ariadne staggered into one of the bedrooms. They had torn window curtains wrapped around their shoulders, like capes. After running circles around the room several times, they fell into the bed and each other's arms.

Ariadne stared up at the ceiling. "Are you guys in some kind of cult? Fuck, I mean I probably should have asked that before whatever happened in the bathroom, but—"

Dionysus smiled as he studied her face. There was something deeply familiar, but he couldn't find it in any particular feature. "Not exactly, no. Cults, plural."

"What?" she exclaimed.

"Never mind that, I was kidding."

"No you weren't. Hey, I don't care if you're in a cult, if it's all like this and not sewing together bodies or cooking meth in the desert."

"More like rambling about Nietzsche in the Bayou," he said.

"Whatever it is, it's great we met. I mean all of us met. I got into theater because of the energy, you know? How it is on stage, but it works off the audience, back and forth, like breathing," she said.

"Sure. Only performers get what you mean though," he said. "You did theater?"

"A little. Local troupes. I sing, managed to get the lead in Orfeo."

"Life can seem to have had a consistent order and plan, as though composed by some novelist. Events seem accidental. Of little meaning. But they turn out to have been indispensable factors in the composition of a consistent plot. So, who composed that plot?" he asked rhetorically.

"Quoting Joseph Campbell at me. Cute." She smiled back at him with those big eyes, but then frowned. "This is weird."

"What is?"

"Tonight. Life. Everything." She nuzzled closer before speaking again. "You know Lilith thinks that we're all... I don't know. Forgetful demigods?"

"What? No. Right? You don't think that you're actually..."

"Well, like... I'm Ariadne now?"

"I think Ariadne is a beautiful name, just like y—"

"Don't even, cheese-master," she said.

"What?"

"I like it too, but don't be silly. All right, so how did you meet these people? And what happened to me earlier?"

"God, it's a long one," he said reflexively.

"Ho ho," she said, laughing, but he didn't seem to get the joke. She put her hands about five inches apart, "Alright, the 'this' sized version then."

"The truth is I don't know how to explain. I'll try. I long had questions no one seemed to share. Identity. Meaning. Existential shit, you know? Around 2002, Jesus and I heard about someone, a teacher who was part of a Secret Society."

"That Mother Hive Brain thing I've heard you talk about?" she asked.

"That came later," he said.

"Hm. I guess a lot can happen in ten years."

"Yeah. All this started even earlier for me, like childhood. Strange experiences in the woods, an imaginary friend who turned out to be real. Recurring dreams. I'll tell you more about that, someday," he said.

"But not today," she said.

"No. Not today. I felt I had to find someone that could help me figure it out. We got wind of him. Gabriel De Leon. How is also a long story and it couldn't matter less. We still went by our birth names back then: Alexi and Meredith...

—

...Alexi ran his hands through the stubble of his hair, flecks of water spraying in every direction. They were in the cabin of Meredith's car. Their only sense of connection to the outside world came from the low purr of the motor. Scenes flew by at impossible speeds, illuminated for a brief moment, passing again into non-existence.

"Make a left here, right?" Meredith asked. The engine hum dropped by a minor third. She caught the shift and laughed. "I'm just getting the image of some twentieth century composer driving drunk and trying to explain how he doesn't need a tachometer to shift, as long as he can hear the intervals."

Alexi checked his scribbled directions in the halo of a passing streetlight. "Yeah, I think this is it."

Meredith glided into the turn. "This is what I get with a philosopher as my copilot. You think it's the right turn?"

Alexi was nonplused. "It might not be. Have you ever read Wittgenstein's On Certainty?"

"You know I haven't." Meredith was scanning for house numbers. Cookie-cutter apartments floated past, their bricks warped by the constant flow of water across the windshield.

"Oh." Eyes passively gazing at the passing buildings; Alexi asked, "Hey Meredith, did you know that your car is a white tiger named Ranesh?"

"No I didn't... where did you get that from?"

"Ranesh has become my spirit guide. He told me," he said cryptically, patting the windshield.

"What are we going to say when we finally meet Gabriel?" he asked, a few moments later.

Meredith spotted the number and found a parking spot. "I have no idea. I kind of hope he does all the talking. You still tripping?"

Alexi stopped, looked up at the stars. "It would appear so."

A moment later, they were standing in a cloud of moths and mosquitoes on what they assumed was Gabriel's porch. It looked the same as the other apartments, the only identifying markers the rusted '111' hanging over the door and a beat up copy of 'Wired' on the ground by the door.

Hesitantly, Alexi raised his hand up to the knocker and felt the cold metal between his fingers. The moths swarming about his head left long trails of white wings, which danced in descending spirals around him. He knocked against the door once, then twice again in quick succession.

They waited an anxious minute, stuffing hands into their pockets and rocking back and forth on their heels, and just as they turned around, preparing to leave, the door creaked open behind them.

A calm voice asked, "Can I help you?"

They turned in unison to meet a tall man of medium build, with nondescript features. He looked to be in his forties, though could just as easily have been younger, or older. His hair was slicked back, and he wore a bathrobe. The faint scent of baked yams wafted through the doorway, as his scrutinizing blue eyes moved up and down, in perfect counterpoint to the tinkling of a harpsichord inside.

Alexi bit his lip and asked, "Why are we here?"

The man smiled with raised eyebrows, pausing just long enough before he answered for Alexi to become a little uncomfortable. "That's a good one," he said, raising his hand to his chin, "but you're going to have to leave."

"No wait," Alexi said, "I feel I was brought here for a reason, I just don't know why."

The man shrugged and asked, "What are your names?"

They replied without hesitation.

"So you've come here to find out why you are here. Interesting," he mused. "Well, would you care to join me for dinner? I have yams and a turkey which is just about done. I'm not sure I can answer your question, but at least I can give you a good meal."

They eyed each other. Meredith shrugged, looked back at the man, and asked, "You are Gabriel, right?"

He nodded and went back inside with an absent gesture for them to follow. They were greeted by the pleasant smell of food simmering in the kitchen, mixed with an aroma which was exotic and hard to identify, something between the cloying spice of an ashram and the lion house musk at the Zoo. Alexi's mind swam as it attempted to sort through the conflicting messages it was receiving. The flickering candlelight illuminated Zen calligraphy, Hindu Yantras painted in deep blues and vermilion, Escher prints adorning the walls of the living room. The antique mahogany bookshelves stood piled high with books, and the lacquered chestnut floor glistened, drawing his eyes towards the far end of the room. The open door of the kitchen cast a steady incandescent beam upon a wrought iron cage, standing tall as a man.

He spied a russet flurry of fur near the bottom and a pair of beady little eyes peering out. Glancing back, he noticed that Meredith was examining the bookshelves and Gabriel was nowhere to be found. Alexi inched closer to the cage, combat boots rapping on the floor, and came face to face with a tiny chattering monkey whose bushy tail curled around one of the long bars behind it.

Meredith ran her finger down the spine of one of the black bound books, pulled it loose, and started reading at random: ...*As detailed in the first essay, plunging into this water is generally a reference to the subconscious, or more explicitly, to the order of life which informs our conscious sensibilities. It suddenly appears to one, as they are making this descent, that they are Jonah in the whale: this power is primordial and to the initiate appears terrible. An encounter with the unconscious leads to a temporary plunge into the abyss. Or in modern terminology, a schizophrenic crackup. It is at its culminating moment always a motion on the part of the individual: a vertical re-organization of models rather than a lateral exploration of pre-existing cultural forms. While the initiation may be into a Gnostic cult or larger societal role, the experience, and the solutions to the problem that it poses, must arise from ones inner life. Now this crack needn't be confused with the medical condition of schizophrenia. It is situational, and may in fact be a necessary life experience for any would-be shaman or artist—the two are in function nearly the same—and so long as the individual is given the tools to deal with the experience, or invents them himself, he will return to the world whole, and what is more, aware of his true depth potentialities. If he remains in that plunge and never comes up for air, he will be lost in the realm of the subconscious…*

Meredith paused a moment, and looked up. We're really in the lion's mouth here, aren't we?, she thought. Alexi was still on the far side of the room, inspecting the cage. She turned her attention back to the book.

…All societies have inevitably created at least one secret society, so the names and specific functions of these Orders are vast. Some of the most famous are the Knights Templar, the Assassins, various Sufi cults, countless Gnostic and Hermetic organizations, the Castrators, the Cult of the Black Mother, the Rosicrucians, the Bavarian Illuminati, OTO, the Golden Dawn, A.A., Freemasons—the list goes on and on. Each of these cults generally has any number of sects operating at any given time, oftentimes enmeshed in squabbling with the others over who has direct lineage from the 'original' order. In Orpheus' descent into the underworld, there is a reaction toward the eternal realization or gnosis these schools or cults intend on presenting: here we see the futile efforts of the individual will and ego to cling, out of turn, to a particular time or impression. This interpretation is strengthened by the fact the Orpheus becomes the figurehead of the initiate within many of these cults, and his myth is a cautionary tale for those who might cling to the mask. The Orphic egg also presents an important formula, representing the potentiality in spirit of the initiate, which may be released through an alchemical process, the initiations. In the process of Ascension the self retains knowledge of itself in the womb of eternity. This is the culmination of an initiation, which may take many lifetimes. While each of these may have different intents than the Gnostic or Orphic cults we're discussing, they all have certain qualities in common. In fact, these organizations differ only in intent and the symbols used in their initiations to create a somatic link to the brainwashing techniques taking place. We can see certain techniques being used across the board to brainwash people, and these are the techniques which have been used by religions and cultures, which invariably develop side by side, and by our modern corollary, media…

Those two reflective orbs regarded Alexi for a long moment; finally, he chuckled to himself and smiled.

Seeing bared teeth, the monkey gave an ear-piercing shriek and sprang forward. The door to the cage flew open, hinges groaning, and Alexi was bowled backwards onto the floor with a grunt. He tried to claw the thing off, but it held on, its iron grip relentless while needle-sharp teeth worked their way along his neck and hunted for a vein.

A series of clicks and chirps came from above and the monkey leapt towards the ceiling. Gabriel's silhouette loomed overhead, his face tilted sideways and wearing an unreadable expression.

"I see you've met Suke, got him all riled up. Come down here, Suke."

He chirped several times more and the monkey dropped back down from the rafters, landing on Gabriel's shoulder and clambering around to find a comfortable seat. "Suke means sweet, in Japanese. Back in your cage now, there you go."

Meredith clucked to herself and looked down at Alexi, still lying wide-eyed on the floor. "Never bare your teeth at a monkey, man."

Gabriel nodded. "Incredibly similar, genetically speaking. Still, some of our social mores differ dramatically. Dinner is served."

The two of them followed him into the kitchen, where he'd already served the meal around a wooden table. The black and white tiles of the floor melted, smaller, then larger in Alexis' vision, and he stood at the entranceway, transfixed. Yin-Yang, broken into trigrams, hexagrams... the I-Ching...

"I'm sorry about my friend," Meredith said, sitting down and taking in a deep breath of the steam which rose from the yams on his plate, "he's still tripping his balls off, I think."

Gabriel smiled and said, "Of course, of course." The wicker chair creaked as he leaned back. "Ahhh. Have you noticed it's been raining for three days straight?"

Meredith nodded.

Alexi still stood in the entrance, staring down at the tiles. He looked up, squinting, and asked, "Do you think that means something? Three... three. And rain. The flood? Yes, here we go: the flood and the ark myth. Genetic transmission. The forty two days of the flood is AMA, the mother, still dark. The forty two judges of Amenti, the forty two-fold name of the creative God. The black mother, the forces of creation in silence."

Gabriel popped some turkey in his mouth, chewed while deliberating on the question, swallowed, and shook his head. "No, I just thought it was interesting."

Alexi pulled himself back from his reverie and took his seat at the table. "This is some damn fine turkey, if I do say so myself. It seems so simple, more wholesome than any I've..." he trailed off, looking at the salt shakers. One black, one white. The pillars in my dream, the passage into the underworld. His eyes remaining on Gabriel, he took the shakers and slowly moved them to either side of his plate.

"You like my salt and pepper shakers?" Gabriel asked.

Alexi continued to stare at him. "I do, very much."

Meredith let out a snort and almost shot masticated yam through her nose.

Alexi turned his attention away from Gabriel, back to his plate, and they continued eating in silence for a few more minutes.

Then Gabriel sat forward and said, "Those above me in the Order would frown on me for saying this, but I'll tell you this much—the real order which doles out initiation, that creates the kind of synchronicities which brought you here and will carry you on to the next step of your mission, is the Universe herself." He leaned back. "Sorry about the monkey, by the way. Would you like some sangria?"

They both accepted, and as Gabriel was filling a goblet for Meredith, Alexi picked up his and held it up to the light, examining the room through its crimson-colored lens.

"A toast," Gabriel proclaimed, "to Love, Light, and Liberty."

They clinked their glasses together, a high-pitched note that faded over an eternity of moments, very much, Alexi fancied, like the ringing of a bell.

Gabriel got up and lit a pair of candles, putting them on the table before walking across the room to switch off the lights. "Incandescent lights get to me, sometimes," he explained.

He picked up a knife and carved off another slice of turkey for each of them, the flesh peeling away like butter. "They say the tryptophan in turkey tends to make you sleepy, you know. But it isn't the tryptophan. Of course, most people find it can be very relaxing, going down into that state. A few try to shake it off, worrying about this and that and what will happen to them while they try to resist in vain, but there's no need to get really tired. It's just pretend drowsiness, so I'd like to suggest you can notice how your breathing is already beginning to slow down, and simply relax." Gabriel picked up his wineglass and finished it off. "What did you find so interesting about my salt and pepper shakers, by the way?"

Alexi shook his head. "It has something to do with dreams I've been having. I keep seeing things which tip me off to that, but when I try to bring light to it and piece it all together, they resist."

"I understand," Gabriel said, his eyes glittering in the candlelight. "Dreams seldom make sense out of their element. Instead of trying to bring them up to you and figure them out, you need to go down to them, deal with them on their own plane."

Alexi nodded and shook some salt on his yams.

Gabriel turned towards Meredith, who was sitting cross-legged in her chair, her long white robes splayed open and revealing most of her chest.

"Care for some more wine?"

Meredith tilted her head forward, a slow smile creasing her lips. "He who drinks of my lips shall be me, and I shall be him," she said, cupping both hands around the bulb and lifting her goblet to accept the libations. The ruby liquid gurgled as it rushed from the bottle and splashed against the glass. Meredith nodded again when it was three-quarters full, and then looked down into her reflection mirrored on the burgundy surface.

Everything around her brightened for a moment as she drank deeply from her grail, various objects on the table catching her attention, crystalline and fixed, standing still in stark contrast to the fascinating interplay of motion on her companion's faces.

Alexi was still transfixed, staring down at his yams and watching the tiny grains of salt melt into them. He didn't respond to the question.

"This wine is good, right?" Gabriel said. "I sometimes think of that idea of kintsugi, the Japanese practice of using gold to rejoin broken vessels. In a sense, all vessels are broken, and all experiences, us sitting here now, awake, the dreams you're talking about, are like the fragments of some long forgotten, broken future past—" As he was reaching across the table to refill Alexi's glass, his elbow brushed against his own and tipped it over the edge. Meredith watched it tumble end over end as it fell, landing with a high-pitched crack and a slight bounce, followed by a raining patter of shards as it struck the tiles a second time and shattered.

The sudden sound startled Alexi so much, he almost fell off his chair. Blinking and looking around the room as if for the first time, he said, "All experience is real, whether awake or asleep?"

Gabriel, beginning to sweep the shards into a pile, paused and looked up. "It's more complicated than that, of course," he said. "But our experience, from a literary perspective, certainly is a palimpsest."

—

"And, well... it was all downhill from there," Dionysus concluded with a chuckle. "Gabriel became a sort of teacher, for a time."

"Hmm," Ariadne said, still staring up at the ceiling, a pillow clasped to her chest. "I don't even know if you answered my questions."

"No, but I'm trying to explain the experience you just had."

"I want to know who you are," she said. "And you're giving me—"

"Fuck, girl. That'll take some time. Do you have somewhere to go? It's like, what. 4am? So check it, later it dawned on me, our little meal was like an introductory initiatory rite. The candle, flame. The cup, wine. Even the plates could be considered a pentacle. You are brought in, your consciousness is altered. There is a sudden shock... and sometimes it sticks."

"Is that book where the Joseph Campbell quote came from?"

"The one Jesus was checking out? No. God! I forgot all about the Campbell quote, but what I was thinking at the time was 'I think this girl has been in my dreams', and then my conscious mind jumps in and is all 'that's a really stupid cliché thing to think, here let's throw a Joseph Campbell quotation out there as a cover, and now you've totally blown it,'" Dionysus seemed a bit surprised at what he'd said. "But what the hell. Let me finish while I still remember the damn thing. '...Just as people we've met by mere chance become leading agents in our lives, so, too, are we serving unknowingly as agents, giving meaning to the lives of others. The whole thing gears together like one big symphony, with everything unconsciously affecting everything else.'"

Ariadne sighed. "M'kay. That's what I meant when I said weird. I know exactly what you mean, but no. Let's just... keep it simple. I like you. That's weird enough."

Dionysus gave the kind of smile which only the mentally enfeebled are usually privy to. "Hey! I'm pretty likable."

She scowled playfully. "I'm just saying. Philosophers are usually assholes. Or autistic."

"We can be crazy, too," Dionysus said.

"Shush," Ariadne said, kissing him.

"This is definitely better than talking," Dionysus said.

She hit him over the head with a pillow, and continued kissing him.

—

What seemed like—and very may well have been—hours later, Mary kissed Jesus' forehead softly and slipped out of bed.

She hugged herself repeatedly. Everything felt renewed. She always wanted to feel like this. An alternate universe where it was spring and she was eleven. Where there were no rules and she could run, fall, and roll in fields if she wanted to, and it didn't matter if she got her dress dirty or scuffed her knee, and no bedtimes and the ecstasy was pure and always free. Jesus had helped her find that place—the two of them had wiled away the night over bottles of Spanish wine and MDA. Jesus was nothing like she expected, in private. Quiet and gentle, subdued. All the posturing, like the makeup, was some kind of armor against a world that had already made up its mind about being bigoted. It must've been like overacting on stage, in the hopes of reaching the back row.

Opening the door a crack, she glanced down the hallway to see Dionysus and Ariadne asleep, curled around one another like two kittens. Her cell phone was in her clothes, which were in... The bathroom. She started in that direction, but a pleading sound stopped her in her tracks. Lilith and Amber were still at it? Good God!

She tiptoed by the supine couple on the bed and headed towards the hall. As she reached for the door, it shot open, seemingly of its own accord. She nearly screamed, clamping her hand over her mouth instead.

"Well come on, then," Loki said, from behind the door.

"Hey, you're still out here," she observed, as she slipped out to stand beside him.

"Where else would I be?" he continued checking both directions of the hallway, not making eye contact as he spoke. "We wouldn't want to be caught by surprise, now would we?"

"Um, no. I suppose not. Who are you looking f—"

"You never know." He finally turned towards her, though his eyes were barely visible through his tinted aviator glasses. "You never know."

She giggled, though he didn't respond with any facial gesture whatsoever. "Where's Artemis?"

"Sleeping. It's my shift."

"Do you sleep?" she asked.

He seemed to think about it for quite some time. "Sure."

"When?"

"Tuesdays, usually," he said, gruffly. "You were, uhm. With. Jesus?"

"Yeah."

"I just wanted to—does she... You know what? Never mind."

She smiled sweetly at him. "Hm?"

"No, really, never mind," he said quickly.

"Why do they call you Loki, anyway?"

"I'm very serious about my mischief," he said.

"I can see that." They fell silent as a man in a business suit stepped off the elevator. Loki leaned against the wall, one hand sliding toward his back, but the man just hurried past and disappeared into one of the maze-like turn-offs.

"So, why are you out here?" he finally asked.

"I have to make a phone call. Tell my parents I'm not coming home. You know, probably for a couple years."

"You don't have a cell? There's a phone in the room, and another in the bathroom, I would assume."

"Well, yeah. But I didn't want to disturb Jesus; she kind of slipped into a trance. And Lilith and Amber... God only knows, and I don't want to."

He nodded his head. "Amen, sister. Alright, you can use mine."

—

"We need to go."

Dionysus opened an eye to see Loki staring down at him through aviator shades. An unlit cigarette dangled from his mouth.

"We need to go," he repeated, nudging him with his boot.

"Huh?" Dionysus managed to ask.

Ariadne flailed. "Tell them to call back. I'm sleeping."

"This is really happening. Wake up," Loki said.

Dionysus slowly got to his feet with the torn curtain draped around him. He could only manage to get one eye open.

"I don't know how it happened, but they found us," Loki said.

That got both of his eyes open. "Who? The cops? We need to–"

"No, no," Loki said. "The fans."

"What?" Dionysus said. "You woke me up for that?"

"See for yourself," Loki said.

Loki dragged Dionysus to the window and threw open the blinds. The riot at the concert had followed them through word-of-mouth, spawning an apocalyptic after-party in the parking lot. There were mattresses strewn about, with half-dressed teens passed out on them. One had SLUT BOY written on his face in lipstick. A furry orgy was in progress, centered around a disreputable conversion van with a clowns-and-balloons mural painted on the side. "Fuck me, Teddy Ruxpin!" cried a voice from within the wildly bucking van.

"Oh. God! You're right, this is bad," Dionysus said.

IX. Invisible Masters

2011

Everywhere I go, in every experience, I see life constantly on the verge of death, the intensity of it almost overflowing, overwhelming me precisely because everything is, from the moment of its creation, so close to its own annihilation. Life exists to the extent that it stands in stubborn and harsh contrast to its own non-existence.

One who is alive, truly alive, experiences Eros for life, as the tension between what we see as being through becoming stands before the darkness, the hallow eternity—not the light!—at the end of the process.

Through this we may discover our second birth, between the secret gravity of our end being ahead and behind us, and our constant attempt to create a beginning, an eternally present moment, right now. It is at first apparent that everything is dying; the undoing, the negation, resonates throughout everything, a Cerberus that barks in warning: 'do not enter, no one ever returns.'

Yet, in passing through the gates he guards, one is immediately overwhelmed by how alive everything is, challenging that pessimistic cry that had set a pall upon the world; all living beings, screaming together 'I am!' defiantly against the coming of the dawn. Should we choose life, accept it fully without doctoring, we must join in to this chorus with all of our strength, become a part of the song rather than an individual standing outside, merely listening in rapt attention.

For those who would cling to a static solution, whether it be a canon, manifesto, or the words of an orator or messiah, I would recommend they take Crowley's words to heart:
'O ye who dwell in the dark night of the soul, beware most of all the herald of the dawn!'" — **Gabriel De Leon**

Journal of Gabriel De Leon, December 2011.

My first waking impression this morning was a hazy glance through frostbitten glass at an overturned trash can. The sound of a dog rummaging through the garbage. The gentle pattering of sleet on the roof. Doppler shift as a car turns on slick asphalt. Sentence fragments, thoughts bisected in a 3 x 3 set of windowpanes on the far wall. If you're really intent on a decent reproduction of the event, lie down and close your eyes. Imagine a chill sensation, a hazy image of a toe with overgrown toenails sticking out of the bed covers, and then a camera pan to the rusty trash can outside. Not a dramatic opening, but it's all this day has given me. Third day of the twelfth moon, two thousand and eleven. None of these patterns bode well. Oh yes, to be sure: the number of panes in my window has control over what the day has in store. It's still dawn, turquoise twilight, and I'm all tangled up in the sheets. What I really want to know is...where is my coffee, when did 7:30am become an acceptable wake up time, and where are all the lithe nymphs I was promised when I joined this God-forsaken 'mystical order'? They promise eternal Love, Light, and Liberty—instead, I get an empty apartment full of books and a pet spider monkey. It just goes to show, never believe what you read in books.

Get out of bed with a wince, because the hardwood floors are about four degrees warmer than ice, and hunt for a pair of socks for what seems like an hour. This is the part of being an Invisible Master which gets lost in the translation: getting up to a freezing apartment and hunting for your socks as you wonder why this morning reminds you of the Moon card and, metaphysically speaking, to menstrual blood. (Menstrum was once believed to be the receptive agent in the birth process, and therefore of great alchemical import.) A beginning to be sure, but for what?

My mind jumps around. I haven't done morning exercises yet. You have to keep yourself invisible because otherwise they'll realize you're still a primate just like them, and the whole game's off. Jesus was wise not to cast himself down from Herod's temple at Satan's request. Pity. But if you want to talk about irony, my mother named me Gabriel. It's a long story why exactly that's ironic in this context but... just trust me, alright? It is.

I carefully slide open the drawer of the chest by my bed, and review recent letters from potential recruits. Reports from agents in the field. Updates from those in other divisions of the Order. I stop on a letter I received from one of these potentials.

I read it once, and then again. I find myself absently running my finger up and down the side of the page, relishing the texture. Now I remember, he's the initiate who wound up in that asylum. I fold the letter thoughtfully and pocket it. The others I replace in the drawer.

Twilight has given way to a rosy dawn; the last sliver of the moon, visible through three panes of glass, is now all but gone. Soon that rosy dawn will turn golden. And thankfully, the dog has ceased his noisy rummaging.

Out the apartment door with my hair still wet, down the block where I wait at the same stop every morning. Each day I catch the 8:20am train with the same assortment of people. This morning is no exception.

As you may have guessed, I am the type of person who catches every detail, but I rarely speak to strangers, unless it is required for an assignment. Subjective investment in a situation mars your capacity for keen observation.

There are three people in the 8:20am crew, besides myself. A wrinkly shell of a woman, wrapped in something coarse and thick—wool or burlap; a bubble-gum popping brunette who always wears sunglasses, probably going to the liberal arts college at the end of the line; and a boy in his late teens. We smile as we board the train. I've been passing symbols their way for months, though they don't know it.

I'm not just a professor of philosophy. I am a member of a lineage which stretches back into ancient history. Exactly which organization isn't important—we make up fronts all the time, just to keep new recruits guessing. It would seem, at first, that a 'spiritual organization' is a real contradiction in terms. Certainly all the base mammalian proclivities show themselves the moment we collect as a group, and territoriality and hierarchy will wheedle its way into even the most high-aimed society. We aren't so long out of the trees, after all. Those loudest in proclaiming their spiritualism are the most suspect, and even the divestment of the material can merely become a form of popularity. Just look at the pot-latch gift-giving culture of tribal Hawaiians. So each Order must be a veil, much as each life incarnation is merely a veil. That makes none of this play-acting any less serious. One does not act a part, one is the part. We trade one illusion for another and are our representations—don't let your reflection fool you. The Magus is more powerful than any God, and the most powerful amongst the legions of the damned is Maya, Lord of Illusion.

Yes, it can get downright lonely, this life. As you go through your day, just remember there are masked ones; it may be that yonder beggar is a King. A King may choose his garments as he will; there is no certain test. But a beggar cannot hide his poverty.

The Order affects the future of the world, not through demographics or tax cuts, but through interaction with people's internal lives. Dreams and symbols conveyed by Nature herself. The downside, is that you never really know what effect you've had. You are the causeless cause, dead to your aspirations as you learn to walk the Hidden Path.

Our eyes are fixed on a horizon thousands, even tens of thousands, of years hence. As the Heirophant, I'm in charge of the young wayward Fallen, who have yet to remember themselves. They begin as outsiders, orphans, call them 'freaks' if you must, who are wading through generations of recurrence. They keep a little bit of themselves when most souls are scraped clean in the great winnowing of Dhumvati. These are something like the cuckoo, who slips into the nest of other birds to lay her own eggs. They hatch, undetected in a nest full of outsiders. From an early age, they know they don't belong, but not why. They usually set out young. I can rarely engage directly, so early. But eventually I find them. Or they find me. So you can imagine, college professor was a good cover.

For millennia, all the Sendiirian Order had was time. Something is changing now, the planet's pulse hastens. Eventually, you reach your destination and you can give that 'special someone' the push they need. I am invisible, hidden between the lines, but always in the back of your mind now.

The train is rattling laboriously over a worn patch of track, which means the next stop is mine. These have all been answers to questions you don't yet have—but you will.

Here's my stop now. See you on the other side.

X. The Revelation of Flesh

2011

Let us sit on the ground and tell sad stories about the death of kings.
—Shakespeare

I was in a grocery store with Stella, and I think I was awake. I mean, I think this was real now. Was. Is? I'm not dreaming? I can't tell anymore. I'm here and I'm always going to be here. Agent 888 in Aisle 8.

I pace in an aisle, and try to ignore that play dough smell, still clinging to my headboard made of cheap plaster and wood, a head lined with wires buzzing 'zzzz' as the moments pull like taffy between eager children fingers. The meat of my body tenses, a canvas stretched over a framework of ancient calcium and phosphorus bzzzt / pig hearts quietly wrapped in cellophane bzzzzpptt / electrical current running through us all. I can feel the weight of the atmosphere, the pressure of miles of air and radio waves and

117

Wi-Fi signals pressing down on my chest. I can't breathe in here, you assholes! I scream, but no one responds.

The pig hearts are all pulsating in unison with my own pig heart, convulsing in the encaged crevasse of my chest. A woman grabs her child close and they rush past this crazy bag of meat and bones that hasn't shaved in a week, oscillating neurotic frequencies in a medium of thin air.

I gasp and reach out for Stella's reassuring hand, but now I can't find it and my hand just hangs out there, awkward and useless. I'm alone; she's in Aisle 9 looking at cat food.

"Should we get the pine stuff?" she asked, really too far away for me to respond conversationally. I grunt, and lurch sideways, my hand still sticking out at an odd angle as if I was a statue or Frankenstein's monster coming to life.

Imagine you're at a party, and you realize that you just took the proverbial 'one shot too many', and you're trying to hide it from everyone and act like you're really okay and not about to puke all over yourself, piss down your leg, or fall over. You have to get out.

"No!" I yelled.

She looked at me and shrugged. "We can't flush the clay stuff, is all."

"This isn't about fucking groceries," I mumbled, pushing the sounds clumsily past a tongue gone thick and limp.

All my life I have denied the truth. High tide is coming. The established rules are a 404. Prison camps. The grim meat hook future for ever. "It's the end of everything. But not. It's like. Fuck. I— I... have to get out of here."

I lurched toward the checkout aisles. Stella followed behind, a crate full of nonsense tucked under her arm. (Cat litter, deodorant, pens, lighters, a stick of butter, celery, milk, and chocolate syrup.)

You spend your whole life locked in struggle against yourself, and some asshole blows by with a head full of coke and breaks every bone in your body. Who is to say that he isn't living more in the moment than you? And who is going to be there in your own private Armageddon to tally up the score?

I had to start breathing through my mouth. Wasn't getting enough air. Oxygen is sanity and there isn't enough. I nodded at the guy ringing up my groceries, and figured it would pass. Can you imagine how sickly and false my smile looked, forcing a crack through my weathered skull? But the checkout guy didn't even notice. A Secret Reality, the Secret Glory, the truth is already written but men do not—

The madness came in waves. I gripped the counter harder. "Boy," I said, trying to smile. "Pine cat litter sure is expensive."

Another wave washed over me and I rode it straight out the door. I knocked a shelf over. Hundreds of cans of Campbell's soup slammed to the floor and rolled around, tugged at by eddies of my madness. I leaped, rolled through the automatic doors, and came to my feet in an all-out run. They wouldn't take me alive.

By this time, Stella could see something was wrong. I stopped, back bent, and arched over my caved-in chest, panting and retching. Her fingers tightened around mine and she asked me what had happened, so I told her. Though how could I really explain?

When I got into the car I was having a hard time breathing properly and I felt my pulse racing again. Let it happen. You can't fight it. Let it happen. The words kept repeating in my head, slowly at first, but then faster and faster until it was just a meaningless stream of consonants and vowels, a babbling brook of broken glass and suffocated dreams.

Everything got dark and far away. The brook froze and then shattered. Bliss. It slammed into my every warm cell coming, coming, coming at the same time and I threw my head back with a terrific "AHHHHH" as I realized that it was perfectly okay. Everything. If I died right then and there. If I had never been born. It was okay that I had no idea what the truth was, and it was okay that none of this would be remembered. No sense in trying to hold on to anything.

Behind it all: the endless, forgetful sleep.

"FUCK ME, FUCK ME, YOU TIMEWHORES!" I screamed. The curvature of space-time was the erogenous zone of the universe, wound inward by gravity, molecules fucking one another so tightly that only the pressure of a sun could give them the sweet release they thirsted for, to ride with the photons in eternity, the timeless heaven of light.

"HELIUM! HYDROGEN! DEUTRIUM!" I wailed, bucking around under my seat belt. I could feel the ancient building blocks of the universe transforming inside of me.

Stella's eyes widened. She subconsciously accelerated, looking over with concern. Couldn't she see the matter of my dense form transfigured into eternal light by the blasts of Gabriel's horn?

She must be able to see it!

"I just figured out how the universe works," I gasped, "but I can't tell you. I have to let it go. This is a test." I told her that sometimes I feel like I'm going to tear myself apart, trying to hold on, trying to figure 'it' out, solve the puzzle... and now, right now, is a free-fall with the kinetic force of a two ton vehicle traveling at sixty miles an hour, before you're staring dumbly at your arm, snapped sideways in its socket, and whose blood is that warm and puddling in your lap? coming and coming and coming—my eyes roll back in my head. Dead I'm already dead oh God Stella coming—

I can see the cells of my head, phosphorescent, then putrefying, the minerals in my bones and teeth seeping into the Earth, carried by rainwater and gravity and wind, moving across the planet, blown into the atmosphere, dead, I've been dead for a millennia already, my mycelial parts spreading spider-web, fractal-like through the universe forever until another SPARK! life comes again and flickers off again so quickly...

My eyes opened, baby new and fresh, tiny universes waiting to be born. We were sitting in the parking lot and Stella was sobbing. I had been speaking gibberish for what must have been hours, in her time.

I felt nothing at that moment, except the afterglow from having been everything. Life is just a beautiful, meaningless spark exiled in an endless expanse. Such a tiny, fragile thing. It flashes for a moment, and then it's gone. How do we reconcile that with this bone-deep certainty that we are the center of a universe? For a moment, I stood in the balance between those opposites. But what do you say? What *can* you say? When she looked at me, it was a look I'd never seen. The eyes of a stranger.

"You need help," she said, and I knew it was her way of preparing to step back. She didn't say it then, wouldn't and couldn't say it then, but it was her way of saying that something had changed, that she had seen how fucked up I really am under the surface for a long time now, but she just couldn't hide it anymore, and she'd stick around a while, because that's what good people do. Soon enough she'd meet someone who liked the same music that she liked, or who talked to her about her favorite band, and pretty soon, she'd be washing his underwear and I'd be that asshole who she had tried to save, but just couldn't.

It was all so clear. I still felt nothing, except this hollow ache in the spot which fondly recalled the comfortable, meaningless mosaic of shared experience. I could see it flickering in the dark, each memory like a pixel on a broken computer screen, and then nothing. The endless sleep makes us strangers to one another.

I knew that there was no turning back. I had committed to this fate, and had to see it through. And I really had to change my pants, because in the process of following the molecules of my body in their whimsical dance through space and time, I came all over them.

—

How can you trace the spiral of your life back to its point of origin?

You may spin around in that darkness, but you'll just knock your head on the pots hanging over the sink. You're in the void, boy. And she's thirsty for you. Lock your doors it ain't gonna matter. Up your drains she coming then, slink into your bed. Like a spider she gonna climb out of that hole in the night. She'll get her parts in you and the worst part is, you'll almost like it at first.

But what in fuck am I talking about? She left. Big surprise. Whether it was a self-fulfilling prophecy, or whether it was just meant to be, it was a month later, almost to the day. A fittingly maudlin, but quiet parting: the sky was overcast, it was drizzling, and she pulled out in our car. Okay, admittedly, it was her car to begin with, but it was also my only form of transportation. She was the only one with a steady income at this point, so

I figured I had a month, maybe two, before the eviction process really got underway.

First thing—before I put on my clothes, before I showered (why bother) —I picked up the phone and I called Bradley. "I am on to you, you deranged fucker. Or are you on to me? Either way, I'm ready."

"Oh, is that how it is, now? How long since the missus pulled out of the driveway?"

I didn't bother to guess how he'd figured that out, and grunted an affirmative. I still felt nothing. Well, I felt ready to die. But like a soldier is ready to die, not like a lovelorn fuck up, living on borrowed time. I looked through the nearly empty fridge, rummaging for something to quell my gurgling stomach. Milk. Eggs. That'll do.

"Our test of mall security showed me a few things," he said.

"Our test?"

"Yeah. You took one for the team. Now it's time for the real Op."

I drank half the milk carton before I realized it had gone bad. A chunk of congealed milk stuck in my throat like stale semen (and my God, how did I know that, anyway?). I swallowed with a wince. "Ready to do my duty for God and country."

"You're really starting to scare me," Bradley said. "Alright. This time we call in the bomb threat before anyone shows up. Maximum chaos, maximum fun. All the Agents will roll in dressed like Santa Claus, a giant fucking parade, one of you crucified on a giant dollar sign."

"Isn't it early for Christmas?"

"Hm. Yeah. Well, they say Christmas comes earlier every year, right?"

"Sure," I said. I threw out the milk. Glug-glug-glug. It shuddered in my hands like a prom queen puking up a gutful of tequila and cake.

"They'll think it's a prank. Boy cried wolf, right?" he said.

"Right. But in reality it'll be..." I trailed off, eyes unfocused.

"Oh? Nothing. It'll just be that. A crazy reality art prank."

I knew with absolute certainty that he was lying.

—

Bradley had a map laid out on an expansive table in the basement. All the Agents attended. All had their shades on. Bradley was ignoring them, placing models on the map meticulously—robots, guns, tanks.

Agent 117 chortled.

"What's funny?" Bradley asked.

"Nothing. It's just... you're playing with your dolls."

"Just for that, you get trash detail," Bradley said, throwing a folder at him. "These are your cover stories, your ID's, and the specs of your Missions. Don't share notes with fellow classmates, kids, or I'll have you raped by a pack of silverback gorillas."

I opened up my folder. It had a drawing of Jesus Christ, with a halo and dressed like Santa, crucified to a dollar bill. Under it, Bradley had written,

"CONGRADDDDULATIONS! You have the most important job of all. Bring the shroud of Turin. (Or a bath towel.)"

I stared at it, feeling a far away pressure in my temples.

"Alright, look. I don't want this." I tried to hand the folder back to him.

Bradley looked me square in the eyes. "There is a fork in the road. On one side, we have you, turning down this Op, and going home to your empty, illegally occupied apartment. On the other, you get to see the sublime in action, the truly fucking sublime, when chaos shatters the foundations of civilization and truth peeks back at you through the cracks. What will it be?"

I don't know why, but I took the folder.

"Good boy."

Agent 777 scowled. "I don't see anything in my mission which requires that fancy map you've got over there. And what the fuck are those miniatures supposed to be? Hovercrafts and tanks?"

Bradley shrugged. "It's game night. I needed a cover for our meeting. Make sure to take some Mountain Dew before you leave."

—

I arrived at the mall parking lot at the appointed time. There I saw all the usual suspects, plus a few faces I hadn't seen before. Agent 777 smirked at me. "I can't believe you agreed to this, man."

"Me either," I said quite sincerely. Why did I?

When the hood went over my head, I realized it was a bit late to be asking myself that question. There was no turning back. We so often make ourselves complicit in other's designs, a passive bystander in our own lives. We'll even let ourselves be tied to a giant dollar sign, dressed like Santa Christ. Apparently.

I wonder, when it's all over, will I talk about how Bradley 'used' me? No, I have to accept my role in my life... somehow.

Hands were moving over my arms and feet now, securing and testing the straps.

"Hey, uh, guys?" I asked, my voice muffled under the hood. "Do you need to make it so tight? Does it matter?"

"Oh, it matters," I heard a voice say.

Then another, "It'd be rude not to have a Christmas present for the Leviathan."

I struggled in earnest then, but it was no use. I may as well resign myself to my fate. It was never my decision, after all.

Then I felt myself being hoisted, the sound of the holiday float coming to life with a deep diesel grumble, the shrieks of what sounded like protesters —amongst them I thought I could make out some familiar voices, as well. I heard the agents playing at police, ordering the protesters to disperse through a megaphone.

Finally, the hood came off, leaving me face-to-face with a mob of screaming white suburban kids, all their slogans blurring together into a word-salad nightmare: 'WE ARE THE 99%—SANTA JESUS DIED BECAUSE YOU TOUCH—OBAMA WAS NOT A BROWN SKINNED—BRING BACK CRYSTAL PEPSI—I SHAVED MY BALLS FOR THIS—HUNGRY, EAT A BANKER!'

'Christmas Wonderland' blasted from the police loudspeakers, drowning out the protesters gibberish.

A bristling line of cops rolled into their midst, as fake snow drifted down from above. Agent 777 winked at me from under his riot gear, right before laying out one of the protesters with his nightclub. Fists and sticks connected with human bodies, and once the chaos had reached its peak, even the protesters were brawling with one another. At that point, all the familiar faces slipped from the scene, leaving a bloody, shrieking mess for the real police, when they finally arrived in response to another bomb threat at the KoP mall.

And there I was, their Christmas lamb, wrapped with a bow.

—

Remember how I said I am obsessed by patterns, that I've always seen them everywhere? Patterns are the glue holding our universe together.

Let me see if I can explain it another way. It might seem that the shortest distance between two points is a straight line. And, see, by appearances, that is right. But straight lines are curved: the amount that they curve is determined by the mass of another body distorting of the fabric of space and time itself.

When Bradley passed through my life, my course was irrevocably changed. When Stella left, there were no other bodies exerting enough gravity to keep me in a neat, orderly orbit. I hurled into deep space. Just a little nudge at that critical moment can change everything.

I looked for patterns and clung to them so tightly, because I was afraid of the chaos. Now it all unravels, unspooling around me like intestines floating in water, sweet slippery tendrils scrubbed clean by the alkaline nothing. Nothing. Nothing matters.

And it's okay. It may as well be okay.

Thirty years looking for meaning in news clippings, the scent of the flowers or garbage I just walked by, my dreams. Numbers, patterns. Only now do I realize. Nothing holds me anywhere. All bonds are illusion.

For now, I continue with the role, a patsy for a fictional art crime. The situation, a lifetime in a cage. The motivation? I am Richard II in his cell, praying that the cosmic weight of thought alone can sustain him in the dark womb. I can see that now. There is nothing here but a mask.

A year I've been locked up here. Years to rot away, but no more tale to tell. What part of N-O-T-H-I-N-G don't we understand?

—

Bradley picked up the phone attached to the grimy wall beside a bullet-proof glass shield. Fluorescent lights flickered overhead. I sat on the other side, feeling fractured. A flash of sympathy seemed to twinkle in his eye and disappeared just as quickly.

"It had to be you. Nothing personal," he said.

I felt the confines of my reality drawn and quartered. "Fuck you, man. Jesus. Fuck you. Why did you do it?"

"A sacrifice had to be made. You understand ritual, don't you?"

"Don't patronize me."

"We need the chaos to instigate change," he said. Like that explained anything. "As in surgery, an action should be done clearly, directly, and with lucidity. Ordo ab Chao, order through chaos."

"That made me deserve this?" I asked.

"Come off it, your Majesty. We don't deserve to be sucked off or shot or starve, we didn't deserve to be born. It fucking happened. Deal with it. But, if you want to pin yourself with some, oh I don't know? ...Complicity, then here you go: every T-shirt you ever bought, every collectible lunchbox or bobble-head or piece of memorabilia. Every porno you ever watched since the time you first learned to masturbate. Every raunchy microwave burrito you purchased from the 7/11. You willingly participated in this deception, and for that you may as well be guilty. So before you judge me for what I chose to do, please realize that your shtick was ineffective and banal. I am productive and effective. I'm sorry that it leaves you on that side of the glass, and me on this side. But that's how it is, and how it will always be."

And then he hung up the phone and walked. Out of my life, forever.

—

The phone rang.

"One last Op," Bradley said.

The voice on the other end reached for a mentholated cigarette from the pocket on the vest of his T-shirt. Bradley could hear it rustle, then the crisp inhale. "Bradley, listen. I told you. You're spun. None of this is even real, man. It's in your head. I think you should probably stop entertaining your paranoid delusions and try to actually get help," he said.

Bradley laughed. "Don't you remember? Don't you see? You've been one of us, all along."

Agent 888 took a deep breath and sighed, insinuating his displeasure.

"Trust me. One last Op, and you're done," Bradley said before tossing his phone in the trash as he strolled past.

So many Agent 888's, so little time.

XI. How To Disappear Completely

2012

There is no coming to consciousness without pain. People will do anything, no matter how absurd, in order to avoid facing their own soul. One does not become enlightened by imagining figures of light, but by making the darkness conscious.
—Carl Jung

Bradley the Buyer once said to me, "Listen, Mike. When there's not enough air to scream, bones to shatter, tears to cry, liquor to drink, all you can do is beat the shit out of some person. And that's how the world goes round."

What a shit he was. This story isn't about him, though. I'm going to tell you how I almost killed myself... no, hold on, it has a happy ending, I swear.

I have to admit I've not been taking such good care of myself. Picture this. I'm alone in a hotel with a single working light. It swings back and forth from a cord like a man on a noose, which is ironic in a pathetic sort of way. This place is a disaster. Toaster. Microwave that doesn't work. Laptop. Toothbrush. A boot through a television. (It was that way when I got the room a week ago, and back then, my life was very different).

Just a week. The past three nights I've half-heartedly tried to kill myself, and every night something—some arbitrary, pointless thing—makes it impossible. One night I spent two hours hunting for my wallet so I could buy a razor. By the time I found it, I was just too fucking tired. Another night, I tried to hang myself with a tie because I didn't have any rope. That didn't work out so well. Toaster in the bathtub? Blew a fuse, and then I had White Rabbit stuck in my head the rest of the night.

It's obvious that my heart just isn't in it. The problem, really, is that I'm not committed to any other course of action either. Life should require a reason. I can't stomach mere survival. Even more than that, though, I can't stomach a world born out of chaos, and that's what really led me here. After my third failed attempt, I've given up on suicide as well. I sit on the side of the awful bed, those hard hotel beds that must have mattresses made from granite wrapped in foam, and drink wine from the bottle, which tasted like it had been fermented in a bucket of dirty socks.

Sometimes that's the end of the story, and sometimes, there's a knock at the door.

A few days ago, it would've filled me with terror. I was on the run from the mob after all, or at least I thought I was. That's a long story, which I'll get to, if you don't mind your life being at risk too. I look through the bubble of glass on the door and see Amelia biting her lip and looking pensive. She'd been here when we first rented the room. When I was still living like a Big P.I.M.P. and thought everything was—

Whatever, I'll explain when she's not knocking.

"Come on let me the fuck in darling," she says, through cheap plywood. When I comply, of course she inspects the room like she's planning on moving in or something. "Fuck, this place looks like someone tried to remake Caligula with no budget, I mean Jesus Christ on a pogo stick with bananas! What did you do to it?"

"Very funny," I said.

There were condom wrappers everywhere. Broken bottles. It looked like there was a naked hooker passed out at the table (or possibly dead), and face down next to a bowl of some kind of powder. I thought I'd been alone in here all this time! And then my eyes fell on it. That thumb drive full of the bank codes of like 1,000 accounts that were used for money laundering.

I'd never thought they would keep hundreds of millions of dollars of assets on a Hello Kitty thumb drive, but I guess that was the idea. I tried to imagine Joey Meatballs carrying the thing around. It was a weird juxtaposition of images.

That's not his real name, but it's what I call him to myself.

"It's been a long week," I said blankly. Where to begin?

"You are a fucking web developer, Mikey. What kind of trouble do you think you can be in?"

I loved how she talked. It was as if she thought she was in some kind of Noir flick. My name isn't even fucking 'Mikey'. It's Mike. But the way she said it, and the way she smoked her cigarettes, it was as if they were all on cigarette holders, even though they weren't. And she was covered in tattoos and her cunt was shaved smooth as a nine-year-olds (which is a style I frankly find a little creepy), but all the same, she thought she was a flapper from the 1920's and I wasn't about to tell her otherwise. But I was going to cut her off, because I really didn't feel like getting browbeaten about how boring it is doing development, compared to her illustrious career as a burlesque dancer who has to pay the house—yes, pay the house—at the end of the night.

"Because it's art," she says. "This isn't stripping. And being an artist you have to pay for supplies, Mikey. Think about it. Like paintbrushes and shit."

Fuck. I had said some of that aloud. I haven't been sleeping well. "Paintbrushes? What kind of burlesque you doing?"

"No, I mean like other artists have to pay for it, too. Anyway, I have a new gig these days."

She's so adorable. I couldn't bring myself to tell her that her argument makes no sense. Most people are paid to dance naked. I honestly don't understand why, but they are. And I swear this isn't some, 'I'm a programmer and I think all women have to be hot sluts to get anywhere in my career and all other women are dumb' bullshit. Most of the web designers and programmers I know happen to be women and they can draw and code fucking circles around the men. Amelia is just so sweet, she comes off like a fucking idiot. She has an amazing sense of aesthetics and she is great at making people feel comfortable—and she has these amazing tits that seem like they levitate, like two participants in some snake oil scam. 'Gravity, be gone! With Doctor Healthfull's Upwards Tonic!' Anyway, am I writing her resume here or what?

"You're looking at my tits again," she said.

To be fair, she'd taken her shirt off and was massaging them with coconut oil. "It helps my complexion," she explained, for like the thousandth time.

"I'm fine with that," I said. "But you have amazing breasts and if you're going to oil them, like, right in front of my face, I'm sorry, but I'm going to stare at them. That's just the deal. Anyway, aren't they a part of your art?"

She shrugged. "Yeah, I suppose so." They must have really needed to be moisturized. "What's going on here, Mikey?"

I sat down next to the hooker and did a big rail of whatever it was. I have no idea if she was an actual hooker, but it's funny to say it like that, right? I mean, that's just what I assume when I see a random naked woman face down in a pile of drugs.

I should be fair though. She could just be a drug addict. "Some really heavy shit has happened this week. I texted you about a hundred times. Didn't you get them?"

She shook her head no, curly hair bouncing across her forehead, her own group of miniature dancers.

"Alright, I'll start where you left off. That party we had on the decommissioned boat. You remember. I mean maybe. First off, I'm sure someone spiked all our drinks. I was worse than Hunter Thompson on an ether binge."

"Yeah, I got pretty looped too," she said. "And David Bowie was wearing a Nazi uniform and filming the orgy that started on that sofa."

"No, no, he only *looked* like David Bowie," I said. "I can't wait until I get to the part you weren't there for. You're ruining my flow."

The hooker groaned and rolled over, falling to the floor in the process. Which was good, I had been too terrified to check her pulse and find out if I had to deal with a corpse.

"Yeah I got a little over enthusiastic, ripped their costumes to hell," she said.

"So, I wound up at this place with a bunch of girls, and the Colonel, you remember, who I worked with at the time?"

"He looked like an undertaker."

"Sure, I guess. Though that night he looked more like an undertaker crossed with a pimp. I hadn't really thought about it, but we roll up with the girls. And the two of us are in guido suits and have like fifty rings on and sunglasses and it kind of looks a certain way. Shady, but it was a crappy hotel, so I had no fucking patience for the attitude the attendant was giving us. It almost got ugly. So. We get in here, and the TV was like that," I point at the TV with the boot sticking out of it. "And the orgy... *Hey,* weren't you there too?"

"Yes, dumbass," she said, rolling her eyes. "Your face was buried between my legs for an hour and you forgot? I sprayed lady juice all over you and, like, the five people behind you, for the first time ever, and you forgot. That was a big moment for me."

I shrugged. I just really had no comeback. You would think I'd remember that. Oh. Now I remembered. Right. And how else would I know about how she groomed?

"Sorry," I said. "I hadn't put it together. I had even more monumental things on my mind, like how I was going to avoid *getting killed.*"

She scowled. "Most boys, Mikey. They would be hard pressed to forget a night like that. I don't know. Maybe that's why I tolerate you. Go on with your sob story, dear."

"Alright. I really am sorry about that. I woke up that morning, and by morning, I mean afternoon, to my phone ringing. It was a man with the most indistinct European accent I've ever heard. He introduced himself as Alfredo Rioss, and he asked me if I was a man who could 'do a job'."

"Which is where you should have hung up," she said. "Even I'm not that dumb. 'A man that can do a job?' Is that for real what he said?"

"I can't make any of this shit up. But yeah. Look, I do a lot of freelance web work, and you would be amazed at some of the clients who need websites. I'm serious. In this saturated market, a freelancer can't be too choosy.

"So I met him in the lounge an hour later. He was in his late thirties or early forties, wearing a crocodile skin hat and unbuttoned silk Bahamas shirt. We hopped in some kind of car, that I'm supposed to be really impressed by. He was apparently selling expensive, rare cars, out of his flat in Laguna Beach, and invited me to come by his place if I wanted to consult. Figuring I really had nothing better to do that afternoon but smoke Spanish hash—and I'd already done that—I went back with him in his convertible. His house was covered with airbrushed, velvet paintings of naked women, which, he told me, he painted himself as a 'divine offering to my Mother Goddess, the mother of Jesus'.

"All the paintings were super eroticized pictures of the Virgin Mary, splayed on top of sports cars in the most lewd poses you can imagine. The Virgin Mary smoking a cigar and drinking a Martini, because she's classy y'know, but getting it up the ass because she likes to party. He used the word classy at least ten or twenty times when describing his own work. It was *amazing*.

"We sat down to talk business. Almost immediately, there came a knock at the door. He got up, and led in a short Mexican man with a briefcase handcuffed to his hand. Getting a Tarantino vibe here? My would-be client told me to hold on, as he inspected the hundred dollar bill bricks in the suitcase. The whole time he had his other hand on a gun in the back of his pants, which I hadn't seen before. Apparently, the take was in, because he let his hand drop out of his pants and waved the Mexican off with a thank you.

"After the Mexican left, he offered me a plate of cocaine.

"Do you know how to sell these cars on the Internets?" he asked. He actually asked me twice, once before and once after doing an enormous rail of the stuff, as if the blow was so strong he had forgotten he'd asked the first time.

"I looked out the window. They sure looked like good cars. Probably."

"You don't know shit about cars," Amelia said.

"Yeah. I know that and you know that... Anyway, he wasn't asking me if I could change an engine. He was asking if I could help him sell them on 'the Internets'. To which I said yes. He drove me back to the hotel and left me with $500 to think it over. I emailed him with all the terms, and he said some friends of his wanted work from me if I did good by him. I didn't feel like bothering to get a nicer hotel. I figured I could stay in the area, do a few quick freelance jobs, and get the fuck out, so I just paid the annoying hotel clerk for a week's stay with the $500. That night, I called up Bradley the Buyer, who showed up with all of his freak friends and pretty soon the vibe in this room was just fucking weird.

"For example, see that walk-in closet over there? It was converted into a cocoon-like sleeping chamber where the kids projected images on the walls that were supposed to mass indoctrinate them into some cult that Bradley was pushing, along with the drugs. Mother hive something. The deal was simple: you show up, you sleep in the closet. Graduates from the closet got the sofa. Graduates from the sofa invariably wound up at one of the safe-house, or, if they didn't pass muster, wandering alone in the desert without supplies. One of the many people who made their way through our home was a girl who called herself the Tooth fairy. She collected human teeth, rarely spoke, and liked to sew feathers and bones into her skin. Man, the Tooth fairy was weird."

I shook my head. I was losing focus.

"OK. A day later I send the guy design comps. We're all looking good. And I'm sorry this story is getting long. I mean, that breast is fucking mois-turized, don't you think? But that night around 3 AM, is when things start to go sideways.

"I get a call from him, asking if he can hit the website which I haven't even launched, with a massive DDoS. Why the hell would he want that? He won't say, but he offers another $1000. Fuck it, right? I do what he asks. He seems happy the next night when he takes me out to dinner and introduces me to a bunch of his friends. These are all characters out of the Godfather, except imagine the scene was directed by some low-life who runs a corner deli and a Lysol-huffing Sylvester Stallone wrote it. I make up names for all of them in my head because I don't want to refer to these people by their real names, even in encrypted emails, you know what I'm saying? Joey Meatballs, Tony Butterfingers, Nunzio No-Neck.

"They're giving me all kinds of scotch and cigars and asking me in rapid fire succession if I can do like a hundred things that don't even make sense. How many editors would it take to run a website, which deals in Bolivian coffee beans? How do I feel about offshore gambling? How long would it take you to create a website that can analyze weather patterns in Panama and cross-reference it with the value of commodities that come through the canal? What kind of web infrastructure is needed to set up a Russian mail-order bride kind of thing, and would it matter if the brides were actu-ally coming from South America?

"It's clear these guys are coked up to their fucking eyeballs, because no matter what I say their answer is GREAT! They're clapping each other on the back and really excited about all the terrific things I'm going to do for them. Whatever they are.

"Sometimes I don't even get a chance to answer, I start, and they're already on to asking me another question. And I mean, none of it makes sense until later I'm thinking about it, and for instance, what do you ship cocaine in? Coffee cans. And... well, I don't really know what the mail order bride things is about, I don't want to know, but offshore gambling is a good way to move money around. Money isn't real. I mean it's not—"

Amelia was zoning out.

"Alright, alright. Get to it, right? The next day I have one more meeting, where they give me a roll of bills and I launch some sites for them. I've this stuff around for them in record time because I haven't been sleeping thanks to Bradley, of course, the parties are continuing to get more and more out of hand, and I'm spending half of my take on drugs and keeping the hotel management off my back. I had also been outsourcing some of it to the Colonel and then a lot of the coding was going to a bunch of Indians. The point is, I get a call. Like, at 4AM. It's from Alfredo. He sounds really frantic. It's all garbled up, like this:

"'It is all fucked sideways. They raided everything.'"

"What's fucked, the cars?"

"'No not the cars, you idiot. The offshore oil rigs. Raided by Navy seals. Cleaned the uh, what do you call them? Servers, the servers. And there is an important item. A very, very important item and it's... it's missing, OK. If Joey doesn't get it I'm dead. If anyone has it and he doesn't get it, they're dead.' He sounded so scared that he wasn't even threatening me. He seemed the type to threaten people when he got scared. 'So have you seen it? It looks like a little, I don't know, it's like a children's toy, like a little—'

"And that's when the phone went dead because I'm pretty sure someone shot him in the head. But I figured he was talking about this."

I hold up the Hello Kitty thumb drive.

Amelia giggled, but hid it behind her wrist when I glared at her.

"I know it's weird but this is dead serious. He had left it in my room during one of his coked up meetings. And I did a little hunting around as secretly as I could and basically it's a collection of offshore bank account numbers that are used for—"

"Shuuuuut up! Holy shit," she said. "You've made me like... an accessory! I could be taken away and—"

"No no," I said. "I've done nothing illegal and... an accessory? You really need to stop watching Law and Order. It's just that I got myself in with some psychotic people and they don't think well, and now I have this thumb drive. Which I didn't steal."

"So give it to them," she said simply.

"If I give it to them, then it's basically admitting that I stole it. I honestly had no idea, but do you think they're going to believe me? That I haven't copied all the data or sold it to someone else? I can't believe that they'll let me live, honestly. It's all just a big misunderstanding, but there's no way out. I've thought it through a million ways. I have to find a buyer for this thing and sell it. These accounts could be worth hundreds of millions."

"You're going to rob the mob."

"It's actually the Italian, Chinese, Japanese, several Mexican gangs—this one drive has the accounts information for all these offshore accounts. I don't even understand half of it. Clearly, it wasn't Alfredo's. I just need to find someone who would be big enough to be able to do something with it. Do you understand why I can't give it back though? It's like telling all those guys I stole their shit. And I can't hold on to it either."

"Destroy it?" she asked.

I had considered it. But this seemed like my one shot—I was just in a lull now—I had no resources. I was sick of web programming. I was sick of being caught up in these crazy fucking schemes. It was time to buy my way out, and if that meant fighting over the meal ticket, well... I put my head in my hands. If I was going to fight back, I needed resources. I also hadn't slept in days. I had to take that into account. I wasn't thinking clearly. But I was fairly sure that I should definitely not give this up, and I should definitely not destroy it.

"Destroy it!" she said again, a little more insistently. Had I been speaking aloud? I couldn't even tell.

"No, listen. I have a plan."

I didn't have a plan. But that's often how the best plans start.

"Oh?" she asked. She had wandered to the other side of the room, gently rousing the hooker who had slid off the table with the remaining drug concoction. With a little moan, the girl smacked her lips together a few times and seemed about to slip back to dreamland.

"Hey," Amelia said gently to the girl. "What's your name?"

"Meissh," she slurred. "Want go to sleep..."

"One minute, OK Meish?" Amelia asked. The girl nodded and plunked down on her elbows, pushing ringlets of hair from her raccoon eyes, black holes which sprouted white centers when she saw the plate of drugs. "Oooh."

"You have 'a plan'?" Amelia prompted again, passing a straw to her new best friend.

"Uh, yeah," I said. I wondered how I could stall just for a minute. I had a mind for planning. I really did, but not on my feet.

"Not so slick, really," she said, unexpectedly.

"Huh?"

The loud thunk of a gun on the counter snapped me out of whatever train of thought I had been on, yanked me out the window, and bounced me along the gravel at the side.

I know they say girls can fit anything into their handbags, but Christ. A Desert Eagle.

"Let's try this instead. You give the thumb drive to me. I don't have to take it from your corpse."

"My corpse?"

"Yeah. Because you'd be dead."

"Oh."

"You'll not have to want for creature comforts, so long as you're loyal. The network needs programmers."

I laughed. At first, it was a genuine guffaw, but when she kept staring at me with razor blades for eyes, it turned forced and then died a sullen rasp in my throat.

"Jesus. You have no fucking idea what you're getting into—" I started. "I mean you're a fucking, a fucking—"

Amelia picked up the gun and pointed it dead between my eyes. "Pow." She winked, put it down. "This plan is better than anything you have."

Meish looked at both of us. "What the hell?"

"I don't have time to read you in. But you will get to spend a lot of time on pretty beaches," Amelia said, pushing back her hair with the barrel of the gun. I prayed she understood how the safety worked and this wasn't some badass act that she'd constructed from those crime shows.

"The plan works like this. I like you... kinda. You code like a demon, but with people, you're like a golden retriever that thinks it's a pit bull. But I've known you how many years now? I fucking *know* you, Mikey. And I know showy criminals like Alfredo. He didn't leave a Hello Kitty data drive here by accident. His life depended on it, but he left it here? No. The drive is yours. The data is his. You stole it because of the mystery of it, because you are bored of your life. It shows in everything you do. Fucking bored and here's this opportunity. You're stupid but you're not stupid-stupid, you know? Come on."

The hole in my memory parted a little bit. I saw my hand, pulling the drive out of the USB slot on his computer, slipping it easily into my bag. "Alright Amelia this is cute but these are serious men—"

A knife flew across the room and stuck to the hilt, very still, very close to my head. "Drywall," I said, trying to smirk.

"I'm a member of a secret order," she said, pointing to the ouroboros burned into her forearm. "We can be pretty serious too. You know what this means? 'Each life is whole, a self-contained round. Nothing outside it'. That's what marriage is supposed to be, you know."

"Marriage?" I almost croaked. "You aren't asking me to..."

She laughed long and hard. "Oh, no, no, no. C'mon, Mikey. You're silly. I didn't say you should wear our brand. And it has a further meaning, to those of us *inside*..."

She lifted her arm, moving the scarred flesh around in the light.

Her tone of voice shifted. Frankly, it scared the shit out of me. "Each life is a whole—an enclosed circle—outside which nothing exist. Our entire universe might be the inside of a black hole. All one cause, a secret unspeakable to those without."

Huh. I really had nothing to say to that.

Her arm dropped. She shrugged. "Alright, whatever. So, listen. We need to get out of here, and it needs to start with a hotel fire. Sometimes, I'll be able to take a bag off your head, sometimes not. You will code. And party. I promise the strangest freaks you can imagine will jet-set in and out of your life as you tend bar and get really good with that Hitachi magic wand."

I honestly couldn't find much to argue with so far. I poured myself a drink. If you find this hard to believe, keep in mind that I had been half-seriously considering suicide just a few hours ago. Sex slave was a step up from suicidal web programmer from where I was standing.

"During our travels, you will organize a Kickstarter for your friends, raising money for your funeral. Tragedy, it was. Very sad. After that, you have no name, no ID, no Social Security card, no citizenship, nothing."

"I get it. I'll be your... programming sex monkey."

She thought for a moment and smiled. "Something like that."

I rolled that around for a minute. I was strangely touched. Plus, I didn't have to take responsibility for my life anymore, which was going to be really nice.

"Heyyy. I'm not a prostitute," Meish said suddenly, clearly running a minute behind the rest of the conversation. "I'm a fucking molecular chemist from MIT."

"Spring break?" I asked.

Meish rolled her eyes.

"Even better," Amelia said. "Though I'm sorry. All your friends are going to have to think you're dead from here on."

Meish sighed. She pulled her hair back, slipped on her glasses, and let her eyes focus for the first time today. "I'm a molecular chemist. I don't really have any friends."

"Amelia," I said, pouring yet another drink. "I concede. Your plan is better than mine."

"The name's Artemis," she said.

Sure. *Artemis.*

Sometimes you have to accept what life gives you, I think.

XII. Wandering Stars

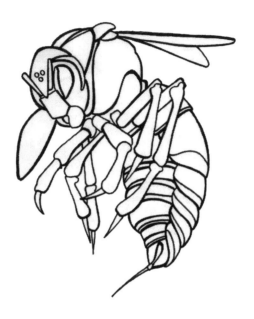

2012

Who does our Order serve?
I think of Her as our mother of birth and death.
She is like a tree, with branches in the heavens of dream, and roots
that stretch to the underworld.
When you offer yourself up to Her, she takes you in and guides your
actions.
When you offer yourself to Her, and pass the gate of your death and
birth, you are faced with a choice: return to the world, like a slate
wiped clean, or, like the Fallen, gestate forever in that dark womb.
But there is a third option, and only She can make it possible.
—Gabriel De Leon

Trevino looked down at a muddy bed sheet sign, tangled in what may have been an herb garden. It was painted crudely to depict the smoldering remains of the World Trade Center, with the words 'GROUND ZERO'S JUST GROUND' framed in smoke.

"What the hell's that even mean?" he grumbled. The previous night's concert had completely trampled the place. The barn was missing chunks of its outer paneling. A rusted tractor lay, somehow mournfully, on its side, crowned by a perfect circle of discarded beer bottles. There were many similar scenes throughout the grounds, but little useful evidence aside from the footage. Someone could probably run an amateur porn business, just off the RedTube posts. Scanning through, he saw things he didn't think there were names for. He flipped open his cell to call it in.

"Trevino."

The voice on the other end belonged to one of the suits. "Report, Deputy Marshall."

"Subjects are in the wind, sir. I tracked them as far as a farmhouse on CR 41, but the mess they made of it... It's like the morning after Woodstock. Nothing here of use."

"We expect more."

"With respect, sir."

"No one's putting this on you, Adam. We need more than felony theft and rotten music."

Trevino walked through the barn doors and flicked a light switch. It did nothing. He pulled out a flashlight and began a circuit of the interior: rumpled sleeping bags and blankets, condom wrappers, cigarette packs...

"You are a tool. We can find another."

His circle of light fell on a stack of fertilizer bags and lingered. It jerked back to a workbench near the door—a rusted car battery and miscellaneous old tools. En route back to the bags, the beam of light lingered on a discarded, pre-paid cell phone.

"Bombs," he said.

"At least."

Trevino swallowed. "No, sir. Bomb-making materials. Two, three hundred pounds of ammonium nitrate fertilizer and electrical components abandoned at their last known location."

"You found fertilizer at a farm, Adam."

Walking back to his car, Trevino's eyes fell on the bed sheet sign again. 'GROUND ZERO'S JUST GROUND'. "Explosive materials, sir. And... literature referencing the 9/11 attacks."

"The combination is... suggestive. Hold your present location. Additional assets en route."

Trevino pocketed his phone and sighed, rubbing his temples.

"God help you little shits."

—

Johny awoke with a start. Keys were rattling at the cell door. His brain manufactured a fantasy about escape, but he shut it down before he even opened his eyes. Hope had no place here.

It was a guard, flanked by a man in a grey trench coat. Heavy-set. He recognized him, the Agent who had questioned him last year about the Mother Hive Brain incident. "You remember me?"

"We don't have anything but time here," Johny said.

"So I hear. I have more questions," Trevino said.

The two of them were left alone. "I want to ask you about the others... the two who were brought in."

"Yeah, sure. They go by 'Dionysus' and 'Loki', now. Or 139 and 506, as I knew them."

"They escaped. Didn't even bother to spring you."

"Look, I've got no love for them, but I know as much as you do."

"Maybe," Trevino said. He dropped a giant file on the table in front of him. Text and email intercepts, various transcripts, maps and photographs all spilled out the edges. "You want me to have the guard get you a coffee? I know you don't get much coffee here."

—

Night fell as they wound their way west. Jesus insisted on keeping the wheel, despite the onset of a bone-throbbingly intense trip. Most of the passengers watched the mile markers slip by, lulled into the trance that life on the road can produce.

Artemis was mid-cabin, cataloging the weapons in their ever-increasing armory, acquired through a rather aggressive donations campaign. When planning tactics, she had advocated the 'philosophy of ninjutsu'.

Loki had nodded, saying, "Okay, sure. Ninjutsu. We'll go with that."

She could never tell if he was just humoring her.

"These mushrooms are hitting me hard!" Jesus yelled. A pair of fairy wings twisted awkwardly around the seat behind her. Her face sparkled with glitter.

Loki replied but it was drowned out.

"I'm sorry!" She yelled over blaring dubstep. "The harmonics of the silence are giving me a headache. I have to keep turning it up to compensate."

"WHAT?" Loki screamed.

"Can you hear my thoughts?" she yelled, eyeing Loki suspiciously. The vehicle began to drift out of its lane as the bass dropped and landed on their heads like the mother ship.

WUB WUB WUB WUB

Loki grabbed the steering wheel. "If you won't turn off this garbage, will you at least let me drive? You're going to fucking kill us."

Jesus batted his hand away, but did deign to turn down the volume slightly. "Hush. I'm at one with the Beast."

An American flag burst in the sky, a malevolent, red white and blue terror.

"Is that Captain planet?" Jesus yelled.

"No. It's Captain fucking America. Pull over. Fuck," Loki said. The girls in the back grabbed weapons and ducked into bunks and closets.

Jesus took a breath and slowed down, pulling to the side. She turned the key. Took another deep breath, both hands glued to the wheel. The interior lights dimmed to a warm glow. "I have this covered," Jesus said. "Follow my lead."

"Okay," Loki said.

A flashlight inspected the interior of the Behemoth like an inquisitive finger. There were several knocks on the window. Jesus tried to smile pleasantly at the stereotypical cop who peered up at her through mirrored shades.

"What can I do for you, officer?" Jesus asked, batting her eyelashes. What kind of mind lurked behind those glasses, she wondered. She imagined it was something like a wasp or hornet.

The officer's mouth opened, but what came out was a long string of guttural consonants.

Jesus swallowed hard. There was no getting out of this one. They may as well have walked up to a random policeman, grabbed him by the shirt, handed him a fistful of crack and proclaimed "I AM THE GRIM REAPER!"

She looked over at Loki, who was frozen in place. No help, there. The girls in the back all gripped their weapons tighter. Artemis moved towards one of the window, looking to line up a shot if need be.

"MMMMMUUUGHHH MOOOOORRZZZ NNNNUUU FFFRRRRRMMMM?" Jesus said, the words spontaneously ejaculating straight from her gut. Her eyes widened in surprise.

The cop nodded agreeably and took his hands off his hips. "Don't let me catch you speeding again," he said, turning on his heel.

Loki unfroze. "What the fuck was that?"

Jesus slowly removed her hands from the wheel. "I... don't know."

The steering wheel began to melt. The speedometer turned into a snake and slithered off the dashboard.

"Loki?" she asked.

"Yeah?"

"I think it's time for you to drive," she conceded.

—

The cop got back into his car and sped off, a Babylon track cranked on his headset.

—

The cop's lights reflected off the window by Dionysus' bunk. He was still napping, but it had taken a turn for the worse. Once drifting on thick rubbery clouds towards some rendezvous with an emissary from an alien race of Libertarian Tree Nymphs, he now found himself kneeling on a smoothly stained wood floor in a cathedral.

Light filtered through the arched blue and red stained-glass windows, which lined the walls, turning everything a royal purple. Tendrils of ivy coated the stones, a knotted network of veins and leaves. Clay pots brimmed over with flowers. Muffled female voices reverberated through the room, dancing to the domed ceiling above. His eyes roved skyward and he noticed that the ceiling was supported by a ring of stone pillars engraved with the outline of hunting cats. They jutted fiercely out of the last ring of pews.

A procession of masked women entered the room. The masks presented a porcelain doll beauty, but their bodies were gaunt, almost to the point of grotesqueness. Stag horns jutted from their hair, which was long, flowing around bodies like orchid flesh drawn taut over jutting bones. What their actual features were, he couldn't tell. They filled the pews, watching him from behind their masks. Occasionally, the women would turn to another and make a hushed comment while pointing at him with a razor-sharp fingernail. Was this a chapel or a courtroom?

He knelt before the Judge's bench. It towered over him, reaching to the bucolic scene above. In the fresco, women pressed grapes with their feet in front of an orchard; a man wearing animal skins stood proudly, surrounded by a circle of cherubic naked women holding wands topped with pinecones.

A shadow passed over him as the Judge entered the room, and hushed the Jury.

The Judge was a ponderous creature wrapped in tattered linens, which trailed out from under his flowing black robes. His footfalls made no sound, but Dionysus could hear the scuttling of spindly insect legs on the floor. A host of spiders followed his every move, and crawled under his robes when he was seated behind the bench.

The room fell silent. The Judge sat unmoving, deliberating.

"Rise, child. Who stands before us?"

"Dionysus," he said.

The Jury began clacking their teeth. Chunk. Chunk. Chunk. Dionysus couldn't imagine a more unsettling sound.

"Dionysus?" the Judge repeated doubtfully.

"I am!" he said.

The Jurors clapped and tittered.

"What is a name?" the Judge asked.

He had no reply.

The Judge stood. The throng also came to their feet, encircling him, shuffling closer as they continued making that awful sound. They removed their masks. There was just a giant mouth there, ringed with clacking teeth, biting on empty air, yearning for something more substantial. He started backing away from them, but quickly ran out of room. His back to the wall, they approached, seeming to relish the anticipation, now they knew he had nowhere to run.

He shut his eyes.

Claws kneaded the meat on his bones, as if it was fresh hamburger. Ensanguined nails sliced his skin to ribbons and tongues lapped at spouts of sticky blood, like red semen. For some reason, there was no pain at all, but he screamed nonetheless, howling glittering gobs of plasma and lymph until he had no lungs left. Bodiless, Dionysus retained a detached awareness of the proceedings.

Their frenzy didn't cease when his body was completely desiccated. Writhing around on the floor like wallowing pigs, their stained fingers ran through clumps of hair, slid between quivering legs. They moaned together senselessly, somewhere between the low braying of a donkey and the snarl of a panther. Eventually, their fervor gave way to a languid purring.

The Judge finally stood and made a gesture with his hand, which the women reacted to immediately. A sarcophagus was carried from a side corridor, and touched ground with a 'whoomp'. They opened the ornate lid and shoveled his bones inside.

They closed the lid. The Judge brought his arms out to the side, as if he himself had been crucified, and then spoke:

"In sure and certain hope of the resurrection to eternal life,
We commend our Father;
And we commit his body to the ground;
Earth to earth; ashes to ashes, dust to dust.
The wind bless him and the waters keep him,
The wine returns to blood again...
This blood feeds the earth;
For out of it was thou taken:
For dust thou art,
And unto dust shalt thou return."

The Jury repeated each line in hushed tones with their heads bowed, hands interlocked. When the Judge finished his curious eulogy, they picked up the sarcophagus and solemnly carried it to a tube behind the bench. They heaved.

He plummeted through slimy water, past clusters of fungus which grew in fat packets around girded edges in the tubing. The sarcophagus fell into the cold deep with a splash that echoed for miles up into the sewers. A single bubble escaped to the surface of the water, sat there a moment before bursting and then all was still.

—

Soft hands moved over his remains, melding them together again. Through a veil of cloth, he could make out the face of a familiar stranger, bringing back shrouded memories of yearnful youth.

He smelled the blooming Datura and crisp pine leaves, heard the trees singing their song—
I am a tree of names,
with branches that unfurl in May dreams
seeds that litter the skies,
and leaves that drink in the Feyn.
This flesh beneath you is an afterthought,
curled amongst my sleepy roots.

My son, you think you're just one of those names,
written on the knotted bark of my shoulders;
Each name a reminder,
a distant star,
twinkling up above the floodplain.
Each name a blinder,
to the destiny our people will one day reclaim.
My lover, look up.
You will wear a hundred thousand names
before laying bare just the one.
Look up.

—

Finally he was able to speak. "Nyssa?"
She smiled and put a finger to his cracked lips. "Shhh. Just a little while longer now."

—

Humming in my bones. This is the part where I look around, and going outside, forget whom I am. I try to look around. Rows of herbs, in labeled bottles above an old stove with gas burners. Dried insects and geodes, fronds of peacock and ferns all perched haphazardly around shelves overflowing with weathered books. There were succulent, but thorny vines and clumps of fungus on a cutting block, and vials of blood. This was a kitchen of some sort, but none of the individual objects made sense. Who eats rocks, vines, or tree bark? Who cherishes moths or cockroaches, delights in rotting carcasses as much as the life that springs from it? And all of it seems faint, otherworldly. The more I pry into the sensation of being here, the more the room pulses around me, fading into a cold abyss and then returning.

Two eyes regard me from beyond this abyss, bringing me out of a final dip into darkness. She is wearing a dress, and I cannot discern its color. Is it blue? Green? Her hair is a distinct electric blue. She gestures with her hands while she is talking. She has been speaking to me slowly, comfortably. Those thin hands look like two doves, her fingers curled outwards like tail-feathers.

I can feel my weight compressing in the chair beneath me, the sensation of my breathing, and now I am really here. All right, what is she saying, now that I can pay attention?

"...The story isn't yet finished, love." She poured wine into a glass. It rushed and gurgled like a brook. "There is one thing you have left to do."

She offered the cup to me. A teakettle in the background whistled, but she ignored it.

"I'm done, I'm done, I'm done," I said. It droned on in my dusty skull. "There is nothing left."

She handed me the glass and smiled. Faint lines appeared around her eyes. "It isn't your place to say. You serve humanity, even if they are tantrum-throwing two-year-olds. Do you give up on your toddler, when he's thrown a ball through the window? You clean it up. Drink this, you'll feel better."

Her lips lightly grazed my cheek, and she patted me on the head. "Then you can rest a while. The humans won't destroy the world, only drown their own empire."

"What is going to happen?" I asked.

"From high tide's water this spring tree will come, the children of summer, then autumn, until finally winter reaches the dark underworld," she said, and I saw now that her belly was round with my child.

"Um," I said. "I think your tea is ready."

Beneath the howling of the steam, there were voices—millions of them, shrill shrieking voices—silenced by the thunder of waves. Mother wiping away buildings like children's toys.

When I looked up, there were tears in her eyes.

—

Dionysus sat upright in his bunk. "I am the Green man!" he exclaimed.

Ariadne rolled towards him. "What babe?"

"Weird dream."

She hugged him. "I couldn't sleep anyhow." Amber's snoring and the other sounds around the cabin had kept her up.

Snoring normally drove her insane. But something about Amber made it cute, instead of intolerable. She was passed out. On her back, mouth wide open, a stuffed Pikachu in a death lock between her legs. "Amber," Ariadne had called over, but the girl could sleep through anything.

Dionysus gazed out the window as she thought. She studied his face, but couldn't read it. "What's up?" she asked, startled somehow by the sound of her own voice.

He nodded almost imperceptibly, and rolled towards her. He laid one of his hands in her lap, but said nothing.

Ariadne spoke instead. "I was just thinking, what if I hadn't bought that ticket?"

"Is that really what you were thinking?" he asked.

"No. Well, not until I said it." She took his hand.

They sat in silence.

Eventually Ariadne spoke. "I was actually thinking about Lilith."

"Me too. I'm drawn to her, but it's like that cliché of a moth to a flame." He paused. "I love you. I can't help myself."

"We all have that problem from time to time," Ariadne said, smirking at him as she ran her finger across the back of his arm.

It was as if Lilith was always right behind her, haunting the cracked mirror as she brushed her teeth, blurry, but still winsome even through flecks of dried toothpaste. Walking home from school as a young girl, her books clutched tightly in the crook of her armpit, splashing through puddles. Lilith's eyes danced in the ripples.

Ariadne couldn't bring himself to say any of that, though. They lay together in silence for so long that he assumed she had fallen asleep, until she spoke. "When you say you love me, what do you mean?"

"Who the hell knows? I'm sure you've had people where, you couldn't explain it if you tried, but everything reminds you of them. They possess your thoughts. Your dreams."

She thought again of Lilith. But that didn't seem like love. "I have," she said quietly.

"I love you to death, but it doesn't cloud my judgment," he said.

Ariadne smiled. But her back was to him. "It just doesn't... intoxicate you. I'm like an old trusty pair of jeans. Comfortable, but don't wear them out of the house."

"Oh, Christ," he said. "Now you're putting words in my mouth."

She laughed and rolled toward him. "I'm just messing with you. Love who you love. But with her..."

"I told you about how I think I first met her, right? In a dream," Dionysus said. "Still haven't mentioned that to her."

"Mmhm."

"It was... kind of terrifying," he said.

"Woe is you. Sounded hot as hell."

"If it wasn't like being thrown to a pack of frenzied reef sharks, it might've been."

Ariadne laughed again, but then looked off pensively.

"Are you pouting?" he asked.

"Ugh, no. Thinking."

"Oh. You always look like you're pouting when you think. So, out with it."

"I'm still trying to figure out where we're headed. Don't get me wrong, nothing has felt so right in my life. But that's just it. This is Lilith's game, and she holds the cards close to her delicious chest. There's no getting off."

"Why would you want to?" Dionysus asked.

"No, exactly. Who would possibly want to get off the magic bus? We're living in a damn MTV reality show. 'Come along with us, all expense paid trip into the rock and roll apocalypse'. I just don't want to get sacrificed to the volcano," she said softly, kissing the back of his hand.

—

Sometimes in bed with Ariadne, she would get that far off look. Is she imagining a conversation? Or locked in embrace or—...?

She doesn't say, laughs it off. She holds Lilith at arm's length but she's always within thoughts reach. It's just a girlish fantasy, everyone has those right? So what if hers was a bit serious—and what is a serious relationship anyway? And so she would veer the conversation into a tangent, until it died in the shrinking space between our bodies, a vacuum of language, her moans an invocation of her secret lover. Lilith, there she is again, slipping behind me with a crooked grin and holding us together with a serpents strength, squeezing, swallowing us... We never truly emerged.

—

The miles slipped away as yet another night turned toward dawn. Loki yawned and stretched, slapped himself lightly on the cheek. Beside him in the passenger seat, Mary was penciling in her eyes. She had been carrying on with Jesus for several hours, but Jesus finally passed out in her mid-cabin bunk.

"Yeah, yeah. I'm beat. And not in the way I like," Jesus had muttered, "I'm going aft," she said a moment later, patting Mary on the head.

That was maybe forty miles back. Loki looked over, saw some kind of introspection was going on in those charcoal eyes, and decided he wanted none of that. He grunted at her once, to acknowledge her presence, but otherwise they sat quietly in that seemingly still place under the endless horizon of the Midwest.

They were set to rendezvous with a shipment of supplies, at a drop-point on a barren chunk of asphalt near a Wal-Mart, at 8 a.m. Artemis arranged this. She had been arranging quite a lot lately. Drop offs. Setting up media distribution nodes. Safe houses. An invisible army of hackers. Integrating dancers with the show—naked and covered with luminescent body paint, they were an instant success.

Loki only found out later they were all martial artists. Not that it surprised him. He'd naturally bristled a little at first, but that was replaced surprisingly quickly with a kind of paternal pride. (Which was a little weird since he found her confusingly attractive, but had already established iron-clad boundaries in his mind? So paternal was fine, he decided, since it wouldn't be anything else). The truth was, this operation was getting to be too much for him to contain single-handed. As she said to him then, "keep your eyes trained dead ahead. I'll worry about our blind spot."

Still, he could feel the heat closing in.

—

They were in the Southwest, planning to turn north next. Campfires twinkled in the night air, a pale reflection of the open sky above.

Dionysus sat alone on a rock plateau, surveying the lights beneath. The wind carried the faint bite of sand and cold with it, and he pulled his blanket closer around him.

He heard the tinkling of stones skipping down the trail, and spoke without moving.

"Ariadne?"

Her footfalls had become familiar. Someone else was with her.

"We've come up here to make you quit your brooding, anti-hero bull-shit."

"I'm not brooding, I'm thinking."

"Whatever." Two hands perched on his shoulders, a chin rested on his head. Another hand reached in front of him, holding a palm full of mush-room caps.

Finally, he turned around to find himself glittering in Amber's enormous pupils. A smirk was plastered on her face. Her hair was up in tiny pigtails, and mischief was clearly in her eyes.

"My God, girls, do you ever stop?" he asked.

Amber just wiggled her hand a little.

Mock sighing, Dionysus scooped up the shrivelled fungus and chewed it slowly.

"You know, I really don't need these any longer," he said, talking around the caps. "I've opened all those doors already. I can—"

"Shut up and chew, Grandpa," Ariadne said from behind, patting him on the head.

When he finished the first handful, Amber showed her other hand. Filled with caps and stems. "Let's have a slumber party."

Dionysus sighed for real now, but took them. "Oh God, wet cardboard," he said, chewing. "You know, that's funny. I used to have slumber parties with girls a lot when I was a kid."

"Oh?" Amber said, after an uncomfortable swallow of caps. "Your parents didn't give you hell?"

"My mother was obsessed with her career and never around. It almost seemed to me as if she wasn't really my mother somehow. I don't know. I guess that's a common delusion."

"I was very close with my mother, before I left," Ariadne said.

"Tell me about those slumber parties. What, did you play spin the bottle or something?" Amber asked.

"No, not really. I had always been more comfortable around girls, I guess. We mostly read to one another, played dress up, snuck out to the woods, and danced under the stars. Fairy princesses, a fairy queen. And the one boy-bodied prince," Dionysus said.

"Oh, come on," Amber said. "No sex games?"

"Well, there was one night. They were arguing about what a penis really looks like. One was saying it was like a mushroom, and the other, I swear to God, insisted it was more like a lollipop."

"Seriously?" Amber laughed.

"It was just natural curiosity. God, it seems so long ago. I think her name might have been Ginny, but it's equally possible my mind is making that up for some reason. We'd already read stories, so what else was there to do but wonder about the 'right' way to kiss and play M.A.S.H."

"Mash?" Ariadne asked.

Dionysus shrugged. "It's a game, that through some arcane process I no longer remember, tells you who you will marry. What your fortune will be in life. That kind of thing."

"Did yours say you'd play drums?"

"No, I think it said I was going to live in a shack. Maybe. I guess not a lot has changed, because here we are. Some part of me, which at the time I couldn't even comprehend, desired something, something overwhelming and a little painful. At the same time, I was not of them."

"Blah blah. Back to the anti-hero shit," Amber smiled.

"I'm not saying... I mean, there were perks. Whether or not they had any other designs on me, I was far better use for kissing practice than a pillow. So while they could trade tips with one another about how to touch them-selves until 'it feels good', I was the only one with a particular object that was—for reasons they also didn't fully understand—taking up their curios-ity. But their curiosity piqued my own interest, about what was happening inside their skirts when they reached inside and started breathing heavier, and so by the end of the night, all of them had held their first penis, and I had, without really having the word for it, seen three girls, one by one turn scarlet, little beads of sweat forming on their foreheads from concentra-tion, and then let out a gasp. For some reason, it felt like a revelation. But I hadn't actually *seen* much of anything."

Satisfied with his story, Amber stretched. "That's my kind of slumber party. Are either of you feeling anything yet?"

Ariadne nodded. "Let's lie down and close our eyes."

—

Hours, eons, or seconds later, the three of them were seated on an air-plane. Two aisles across. Dionysus guessed it was a 767 wide-body, and didn't bother to wonder how they got there. He glanced at the pamphlets in the seat in front of him, but only found a couple of palm-sized rocks.

The engines thrummed along pleasantly, interrupted by an occasional cough.

Ariadne turned to Dionysus. "How did we get here?" she asked.

"How long have we been here?" Dionysus replied, shrugging helplessly.

The three of them sat silently for a moment. A flight attendant passed, asking if they needed anything.

"Ginger ale?" Amber asked.

Squinting out the window, Dionysus only saw blackness at first, and then flashing lights at the end of the wing. Wrapping his hands around the glass to block out glare, he moved closer and waited for his night vision to adjust. Instead of seeing the tell tale lights of a city, he saw a black shape shoot across the wing.

"What are the chances, do you think, that a marsupial or simian could survive on the wing of an airplane, travelling at five hundred miles an hour, at thirty five thousand feet?" he asked, pulling away.

"A what or a what?" Amber asked.

"A marsupial. Like a... a simian," Ariadne said.

"Like a, um. Lemur. But meaner." Dionysus squinted out the window again, chewing on one of his nails pensively.

"Oh," Amber said.

The plane suddenly jolted, lurching violently to one side. The lights flickered, and oxygen masks descended from the overhead compartments like flaccid testicles.

"Those look like—" Amber said.

Ariadne giggled.

Everyone else in the cabin screamed for their lives. An announcement blared through tinny speakers. Something about imminent destruction. Dionysus ignored it.

"Bloody things are tearing the engines off," he said. "Just like in the Twilight Zone." He took another look. "They don't really look so much like marsupials, now."

Ariadne laughed hysterically as they plummeted through the clouds and into a shopping mall. Metal sheered and shrieked as glass powderized into the air in a rainbow cloud. It twirled gracefully around the wreckage, like dragons on Chinese New Year. Books, stuffed animals, overcoats, and televisions poured from the shelves as they shuddered past the jewellery aisle and a flock of slack-jawed housewives. The plane's double tires splattered all the would-be shoppers who had the misfortune of being in their path. They popped like cherry tomatoes and left a red smear all the way, from what was left of Macy's down to the food court, where the shattered vehicle finally came to a lurching stop in front of Taco Bell.

All was silent in the cabin, charred black with smoke and fire. Outside, the lights of rescue vehicles flashed, but there were no survivors, and no vehicles.

Dionysus turned towards Amber, about to comment on how odd it was that they were still alive, when he saw her bite her lip. She sighed and closed her eyes. Ariadne was licking her ear and running a hand between Amber's slowly parting thighs.

One of his hands wandered under Amber's shirt, finding her pierced nipples already hard. The other gently lay on top of Ariadne's damp fingers as they explored under Amber's skirt.

Looking at him through wisps of Amber's hair, Ariadne smiled and hiked up her skirt further.

Taking the hint, he leaned over, kissing his way up her thigh. She shivered appreciatively. As he leaned forward, he felt his hands sink into the dust.

He looked around. They were on the plateau. Drums beat in the distance. The fires that clustered about the Behemoth had burned low.

"We weren't on a plane," Dionysus said matter-of-factually, looking up at Ariadne, past Amber's now exposed breasts.

"Huh. Guess not," Ariadne said.

Dionysus shrugged, and then leaned forward again.

—

They passed out in a contented pile shortly after the sun crested the horizon.

Ariadne drifted in sensations, untethered from time and space. Her mother was smiling above her. She was atop a picnic table, surrounded by a crowd of wrinkled faces. She put her foot in her birthday cake. Three candles and such tiny toes. The sticky icing oozing between them turned dry. The smiles turned to frowns. Now she was on a beach. Sun-blinded and breathing in the smell of salt, sand and crabs baking in the heat.

Her fingers closed around another hand. An electrical circuit seemed to close as their fingers intertwined.

She was grounded, fixed again in place and time. She rubbed her eyes, and was surprised by what she saw when they opened. No longer on that ridge. Amber was nowhere to be seen. Dionysus was curled around her, as he so often was. They were both in a labyrinth of stone and forgotten memories.

"Hey," she said, running the back of her hand along his cheek. He mumbled to himself, but didn't stir.

Changing tactics, she bit his ear.

"Fuck!" He flailed pointlessly, and then looked around. "Where's this?" he asked absently, as he stared at a baby hanging from a tree above him, squirming in a glowing amniotic sac. The rope she had followed before branched off in places, taking on a veiny texture as it ran along the base of the otherwise barren, baby-laden trees. This cord looped in spirals into their navels. Whose babies were they? There was no way to tell. They were oblivious in their little worlds, awaiting some future revelation.

"I don't know. I've been here before, though... I think," Ariadne said. She started to stand up, but he grabbed her arm and pulled her close.

"Does it really matter?" he asked.

She held him close and thought for a moment.

"Except—"

She was cut off by a sound that sent a shiver through her. The howling of steam and gears. Some kind of beast, with the force of a locomotive. She was on her feet and running before Dionysus could get a word out.

He chased after her. "Hold on!"

She didn't reply, though she did cast a horrified look over her shoulder.

"Listen—Hey, stop!" He caught up with her, grabbed her. She shook in his arms. "We're dreaming."

"Together?"

"Yes," he said. "Look."

Behind them, the creature was galloping through the labyrinth, uprooting trees, shooting sparks from under its metal hooves. She was jolted, but he held her still. "Look at it. Trees with fruit babies. A ...Whatever the fuck that thing is..."

It almost had them. She closed her eyes, tears leaking from between her eyelashes. What would it be like to be gored to death, impaled through the cavity of her chest on one of those rusted horns?

"Look," Dionysus said again, gently this time.

She did. Everything seemed to slow and turn to white, a warm snowstorm that blotted out everything save the feeling that she was going to be alright.

Dionysus yanked her out of the light as it blew by, a steam train of peculiar design. Not horns but exhaust vents and elaborate railings and fixtures. The light had been its guide through the gloom, and now it rolled past the labyrinth and pastiche city beyond, from there winding further down a steep incline, finally vanishing into darkness in the boughs of a forest at the absolute limit of their sight.

"I almost—" she said falteringly.

"I know," he said. "But I got you."

She smiled.

"I've been here before," he said.

"Yeah, me too."

"But never with this—" he said, motioning toward the rope.

"Oh," she said. She picked it up, as if that might convey some further knowledge. It was wet and slimy, as one might imagine. "Do you trust it?"

"Well, I mean. How else are we going to get out of this maze?" he asked. Looking ahead at its full extent, Ariadne was forced to agree.

—

There was little movement in the desert during the day, aside from the rustling of dried brush in the wind, or the occasional Imperial woodpecker, hacking a home into the side of a bloated saguaro. Everything around them was silent, implacable. Hungry and patient. Nothing would be spared the thirst of the howling wind. The lizards sat and waited for carrion. They had time.

It was near noon. They'd spent several weeks now at a safe house beneath the Santan mountains.

Artemis paused to survey the girls, all of them dutifully repeating the Xing-Yi form she had just demonstrated. The sun scoured their skin, cooking out weakness. She caught Ariadne making a common mistake and corrected her. She had them repeat it again, and again. "Okay, better. Now show me the next move, where you fall into san ti and redirect."

Dionysus fell out of stance, and said, "If an opponent advances with force, yield by rolling around the perimeter of that advance. Retain contact, retain control. Your opponent winds up over-committed. If we match force with force, we lose."

Loki stopped at the apex of a push-up, and cocked his head in Dionysus' direction. "You like talking just to hear yourself speak, don't you?"

Dionysus shrugged. "And you like doing push-ups while you smoke. Don't harsh my mellow. Reality is what we can get away with. We've dropped that rhetoric before, probably between essential oil rubdowns at Burning Man. But this isn't just goofy post-hippie bullshit. Let's consider the tactics of those who are likely to oppose us— OW!" He was stopped mid-rant by a speeding pebble.

Artemis laughed and reached for a larger stone. "Let's consider the tactics of shut the fuck up and get back to work. You've got a show in six hours, and another initiation ceremony after."

—

"Buckle your seat belts, boys!" Jesus yelled, an unlit joint flapping from her lips, as the wheels spun and a cloud of dust shot out the back. They were headed to the venue, some warehouse on the outskirts of Phoenix.

Dionysus' knuckles whitened on the seat beneath him, but he kept his mouth shut. He hadn't seen Jesus so playful since before they'd been hospitalized. She was reckless when she was happy.

Deciding Jesus was probably best left alone in this mood, he turned his attention to Lilith. She was sitting across from him and sipping on cold green tea, gazing introspectively out the window as she scribbled in her notebook.

—

Please, the Graveyard asks, please just rent me that coupe of a body, it looks strong enough to erase the dim memory that clings to this house of bones. The more you suckle in your stony sleep, the more you yearn, until your heart could drink the sun. So you toss and spin the endless round, again you draw in air and stink in infant lungs.

Let those lips be my lips, and taste what they might, those firm legs, a chest not caved in on itself—how much fun we'd have in a body like that! My friends and I could all take a turn. Just once around the lake. Or we'll race it up the side of K2, if you have the stomach for it. We'll have a contest and see who can make you cum *until you lose all your hair and start seeing dead Gods everywhere you turn. $500 prize.*

What do you have to lose? After all there is only tonight, tomorrow you will wake up and remember the only thing your freedom likes is the look of lovers in the rear view mirror. Don't look at me like that, you don't know what my car is like. They don't make this model any more. It has a chainsaw for a driver's seat and the engine is made of broken promises.

One hundred thousand lives on this thing was some feat, though eventually every day becomes the same, no matter the details.

To no longer yearn for rippling color, no longer dream of pinwheels of noise— just silence, just peace. The freedom of no taste, nothing on the wind or the horizon. That is my freedom. You're not there yet. Your hands still pray, your eyes still water, your home is still empty. You think freedom is being able to outrun the sunset.

But soon your resting state—
(which is a silent scream)
Your open arms—
(which still can't reach far enough to hold anything but themselves)
Your puffy eye sockets—
(that are like two cracked windows looking out to nothing but this manicured garbage heap of a city, the clouds rising over an old laundromat that runs all day and night though no customers ever enter or leave) —will no longer be lost in this idle shuffle. You won't waste what you can't swallow. Won't remember that your friends all went away, all died, and replaced your beautiful memory with their pain.

The memories that stick around hunger, mourn, and clamor. Tired of one another so long ago, a marriage of inconvenience in the best of days, but in the end you had only each other.

Keep running, Lilith; your Sun hasn't yet set.

It'll take many cycles before you'll see the truth and replace all your Something's with a branch from the Winter Tree.

And then that sun won't be darkened by your hidden frown, the birds won't fret over your problems, and everyone will be just fine. They are nothing to you but what you've already forgotten.

Each time round the potter's wheel, you take on more clay. Fallen you are because you just see the curse, like tangled thorns growing amidst blossoms, and not those blessings, like the petals that fall. Your mind always turns toward its source, a stone stained. That's your bloody benefit, your sacred temple in an abattoir.

The parts shuffle, but the players remain the same, as if changing the place settings will make them love you. A universe shrunk to the size of your clenched fist, the jaw that dislocated itself, a hand-sized map of a war zone. When you walk in you bring all the world's tragedy with you in that open casket you call a heart.

How many lives have I lived? I can feel those lives stretching out beneath me like a jagged chasm, the mouth of something subterranean, lustful, and frail, something that hated itself so much it was transformed into a living God and you all worshipped at her Altar.

But she lives above not below, between ribs of bony brier, crowned by silky nettles, cheeks like upswept ivory, hard and hot, a heart in my hands, pumping icing to a mouth starving for a taste of that sweet bloody Nothin—

—

Hopping across the cabin, Dionysus landed next to her roughly, jarring her hand. Luckily, the seats were well cushioned. He draped his arm over her shoulder.

She forced a smile, but didn't turn towards him.

"I was writing."

"What's going on in there?" he asked.

"This is the point of no return," she said cryptically.

"For the band?"

She shook her head, her long hair dancing across her bare shoulder. "Oh, not that" she said. "My dreams have all led me to this point. I mean, what are the chances any of it would have come true?"

"You mean, what? Fame?" Dionysus asked, not following.

"No…"

He nibbled her ear.

"Boys! Jesus." She slid out of reach, and then rubbed the back of his head affectionately. "This is hard to put into words."

He sat back and folded his hands. "So, your dreams—"

"Sex, always sex," she said.

"And you accuse *me* of—!"

"OK," she said, looking into his eyes like there was a puzzle there she was trying to solve. "When did we first meet?"

"At that bar," he said quickly.

"Are you sure? You seemed to recognize me."

His eyes narrowed. Fine. "A field of wheat."

"When I see people out in the crowd at the show, I remember. I see them. I have visited them all," she said.

"When did you… I don't know to ask—know you were Lilith, and not Lola?"

"They're just names, and I've had so many names."

"Yeah, but—"

"I've always known, this time around. But it wasn't until I found more of us that I knew for sure it wasn't an elaborate fantasy. Then I knew what I had to do."

"Let's pretend I know what you're talking about. What is that?"

"What?" Lilith asked. She had a faraway look in her eyes, and in that moment seemed withered. It was gone the next time he looked.

"What you 'have to do'," he prompted.

"Oh. Apocalypse is revelation. Isn't that what you're going on about in those podcasts of yours? I'm going to part the veil... Stake my claim on *this* side of eternity," she murmured.

He sighed. "You're right. I don't know what you're talking about."

She turned towards him with a devilish smirk. "Just the way I like it." She grabbed the back of his head and kissed him unexpectedly.

"Are you kissing my man?" Ariadne stood in front of them with her arms crossed, but couldn't maintain the facade when they turned to her with expressions of mock shock.

"Yeah. Wanna fight?" Lilith asked.

In reply, Ariadne took a swing. Lilith caught it, and pulled her in for a kiss. Green tea splashed all over Dionysus' lap.

"Want to finish this for me?" Lilith asked, handing him the mug. "I need to teach this girl how to fight. That was a terrible left hook."

Dionysus got up to follow.

"Private lessons this time, sorry."

—

The show came and went. And the one after it.

Ariadne and Dionysus were rocking in their warm nest in the only home they knew now, their little boat on a sea of mountains, plains, and deserts. Ariadne sighed. "I had a dream. I saw her—Lilith, I mean—holding a violin, but it seemed like a body, with taut sinews and pulsing flesh. As she played it, I became terrified I'd lose control. I don't know what the fear was, dreams are weird. Eat a baby like she claimed to?"

"She claimed to eat babies?" Dionysus asked.

"Well no, that's what women used to say about her in ancient Babylon, so she says."

He laughed. "Wow, three thousand year old hearsay."

"That's history for you," she replied.

"So it is. And Lilith is stroking this Geiger violin and you're afraid of losing control of yourself."

"Like that film, uh... The Witches of Eastwick," Jesus added from one bunk over.

"Huh?" Ariadne asked. "Never heard of it."

"You're fucking children!" Jesus yelled at Dionysus, playfully.

"You've been sweeter on Mary than any women I've seen you with since. And she's what, nineteen? Twenty?"

"I dig her, yeah. But you'd better believe she's seen Witches of Eastwick."

Mary poked her head out from behind the curtain to nod, and then disappeared back into the shadows of their bunk.

Dionysus shrugged. "Fine. Alright, so what was the point of interjecting that little piece of trivia?"

Jesus turned around in her swivel chair, and set up the projector as she made herself a White Russian. The cubes clanked tersely, making Dionysus wonder if he'd inadvertently pissed her off. Male or female, Jesus had always been a Pisces. Or maybe there was some other reason she was so moody. Maybe lifetimes of stubborn martyrdom. Either way, she wore a smile, along with her Kahlua and milkstache, and soon they had seen the movie.

After, Jesus said, "Mostly, I just hadn't seen it in a while. But it doesn't take Freud to see what kind of organ Lilith was rubbing on. Ariadne, you want to shag her rotten."

Ariadne blushed but said, "Duh. Who doesn't? But...That's just it. Sex is sacramental. Like, you have to respect it. Same as a psychedelic."

Lilith slid beside Ariadne, who did her best not to look mortified. There's never much privacy on tour.

"I respect the people I fuck as much as they respect themselves. That simple. But I'll go easier on you next time," Lilith said, patting her behind.

"Don't go easy on me," Ariadne mumbled. Then, "That's what I'm saying! —"

"Ohhh," Lilith chuckled. "Of course. You're a top from below girl, aren't you?"

"I guess..." Ariadne said.

"I know just the thing," Lilith said, but then wouldn't speak of it the rest of the night. As the others started to drift off or zone out, she leaned over to Ariadne and said, "I want to propose a project. Start keeping a dream journal. I want to talk to you about them every week. Let's make them happen. Is it a deal?"

"My dreams get pretty weird."

"Are you kidding? That's why I'm into it! Conscious fantasies are so typical. If you want the real shit you need the balls to get surreal."

"The labes," Jesus offered.

"Yeah," Lilith said, grinning. "The labes."

—

It was business-as-usual inside the studios of the Conservative News Network. In the minutes before they went on air, Melissa Allbright, their star talking-head, strutted around backstage yelling at her personal assistant (the coffee was cold, and too bitter), popping pills (Prozac 25mg, Ultram 50mg, Adderall 10mg, Xanax 1mg, Calcium 500mg), and throwing pencils at the audio tech (menopause was a bitch).

Despite all the medication, it wasn't until the cameraman reached the silent two... one... of the countdown, that Melissa smiled for the first time that day.

"Good morning. We have a special show for you today. The members of the controversial rock group Babylon have agreed to join us live via satellite. They have been blamed with a rash of domestic terror incidents. I'm going to get some straight answers out of them, about this disturbing new trend. Lilith, Dionysus, Jesus, and Cody. Welcome to the show." Melissa's worn, makeup-caked face took up the screen. She seemed composed of equal parts Botox and conservative indignation.

The feed showed the faces of the group, seated inside the Behemoth. Dionysus, shirtless with a feather boa, his hair now shoulder length and matching his sky-blue eyes and nails; Cody looking weather-worn except for a youthful smile from under his broad hat; Jesus in a neat pin-stripe suit, her hair slicked back and glistening; and Lilith, in sweatpants and a faded Cure t-shirt.

"Happy to oblige," Lilith said, smiling sweetly.

"I understand that you're entertainers. Shock rockers like Marilyn Manson have been scaring money out of audiences for years. But what *you* do is dangerous."

Dionysus jumped in. "Really, that's what you have? Don't want to talk about the music, or the fact we've got nearly major labor following in just six months with only private backing? I'll talk about being in a mental hospital, or about how Jesus being trans isn't an 'abomination' as you said on your previous show. We get the tired post-Columbine rhetoric, OK. Why don't you—"

"—Look. We are a country at war and for you to spread your message of anarchy and sexual perversion—there are real stakes, here. We need to stand united in defense of freedom." Her response was practiced, even bored.

"I think freedom is doing just fine without our support," Dionysus said.

"I'm sure many of the viewers today would tell you to get out of our country, then," Melissa shot back.

Dionysus nodded. "I'm sure many of ours would say the same about you. If they watched. But ohhh, they're watching today aren't they?"

"I bet they have a nice bunk warmed up for you in Gitmo," Melissa said dryly.

Before Dionysus could reply, Lilith jumped in. "Hold on. I'm sorry Melissa. I want to go back to something you said earlier. Did you say 'sexual perversion'?"

Dionysus looked over. Why was she taking the bait?

Melissa turned to Camera Two. "That's right. The Concerned Christian Parents League has charged you with converting children to Paganism. They've accused you of sexual deviancy with minors. These accusations have teeth. We have managed to secure a video of you having sexual relations with an underage fan..."

A web-cam video played in the feed, partially blurred. It showed several seconds of Lilith and Amber's bath-time, shot from some sort of hotel security camera. When they cut back to the Behemoth feed, Jesus was using her reflection in the camera to apply lipstick, smearing it around a bit for effect. She leaned back to reveal Lilith's calmly radiant face.

"Yeah. I'm bisexual. Sorry you had to find out like this, Mom!" she said. "But she's twenty, not underage. By the way, if any of you want to see the full video without those annoying blurred areas, there's a version available on our Darknet site. WWW dot join my cult dot org."

"No, that's..." Melissa sputtered.

Lilith reached out towards the screen. "Thanks for talking with us, Melissa!" She cut the feed suddenly.

For a moment, there was just dead air. Melissa blinked in shock. "Well, that was what we've come to expect from this sort of fairy-tale anarchist liberal agenda."

"We're out," Camera One said, shaking his head and chuckling. A bunch of the guys around the studio were already using their mobile devices to hunt down that video.

Trevino was pacing back-stage with his cell phone to his ear. The coffee-inept PA, trying to be helpful, asked him "Did you find them?"

Trevino continued pacing for a moment. He stopped suddenly, and smashed his cell phone on the ground.

"Guess not," the PA said under his breath.

"I know where they are, idiot. Melissa, you just gave them a free ad spot on a national network. Can you at least rework it for other time-zones?"

Melissa frowned. "Why? That piece is going to be great."

Trevino stomped on his phone one more time for effect, and marched out of the room.

—

Loki sat at a workbench surrounded by electrical components and miscellaneous tools. A Hazmat respirator and reflective goggles obscured his face. A GLOC stuck out of his shoulder holster. A flag with Babylon's symbol hung behind him, the snake in white on blood-red fabric, and the sigils in black framing the negative space.

"Welcome back, friends and neighbors! In previous episodes we've covered comms, tactical planning, ran some practice ops. Now it is time for a little theory. And to help us with this, I'd like to introduce you to a little friend of mine."

A sock puppet dressed as a jihadi and branding a miniature AK-47 popped up from below the bench.

"Hello, sock puppet jihadi, how are you today?" Loki asked.

"Fight them in the streets! Death to the infidel!" it screamed in Loki's falsetto.

"Just take a look at this poor bastard. He wants to get himself killed, and if he starts popping that thing off in public, he will. His fight stems from a basic misunderstanding of what a State is, what it's designed to do.

"States are protective rackets. The Invisible Hand needs a visible fist. It keeps the streets clean enough to keep the cash flowing. Those nasty other guys, with the ugly flag or no flag at all, the State exists to murder them, and their whole fucking tribe the moment they fuck with what's yours.

"Pay your taxes, don't dodge the draft, you get to walk the streets unarmed. Go around shooting people and blowing up police stations, you'll get what you get.

"You don't arm wrestle Leviathan, and you sure as Hell don't come at him with a cap gun. Not more than once, not if you want to win.

"What you do is, you make him look like a bully to his own people. You poke him into blind, violent over-reaction. You trap and confuse him, mock and bleed him. Money. Markets. Security. Identity. Legitimacy. These are your targets. Your every action should be considered, to create the widest possible disruption with the least effort and the least violence. Leave Leviathan stomping in idiot rage. Confiscate their bottled water while Rome burns. And when he hurts his own people, you'll be there with a kind hand and a comfy couch. And your recruiting pitch. Build your tribe. Build it smart. Stay alive.

"He'll be blind, broke, and friendless, with blood on his hands. You'll be alive to build your new world."

"Cut," Dionysus said.

"Hey, that was great," Artemis said.

"I hope it doesn't matter that it's all bullshit," Loki said, pulling off his goggles. He blinked, staring up at the ceiling. What the motherfuck were they doing?

—

Lilith sat in a throne they'd built in their off hours at the desert safe house. Elk and deer skulls, elm and woven willow, talons of owls and wolverines, snake-skins and resin-bound scorpions all found a nest in the structure. It was crowned with a seven-rayed sun. Not yet lacquered, but finished enough, apparently, for her to sit back and sip wine as she watched the seven newest initiates stripped and lashed to its massive base. From her perch, she directed the ritual with casual aloofness, Ariadne's dream journal folded under her arm.

After they were plied with drugs and music as the sun slipped beyond the crest of the mountains, and the wide sky seemed to swallow their suddenly chilled skin, then her Sisters would tease until words turned to glossolalia, and then out came the ouroboros brands from the fire. They would scream over that quick snake hiss of scalded flesh, and then they'd fall silent. But soon that silence would turn to murmurs, to pleading, as the Sisters again led them into the current. Lilith called out to the desert, and it responded.

The outer circle grew.

—

Dionysus hunched in front of the microphone, his voice maintaining a conspiratorial whisper throughout.

"I know some of you are listening out there. I know you see the signs, though you don't know how to read them. You'll have to come to a show for the experience. I can't read it into you. Doesn't work like that.

"But think of this. Imagine, a century ago, the first cars were coming off the assembly line. There was an untamed frontier, and that became America's first unifying myth. America really did git 'er done. She was willing to do anything to make it happen. Lie, cheat, and steal. Genocide. Anything was possible to the crazy bastard willing to risk it all. At least for those lucky enough to be born rich, white, male, and willing to take on that post-Enlightenment ideal of Manifest Destiny.

"A century later, we see what that myth of has delivered: a white hot moment of high petrol fuel, in geological time just a hit of crack rock. The addict knows only ash will remain, that it was their rent money—that they can't keep going like this. Yet they do, like a cockroach dragging its broken body across the floor, its abdomen an empty husk, most of its legs floundering as if in severe palsy.

"We all knew. We were all on the take. We burned through the world like addicts. Like addicts, we used each day to leverage the future, and soon started hocking it as well. Next month's paycheck. Next year's. Our children. Our children's children. We used one another, as we always have, like users and pushers. The analogy is so sound that it's facile. Governments wage false wars on drugs because the psychology of user and abuser is one they're familiar with. No surprise. And yet the shock in our voice was genuine, when all our accounts ran dry, when our friends were no longer assets we could drain. Then comes denial, bargaining. Then comes the mad power scramble. If we want to know the future, just imagine David Hoyle dragging himself slowly across broken glass in the awkward silence between commercial breaks, and you've got a pretty good idea."

"It's about to get choppy. Get ready. See you at Rushmore."

XIII. Stray Bullets

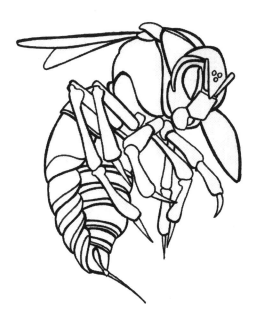

2012

Statement, 'Chloe', Agent Trevino's Records. 7-14-12
There are so many of us living on the road. Tribes, gangs, call 'em what you like. Some follow Babylon around, sure. You think it's all about them? You got it wrong.

Our parents, they say get good grades, do this do that, get a $80,000 school debt, get that job and it'll all be dandy—for what? We had our failure pushed back on us time and again and finally said screw this. Doing what we had to, to stay alive. I'm not proud of all I done when I was riding with them.

It was a form of entrapment. Take what you can, absorb, slay, or flee. But I think some of them really got off on it. Maybe they had felt powerless all their lives, and now it was their turn. Who knows? And some of us really wrestled with it. I know I did. But now... I can't help seeing it as a bunch of silly girls. Silly girls under the costume, playing dress up, hide and seek, skin the redneck. None of us are ready for how ugly the world can be.

Survival demanded we have a pack. I wondered if our prey always deserved it. Usually we selected men. They might be pushy, or reckless. Sometimes they were just sad. Dull, crude, even cruel, but still just sad beneath it all. Those were the ones who cried before the end.

Sometimes they deserved what we done. Like one night, a man with stubble like a thousand needle pricks went under not a moment too soon. Calling me a dumb cunt. We left him hanging from a tree, still alive, and worse for it.

Sometimes none of it made sense, though. A boy with hazel eyes specked with gold held my chilled hands outside one of the few working gas stations we'd encountered in weeks. I could hear the girls out front, haggling with the owner.

I leaned in close, I'm sure he imagined for a kiss. But I whispered something like "Get up, walk further behind the building, then keep walking toward the woods. Don't stop. Don't look behind you."

He looked at me with confusion, a kind of pleading behind it. 'Don't you like me?'

Sure, I like you, stranger. And your beautiful eyes. Maybe the girls would leave him alone. After all, we didn't just assault everyone we met. But if they attacked, there's no way I could stop it. I kissed him once on the hand, which was so cold that I paused a moment and rubbed it with my hands. I guided it between my thighs, where it was much warmer. Then I shoved him forward. "Go!"

Even more confused than before, he started lumbering toward the forest.

When the others caught up with me, Jez knew somehow. She was the head of our pack. I think she wanted to be Lilith real bad.

"Not everyone deserves to be a meal," I said.

"You thought he was pretty. Wanted him to pin you against this wall—" and she grabbed me firmly by the neck and pushed me against dingy cinder block.

The other girls giggled at the show. At first, I resisted. I felt a bit ashamed, and that she was taking out some kind of anger on me. She was certainly rougher than usual. But I didn't resist, not really.

I was breathing heavily when she pulled away, leaving me suddenly cold and hollow. "Just make sure you don't drop your guard around the wrong one. Men are people, and all people are dangerous."

"Like you?" I asked, my voice raw.

She got a dark look. "Yeah. Like me."

I knew I had to get away from them then.

—

The Behemoth huffed up to a derelict gas station in the middle of nowhere. Broken cars and tractors encircled the attached garage. Crickets serenaded a sliver of moon.

Loki and Dionysus hopped out. Dionysus looked up and wondered if it gives birth to his first son. But that just happened in dreams—

"—I'll pay. Fill her up," Loki said.

"Sure," Dionysus said, still contemplating the moon. He raised a finger into the air, and waved it, as if plucking a string. "Did you feel that?" he asked.

"Feel what?" Loki asked, looking around.

"That moment, just there. It's gone now. That moment... was the high point of Western Civilization. It's all decline, now," Dionysus said sagely.

"Uh huh. Diesel, remember. I don't much care what Derrida and Buddha have to say on the subject. I don't want to drain and flush a fuel system tonight."

Dionysus waved him off. He looked up to find a large spider rappelling down from above. "Ugh." Then he noticed that there were spider webs over everything. Legs wriggling, half in sight.

"The hell?"

—

Loki discovered that the attendant was a one eyed freak of nature in overalls. "Wut git you for?" it asked.

"We're filling up the... uh." He found himself staring at rows of half empty shelves with products hidden under a thick layer of dust.

The attendant scowled and gritted his misshapen teeth. "Huh?"

"Never mind. Here's money." Loki slapped a small wad of bills on the counter.

"Huh?" the attendant asked, again.

"This is surreal," Loki muttered to himself.

—

Loki made a beeline for the vehicle. "Sorry it took a few minutes. The creature in there was barely mammalian. English was a challenge."

"I was beginning to wonder," Dionysus said. "Moon's pretty, though."

"Yeah, okay. This place is creepy. Let's go," Loki said.

"Like a psychedelic but awful horror movie," Dionysus continued. "Did you see those spiders?"

The screeching of car tires cut off any forthcoming answer. A beat up Cadillac convertible tore out of the garage, pulling a hard turn that lifted it up on two tires. Jesus flicked a cigarette out of the car as it shot past.

"Great," Loki said.

—

Jesus had been lying on her bunk staring at the ceiling. A cigarette, burned down to the butt, still dangled out of her mouth, with a trailing snake of ash.

"I'll pay. Fill her up," Loki's voice floated in through the open window.

Jesus was clearly dressed for a night out—PVC rubber, big shiny pistol—but had nowhere to go.

Lilith pulled back the red velvet curtain to her sleeping area. Amber and Mary were both passed out in her bed, naked and snoring softly like kittens. Lilith stumbled out, wearing nothing but underwear and combat boots. An unwholesome glow radiated from her. Bite marks and scratches stood out raw and red against her paleness. She stared at the revolver on Jesus' belt, blinked, and took a long pull on a bottle of vodka.

"I'm sweaty, I'm sore and these fuck monkeys just didn't know when to quit."

Lilith went down on all fours, forehead-to-forehead with Jesus. "Steal me a car, you!"

Jesus looked out the window. "Have you taken a look out there? I think we're on the set for a Deliverance remake. There can't be a—"

"I don't care. Steal me a car. Let's go out and have a little fun." She thumped Jesus playfully on the shoulder as she sat back on the bed, nearly sliding off the edge.

"Oh, fine," Jesus said. "But put on some clothes."

—

The Cadillac wasn't too bad, Jesus thought, once she got it up to speed. Her purple hair and strips of fabric and yarn blew back in the nighttime breeze as they shot down winding roads. Lilith leaned out the side and yowled as they passed a diner. She was still working that Vodka bottle.

Jesus finally broke a smile. The speedometer gunned up; eighty, ninety, one hundred... she slammed a sudden turn. The car fishtailed. Lilith laughed hysterically.

They spun off the road and bucked violently. Jesus gritted her teeth and hit the gas.

"Lilith. Vodka. Inspiration. Please!"

Lilith handed her the bottle, and she finished it as they raced across an already harvested cornfield. Jesus grinned and slewed back and forth, coaxing the wheels to skid, sliding the huge convertible about like a rally car.

The wheel got out of her control again. "Fuck you, we are *not* going to flip!" The car rose, resembling a whale preparing to breach, and only at the final moment did it set back down in a blast of dust.

They stopped in the middle of the field. The beam of the headlights shined on a cow, which let out a moo, but didn't seem perturbed enough to move.

The silence seemed to drown out the crickets. Jesus looked up at the canopy of stars above them. She leaped out, and lay on the hood. Lilith joined her.

—

The stars seemed to pulsate, as if they were bioluminescent fish bobbing atop a verdant sea. Jesus' breath slowed. She went completely slack on the hood, still warm beneath her, and approached the speed of light. Epiphanies sucked back into the depths of her mind as her thoughts slowed from microseconds to minutes, minutes to months, months to centuries. The more profound, the further back they hid. It was as if she'd already known everything, and the hiding was just a game, something to do while the fire ants stung their prey, as black holes sucked everything past their event horizons, as nations rose, and people died, loved, and suffered and themselves came to know.

The stars spun, stuck in place, and then time itself froze. A universe of glass. Under the glass, entities streamed information into her, in the code she thought in before her thoughts became language. She began to realize that these entities were nothing more than fractal masses of that code, aware of themselves, and aware of her intrusion into their realm. There was no form. There was only the color red, a sense of distance, thought entering her and leaving her like breath. Jesus herself was nothing more than a passive transponder, suspended in bliss, wetness, warmth. Words drifted into her in this timeless space...

—

They say she built a family about her, before riding out. Back then, she had avatars, maybe even people who didn't know whose purpose they served. Around this family must have rushed the legions—imagine it, thousands of people scrabbling out a living in the shrieking hell of the deep desert.

Long she slumbered in the deep desert. A carapace grew in the Allurah, like a hard obsidian hermit crabs shell, and like the crab those desert wanderers took refuge there, calling New Babylon their home, never knowing. Traveling in her lands is to always be watched, though one can no longer actually look her eye to eye. Now New Babylon itself is her face, her glass-lidded eyes, her ivory teeth. The bazaar her smile. The red sunset her hair.

As I approach the city, I can feel her, curling up beneath it like an embryo, dreaming in the amniotic fluid of the Underworld. For 1,000 cycles, she's amassed her strength, and it won't be long, now...

She will rise.

—

Time returned to its normal pace, and she was again Jesus. "Would it be totally nuts... I mean, totally fucking nuts, to say I think I'm thousands of years old? Or was that place the future?"

"Oh? Nah," Lilith said.

"Oh well. 'Cause I'm totally nuts," Jesus smiled.

"Though I'd guess you are a great deal older than that," Lilith said.

Jesus slumped backward, as if totally spent. "I'm hungry."

"I think we passed a diner somewhere back there."

"Pancakes," Jesus said, hopping off the hood. "Fuck yes."

—

It was indeed, as the sign said, a diner. It had no name beyond that, and clearly no aspiration towards greatness. The sky was beginning to turn a brilliant blue as they entered.

Jesus plunked herself down on a stool and motioned to the waitress. She was the archetypal kind of diner waitress, who looked like she might have been attractive in her glory years. The Peloponnesian War, maybe. She did her best not to react to their appearance.

"Coffee, please," Lilith said.

The waitress turned to Jesus.

"Yes. And pancakes," Jesus said enthusiastically.

The waitress did a double take as she was about to go. She stared openly at the pistol sticking out of Jesus' belt. A .45. Not easy to miss.

"Huh? Oh. Right. Silly me. I totally forgot. I'll put it in my car and it'll be our secret, okay?"

The waitress nodded dumbly.

Jesus got up and headed to the door.

Lilith lit a smoke. She heard the door slam twice behind her.

—

"Trannies aren't wanted around here," a voice behind Jesus said. She stopped, several paces from the entrance. She didn't turn around.

"Get in your car with your whore. Leave," he continued.

"Are you stupid?" Jesus asked.

"Huh?"

Jesus could hear gravel crunching as he approached her. She reached into her belt and spun, leading with her shiny pistol. He stared down its barrel from the wrong end.

"My friend here speaks louder than I can," Jesus said. She had always wanted to say something like that.

He froze like a possum in headlights. Jesus cocked the hammer.

"Don't walk," Jesus said. "Evaporate."

He remained stuck in place. Jesus swore she could hear the gears in his head groaning with the strain of cognitive dissonance from getting Clint Eastwood-ed by a hermaphrodite.

At that moment, Lilith came out of the door, and it slammed behind her. With a crack that echoed across the horizon, the gun went off. Its brutal force lifted the trucker. Blood splattered everywhere as his body fell sideways heavily.

"Shit," Jesus stared at her fingers as if they were to blame. "I didn't mean to. ...What did I...?"

Lilith ran over to the body. She was grinning.

"I didn't mean to..." Jesus repeated, her eyes unfocused.

"That's like a Jackson Pollock, isn't it?" Lilith said, tilting her head to look at the remains of his head.

"Huh?"

"The brains. Never mind. We'd better go."

Jesus took several steps backward. "Yeah..."

The two of them jumped into the car and took off.

Inside, the waitress was blubbering on the phone. "That's right. A coked out prostitute and a transvestite with tits! Splattered poor Ed's head all over the parking lot."

—

Jesus tapped on the window with the handle of her gun.

Loki opened the door. "We should have just left you assholes."

"Joyride, sorry," Lilith said.

Jesus entered silently.

"What happened?" Loki asked.

"We were going to get pancakes, but got distracted," Lilith said.

—

"Description match. Lilith and the tranny," a young cop said to Trevino.

"Her name is Jesus."

"Doesn't seem right, calling it that," the cop said.

Trevino stared at him a minute and shook his head in disgust. "Anything physical?"

"I just wouldn't fuck anything with a dick–"

"Evidence," Trevino said flatly.

"Oh. Casing. Tires." He shrugged.

Trevino grunted. He peered down at the chalk outline where Ed's remains had been minutes before. It was stained black around the head region.

"If we can bring one of them in and work them with the witness statements—" the cop said.

"Good luck with that." Trevino turned and walked back to his car, scowling.

He met his own gaze in the rear-view mirror. Exhausted, sunken eyes returned the stare. They closed. He took a deep breath and went perfectly still. Then, in a flurry of rapid motion, he slammed open the glove compartment, pulled out a napkin, and held it across the steering wheel with his pen out. He wrote "GROUND ZERO'S JUST GROUND" crudely, with his left hand. Crumpled the napkin in his fist.

He got out of the car and approached the waitress. She was leaning outside the front door, hands shaking as she sucked down a menthol cigarette.

"Would you mind showing me where they sat, ma'am?" he asked.

Stubbing out her smoke, the waitress nodded.

A few minutes later, Trevino stormed out.

"Did you look under the table?" he asked the cop.

"Yes. Nothing."

Trevino held up an evidence bag with the napkin inside. "This isn't nothing. Write it up."

"I didn't find it."

"Write it up and you didn't miss it, either. Do better, kid."

"Yes, sir."

Time to call the Suits and ask for more resources.

XIV. Birth of the Syndicate

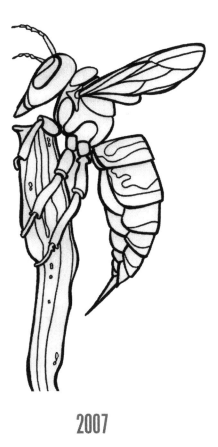

2007

There will be in the next generation or so a pharmacological method of making people love their servitude and producing dictatorship without tears, so to speak, producing a kind of painless concentration camp for entire societies so that people will in fact have their liberties taken away from them but will rather enjoy it.
—**Aldous Huxley**

It took Bradley a long time to realize that the horrible buzzing wasn't emanating from a three-foot tall green goddess with udder-like breasts. Hathoor the cow-goddess had somehow been jumbled up by his subconscious, now sharing cognitive space with the green-skinned alien that Kirk tried to fuck, and the backwards-talking dwarf from Twin Peaks. She was hovering above him, her mouth wrenched open in an eternal, orgasmic wail—that electric heat scraped his eardrums with razors, gutting his miserable brain like an acoustic fishhook. Stuck on the end of the hook, he flopped and floundered, dragged slowly from a far more pleasant realm.

No, not a fishhook. It was an alarm clock. This meant he had to go to work. A treadmill, headed nowhere. The wailing cow-teet Goddess had abandoned him to this cold world of concrete, business briefings, bullshit, and the only Gods he had left came in Grande and Make-My-Heart-Explode-All-Over-Your-Shoes sizes. That cruel gutterslut. The ungrateful whore of a cunt mother of a b—

He couldn't remember the night before, though the drool ringing his mouth was a good indicator that it had been far from pretty. Fragments began to cohere, and his eyes widened and then slammed shut.

Yeah. He had crashed a company's stock and smeared their public image because he was bored and Wild Turkey was a hell of a drink. An empty bottle, an empty apartment, and a horde of empty people who would do anything to—He rolled over and fell straight onto the floor. Train of thought derailed. Again.

The alarm continued ringing from one room over, droning on like an unfed baby.

He finally reached the alarm and threw it. Hard. Good thing he never had children. He tapped keyboards and mouses as he made his way to the harsh glare of the bathroom, knocking computers out of their binary dreams. After brushing away the residue of last night's dinner, he sat down in front of a monitor and started scanning the headlines over a cup of unsweetened black coffee.

He was mostly looking for Google alerts linked to Europharm's recent 'product releases'. Europharm was his employer. One in a long line of corporations he'd infiltrated. Bradley had everything there was to be had on them. Documents, files, video and photographic evidence, financials. Every piece of information that passed through the company was available to him, from the sickening and puerile emails passed between certain secretaries and middle managers, to the top-level deals with other corporations and bodies of government.

Right now, some eleven-year-olds were strapping bombs to their chests and calling themselves the Youth Resistance. That couldn't be causally tied to their products, despite the fact that the members of this little cult had more chemicals than blood in their veins. Legal got them off with a slap on the wrists but the press—diligent little public servants, always in search of the biggest scare-hypnotic they could find—were still working their street-corners.

The worlds of PR and SEO had merged. You just needed two words mentioned next to each other in a newscast and pretty soon, they may as well have fucked each other for the past decade. Bradley only knew that he had to keep his finger to this pulse, as when you want to bring down Goliath, it's best to sling someone else's stones. Better the Youth Resistance than him, when it came time to lose a pound of flesh in the courtroom. (Or to the court of public opinion, which super-sized that order.)

"Nice," he said to no one in particular, leaning back in his chair. Asshole execs had assumed this story would be buried beneath the fold. Instead, it was getting top billing. 'July 7, 2007. EUROPHARM CHEMICALS LINKED TO YOUTH RESISTANCE SUICIDE BOMBERS'.

Had a certain dadaist ring to it. Just like he'd said, bold in the fucking New York Times. But no one ever listened to him.

Those on the board would get theirs. They'd all get theirs.

He almost fell backwards, and quickly sat up straight.

—

The Europharm AG boardroom glowed with a diffuse light, emanating from behind frosted glass globes positioned at regular intervals along the slate walls. Bradley recognized a number of the faces around the table, the sinister cabal of leeches who sat on the board of directors—the head of marketing, the Vice President with his classic comb-over, the rat-faced CFO —all men of note, who held onto their positions precariously under the critical gaze of the company's CEO. There was some unspoken executive rule: Stereotypes only are allowed past this line. Bradley imagined they drank their morning coffee after crawling out of sarcophagi hidden some-where on the mysterious thirteenth floor.

The present CEO's predecessor, Mark Greenwald, had increased profits by a wide margin. Ironically, Mark died from complications from Effexarin, a drug he helped market. God giveth and He taketh away.

Before Mark's passing just a couple weeks ago, he handpicked Al, the current CEO. The board took umbrage with this decision, but, through a series of Shakespearean power plays and a healthy dose of good luck, Al maintained the CEO spot. Quite simply, Al beat the board's first pick to death with his own mother's arm, and ripped the face off the second replacement. Eventually the board had to bow to the unremitting will of their new Genghis Khan.

This group of desiccated mummies leaned towards the shiny mahogany table, waiting on Al's reaction to the vice president's most recent sugges-tion. This was the first time Bradley actually sat in a meeting with Al since the changeover occurred.

What Bradley found at the end of the table shocked him so completely, he almost dropped the report in his hand. He looked from one sweaty suit to the next. They were all subconsciously holding their breath, eyebrows raised expectantly. None of them seemed concerned with anything aside from Al's acceptance of their ideas—expressed with guttural hoots, arm flailing, or cooing.

They weren't distressed by the fact that Al, their CEO, was a chimpanzee.

Al crawled onto the table, shot a wrinkled pink hand up into the air, and let out a grunt before it dropped down, knuckles rapping loudly. There came an audible sigh from the crowd. Apparently, they interpreted this as approval for the advertising budget. A $500,000 campaign, green lit with the wave of a hairy arm.

In an attempt to regain his composure, Bradley straightened up and cleared his throat. "I know this isn't a PR meeting, but, I wanted to bring up the piece which was recently published in the New York Times."

"That's not what this meeting is about," Dave, the Head of Advertising interjected. "You're just here as a favor."

Bradley generally reported to Dave. Bradley's contempt for this beast had nearly shattered his impeccably obsequious façade when they spoke privately. His cover would be blown, and that could get ugly very fast. He wanted to squeeze Dave's T-bone steak neck until his eyes turned to foam.

The Beast. That's what he called Dave to himself, reciting it over and again in a hate-mantra incited to invoke the Gods of malice that'd let him hold cover just a bit longer. It wasn't just because the man was evil, the very embodiment of the abomination that beset the fall of Babylon. It was the way he wheezed when he breathed, as if he wasn't even human. The veins that stuck out of his eyes swirled in place like gray worms. The bulge in his strangely fitting slacks made it look like he was wearing a diaper when he waddled around. Bradley wasn't sure how much of his anarchistic worldview actually leaked in these instances. Possibly too much.

They were still in the boardroom. He was eye to eye with a chimpanzee. A chimpanzee valued at six-point-two billion dollars. No time for such day-dreams. "I'm sorry, what were we talking about?" Bradley asked.

"The New York Times article that you're about to waste our time with," Dave said.

"Let him speak," one of the lawyers said, after scrutinizing Al's face. "He is curious to hear this."

Al sat down on the table and lobbed a fountain pen at Dave's head, which missed by a narrow margin.

"See?" the lawyer said, shrugging. Dave fell silent.

Bradley tried to stare straight ahead without matching gazes with any-one. "Let me just read the article... you at least need to think about drafting a counter-story or a press release."

Al circled his fist in the air a number of times and then defecated.

"He wants you to paraphrase," the CFO explained over his bifocals. "His time is precious." He then gestured to one of the assistants waiting in the shadows, who quickly swept in with machine-like efficiency to deal with the ape droppings.

Bradley sighed as he tried to avoid staring at the pile of chimpanzee dung in the middle of the boardroom table, as it was removed from sight. "Dr. Andrew Mosholder, a senior epidemiologist for the FDA. *Moss-holder.*

The hell kind of name is that? Anyway, he, uh, found that children given antidepressants were nearly twice as likely to become suicidal as those given placebos. This you know."

"Easily ignored by doctors so long as we provide sufficient incentive," the CFO continued dryly.

"A second series of similar tests were undertaken, in the hopes of proving the first series—" Bradley looked around the room. Everyone was staring at the chimp, waiting for a reaction. "Fuck this. I just want to be sure you understand the kind of business you're in, before I unleash unspeakable war and unholy vengeance on you and the rest of your kind."

As Bradley spoke, Al wandered off the table and fell asleep in his chair.

"I'm sorry Don, our CEO doesn't consider this worthy of his time, but we will talk about it later." Dave said. "Now let's move on, shall we?" He waved his hand dismissively in Bradley's direction.

Bradley shook his head, heat rising to his cheeks. They hadn't heard a word he'd said. "Yes, sir."

He turned and left.

—

The rest of the day, Bradley couldn't focus on his work. Suddenly, he emphatically pounded his skinny white fist on the desk. Something had to be done. It's time for The Plan.

—

Later that afternoon he entered Dave's office, carrying his laptop under one arm and his lunch (contained in a paper bag from McDonald's) in the other. Dave's horse-faced secretary was too focused on typing out a text message on her cell phone to bother acknowledging his existence.

Dave sat behind a massive desk, silhouetted before floor-to-ceiling windows. Bradley stood in front of the desk for a moment in silence, broken only by Dave's laboured breathing. Bradley felt like Luke Skywalker confronting Jabba the Hutt.

"You wanted me?" Bradley prompted, resisting the urge to deliver Luke's line. If Dave caught the reference it would be all the worse for him, and if he didn't it would just confuse him.

Still not looking him in the eye, Dave slowly opened up a drawer on his desk, and pulled out a cigar. After running it under his hairy nostrils as he inhaled deeply, he leaned back and pushed a button, turning off the smoke alarm.

"Yes," he said at length. "Have a seat." His blood-shot eyes finally locked with Bradley's. They were the eyes of a reptile. A stony, stupid and yet ruthless cunning lurked there, that constantly asked: 'can I eat it, or will it eat me?'

Dave clutched the cigar impotently between his teeth as they stared at each other uneasily. Instead of speaking, he crossed his feet on the desk, which was bare except for an ashtray and a thick glass with a tell-tale pale amber puddle inside–the remnants of Glenlivet on the rocks, left out too long.

This was meant to demonstrate his superiority in this environment; however, Bradley was too busy thinking about alcohol. Bradley was a fan of single malt himself. It was liquor well suited to back-room meetings.

It wasn't right for this meeting, however. Scotch was a drink to be shared between co-conspirators. The plot he was about to unleash called for a couple shots of tequila, which was generally a far less Machiavellian liquor. He doubted Dave would catch his sinister intentions if he asked for Cabo Wabo, a brand owned by a rock star, which seemed fitting, overall. But, no. This plane would have to be landed sober.

"You are an idiot," Dave said, breaking a measured silence. "Sometimes I really wish we didn't hire any of your kind here, but it seems that if we want an IT department, there isn't any choice. Otherwise, you'd probably be homeless, handing out socialist pamphlets on street corners. But I am a nice guy. You know that right, Bradley? So let's talk a little bit about business, shall we?" He lit the cigar. Each breath sounded like a death rattle.

Bradley pulled a chair up to the desk and gingerly put his laptop down on the floor. "Sure, let's." He could smell scotch on Dave's breath from ten feet away. It cut right through the pungent smoke. I warn you not to underestimate my powers, Bradley thought to himself.

"What is this nonsense, with you busting in on a boardroom about unholy vengeance? You are in the presence of a God, son. If you are going to continue working for this company, you need to realize that your first concern must be growth. Growth must be your God. He is a hungry God, Bradley. A hungry, vengeful God." An edge of genuine fear made his voice tremble.

Bradley froze. This was unlike Dave. Corporate brochures, countless awkward and tedious meetings, sure. Maybe Dave was trying to bring him in on the 'inside'.

"It watches your every move. Do you follow me? I want you to go to sleep at night thinking... how can I keep it fed tomorrow? If you don't feed it, it will eat you. You are a cell in the body. You are little... tiny... you are tiny Bradley, do you understand that? *Tiny*." Dave was chewing on the end of his cigar as he spoke. A brown froth lined his mouth.

Bradley rummaged around in the paper bag he brought in with him, nodding absently. "Yes sir."

"Your bleeding hearts are small. You gotta have passion. Real strength, to kill millions. If one person out of a thousand dies as a result of our medication, there's an outrage," Dave growled. "They don't understand true power."

Bradley nodded, giving an almost mischievous smile. If Dave had been paying more attention, that smile might have made him wonder. He might have wondered why Bradley was opening packet after packet of ketchup, without anything to put it on.

But Dave wasn't wondering much of anything at all. He was so hammered his face was numb. He continued, "When I was your age, kids were crying up a storm about a couple of slants getting blasted in Mai Lai. Fuck them, we were trying to crush Communism. We had to get out of the jungle but we won the war, goddammit. And one day, he—" Dave dropped his drink. "Bradley! What in the hell do you think you are doing?"

While Dave was speaking, Bradley had dropped his pants, and proceeded to squirt ketchup over his genitals, all the while nodding his head agreeably, conversationally.

Bradley and Dave regarded each other awkwardly over the slop-slop-slop sound of his hands doing their work below. The cigar fell from Dave's flaccid lips, making a wet splat as it landed on the desk and stuck there, hissing amidst a cloud of ash and smoke.

But there was no other reaction. Dave was apparently far more insane than Bradley had assumed. There was no brain to shatter. Dave was a simulacra, a shell of a man who existed merely to serve his God, the Leviathan—tyrant of the virtual beyond. Lord of Europharm AG, and all Corporate Egregores.

Bradley kept a wide smile as he proceeded to masturbate, ketchup splattering all over the expensive rug. The smile grew, but this was getting awkward. Dave wasn't moving, only staring with an increasing look of curiosity on his face.

What was supposed to happen next? In hindsight, maybe calling it a 'plan' was getting ahead of himself.

Nothing to do at this point but run.

Finally, Dave reached for the phone to call security, but Bradley was already gone.

As he flew down the steps, an uncomfortable slimy feeling between his legs, Bradley realized he had been planning this for months, maybe even years. Not the ketchup stunt, that was just a sudden flash of genius.

There was something very, very wrong with this world. The question was, what was it and what could he do about it? It had been bouncing around in his head all this time, it had even been the subject of his dreams —when three-foot-tall naked green women didn't occupy him. Dave's drunken rambling about cells in bodies had given him an idea... a terribly wicked idea. Simple and profound. Leviathan was a weakling compared to the Gods he could help invent. His feet pounded on the stairs as his thoughts spun.

Cancer starts with just a couple of cells, after all. It is the revolt of the few against the many, when the many are fat and insane. Cells, agents of the invisible hand. The beehive buzzing of the brain.

Maybe the analogy didn't hold, exactly. He had more pressing things to worry about, anyhow—like evading the guards.

—

The autumn months of 2007 moved towards winter. Clumps of auburn leaves were replaced by an unsightly gray sludge. The bustle on Park slope was a perpetual blur, viewed through the window of Bradley's makeshift office in the front room of his apartment.

Not that he looked out on the outside world much – his primary contact with the outside was through Xi Ping Bo, who brought his orders from the corner Chinese store regularly, by bicycle. There were other options in the area, but Xi Ping was his favorite. Maybe he just found his name amusing.

Bradley had been gaming corporations since middle school. Hacking, playing the market, but he never knew why before. Yet again, he'd banked against Europharm, fucked them over all across the news, outed them to the government anonymously, and raked in some back end off his investment in their competitors. He lived in a modest apartment and endured the commute, and kept saving. This was no different than before, except now he had The Plan.

Subversion had been his modus operandi. A means unto itself. Not anymore. He would use the money and techniques learned through that interaction to fund social viruses, which would spell the end. For the Pharmaceutical industry. For all industries founded on imperial ownership notes.

Crushing major corporations and causing civil upheaval took planning and skill. This was why he needed to recruit the help of some of the most brilliant and eccentric minds in computer programming, economics, media, and social engineering. Ontological terrorism on this scale was a long con. He had to settle in.

In the end, no one would know where it originated. When that time came, he would be long gone. He would be in Thailand, or Switzerland. The image of that flaccid cigar falling from Dave's slug-like lips would taint his nightmares until his dying day. He didn't want to be Dave 2.0 in twenty years. That image was reason enough to drag the Western World to its knees. Blue screen of death. Hit Ctr-Alt-Delete. Pray for the best.

Over the course of months, he dabbled with countless approaches. With the nest egg he'd saved, he had time to research. He had time to skulk, plot, and eat copious amounts of greasy Chinese food. Pages of notes collected first in vast piles of napkins, wrinkled and stained with coffee rings. A couple of napkin ideas graduated to a notepad.

Many of these notes later got the red pen, writ large: 'not feasible', 'unnecessary', 'stop eating Lo Mein after midnight', 'magnificent tits!', and so on. He gathered information on the groups and individuals he would need to contact, he charted out all their first, second, and third tier contacts, and determined at what point their cell would need to be activated. He barely slept, no one saw him, and the few friends he used to have were long since convinced he had gone entirely insane.

When he was done researching, he started making phone calls.

—

First on his list was the Colonel. His guess was that his moniker originated with Colonel Kurtz, from Apocalypse Now, Coppola's modern adaptation of Heart of Darkness. Kurtz had gone beyond the realm of the Military's command, had gone beyond the realm of sanity, and found a strangely pragmatic reality out there, in the tangled roots of the mango trees. Of course, this Colonel looked more like Klink, from the Sixties television show Hogan's Heroes, if he was fronting an Industrial band in the Nineties.

Last he heard, the Colonel was making a killing on some web start-ups, and blew that killing quite literally in white-hot blasts through the septum. He did it alone, he did it at the great parties he threw at his pad, and he did it while he worked. Chances are, soon he'd do it subconsciously, while he slept. Bradley could imagine his hand slinking around the top of his bedside table like a tarantula, quivering atop the glass when it sensed its prey was near.

He made a quick call to soften the Colonel up. The real conversation would happen in person, over a line or two. Bradley honestly wasn't fond of the stuff but he'd make an exception to close a sale. Or in this case, investment. When the Colonel answered, Bradley heard hysterical giggling in the background, loud enough to overpower crashing electronic drum machines and distorted vocals.

"Speak," the Colonel said. He obviously knew who was calling from his caller I.D. Two years, and that was all he had to say. Typical.

"Colonel, it's Bradley—" he started automatically.

"I can read. OK, go to town girls. Now. Like a vacuum cleaner... Though you might want to have your number protected. I could find out where you live...," he hissed.

"You've known where I lived for years. Anyway, I have a business proposal for you. It's not just money... it's... something bigger than that. Do you remember that ongoing conversation we had back in school with Professor De Leon... about the nature of reality? About shifting the geography? Well I have something which could be bigger." Bradley spoke rapidly and loudly, hoping he was being heard over the music.

The Colonel hummed to himself when Bradley finished speaking, and then replied with what sounded like bemusement, "Great, I was wondering how long it would take you. Making these porno videos is totally sucking out my soul."

"Porno videos?" Well that explained the background noise.

"Yeah," he said, "I'm making one right now. Thank God for DV cams, and coke whores. Girls these days, they'll do anything for a gram. It's sad. Isn't it, honey? Anyway, it passes the time, but I'd rather do something more subversive."

He hadn't said otherwise, but Bradley knew he wasn't actually participating in the films, either. The Colonel was rather particular about making flesh on flesh contact with anyone, even in passing. Most of the time he wore tight leather gloves, layer upon layer of clothes. It was such a straightforward mechanism that psychoanalysis seemed unnecessary.

He was still talking like a jackhammer, probably swimming in a deep, invigoratingly cool pool of dopamine. "So you're at it again huh? Let me guess, the entire business world is like... different organs in the same organism. Like, oh my god!" Hearing the Colonel try to talk like a Valley Girl turned Hippie was almost more than Bradley could bear. "And you want to become an organ and then, like, pull the plug. Or fill the body with confetti or something. I'd rather an army of monkeys, or a pet elephant. Or an M-1 tank. But your plan sounds grand, too. *Jesus, finesse, c'mon...* Though I have to tell you I don't think humans are fit to govern themselves. How about tomorrow night, your place? *Me love you long time. Spit or swallow girls, make up your mind.* Oh, wait. Tell me why I give a fuck, again?"

Bradley cracked open a book on his desk. Bibliomancy. He opened to a random page. "One must be free to learn how to make use of one's powers freely and usefully. The first attempts will surely be brutal and will lead to a state of affairs more painful and dangerous than the former condition under the dominance but also the protection of an external authority. However, one can achieve reason only through one's own experiences, and one must be free to be able to undertake the-"

The Colonel spluttered, shooting spit as he cut Bradley off.

"-Hey! Please for the love of everything holy, tell me you aren't reading Emmanuel Fucking Kant to me right now."

Now he was the one being cut off, by a baritone voice in the background bellowing "oh God, oh God, OH GOD!"

The Colonel relaxed. "Eh. Money shot. You harpooned your whale, Ishmael. Now get off my ass. I owe these DNA coated foundlings a line of shitty mob coke."

—

As he continued making phone calls and everything fell into place, he started to feel the dominoes had been set for years... maybe even decades.

In the end, it didn't matter. Was God's hand moving him, or was he a part of God's hand?

XV. Rushmore

2012

As for sculptured mountains—Civilization, even its fine arts, is, most of it, quantity-produced stuff: education, law, government, wealth—each is enduring only as the day. Too little of it lasts into tomorrow and tomorrow is strangely the enemy of today, as today has already begun to forget buried yesterday.

Each succeeding civilization forgets its predecessor, and out of its body builds its homes, its temples. Civilizations are ghouls. Egypt was pulled apart by its successor; Greece was divided among the Romans; Rome was pulled to pieces by bigotry and bitterness much of which was engendered by its own empire building.

—Gutzon Borglum

Dennis walked down a dusty highway. Thunder rumbled in the distance.

"Fuck," he said, to no one. His head, wrapped in an American-flag bandanna, hung a little lower. He was just a kid alone on the road, like so many at the time. America the Once-beautiful, like a prizefighter long past his prime, trying to squeeze into those old shorts. Or... hell, something like that.

The skies opened up, and those thoughts fizzled. Soon, he was trudging through quickly forming puddles. Spitting out a mouthful of rainwater, he stopped and looked down at himself. His shoulders drooped.

Streams were already forming in the gullies along the side of the highway. At that pace, it would be a flood in no time. The weather kept getting more freakish, he thought. "Fuck. Fuck. Fuck."

Headlights pierced the murkiness ahead. He didn't notice at first, but when he did, he stopped and began waving his arms.

A luxury sedan pulled over. The driver, a kid with black-dyed hair and pathetic facial hair, looked at him through his Matrix sunglasses. A red head leered at him from the back seat, and an emaciated ice princess rode shotgun. He doubted she was capable of facial expression, aside from a perpetual look of surprise painted about two inches above where her eyebrows should have been.

"Where are you going?" the boy asked.

"Rapid city, South Dakota," Dennis said.

"That's... really far to walk."

"Yeah. Can you give me a ride?"

"Only if you can handle riding with us."

Dennis frowned. "Your name is Morpheus, isn't it?"

"No, it isn't." Morpheus said, blankly. He lowered his sunglasses and tried to give a piercing stare. "We operate on a different level."

"Okay. It's cold, it's wet, and it's possible my fiancée ran off with a friend of mine. So..."

"Get in."

"Thanks." The girl in the back moved over, and he hopped in.

Morpheus cranked up the music. It was surprisingly good, Dennis thought, like a harder-edged alternative-universe version of Seventies prog, mixed with dubstep and psytrance. Just when he was starting to get into it, the ice princess rolled her eyes and turned it down.

"Turn it back up!" Morpheus whined.

"Do you want me to keep blowing you, or not? Listening the whole way will totally ruin the show for me. I want it to be fresh."

He sighed, but let it be.

"Asshole," she muttered under her breath, and then turned around. "What's your name?"

"Dennis. Where are you headed?"

There was a muffled, banging sound from behind them, but no one seemed to react.

"To see the best band ever," Morpheus said.

The redhead smiled. She gave an awkward laugh and tried to move closer. Dennis, not so subtly, leaned in the other direction. He marvelled at how much she looked like a pug.

Then there was that banging again.

"I think something is wrong with your car," he said.

"Oh no," the ice princess said. "That's the guy who owns this thing. Total suit."

"Man! You should have seen him!" Morpheus said.

"Terrific," Dennis said, wishing he was dead.

—

Dennis' head knocked from side to side as they continued down smaller side-roads. They stopped suddenly. He had been drooling on himself, he realized.

"We're here," the redhead said. She was lying on his lap, but thankfully bounced out the door before he had to dislodge her himself.

He rubbed his eyes. "Here?"

"You'll thank us later."

"Uh-huh."

—

Morpheus tapped the key chain, and the trunk swung open. A man in his mid-fifties struggled against the cocoon of duct tape wrapped around his body. His eyes bulged from screaming into a gag for hours.

"What do we do with him?" Morpheus asked.

"Let him go," Dennis and the redhead said at the same time. This led to a really awkward moment where she stared at him adoringly with piss colored eyes. Dennis was finding it hard to see how any of this was better than dying in a flood, hours before.

"Kill him," the ice princess said, derailing his thoughts.

"*Kill* him?" Dennis looked around. "The fuck are we? The fuck is wrong with you people!"

Morpheus tossed the keys into the trunk and slammed it shut. "There. He won't be able to get out, now."

They stared in bewilderment at the trunk and then him in turn.

"Typical," the ice princess said. She smacked him on the head, hard.

"I guess we're all walking," Dennis said.

"Huh?" Morpheus asked.

She sighed. "You locked the fucking keys in the truck. How do you plan to drive away?"

It finally dawned on him. "Ooooh, right. Sorry. Well, we're here anyway."

They started down a path.

"You stole a car to take me on a date. Why? Because you don't fucking have one. Who does that?" the ice princess asked.

"Pretty cool, right?" Morpheus said, grinning.

"It shouldn't be far," the redhead said, looking off to the misty hills.

—

They made their way through rocky terrain, spotted with pine trees. Dennis saw a shadow moving off to one side. "What is that?"

Morpheus squinted. "Oh, probably another fan."

"Fan?"

"Yeah. Don't worry about it."

"Alright," Daniel said, still worrying about it.

More shadows in the near-darkness. Then he saw what looked like Christmas lights. As he got closer, he saw that they were in fact Christmas lights, wrapped around the bulging form of an old man dressed in a sheet. It was stained and painted with an incomprehensible script.

"Hello fellow travelers," the man said as they approached. He had a staff, which was clearly a broomstick with a pine cone glued to the top, and a bushy white beard.

Dennis walked right past him, careful to avoid eye contact. A former East Coast city dweller, he knew the power of avoidance. Once you locked eyes with a crazy, you were in their world. The man ranted to another group as he fell out of earshot about "Draco dragons" abducting teenagers to steer his "white-powder time chair," and something about reptiles eating human pineal glands.

As they continued, he saw a series of glowing orbs leading a path through the pine forest. First, clusters of people here and there, then a torrent of them, like Atlantic salmon coming home to spawn. This mass of bodies converged at the lights, and following them further in.

"They're like will-o'-the-wisps," the redhead said. "Guiding us to Babylon."

The forest thinned, and Dennis saw the stolid faces of the presidents, lit artificially from beneath. But that is where familiarity stopped. It was as if Burning Man had formed an independent, nomad nation and decided to take over Mount Rushmore.

—

Eighty yards above the mob, Trevino waited with a spider's stillness.

"Target acquired," a mercenary beside him said. He was looking through the scope of his AR-50 sniper rifle.

"Not until my order," Trevino said. His voice carried via his headset to men positioned all around the perimeter. Babylon's security apparatus boiled off doubt that the crew he faced here was a dangerous one. Either Babylon hired a crazy man for too much money, or these little psychos were getting organized. The suits were onto something, and they couldn't tell him what.

He had spent too many nights on too many rented beds, splicing and peeling back the memories of their meeting. Those three were inarguably criminal, fine. A case could be made that he faced a fledgling, domestic terror cell. But sending him out with a gun and an order to assassinate three American civilians never sat right. And then he saw just how many others there were. Could they really cut off the head and think it'd all just go away? For months, he struggled with that one. But it's like arm wrestling yourself. Either way, you lose.

"Let me reiterate that if you screw this up, hundreds of unarmed American civilians could die. This has to be surgical," Trevino said.

He caught himself grinding his teeth. The mob's formless susurrus gained rhythm, becoming a chant of 'Bab-a-lon, Bab-a-lon', moments before his targets came into view. Three girls came first, sweeping the area with their eyes before taking positions around their makeshift stage. Another followed quickly with a handful of others. They seemed to be their superiors, gauging by body language. They were also mostly naked, but well armed.

Loki strode into view, a blur of activity, cigarette clutched between his teeth. He was waving his hands, directing the girls. Next the band appeared. First came Cody, wearing a bemused, 'aw, shucks' smile and a wide-brimmed hat. Dionysus and Jesus followed, chatting amiably and reeking of nervous energy. For a moment, they lingered in loose formation with their security, a pair of triangles near the base of the makeshift stage and control area: two watchers and their superiors standing hard and calm, the three musicians fizzing and bouncing in place.

—

"Dancers are in position," one of the girls said over the com.

"Security perimeter set," another replied. "Can we get this party started?"

Loki cocked his head to the side, crunching out his cigarette quickly under his boot. He spoke into his headset. "Widen the perimeter; something's not right."

—

"I've got the shot, sir."

"No, I said hold," Trevino said.

Loki was walking behind the Behemoth. In seconds, he would be out of view.

"I'm taking it."

"No!"

Dennis walked in front of the line of fire at the exact moment Loki passed from view. If his fiancée had decided to dump him another day, he might have been at home watching TV. Instead, he was at an outlaw at Mount Rushmore. This moment, this spot, in the sights of a rifle held by a man who really liked shooting people. The Universe was playing one of her many cruel practical jokes.

Bam! His chest exploded, organs and limbs tossed into the air like confetti. The force of it ripped the leg off the red head standing behind him.

"Jesus. Fuck. Go, go, go! Take them!" Trevino yelled.

—

A semi-circle of mercs in body armor emerged from the pines, their weapons drawn. They proceeded directly towards the band, which had already disappeared from the stage.

"Civilians, stay where you are," one of them said over a megaphone.

Some froze. Some tore off into the woods. But others, seemingly oblivious to common sense, charged instead. They screamed, cursed, and hurled what they could get their hands on.

The deafening sound of the mercs return fire seemed to echo in Trevino's eardrums as he watched, and long after.

A half-dozen of the rioting audience bore down on a merc. His rifle discharged uselessly into the air as they tore at him with broken bottles, fists, and teeth, before concentrated gunfire chewed them to pieces.

Audience members entered the fray with handguns they had stowed in their bunks. Morpheus jumped from behind a rock, firing off a single shot with a pistol before his face exploded in a whiff of bone and vapor.

A second shot cracked from beside Trevino, ripping a chunk into the side of the Behemoth, but missing the engine block.

The sniper beside Trevino let out a groan, and seemed to flail in the dark before slumping forward.

He continued to twitch spasmodically as Trevino crawled away.

—

Dionysus, Jesus, Cody and Ariadne fell back to the Behemoth as planned. They held position, gaping, surrounded by a skirmish line of their security detail. Their faces were studies of contained fury.

Loki and Artemis could be heard screaming orders. Several mercs dropped in their tracks as they advanced, bolts sticking out of their necks.

As though from the ground, Artemis emerged from a shadow, blade drawn. She slid it under a mercs jaw, and then dropped and rolled out of sight.

Smoke grenades began to sail over the heads of the rioters and into the remaining skirmish line of mercs. They were quickly blinded, and the rioters surged forward. Loki snapped a 'thumbs up' at the girls who'd just tossed the grenades.

He dropped one last grenade, almost at his feet, and was immediately obscured by brightly colored smoke. Near the edge, security formed a loose screen, picking off mercs with their crossbows before the smoke rolled over them as well.

The following moments were a nightmare of flailing limbs, muzzle flashes, and dying teenagers.

Loki popped up again, putting two in the chest of a nearby merc. Suddenly, every inch of Loki's body felt icy cold. It wasn't fear, just a thought – the man twitching at his feet had probably suffered through twelve years of tedious public schooling, the ins and outs of life on the street after a war, possibly a loveless marriage, a host of unrealized hopes and dreams, just so he could bleed out in a field full of plastic cups and dead kids.

He shook his head. Two seconds wasted navel-gazing in the middle of a firefight. He needed to stop spending so much time with Dionysus.

Loki and Artemis regrouped behind the stage with the remaining security. They nodded in unison. Time to go.

They trotted alongside the already moving vehicle and jumped aboard. Small arms fire dinged the armor as they sped off.

—

Dionysus switched places with Loki once they'd cleared the immediate area.

"We're all here... no, wait. Where's Lilith?" Dionysus looked around frantically, re-counting the people in the vehicle.

"I don't know. Right now I'm trying to save our asses," Loki said.

"We need to go back," Dionysus said. He watched the chaos of flashing lights and scrambling bodies vanish into placid twilight.

"No way. Can't save anybody if we're all dead. Got lucky. Would've owned us otherwise. That was a hired assault force."

"Hired?" Dionysus asked.

Loki grunted. "Everything's getting privatized these days. Y'know—"

"—Dionysus?" Ariadne asked, weakly.

Dionysus looked down. She was lying on her side, blood was pooling all over the floor around her.

He pushed down on the wound, but more blood gushed over his hand. "Oh, fuck. Artemis! Cody? Jesus?"

Jesus and Cody flattened themselves against the wall as Artemis tore past and attempted to bind a wound in Ariadne's upper arm with a T-shirt. She was in shock, barely conscious.

"Gonna be fine. Gonna be fine. I've got you. You're gonna be..." Dionysus looked at Artemis. "How is she?"

"Shut up." She continued working.

"Talk to me," Loki said.

"They shot her," Artemis said over the growl of the engine. "Went right through her arm. Looked clean but then it spurted."

"Deep brachial?" Loki asked.

"No. Pinch the axillary. She's going."

"Dionysus..." Ariadne said.

"You'll be fine. You've just lost a lot of blood." He looked with concern at Artemis. She shook her head.

"Listen," Ariadne said to him. Her voice was barely a whisper. "Time is the dream. I'll see you—" Her eyes rolled back. She was breathing, but barely.

—

Dionysus was covered in blood and she was gone.

Silence fell on the vehicle as it sped off into the night. He looked down at the body. Suddenly a thing, a rigid object. Soon it would leak fluids, putrefy. Turn to mineral. Seep into the water and rejoin the ocean.

Their first real conversation returned to him, as if he was meeting her all over again. He had promised to tell her the story of his 'imaginary friend', of his name. There were so many things he'd wanted to tell her. The opportunity never presented itself.

Now the door was shut, and he was in the same loneliness he had once known. But this was even worse. It's different, what you've lost and what you've never known.

He sighed, closed her sightless eyes. Then he rested a hand on her forehead, stroking her hair as he always did when they were talking in the twilight hours before sleep. And he told her the story of his childhood.

—

"She's really real, Mommy," I'd said. Three times, I thought, was the magic number. Tell anyone, even an adult, something was true three times, and they had to believe it. Not so with my Mother. She stared at me sternly from behind the slit of light cast through the door.

"Mommies have to sleep. I don't care what your imaginary friend says. No more going outside at night. No more. Just please! You're scaring us, okay? Or we are going to have to take you to some kind of specialist?"

That year was probably the most Mother ever loved me. Father left and there was something left unspoken that said I was a part of it. Father had given birth to a freak, and Mother was saddled with it. That concern became impatient concern and eventually something resigned and cruel, but that's jumping to what I know now.

Back then, well, I didn't really know what any of that meant, but the way she said specialist made me think of ET. I imagined I'd be hooked up to all kinds of machines, and the Doctors would realize, to their amazement, that I wasn't even a human at all. With flat expressions painted atop their deep existential terror, they would tell my parents, "I don't know what that is, but it isn't one of us."

That would explain a lot. I was frankly pretty excited about the possibility; I would have so many friends just like me! And I was a little disappointed whenever a test came back that said that I was a human like everyone else. Blood type AB, so I was rare, but only as an inconvenience if

I needed a transfusion. IQ of 156, super smart, which to kids my age also meant 'FREAK, TOTAL FREAK'. But more importantly, I was trying to tell my mother that my friend was real. She ate blood and lived behind our apartment in the forest. She whispered secrets in my ear while the humans slept.

It might seem that I'm giving a lot of credence to the imaginings of a child. But I had never thought like a child. I didn't really think like an adult either. I remember wondering, even back then... well, what am I?

Descriptions fail us. What's it matter whether I was born into a male or female vessel? These are all quirks, little fragments cast to the current, making a momentary configuration and then taken by the chaos of that ocean. There was nothing structured or organized, no pattern I could curl myself into and call Me. Something lurked underneath it all, like a seed waiting a time to make its treacherous journey upward. The name my mother gave me felt fake, pasted atop my real name.

And as a presence in my life, my false mother was a just shadow on the wall, first glimpsed through dangling stars, suspended from the ceiling by strings, and then, still a figure in the background, like the furniture in the apartment. No siblings save the wide night sky.

The first realization I had as a child, the first I could really hold onto, was that I was alone. So I held to the idea. I was a star child, a wanderer from the moon.

That is, until I found my imaginary friend. My view of my place in the Universe changed when I met her, though it took time to really show just what a profound change her presence, however distant at first, had on my life.

Not that orienting myself in relation to Her made life easy. Nothing quite made sense; none of my parts fit quite the way they were supposed to. It was a shock at first to realize that I was not just male-bodied, but also human-bodied. I had five fingers and toes like everyone else, but something had mutated in my soul. This year I was introduced to Nietzsche— Zarathustra was a fitting, if somewhat odd birthday gift from my present therapist, certainly the most tolerable of the bunch—and I found that he had a word for this, a whole slew of them in fact.

"What is great in man is that he is a bridge and not a goal."

A bridge to what? I wondered about the first fish which had learned to walk, like Tiktaalik, neither quite a master of the water or the air, but a struggling thing trapped between two worlds before it could leap, before it could run and fly. Such a sorry little thing, flapping, gasping, and lost in primordial muck. I wondered if I was that kind of mutant. Sharing thoughts like that really caught the attention of the team of psychologists that my mother, a psychiatrist herself, spent a quarter of her income on.

My mother reminded me of this fact constantly of course. She had to tip the waitress fifteen percent and not twenty percent, because of how much she was spending on figuring out what was wrong with me. Like a silent kick under the table with steel-tipped boots: YOU ARE KILLING ME SLOWLY.

I was limping and half-broken, I knew my mother was right in a sense, but not for the right reasons, and the psychiatrists and therapists alike were running in the wrong direction as well. They wanted to make me more like Homo Sapiens, but what I needed was a guide to run hard and fast in the other direction.

My imaginary friend was my only proof I wasn't entirely alone down here. My hunch was that She was such a being.

I was being watched, though it seemed there were places She preferred and places that She would not go near. I felt She followed me into dreams as well, perhaps there most of all. I slept with Her nightly. Alone in the shower crying so hard you feel that the water will take you away, that you will turn entirely into tears and mucus and flow through the drain, and yet somehow She could find me even there. But never in a shopping mall, and She really didn't much like cars.

She wasn't human Herself, so She didn't know how to care about me the way a human mother might, but as time passed, I could sense that She did feel the need to protect me. Maybe She loved me? If so, if She did even a little, I think She must have loved me more than my own mother did.

This is where a therapist's eyes perk up. A distant Mother, you say? A projection of the Mother archetype, you say? I see where you're going with this. I'll play along. And it's not as if I'd seen Her yet, I mean, physically seen Her.

The first time, I must have dreamt it. I think? She had perfectly white skin and blue hair, and when She opened Her mouth an albino snake slithered out, coiling around Her until it plunged again into Her cunt; everything white, all hairless, except her eyes, ringed with thick blue lashes, eyes like sapphires, blue hair. She squirmed and moaned. I couldn't tell at first if the endless coiling of serpent was tearing her apart, but it became clear it wasn't pain.

She was an apple in a garden of throbbing flowers, so heavy with pollen, begging for the bee, and the buzzing bees carrying it flower to flower. Parthenogenetic.

To go further, we actually have to go backward. This is something psychoanalysts learn quickly. You see, my insistence on my imaginary friend began a history. Whether she was imaginary or not at first, this imagination changed the entire trajectory of my life.

Age nine. My therapist, the first, was dimwitted. I told him so. His analysis of my first dream was pathetically Freudian, and in a way that Freud himself would've been embarrassed by.

But I remember being able to peer across the table and make out his notes, which made him a bad poker player as well as a bad psychoanalyst.

He thought I had a sexual fetish, developing around my mother, which I was projecting onto the safe image of this 'imaginary friend'! Blah, blah. Next!

Age ten, psychiatry. A man, half-dead, as if his soul had cataracts. Ritalin and liquid Prozac smudged the year like pastels on fine-toothed paper. One thing was clear. Once those meds took effect, my friend left me. I didn't feel Her on the crisp autumn breeze. I knew that my heart beat alone when I ran through the forest. Either She was a figment of my imagination, or the drugs blocked Her out somehow.

With Her absent, the other kids suddenly seemed to notice me. It was as if She conveyed an aura of protection, even that She had cloaked me from their attention. For years, I went along undisturbed, unnoticed.

Suddenly, everywhere I went all the children saw me and, while the girls seemed merely perplexed and intrigued; the boys, almost to a one, were overtaken by an incoherent and singular hatred for everything about me. My shoes, my hair, the way I breathed, anything could, at any moment be singled out as the reason that I should be beaten unconscious with a stick.

It was like there was a spotlight on me everywhere I went. Eggs cracked in my hair. Face bashed bloody against bathroom porcelain. Broken glass shoved places glass shouldn't go. It all blurred together, and after a while, I stopped even trying to fight back. They'd punch me, or push me, and I'd just fall and lie there, while they kicked me, until one would stop, because I wasn't even showing emotion. And then the others would stop, and look down at me, panting, no longer feeling the rush of power, and they would run off to play football or baseball, or whatever it is that normal kids did. I'd shake it off, inspect the bruises, brush off my books, and get back to reading.

Age twelve, I got very sick. It was like Her absence created a void, and something had to rush in to fill it. A psychiatrist and two therapists, none of them saw what was coming next. One day, I finally lost control. Teeth shattered under hate-wielded rock. Blood, nerve, saliva, his eyes rolled back. And I grinned wildly. Fucker thought he could take the small quiet one like everyone else had. "Think again," I said aloud. I licked the stone clean of his blood and tossed it to the ground.

One blow. I had accepted torment and torture for years, but all it took to end it was one blow.

He was still breathing. I knew how easy it would be to step on his throat and end his life forever. I'd always stopped because something inside me knew how easy it would be to kill them if I fought back at all. And then, what, prison?

There would be no more parent-teacher conferences or hand-wringing counselors. They don't deter bullies, just embolden them in private. Humans are monkeys who still respect the club most of all.

I leaned down to him, eye-to-eye, and I said very calmly, "Tell your friends that if any of you touch me again, I will tear the life out of you. I will make Christmas wreaths out of your intestines while you are still alive to watch me string lights around them. Do you understand?" It was the voice of someone else speaking through me.

He gurgled and cried. I slapped him. "Do you understand?"

"Yes."

I sighed and thought about when he had thrown rocks at my head. When he'd smeared eggs in my hair. When he'd broken a soda bottle and tried to shove it into my ass. But I wanted to meet Her, finally, and I don't think she took trips to juvie.

And that was the end of my stint with the meds, and with public schooling.

They wanted me on stronger meds but I tossed them all. And I waited. And waited. Almost four years to the day. By then I was in a special school, a school for smart but troubled children (now my Mother only tipped ten percent, and she would actually apologize to the waitress on my account), but I would otherwise be in high school by now. Music became my world and I almost forgot. But we can't hide from ourselves, and I felt that She was in my blood.

The leaves were blowing against my window, scratching like thousands of little rat paws. I felt what could only be described as a presence. Not a ghost or anything, but the hair on my arms did stand up.

At first, I saw only my own reflection, lit by the candles I had set on my art table.

The reflection obscured anything beyond. My face was at that awkward point between childhood and adolescence, when you can't tell if the baby fat will grow and fester a colony of pus-filled pimples across the territories of your puffy cheeks, or if they will vanish, leaving a more handsome outline.

Then I saw through myself, and there she was. Just for a minute. just long enough to know that this was no trick.

She was there, and I was, by the rules established by the DSM and all the companies like Europharm AG, insane. Quite perfectly insane. I knew what looked back was not human. Pale, almost translucent as ice, eyes with teeth, the mouth I had dreamed about. Hair blue as the liminal sky. But surely, I had invented Her.

If She was something you could touch, that would change everything. I'd felt Her before I'd dreamed Her, dreamed Her before I smelled Her on the wind, following Her scent to a perfect pine circle in the woods. Still no sight of Her, just an affirmation felt in the wild places, the few not claimed by industry, covered over by asphalt, coated in poisons. Over and over, a hope to meet Her eye to eye.

Her hand came to the windowpane and left no mark. She was naked, and speckled with blood. Then She was gone. But Her voice resounded in my head, "Dionysus," it said, "come home." That was the first I heard that name, but I immediately knew.

Only a slight glaze of breath on the window remained, breath that I just knew smelled like blood and tasted like milk and lavender.

For some reason at that moment, I picked up the copy of 'Zarathustra' by my bedside and read aloud, wherever my eyes fell, "...Whoever is the wisest among you is also a mere conflict and cross between plant and ghost. But do I bid you become ghosts or plants?"

I realized then that She was both of these things, a ghost though no longer a living human, a plant, tendrils, vines, and bees, and now that we were changing the Earth, She too was changing, feeding now more on blood than moonlight.

The candles had burned low, leaking a congealing mess of beeswax onto my drawing. I looked out the window. The breeze that hit my face was still mostly a mix of summer humidity and the smell of growing things, but there was the faintest hint of the autumn to come. In that hint I was finding Her. The smell.

Everything went blank as I crawled out of my window. What followed were a series of images, pieced together as if they had been a part of a dream, but I know that they happened. Or is it that all of our lives really are a dream, like that Taoist saying about Zhuangzi, and we just toss it off as cliché or silly?

Do you know that one? It goes like this. Once Zhuangzi dreamt he was a butterfly. He was a butterfly flitting and fluttering around, happy with himself and doing as he pleased. He didn't know he was Zhuangzi. Suddenly he woke up and there he was, solid and unmistakable: Zhuangzi. But he didn't know if he was Zhuangzi who had dreamt he was a butterfly, or a butterfly dreaming he was Zhuangzi. Between them, there must be some distinction! But what? That is why so many of us are quick to dismiss this story, because we are going about our butterfly business and nothing has startled us awake, at least not yet. But let me tell you, when something does, you just might find yourself thinking about this story.

After I had left the window, I followed the scent of autumn into the woods which surrounded the apartment complex. There was a wildlife sanctuary nearby, and so the cookie-cutter bloat of suburbia just seemed to disappear, once you were far enough in. Many times, I lost the scent, and found myself standing in the darkness, illuminated only by the moon, feeling very silly and a bit frightened and exposed.

It was night-time, and I was in my pajamas. I wasn't even wearing shoes, I'd slipped out after her so quickly. And even if there were no supernatural dangers out here, there were likely natural ones, like crack-heads or bears. But I didn't care, or at least I couldn't afford to. She was more important than anything, because She was the only thing in this world—of this world, and yet not of it—that I felt might be able to explain the mystery of my existence, of how I too was a part of this world, and yet not a part of it. How I had been born, as it were, out of place and time, into a society that I did not belong in, and yet called to some purpose that I still did not understand.

Eventually, the trail that I was following stopped, and I was forced to break off into the underbrush. Sharp vines lashed my feet. I could tell I was bleeding, and oddly that redoubled my certainty that She was out here with me. I could even hear Her breath on the wind—sniffing my blood, keeping at a distance, but so tempted by this morsel, which had wandered into Her garden.

I felt pretty silly doing it, but I had no choice. I stopped and spoke as loudly as I could. "Are you out there? I know you're out there."

The leaves rustled in the wind, and it sounded like laughter. I saw the faintest purple light up ahead, and followed it as it guided me around a bend in a hill, and down into a valley. This was a part of the forest that I had never discovered, despite years of wandering. It was as if the woods had parted, revealing a new path. And at the end of it, there was a perfect ring of pine trees.

They were like scraps of black cloth, tossed across a purple background. A hole in time and space. I could smell the strong pine scent, wafting up to me, and I knew, somehow, that this circle was sacred. There is nothing, absolutely nothing, sacred in the world that I had been raised in, and suddenly being shown a sacred place, I was filled with a kind of terror I can't describe, if you've never had such an experience. A bear, a crack head, these are known dangers. The sacred hints at some unnameable reality, hiding beyond bone and marrow.

I took several steps further until I was at the very edge of the pine circle. I knelt and smeared the blood from my cut feet and arms across the bark of the trees at that natural entrance. And there I sat, for at least an hour, listening to the wind, suddenly not so driven by expectancy.

I felt something gathering in the darkness, like a blanket of moths rising from their bed of pine needles. I finally found the nerve to stand, but I could not, I simply could not enter the circle of trees.

"I love you," I said aloud, and then I turned around and made my way back home.

At the end of it all I found myself in bed, covered in mud and pine, crawling with ants and ticks, sticky with sap. I hadn't found Her, but I had the weirdest feeling that She had been testing my resolve.

That night, like the night before, I drew a ring of candles and began drawing an image of Her.

That night, like before, the wind picked up and She teased me with scents and images just outside my reach.

There was a mirror on the opposite wall, and for a moment I saw her standing outside my window, watching me. Milky-white and naked, but where I had been vulnerable in pajamas, her nakedness was like a suit of armor.

When our eyes locked, She took off into the woods, silent as an owl.

Ripping open the window, I tore after Her, down the footpath, into the woods. My mother must have heard the commotion and called after me, but I didn't bother to respond.

"Stop!" I yelled, rounding another wind in the path of pine needles, before I tripped and rolled, banging against roots and rocks until I came to a stop in the pine circle. Our circle. I had crossed the threshold without realizing it in my haste, and lay there in the middle of the trees, looking up at the moon above. I heard the lightest padding of bare feet—I knew she was coming for me, but I didn't move or make any sign.

I knew She was dangerous, a creature built to hunt. But there was no turning back. It was this or going back to that apartment and living the lie. A name that was not my identity. A world that was not my world. I had to know.

I could tell that the hand which wrapped around my throat was strong enough to easily crush windpipe and spine. She could rip my head clean off my body and drink my spinal fluid. Our eyes met, and this time I couldn't think of what to say. Her face was mostly in shadow, but I knew exactly how it looked. I knew every pout, scream, or yawn which could possibly grace her features. She relaxed her grip, but only enough to allow me to speak.

The scent of night flowers filled my nose. She didn't blink, studied my every minute movement. "Are you my...?"

"Am I your what?" She asked, the first time I'd ever heard her voice, not just in my head but a real voice, vibrating in the air.

"Mother. Are you my real mother?"

She wrapped her legs around me. She was pale as moonlight, and about a hundred times stronger than me.

Our mouths locked and I was inside her—
After you're born, you'll have a lot of time alone.
Time to pick yourself apart and forget what you are.
Time to hunger and yearn, and lose yourself in your desire.
Life will be your exile, death your rebirth. A stranger, you must hide in plain sight. You can grit your teeth and pretend you're like those around you, keep silent to the lonely visions of your ancient curse, or preach it from the mountaintops.
Where will be a place for you? Only dreams, and nightmares especially. You can even pass as a human being. Just don't fool yourself. The more you become yourself, the less human you will be.

To the people of this world you're but an abstract drawing of their hopes and fears pasted to a Popsicle stick, a paper mask dragged around by a ragged grave-yard of hungry dreams. That's all the Fallen are to man. Never forget.

I am with you always. We will not meet again.

—

Dionysus was still stroking Ariadne's face, now grown cold. "I still remember the song the trees sang to me, calling me 'Dionysus'. I still remember when Nyssa gave herself to me, inviting me to join in that final embrace—hold tight and don't let go as we sink to the bottom of the world. Hold on. Hold on. We are almost there."

XVI. Dreaming Darkly

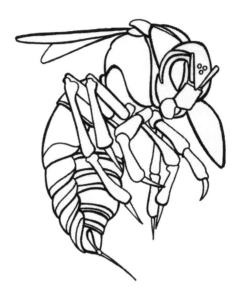

2012

We pretend to hold being true to one's self as a high virtue, but what does that mean? So many self-help gurus spout platitudes along these lines. "Listen to your heart," they say, and everything will fall into place. Their hand is outstretched for your donation or reverence.

Yet hearts don't speak, and nothing in this world moves because we listen to some inner voice. What do psychologists say about listening to voices?

My method with my students was to bring about a confrontation with the self. But what is that?
—**Gabriel De Leon**

Trevino stood in the field where the audience once stood. He was surrounded by bodies, many of them the age his children could have been.

It wasn't Mai Lai. Mai Lai happened to 'other people'. The Kent State massacre had a body count of four students. He looked at the empty, staring eyes of a dead girl. Maybe seventeen, all-American, except for the bullet holes, the face that looked like a jack-o-lantern carved by an eight-year old. She wasn't a terrorist; she was a kid out past curfew. And here was a field of them.

He lit a smoke and looked away. Someone was going to hang.

Lilith entered Trevino's field of view, surrounded by mercs, her hands cuffed together. She was a mess of ripped fishnet and blood, but seemed unharmed.

"Take her to interrogation," he said.

"Sounds fun," she said.

"It shouldn't."

She flashed a winsome smile before being carted away. He shook his head and looked up at the faces of presidents, long dead, dreaming darkly.

—

Trevino paced behind the one-way mirror, flicking a Zippo lighter back and forth in his hand. On the other side sat the most appealing creature he had ever set eyes on–forget that she stood for everything in the world that he loathed. She was still wearing the form-fitting leather outfit she wore on stage. Her hair cascaded around bare shoulders.

She was like a sphinx when they arrested and cuffed her. Her composure seemed scripted, but nevertheless, impenetrable. Trevino, a veteran of countless firefights, one official war and many unofficial ones, knew a fanatic when he saw one. They were the worst. Can't lean on them, not really. You can only play into the game and see where they want to lead.

"I'm sorry, but you can't smoke out here, Marshall," a merc said. Like all the rest he was two hundred fifty pounds of sweating dynamite, wrapped in kevlar. The suits had sent them when he requested forces, all with the same triangle logo. Were they J-SOC? Some private firm? Trevino knew better than to ask. They followed his orders, mostly. But only because the suits said so.

Trevino stopped pacing, and met the merc's gaze. "Does it look like I'm smoking to you?"

"No, I just..."

He flicked the lighter closed a final time. "It helps me think." He looked back at their prisoner. Lilith was casually inspecting her handcuffs.

He marched into the room.

"I am Deputy U.S. Marshall Trevino." He tapped out two cigarettes and pulled out a chair.

"The good cop routine, then?"

"Might be taking you to a firing squad, too. It's just common courtesy," Trevino said, looking back toward the mercs who were probably glaring through the video feed.

"Sure. I'll have one." She leaned forward and indicated for him to place the smoke in her mouth.

He lit both cigarettes.

"There's no 'routine'. We have you as an enemy combatant—a terrorist. So we can get to the thumbscrews later." He scrutinized her, and realized it was a lie. "They didn't take off the cuffs?"

"Nah," she said, "I prefer it this way."

She locked gazes with him. For a moment he could think of nothing but the image of her, still bound, on her hands and knees. Trevino blew out a cloud of smoke and finally sat.

"Let's get to it," he said.

"Let's. You can't control this," Lilith said, for some reason now inspecting her nails. "Too much momentum."

"I want to know plans, dates, and targets."

Lilith laughed. "Plans? Silly. You don't understand what's going on at all, do you?"

"Why don't you explain it to me?"

Lilith thought for a moment. "Alright. I saw this show on the Discovery Channel about ants. It was amazing, watching them move together. Attack together. Flee together. They would even drown themselves to let other ants traverse a stream. Now, sure, they have a queen, but she's just their bloated sugar momma. No one is giving orders."

"I don't understand wh—"

"I'm answering your question, Mr. Trevino."

"Agent Trevino."

"Okay, sure." She leaned back. "You'll make legends with your bullets, martyrs of a rebellion which didn't even exist until you started firing."

"We didn't create this thing," she continued when he just sat there. "This nation was ready to fall."

"Bullshit. Who funded you?"

"Please. Protesters will knock down your gates if you lock them away. If you make this happen, you'll find you're outnumbered. You'd have to kill us all."

"That might be the outcome, yes," Trevino said, grimly.

"I'm not talking about the band..."

Trevino didn't want to go where she was leading. "There's no way your idiot friends organized this. Last I dealt with them, they were a group of disorganized pranksters. Suddenly it's a fucking insurrection. Who's backing you?"

"Hey, could you move the ashtray over here? Thanks honey. No, you don't understand. You think individuals create history? Everything happens because of something else. It's only in hindsight that we call out a Hitler or an Einstein and say, 'There. That's where that started.'"

"You're saying—"

"How did it feel to kill all those kids?"

Trevino boiled for a moment. He stubbed out his cigarette and reflexively reached for another. "Get to your point, if you have one."

She savored the last drag of her smoke before putting it out. "I don't usually allow myself. Singer, you know. Although Bowie smoked, go figure. Okay. How's this for a point? I can give you more than information. I can give you the band. On a platter like roast pigs. Apples in their mouths. Actually, no. I'm picturing that, and it's just gross."

Trevino scowled, his face crinkling like worn leather. "You mean you intend to, what? Defect?"

"There's something sexy about double agents. Don't you think?"

"Why would you do that?" he asked, not taking the bait.

"You couldn't possibly understand. Let's just leave it at 'bitches be crazy'," she said, cocking an eyebrow.

Trevino sucked in another breath of burning tobacco and fiberglass and god knows what else. Sometimes, just for a second, he wondered if the entire world, everybody from the cardboard-box, ten-layers-of-clothes and reek-of-cheap-alcohol-and-rotten-meat 'go'way tryin' ta schleep' homeless to Mary-fucking-Teresa were toys in the attic. God existed, and he was at the tail end of a seven-billion-year PCP binge.

He shook away his thoughts. "Guess I'll have to. But if I find them with a goddamn army, we're going to take them."

—

As Lilith was escorted to a holding cell, Trevino flipped open his cell. His eyebrows knitted together as he stared at the number displayed on the screen. The door slammed, and he was left alone with his thoughts.

The pieces didn't fit.

Finally, he pressed the green button, and waited for the expected voice on the other end.

"Adam?"

"Sheila. Yeah, it's me. I just needed someone to talk to, who isn't directly connected to any of this. Someone with a clear head."

"You still on that assignment?"

"Yeah, that's what I want to talk to you about..."

"I'm really surprised you got a promotion out of what you did," she said. Her tone caught him off guard. "I'm sorry?"

"It just pissed me off a little. I thought I'd hone up to it right off the bat. Partners, our primary suspect vanishes into thin air when she's in the box with you. And now you're gunning to work federally. Whatever."

"You sounded pretty fucking... what's the word... conciliatory with those answering machine messages you left back when I—"

"—Just forget it, okay? I saw the reports. You caught one of them. Glad to hear it."

"Sheila, Listen. The mercenaries blew the op. This is getting really ugly. At this point, there's no option but to blast them off the face of the planet. I get that," Trevino said.

"What's this really about, Adam? You're not wondering if they're legit, are you?"

"I'm wondering if any of this is legit."

"Adam. Repeat after me: these are terrorists."

"That's not what I meant. It was rhetorical in the first place. I was trying to get to a point."

"Get there. I want lunch and I know you hate it when I chew on the phone."

Trevino reflected on what Lilith had said a moment earlier. "I'm going to have to call in the guard, or we need to outsource this to people who aren't... Look. I'll have no trouble sleeping if I put a bullet in the heads of the initial targets. What is eating at me is that there's a really thin line between civilian and combatant, here."

"These are terrorists."

"That's what I'm getting at. Do you have any idea how many fans they have? What happened at that concert was a bloodbath. This story is going to out, and we don't even have our damn suspects. Where does it end?"

"Oh. Okay, I get it now. You called me up right before my lunch break to try to assuage your conscience. Then you can go in there and make a dirty job seem patriotic somehow. I won't do it."

"I wouldn't—"

"Adam. You're so naïve sometimes."

"These are people's children."

"So are Iraqis. They don't pay me to sort this out. I'm hungry. You want the job? Do it. Your job is to catch them, not worry about PR fallout, or your damn conscience. It's too late for any of that now, Adam. I'm just being straight with you. Will you listen to what I say very carefully?"

"We worked together for years, Sheila. I trust you."

"This has to look like a war, or else you're fucked."

The phone went dead.

Well. This was definitely the most bizarre case he had ever worked. He sat down and lit another cigarette. He'd smoked a lot more and slept a lot less, these past few months.

XVII. Retribution

2012

There is no choice, save to be what you are.
—Gabriel De Leon

How long have I been dreaming? Am I awake?

They gave me something—some pharmaceuticals, a long time ago. Though they were meant to help with my burden, instead, these poison tablets shattered my world, leaving me in endless gray hallways.

The smell of mold tells me I'm back at Pennhurst. They must have caught me, somehow. The underground labyrinth beckons, calling out from its unseen heart. Fascinated and horrified, I drift through the catacombs towards this center, following the etchings on the walls like a spool of thread, winding in, and down.

The walls are adorned with murals gouged with bleeding fingernails and sharp sticks, children's paintings and graffiti. Stuffed animals. Broken umbrellas. There are boxes full of trinkets, probably deeply meaningful to some person at another place, in another time. Letters written in graphite and crayon. Old bottles of perfume. Rusted keys. A beat-up tricycle. The memories and scattered possessions of the fallen, the neglected, and the abused.

It—whatever it is that draws me here—directs my attention to a room numbered '333'. I press my face up to a smeared window and look inside. I can make out the figure of a young man, bathed in seductively flickering blue light.

He is completely naked, but for the restraints binding him to an upright table. His eyes stare, lidlessly, at images on a screen before him: mother, father and child, clasped together in a blurry family portrait, over-saturated and scratched, like a distant memory; a boy and girl holding hands, there and then gone, a flicker of hope in black and white; banners and flags; girls dancing in sequinned dresses as fireworks erupt behind them; the quivering, painted lips of a girl, naked, vulnerable, in ecstasy; the glint of a wedding ring, parents in the background, pantomiming happiness as they feel their own end moving inexorably nearer; computer screens, printouts, spreadsheets, gray slacks, then a fading image of wrinkled arms, wreathed in medical tubing, and the lonely darkness, as the words 'Happily Ever After' take the screen, and remain.

"I've never liked old movies," I said. I don't know if that's true, don't know who I am. But I know that film isn't my story. I'm something different.

"And how are we feeling?" the doctor asks. He is an older man, built like a bear. His breath wheezes as he stares me down. In his eyes, I can see a maze of clockwork and tubing, like an Escher drawing in miniature.

I look down at my hands. Wrapped in bandages. I remembered staring at myself in the mirror, my face distorted by rage. What I saw there was unfamiliar, though I recognize it as my own. The mirror shattered. Silver splinters float around me.

"How are you doing today?" My eyes don't rise in response to the voice. Gauging by the latticework of angry gashes, not so well. I am tied to a wheelchair. Not well at all.

I could feel his eyes searching for something. My face was a mask, a dead weight fashioned of heavy and soggy clay, so it was unsurprising that he should be stonewalled. I still haven't moved, or met his prying gaze.

Instead of replying, I turn to find bubbling and cracked paint. Columns of mold. Shelves of rat-gnawed feces. "Where am I?"

"Unit A, Modular 3. Pennhurst."

This was unlike the sessions I recalled. I had been facile, detached. Safe in the knowledge that I could run circles around the doctors and cage them in a prison of words. No, it was different. I am exposed. Naked.

I look down at my arms again. The slashes are puffy and oozing in the first stages of healing. Why am I here? The answer is in that web of dried blood and new skin. Who am I now? That question hangs around me like smoke. It chokes my vision, steals my breath.

With great effort, I peer up at the impenetrable eyes of the doctor. "Where is she?"

"Who?" Behind him, a wall of clocks tick and whir.

"Ariadne. Where has she gone?"

His fingers absently drum on his desk. "Who do you think you are?"

I hear footsteps behind me. Orderlies cart me away into cavernous, dark tunnels as the clocks simultaneously chime the passage of midnight.

—

I'm flocked by a procession of ghosts. They are dressed in rags, their stained underwear wedged between chicken legs, their eyes like black glass. It's hard to believe these creatures were ever human. One of them pushes past the orderly long enough to lay a hand on my forehead.

"Coram sanctissimi Sacramento, sive in tabernaculo asservato sive publicae adorationi exposito, unico genu–" she says, before being elbowed in the ribs and pushed aside. The orderlies have to use more force to keep the gibbering masses back, as they scramble to touch me, begging me to release them from the prison of their atrophying flesh and bone. Their hell is all around them. Only death brings serenity, in forgetfulness.

Their faces remain serene as their bodies sustain crippling blows, cushioned by religious ecstasy.

—

The orderlies toss me into a ring of pitch. It is too dark to see anything, aside from the lights of the hall reflecting in the stagnant water that pools on the floor, but I can tell there is something dead in here with me. It drives me a little mad—being unable to see it, unable to know what is rotting, possibly feet from the wheelchair I'm strapped to.

"Bring me the patient," I hear him call down the hallway. Orderlies drift into view somewhere in the gloom, and nod mutely. The wheels on the wheelchair spin in lazy circles as they approach, like a ship appearing from some distant shore. Of course, that alien land was his office of clockwork, and what lay between was a series of cubicle-like rooms with barred doors, single toilet, and walls coated with intricate patterns of mold and fungus. They enter the final dark of my solitary confinement, and strap me to the chair. I will be brought to him again.

—

His eyes meet mine with indifference. I peer over his clipboard, and notice that it is just a series of check boxes. The details of our lives reduced to multiple-choice questions.

"Why do they think I can save them?" I ask.

"Who are 'they'?"

"The other patients. They think I can save them."

"Do you?" he asks.

Before I can answer, I'm wheeled out of the room again, as the doctor nonchalantly makes a couple of tick marks on his psychological tic-tac-toe board. His eyes are no different than the watch faces behind him, all staring into time as empty as the vacuum of space.

"We're all just being processed," I say to the orderly, as he leaves me in the dark with my invisible, dead friend. "Ground to cement."

The orderly doesn't make any sign he's heard me.

Now that I think of it, I've never seen their faces. Ariadne, where are you?

We're all alone here. Truly and utterly alone.

—

I was left in darkness for eternity. But something stirred in that dark, and finally freed itself with a pop, and a gout of fecund liquid that mingled with the filth of the floor. A pale light, a hazy red-orange like a blood moon intruded in the circle of pitch. Despite my search for Ariadne in the starless sky, as if those far off poets of light failed to join the hunt, I never found her. I breathed the graveyard scents of the labyrinth, but never found her.

Yet Ariadne had been with me all along, her body supine, half twisted in likeness of a nautilus shell washed ashore between the four trees of the world, to which I have been long chained.

—

When the building itself is the stick, then a mere smile serves as a carrot. A moment's reprieve from the dank and the dark. A little food that doesn't taste of corpses. Why, how do you do? Mm, yes. Now do whatever I say, thank you. Like getting a rat to push a button. The other patients could be managed in this way. But not this one.

These monsters may have broken the other inmates, but I feel something inside me that can't be chewed up and homogenized. I focus on that part of me, feel it grow stronger. I feed it everything else in me, cannibalize myself. Focus on that center, the center of the labyrinth. Find it.

—

Again, I face the doctor. "I'm on to you," I say. "You're the motherfucking Leviathan."

"What?" he says. His face, usually devoid of human emotion, shows the slightest sliver of concern.

"I had a dream the other night that I woke up, dizzy and nauseous. You see, in the dream I woke up. So I was confused. I thought that the dream was my waking life, and my waking life was the dream."

"Have you been taking your medication?"

"No, listen. You'll like this. I felt something inside of me that was indigestible. Indestructible. Timeless. But it was inside me, I mean literally inside of me. I had swallowed it. My stomach... it ballooned out like a condom bloated with cocaine."

My stomach began to bulge and contort. I took my hand and raised it over my head dramatically. The doctor writhed in fear.

"I shoved my hand down my throat... my whole hand... and vomited up an iridescent rainbow. It shredded my insides as it lurched out of me, a hailstorm of diamonds and esophagus. And so–"

With a sound like a cat hacking up a hairball, thousands of diamonds poured from my mouth, clattering wetly to the ground all around me. The doctor ducked behind his desk.

"I woke up laughing. You can't digest me. You have no idea who you're dealing with. Coming for me? I'm coming for you. Do you hear me? I'M COMING FOR YOU."

I grabbed the doctor and began cramming diamonds down his throat.

—

Dionysus woke up in his bunk, laughing hysterically. "I am coming for you!"

He rolled over, his hand naturally hunting for the spot where Ariadne normally slept. All he found was her favorite T-shirt. He blinked, and then frowned before he balled it up and held it close to his face.

Loki pushed back the curtains. "What are you going on about?"

Dionysus shook his head. "Crazy dream. Poetic, dark. But listen. In the hotel... the night we met Ariadne. She said Lilith told her we're all forgetful Demigods. I mean for real."

"All of us? Like, everyone?"

"Well, no. Not exactly. I'm not sure how it's supposed to work. But... I could tell something happened in that bathroom which really got into her."

"Just Lilith's magical mystery pillow talk. And possibly her tongue," Loki tried to smile, but it broke. "Look, she's gone. They both are."

"No. Listen. I remember something Ariadne said to me once. She discovered that in Greek myth, Ariadne and Dionysus were married. That she died...and that, later, Dionysus went all the way to the underworld to recover her. Ariadne took it seriously, she told me I had to promise her that I would always come after her, always find her. I thought it was both sweet and kind of foolish. I told her how many contradictory stories there are about Dionysus and Ariadne. She'd have none of it. I made the promise, despite myself. I said 'always will I search for you, always will I find you'. I thought it was silly, but I meant what I said. Right before she died, she said she'd see me again. She died believing it. I guess—"

"I'm sorry," Loki said, "I don't really do sentimental."

Dionysus nodded. "If it's true, if it's true... consider there might be more of us. Consider that one may have grown more powerful than the rest."

"The Leviathan?" Loki asked.

"The Leviathan," Dionysus said.

Loki scratched his chin. "Aren't you the first to say that all these things are metaphors?"

"Yes. Symbols."

"Ok. So?" Loki asked.

"That doesn't make them any less real."

"This is where you lose me."

Dionysus shook his head, and then stared at the ceiling. "And what rough beast, its hour come round at last, slouches towards Bethlehem to be born?"

Loki thought. On the one hand, it was possible his best friend was losing his mind. On the other... No, he was probably losing his mind. "This is where I'm supposed to call you crazy and get back to work, but... look. Is this revelation going to help you fight a war against the flesh and blood agents who are likely hunting for us right now?"

"Probably not," Dionysus said.

"Then it changes nothing, so... Shut up. Win today. Play demigod tomorrow."

Dionysus nodded. "I miss her already."

"I know."

—

They headed deeper into the Black Hills, a place where tree-lined plateaus and cliffs jutted from pale fields, an oasis within the plains, secluded and loud with thunder, where, in the shadows cast from this sacred landscape, they buried her.

Dionysus cleared his throat, and spoke after they had interred her body.

"I want to talk about Ariadne. I need to talk about her. But I can't. I see her face in my mind, and I— The words just stop making sense. I can talk about this place, though. The place where she was shot and died, along with so many others. They have become part of a larger history. The land was sacred to the Cheyenne, before the Lakota took it. And then it was taken by the United States. You all know the story, even if you don't know the story. Custer, in his bright-eyed hubris, pushed his men for days, and many tribes beset them. For a moment, their plight seemed something other than hopeless. But that victory was their failure. More white men came, and the Black Hills were overrun. Later, four presidents were carved into the southern face of the mountain once known as Six Grandfathers, to drum up the tourist trade. You see? Here, one myth was written atop the next. Here, proud people stood and died, only to be commemorated by monuments for gawking tourists. And here is where we are going to make our final stand—"

Everyone talked at once now, but Loki was the loudest over them. "A final stand? You stupid bastard!"

Jesus almost choked on her hit and glared at him, but now they all fell uncomfortably silent. And then, as if on cue, vehicles began rolling in from the horizon. Fleets of motorcycles, banged-up flatbeds, RVs, all painted in bumblebee pattern in homage to their vehicle. Artemis and Loki scampered to the top of the Behemoth with binoculars. Loki began laughing. It was a dry, cracking sound, like a music box shattering.

"I rather preferred it when you were yelling at me," Dionysus said. "What do you see?"

"Hippies," Loki called down. Then he climbed down the side, shaking his head. "Hippies and Burners and Bikers. A last stand? We're dead. They're all fucking dead."

Throughout the nearby canyons and fields, or clustered amongst the pine trees, they could see more groups encamping as the sun set. Tents going up. Rifle racks coming out of SUV's. People doing yoga. The flicker of camp-fires. Pleasant conversation and laughter. His shoulders shook with rage.

"That's... hundreds. Thousands are going to turn this into some stupid gesture. Man the barricades! Let's transcend humanity, man! Let's all die for liberty! The Grand-Fucking-Gesture. We're dead. We're surrounded. We're buried."

"Hey," Dionysus said. "Listen to me."

"The one thing a State can kill, the one thing it can handle, is an army. It's what they do. It's their damn job. You and your god-damned cult, peasant crusade bullshit..."

"Hey," Dionysus said, more emphatically.

Loki stopped and collected himself. "Yeah. Sorry. It's just... I tried."

"I know," Dionysus said, standing to his full height.

"I did my best. I did. I..."

"Rode a tidal wave into an iceberg."

Loki grinned. "Something like that." He flicked his cigarette. "See that? They'll say a falling star marked the hour of your passing. You poor, martyred bastard."

"A little respect for the dead, if you please."

Loki shook his head, and then shrugged. "The Grand Gesture. Fine. This ain't Megiddo, but it'll do."

"I want to live like anyone else, but this isn't about us. It never really was. It's about them, those desperate people out there. So, Loki, are you ready to die like a God?" Dionysus asked.

Loki shrugged again. "You know why I initially picked this name?"

"No, actually," Dionysus said.

"It wasn't any of Lilith's ideas about demigods or 'Fallen'. It was because I've always taken the side of the underdog."

"I thought you said it was because you took mischief seriously," Mary said.

"That too," Loki grunted. "Alright. Enough bullshitting. Artemis, get me a topographical map of the surrounding area." He motioned inside the vehicle, and they set up around the cabin.

Jesus eyed Dionysus. The two of them perched in the passenger seat, nodding at the others walking past. "I heard what you said from your bunk. The other night, when you were talking with Loki."

"Yeah?" Dionysus asked.

"Every time," Jesus said cryptically.

"Huh?"

"It ends in blood. Every god damned time."

Loki inspected the map. He and Artemis started circling areas. "Ain't ended yet," he said over his shoulder.

"Nailed up, torn up, hacked up, shot up..." Jesus continued.

"Slow down," Dionysus said.

"I've been poisoned. Beaten. Do you know how many times Christians have killed their own savior? I've frozen in the pews. I've been staked out for lions."

"Tigers. The stakes were your own spears," Loki muttered, not paying attention to his own words.

"Wait. What did you just say?" Dionysus asked.

"Huh?" Loki asked, genuinely confused. "I didn't say anything."

Jesus and Dionysus eyed each other. Dionysus put his hand on Jesus' shoulder. "Hey, walk with me."

The two of them made their way out the door of the Behemoth, eventually sitting on a rock. The crickets filled the silence between them, seeming to recede when they again spoke.

"Why?" Jesus asked. "You know how this ends."

"That's my point," Dionysus said, "we know, whether we know it or not." He glanced back towards the Behemoth, where they could see Loki and Artemis still deep in planning, and a flock of girls gathering around them, taking orders. "But we don't die. Not really."

"I die every time," Jesus said, looking up at the fresh crescent of moon, rising like an angel from the dim shadow of the mountains.

"Yes," Dionysus said. "And you get up, every time. 'From thence to rule the quick and the dead'. You bear their sins and die in the desert. I synthesize a new order and have to reclaim what I've lost. Loki invests a net and they bind him with it. Every. Time. And we keep coming back."

"Cycles. Circles. Over and over and I'm sick to fucking death of it," Jesus said. She had pulled out makeup and was using it in some semblance of war paint.

"Spirals. Not circles." Dionysus paused, and then motioned toward the 'war paint'. "Can you do me next?"

"Sure. Same difference, from the cross."

"No. We're born into the world we made, don't you see? We can't help changing the world, leaving it redeemed, redirected, empowered. No matter how many ways they dream up to slaughter us, no matter how addled and useless we feel... Let me tell you something I've learned about apocalypse," Dionysus said.

"What's that?"

"Apocalypse isn't the end. That's the destruction that precedes the apocalypse. The rupture creates an ouroboros, so the currents of the past flow into the future. The apocalypse is not the explosion, it's the revelation cloaked in the silence which follows."

"The moral arc of the universe..."

"Is way, way bigger than any of us," Dionysus said.

Jesus lit a smoke, and lay on her back. "I think this time I want to explode, to burn, burn, burn like a fabulous yellow roman candle exploding like a spider across the stars..."

"Huh?" Dionysus asked.

"You'll see," Jesus said, puffing away placidly.

—

From inside an armored SUV, Trevino scanned the dawn horizon with binoculars. He watched them, looking like the children of the sun. A flock of figures running, falling, laughing, speeding across the plains in the dappled shade, until the last lonely cloud was banished by the light. Soon, a rain of gunfire would fall from that empty sky and soak the ground in silence. He muttered a stream of orders into his headset.

"...Got it. Draw fire to their south east, we're go for insertion. Maneuver and counter-fire only. Remanding the principals alive is top priority." Trevino swiveled the mic away from his face, which he wiped with a sweaty hand.

"You're kidding yourself," Lilith said. "They're here for blood."

"Those kids are armed. Can't just expect us to take fire and not–"

"–kill every hippie terrorist you set eyes on?"

He sighed. "We want the same thing, here."

"I doubt that very much."

"You're right. I could give a shit what you want, past those three in custody. Show trials, martyrdom, I really, honestly, don't give a rat's bleeding asshole. Bring them to me and this–" he waved at the desert out there, and the idiots who were about to die "–ends."

"Well, I'll lead you to them. That, we agree on." She lifted her handcuffs, which Trevino unlocked. "One other thing."

"Yes?" he asked.

"I need a firearm," she said evenly.

He laughed.

"I'm serious."

"What could you possibly need that for?" he asked.

"There's a chance they won't come willingly."

"Sure, but that's your problem, not mine. I'm not taking the liability for..."

She sighed and leaned back in the seat, one foot up on the dash. "Fine. A knife, at least."

He shook his head.

"What, you think I could take you with a knife?" she asked.

"No, I just—"

"Because I could've taken you out hours ago, if I wanted to."

He shook his head. He couldn't believe what he was saying even as he said it. "Fine, fine. Whatever. Take my utility knife." He reached down and handed her the sheathed blade, which she slipped into the elastic of her skirt.

"That wasn't so hard, right?" she said, and then she blew him a kiss and opened the door.

"We're tracking you," he said.

"I'm leading you," she said, shutting the door. Trevino was left to ponder that, as she disappeared into the rocks.

—

"On my order," Trevino said.

The Sun had begun its long journey across the sky. He expected it to be over quickly.

—

A girl blinked up at the sun. Purples and yellows blended into a surreal orange as the early light of the day passed through layers of dust. Dogs basked quietly in the shade as people sat on blankets and quietly enjoyed the vista, bare-chested men weaving between the patchwork with platters of fresh fruit, women laughing and dancing, heedless of threat, though many at the perimeter sat waiting, weapons in hand, eyes on the horizon as if their enemies would descend from the gates of heaven.

"Follow me," a man in shaolin monk robes said, waiting for his companions to emulate his motions. "This is Monkey Steals Apple. It's a Bagua form that comes from the water element in the five element cycle–"

A girl struck the same pose as her friend and held it, smiling beatifically. Her head exploded with a wet pop. A far away gunshot sounded, a moment later.

In the seconds that followed, there was a great deal of screaming and scrambling, people grabbing weapons and aiming them at random. From the tent behind her, Cody emerged, blinking. Gas grenades landed all around him, adding dense, colored smoke to the maelstrom of chaos.

He squinted at more gunfire in the distance. With each crack, like a woodpecker chipping away at a saguaro, a head or chest exploded. Soldiers strolled through the clouds, easily offing anyone who moved. Cody dropped to the ground, curled into a ball, and closed his eyes. When they had passed, he began crawling away from this meat grinder.

—

Lilith serenely walked down a steep-walled canyon. Bullets pinged off the rocks around her, explosions sounded in the distance. She continued as though in meditation.

She thought fondly of training the girls over the past year, firelight conversations, half-remembered nights spent drinking salty kisses. The memories didn't haunt her. Alone, her mind was clear, like a mirror without an expectant gaze.

She could finally see the future. The bower of dream would creak and crack with all the babies yet to be born, all her daughters. They ripened and burst in fields of wheat, and whether some were given as sacrifice, even their blood greased the cogs and wheels of the Leviathan's broken cities and barren fields until they flower. The high tide would come and pass, the Leviathan and his civilization would be dragged to sea with it, leaving a new land to pass through the long winter after the fall before turning again toward summer. And in that Alterran her children might flourish.

—

Jesus filled the tank of a dune buggy with gasoline from a portable container. She topped it off, and then splashed the remainder all over the vehicle; madly duct-taped a bunch of prepared dynamite to the chassis, and prepared herself for an adequately flamboyant martyrdom. A radio at her belt squawked. It was Loki's voice.

"They're in the canyons, we've got 'em. Fall back to rendezvous point A. They're–"

Jesus shut the radio off and dropped it. She strapped herself in and started it up. Taking a deep breath, she gunned the engine.

—

They lured mercs into dead ends, coming at them from craggy overhangs and then slipping away. They baited and teased them, using the landscape to hold off an immediate slaughter. It was an old approach, old as Thermopylae, but in this terrain the mercs had little choice—either give up pursuit or take the punishment in the struggled for an advantageous position.

Loki perched silently on the side of a plateau, surveying the pass below with binoculars.

He spotted a group of mercs. Apparently, his mines had taught a harsh lesson. Caltrops, in clusters every three or so feet. Bury the mines in the ground in-between. This company was down to a handful of men, but there would be more not far behind. Artemis flashed him a sign to wait until they were in the middle of the clearing.

He made a couple of quick hand gestures to the group positioning themselves on the opposite bluff. Artemis caught his signal and made signs to the rest of her group. They moved into position.

—

Loki grimaced at his radio, wishing he could reach through it and stop what he heard on the other end.

"I think they got Jesus," he whispered to Artemis. She shook her head sadly before turning her attention back to the movement on the hill opposite their perch.

An engine roared from overhead. Dionysus gawked as Jesus sailed through the air in a dune buggy, arcing down towards the merc squad, revealed from their camouflage with waving arms and shrieks of surprise. They fired as she descended in an explosive fireball that rocked the canyon.

Chunks of metal and blood fell around them like rain. A whirling, flaming cross—the dune buggy's roll bar—nearly speared Dionysus as he rolled to his feet. It stuck upright in the ground and quivered like a tuning fork.

Loki and Dionysus looked at each other in shock.

—

A hawk circled above, keening bitterly. Loki fired a single shot, drawing a merc's attention. He slipped from sight.

Artemis' group, who were positioned on the other side of the ravine, rained rocks on them, the rest unleashing a silent volley of razor sharp crossbow bolts. There was sporadic return fire. She dropped to one knee and took aim.

Warm blood drenched her before she could fire. She flattened immediately, instinctively. Beside her was Amber's corpse, still spurting blood but the personality had already left her eyes. Sniper with a high caliber rifle.

.50 bullets blast through a body, shred and explode soft tissue. Half of Amber was quite simply gone.

No time to vomit or scream at the unseeing sky above. Anything but machine-like detachment would just slow her down.

Everyone else fell behind cover. The slightest movement in her peripheral vision gave away a sniper, and another merc approaching with a sub-machine gun on a path with spotty cover of thistles and dead trees.

She gestured over her shoulder and then counted. Closed her eyes and visualized the merc walking towards them. Kept the image playing in her head. One... two... THREE. She popped up like a prairie-dog, her bolt flying where her mind's eye placed the moving target. It lined up, and he went down with a gurgling howl.

A chunk of rock exploded behind her, sending a shower of pebbles into the air. The damn sniper. They didn't have anything that could take him out at that range. "Fall back," she said.

The group seemed to melt into the rock itself.

—

As they wound their way further into the cliffs and plateaus, Artemis held up a hand. The narrowing crevasse split in two directions.

She glanced at Loki and he nodded his head. They should break up. She pointed to herself, Mary and three of the other girls who had worked security, and motioned towards the left passage.

The rest clustered around him. "We'll regroup at the cave," he said to Artemis, quietly. And they were off.

Artemis' group moved through a winding path of loose rocks and shrubs. Ahead, Artemis knew, there was a glen of squat trees with broad branches, which created a sheltered canopy. Despite the far off sound of gunfire, birds continued to chirp here. In the shadows of the cool rock faces, many small plants and animals could find a daytime shelter from the unrelenting sun. The path rounded a corner and pitched at an incline here, ending in a deep bowl. This was the spot.

Position over there, she gestured. She could sense the troops following them, but they were a little ways off. Supporting fire.

"Where will you be?" Mary whispered.

Artemis pointed to a ledge, maybe seven feet up the side of the wall, which was angled away from the path they had just emerged from.

Mary gave her a concerned look, but she waved it off.

—

Along with providing the tactical advantage of location, the glen seemed to act as an amplifier for sound, within the stone passageways between the plateaus. The footsteps of approaching mercenaries could be heard. Eight of them entered the clearing.

Artemis took a deep, slow breath. Time itself seemed to slow. Taking aim with her repeating crossbow, the one in the rear went down with barely a whimper.

One.

As she predicted, the group whipped around and fired a burst at her hiding spot, but she had already dropped, falling into a roll, both to lessen impact and make up some of the distance between them. A cluster of birds took flight from the trees.

She came out of her roll, firing another shot as she went. Spraying crimson from the neck, he fired wildly as he fell.

Two.

She was in their midst. Several sub-machine guns were swinging in her direction. Moving on instinct, she dropped like a bag of rocks, wrapped her legs around one of the soldiers, and rolled, using her momentum to uproot him. His head connected with a nearby stone with a dull smack.

Three.

She was on the ground, and exposed. She made a mad leap to get behind cover.

The force of impact twisted her around and nearly knocked her down. Shoulder. Keep moving. Now in position above, the girls opened up on the mercs. Bolts whistled in from the trees, hamstringing one soldier and harpooning another through both arms.

She let out a howl and lunged behind a wounded merc, wrapping her arm around his neck as she slid past. One of his dead-eyed comrades slammed several bullets into his chest, blowing organs all over her already blood-soaked shirt. She shoved him into the soldier who had fired, and shot him in the chest before he had a chance to recover.

Four. Five.

The merc in front of him grinned, thinking she had missed, only to see his comrades fall face first beside him, grotesquely beatific like Saint Sebastian, with bolts in both arms, and one in the chest. This seemed to startle him. Maybe he dimly recalled the famous painting his fallen comrade's body so resembled.

He looked back up in time to see Artemis' face rushing towards his, shrieking like a Valkyrie as she came. At the last moment, she lowered her head, knocking him back several steps.

Sensing danger from behind, she dropped and rolled behind a boulder. A hail of bullets perforated the chest of the stunned soldier instead of her. She twisted around and put another bolt into the neck of her would-be assailant.

Six. Seven.

There was just one left, but he had his gun trained directly on her. However, he didn't fire, as her semi-automatic crossbow was aimed at her favorite target, the jugular vein.

"How many shots you have in those things?" he asked.

"I guess there's no chance you could just leave?" she asked.

"No way, bitch," he said. When another series of twangs came from the direction of the trees, she rolled to the side like a barrel down a hill. The bolts found their mark. Sure enough, on his way down, he fired off a burst where she had been, the bullets shattering rock and skittering harmlessly around the glen.

Eight.

She groaned. Her arm was stiffening. She gingerly peeled back the torn cloth around the wound and was pleased to see that the bullet, though it had torn some muscle, struck at an odd angle and didn't embed or hit anything vital. The proximity of so much gunfire had quite literally deafened her, at least temporarily. The adrenaline was wearing off.

"Fuck. Guys–" she said, wearily.

The ground trembled.

"Take cover!" she screamed, rolling into a defensive crouch.

—

Trevino's SUV rolled through the carnage of the main camp, towards the canyons.

"Lost contact with Gamma and Delta squads," a merc reported over the hiss of the radio. "Beta reports zero casualties in main camp."

"Hundreds. Hundreds in the main camp, you..." Profanity failed him. But had he really expected any different? "Beta, condition?" Trevino asked.

"Insurgent elements contained in canyons, mesa secured. We have heavy weapons solution, repeat, have solution."

"Go," Trevino said hollowly.

"Beginning bracketing bombardment," the merc repeated.

—

In the cave, Loki was crouched over a series of rocket tubes, fussing with fuses and checking caps. He looked up as Dionysus entered, then returned to work.

Loki nodded to the others, passing them rocket tubes as they swarmed out of the caves.

"The camp's a pile of dead kids. We're down to two teams in the core..." Loki said.

"Artemis thinks we can win this. She–" The ground shook with a distant explosion. Dionysus' eyes widened.

"Artemis is a believer."

There was a second, closer explosion.

"That's artillery–" Loki started.

A series of rhythmic explosions continued. Loki stopped, troubled by something in the timing, but Dionysus got there first.

He grabbed Loki and leaped for the cave mouth as there was a final blast and much of the room collapsed in dust and hoarse screams.

—

Dionysus opened his stinging eyes, but all he could see was darkness, swirling dust and smoke. There was far off rumbling and screaming, then silence. He imagined all his friends, dead. He imagined himself dead, starving slowly in the bowels of the mountain. Then he heard coughing, and a gentle click as a flashlight cut a path through the swirling ash.

"How—?" Loki asked.

"I'm a drummer, dumb ass." They grinned through a coating of blood and dust. They were alone. When the dust and foul smoke cleared, they could see the entrance to the outside was still partially open. There was no sound save the thrumming in their ears.

Loki looked around. "Eh. Well... looks like we've got water, food and a collapsible entry. Worst case, we hide out for a month or so."

"Artemis? Mary?" Dionysus asked, feeling a bit numb.

Loki shook his head. "If they're smart, they took cover and are high-tailing it out of here. This is over. We fought well, but you can't argue with physics."

Dionysus nodded, and picked up a handgun. The two of them went down on their haunches. A couple minutes passed before Dionysus spoke suddenly. "When asked of heaven, I said, the Sun was once a brothel of joy. But it was here and nowhere else. Before it drank the spirit of the last free people. Their eyes grew dark, their bodies still, yet still restless, their dreams no longer spoke wisdom, but merely churn something meaningless like stones clattering to the red earth, forever."

"Huh?" Loki shook his head. "Wouldn't you rather be playing cards or something?"

"Nah. You always kick my ass in cards or chess. It's not fun." Dionysus shrugged.

"Seriously, man. Okay, I have my breath back," Loki wiped his eyes with the back of his hand, blinking. "Hey. Is that Lilith?"

There she was, walking by the entrance to the cave, looking like she was on a casual stroll to a picnic.

"Lilith!" Dionysus said in a hissing whisper. Loki shot a glare at him, but he didn't catch it.

Loki closed his fingers around his blade as she approached. "Good to have you back. We're probably it. You know that."

"No one else needs to die here," she said.

"Huh?" they said in unison.

"I made a deal with the Marshall, Trevino. They've been spying since the start. Some policy or some bullshit. So let's end the act, alright?"

"Lilith. Since when did we start negotiating with feds?" Loki asked.

"It's at least worth thinking about," Dionysus said.

Loki locked eyes with Lilith. "No, it's martyrdom. I get it. This was all you, wasn't it... I planned your war, drove your chariot, guarded your damn doorways, but this does it. Count me out."

"Don't do this," Lilith said warily.

Loki unsheathed his knife. He began to move into a defensive posture.

Faster than he could have predicted, Lilith shot past him. Now she was behind him, dagger to his throat, and other hand on the elbow of his primary arm.

"Wow," Loki said.

"What are you doing? This is nuts!" Dionysus said.

Loki shook his head. "She's gonna feed us to the Feds, don't you get it? We're a goddamn sacrifice. Just like we did with Johny. All this, the band, the movement..."

Lilith looked at Dionysus as she whispered in Loki's ear, "You always were a bit too smart for your own good. Till next time, friend."

"You better hope not," Loki said.

Dionysus shook as he watched blood pour from his friend's neck into the thirsty sand. Their conversations had been a constant part of his life for more than a decade. It had shaped their ideas about both themselves and the world more than either cared to admit.

But there was nothing he could do. So far from medical assistance, there wasn't even a point in trying to help.

"Why?" was all he could force between his teeth.

She looked at him blankly. "You're like a kid asking why the sky is blue."

"You built us up, just to have us publicly disembowelled? Is that it?"

"Look at you, your animal body quivering. Your mind spinning. See Loki dying on the ground there? Look, he's clawing towards you, desperately fighting. Fighting. There's nothing to fight! Let go. It's the price of becoming a God." Hands on her hips, so certain.

"Slough off this mortal coil, is that it?"

"Something like that," she said.

"Then you should thank me."

"For what?" she asked, the subtlest trace of confusion tainting her placid demeanor.

"Setting you free," he said, with crushing finality.

She was gazing into the dark barrel of a gun. Her eyes widened in horror.

The darkness went white, then womb red.

—

Dionysus stood frozen in place. Her words rang in his head long after the sharp crack of the gunshot echoed back at him from the impassive walls of the cave. Smoke slithered out of the barrel of the gun. Her shattered body, still twitching, spurted black blood.

The gun in his hand did not shake. He felt no remorse, no rage. He was merely a channel for what had to be done. How it was that a brutal act of revenge elevated him to some kind of Demigod-hood, he wasn't sure. But the certainty was there, sitting comfortably in the part of his stomach that usually housed fear and doubt.

—

Oh, Lilith. You wanted to fuck your way to immortality. You wanted to make them pay. You wanted a great party where everyone was brilliant and beautiful and fit neatly in the palm of your hand. But instead, it was silent and awful, no one knew and no one cared, they just wrote their profane part on that blank body, blue-lidded, seductive, and empty. Everyone could have their turn with her, Babylon, queen of the whores, Babylon, who promises the world between her thighs.

Time is laid out before us, clean and bare, whole. It fools us into thinking we are free. Time, erotic in its blank submission, a body that needs you to fulfill its desires, and write your life story on its flesh.

We must act, we must fight, and we must scuttle in the dirt to appease that body. Life demands a performance. But we have foresight. Unlike those pill bugs you once told me of, your first memory—a child of just four, in the garden, dirt to your knees and elbows, the insects squirming about you. The only difference between their struggle and our own: I've never seen a pill bug seduce the world. So don't deceive me with those lips and hands, with that smile that hasn't changed since you were four because it always—always!—got you what you wanted. That is the great lie, that in losing ourselves in one another we are free.

Heavy on the horizon now, I hear a churning flock of birds, fighting over these two carcasses, still holding their knives, still holding one another as if lovers at the end of the world.

The party is over.

—

Trevino watched Dionysus through his binoculars. He was walking alone, shirtless, fearless of gunfire. Directly toward their position.

Normally at this point in a mission, he would feel professional satisfaction, even elation, but this time he just felt sick.

"Confirmation," a voice crackled on the radio. "He appears to be unarmed."

Trevino shook his head. "He wants us to take him. Cover me."

"We have the shot."

"He's mine. Do you hear me? Don't fire without my command."

Trevino stepped out from cover, his arms open. Two mercs followed.

"Dionysus—" Trevino said.

Dionysus stopped, but didn't turn.

"—it's over."

Dionysus piercing eyes were like a spot of pure snow on a red and muddy battlefield. "There's nothing you can do to me that hasn't already been done."

Trevino turned to his men. "Stand down."

They appeared unsure.

"Stand down," he repeated.

Trevino approached Dionysus, who put out his hands in expectation of handcuffs. Trevino shook his head. "Five guys with guns pointed at your head. I'm not worried."

"You've spent years tracking us. The first case, this one. Well, here I am. But you're not smiling. Why is that?"

Trevino had nothing.

Dionysus looked thoughtful. "For some reason this reminds me of a story I heard about a samurai. He was sent by his Daimyo to kill an official of some kind. And before he could land the blow, the official spit on him. The samurai... he just sheaths his sword and walks away. Do you know why?"

He got no reply. "If he had killed him at that moment, it would have been personal. Tell me. Is this personal for you?"

Trevino grunted. Dionysus hesitated a moment, reminded in that gesture of Loki. But it was gone. This man hardly resembled his dead friend. Maybe Loki was right, maybe he did just like the sound of his own voice.

"Eh, anyway. Certainty can be so attractive, especially when you've been uncertain all your life. They wanted to know what it felt like to know something to the bones, to *deliver* it. And all the petty bickering, and posturing, and back-biting of the world magically became someone else's problem. Now look at them."

"Yeah, whatever. Loki? Is he dead or alive?" Trevino asked.

Dionysus shook his head.

Trevino sighed. "Look. I called off the slaughter. I just want you and Jesus."

Dionysus shook his head again. "Called it off? Haven't you killed nearly everyone already? Let me ask you something. Why do you think you were sent after us?"

"You're an escaped convict. You—"

"—you're not stupid. I can see that now, looking in your eyes. Simple, but not stupid. Why you?"

Trevino nodded grimly, despite himself.

"You are a disposable and desperate pawn in the service of a mad God."

"Gods? You're insane."

Dionysus looked off into the vast stretch of sky around them. "Alright. Let's find out. The men you work for dictate the course of bloody history from behind a desk. But you can't comprehend the risk we pose to them. I could shoot the messenger, it changes nothing."

"You're going to threaten me, now?"

Dionysus spread his hands wide. "I'm not the one you should fear."

Trevino had considered this as well. Hundreds of miles away, would the three Suits sigh together like wearily triumphant surgeons when he called it in? If the lunatic were right, would they kill him?

He pictured himself laid out with the lumpy quiet of a cadaver on the conference table, with the Suits surrounding him. Their hands adjusted his tie, pinned his credentials to his lapel, fussed with his hair. Martyred, a Saint Stephen full of hollow point slugs like bloody mushrooms.

Is this what their predicted outcome was?

Dionysus continued. "Look at the chess pieces. Look at the board. This isn't about the acts of individual people. Though if you were to work with us, as a plant—"

Trevino shook his head, half following, and half ready to lock him up in the asylum himself. "Plant? Please. What you said about the movement, whatever this is... Lilith said something about that," he said.

"Did she?" Dionysus asked, sounding honestly surprised.

"Yeah. I still don't know what either of you are getting at. Were getting at. Look, you know what happens now."

"You kill me," Dionysus said nonchalantly. He turned around. Trevino shook his head again, and then slapped on the cuffs. As they started walking off, the mercs moved to follow.

"I can handle this," Trevino said.

They eyed each other suspiciously. "Yes, sir."

—

They made their way through a maze of brambles, Dionysus in front and Trevino behind, gun in hand. The sun was beginning to peak the top of the bluffs.

"I don't hold blame," Dionysus said. "The Leviathan comes from us all. We're all haunted by the immortal ghosts of our ancestor's ideas."

"You're looking death in the face, and talking about... I don't even know."

Dionysus looked up at the swirls of cloud, which radiated those last rays of the unseen sun. They seemed frozen in time, as if those clouds might hang in the sky forever, though he knew better. "Time's a cruel joke that eternity plays on us," he said.

Trevino chuckled darkly. "I'm beginning to wonder how you could possibly be behind a terrorist uprising."

"I wasn't. If you kill me now, you would always do so. Choice isn't fixed, but whom we are in a given moment... Well, let me ask you... Are you the kind that kills an innocent fool?"

"Stop here. Kneel," Trevino said, his voice less steady than he would have liked.

Without any argument, Dionysus knelt on the pebbles and cracked earth beneath him. "Maybe you are. Though for some reason, I don't think so."

"You know I have a gun to your head?"

"No, you don't."

The gun dangled limply in Trevino's hand, pointed nowhere in particular. It trembled slightly. None of this made sense.

Dionysus breathed with the cadence of the crickets. A moment of peace and stillness. The gun discharged loudly into the chill air.

Shaking his head at what he was doing, Trevino unlocked his cuffs. "Disappear. Do you understand? Just. Fucking disappear."

Eventually, Dionysus heard footsteps padding away.

—

Trevino picked his way back across the brambles to the mercs, who waited in the idling SUV.

He holstered his sidearm and tossed a pair of bloody handcuffs to the merc riding in the rear before climbing into the shotgun position.

"Got any water?" he asked.

Accepting a canteen, he drank deeply. "I've never executed a man before. Get us out of here."

After another swig, he flipped open his phone.

—

The Suits sat expectantly with a speakerphone and a manila file folder on their table. One of them activated the phone.

"Go ahead, Adam."

"We're finished, here."

One of them pulled the folder to himself and opened it.

"This is confirmed?"

"Sir. It's finished."

"Well done, Special Deputy US Marshall Adam Trevino."

One of them brought a heavy, old-fashioned stamp down on the first page of the file. Trevino's world-weary personnel profile photo was marred with a 'KIA' in red ink.

An impossibly loud gunshot played over the speaker. They deactivated it, closed the file, and pushed it across the table.

"Notify human resources."

—

Dionysus walked alone in these carrion fields, under the canopy of the stars. Seemingly still, always in motion. He was alive, he was free. A speck of light, momentarily flickering in the void, and then vanishing.

—

Many of you know me by now. This will be my final broadcast.

I escaped a fire-storm in the desert to be blanketed for all eternity under forgetful snow. The worst winter in recent memory. It patters like a million fluttering eyelashes against the ground.

Yes, the snow makes a sound. It's an ever-present 'hussssssh', though I can't say who it is telling to remain silent. Amazing, that something so fragile can crush and bury people alive. It calls to mind an article by John-Ivan Palmer about the man who beheaded Yukio Mishima.

Let me explain. He said that there exists an onomatopoeic sound for absolute silence. The Japanese word for silence is 'sin', pronounced more or less like 'sheeeen...' with the sound trailing off at the end. Like 'whoosh' is the sound of a sword cutting through the air, and 'gurgle' is the sound of blood spurting out the neck hole, 'sin' is the 'sound' afterward, when all is done, the bodies removed, everyone gone home, and only the silence remains.

That silence could be the sound of our resignation. Not blood spurting from a wound. Just the whimper of a world sucking sustenance though tubes. No bang. No surprises.

That's the sound I am hearing now, as I watch the snow fall in electric blue night. One snowflake, another. They add up, soon my past will be even less than a memory. But the myth of Dionysus... that is something altogether different.

What is the greatest act a person can take? Is it the greatest sacrifice? Certainly, the suicide bomber has been convinced of this. We look away in discomfort or snub our noses at such fanatics. Mostly, I'd say, rightly so. They've been duped. They've been sold a unicorn and paid for it with flesh, blood, and mortar, and not all of it was theirs to sacrifice.

But there's another side to this posture of disengagement. It turns us to good cattle, good consumers. Good slaves, who do our master's bidding because it is easier that way, easier than challenging and possibly facing death as the repercussion of our actions. Maybe this was the future that Yukio Mishima saw for his dying Empire; a future so bereft of honor and dignity that the only thing he could do in response was shove a blade through his innards. The death of a warrior, not a writer. His suicide could then be seen as a final transformation: writer into warrior. Thinker into actor. But this transformation is only complete when it resonates with a culture. When those ripples reach outwards across the years, transform entire civilizations. We all know the power of a martyr.

This was not Mishima's fate. He was a man, in so many ways, out of step with his time, a relic. To mix metaphors, if a man can become a metaphor, he was the final gasp of a dying mythology. The modern narrative on suicide, even in Japan, is not what it was. To the West, his was the death of a coward. We sigh sadly at the thought of Hunter S. Thompson blowing his brains out, a sound not unlike a book dropping heavily to the floor, or so said his son Juan. What poetry, the final sound for a writer to make. A book falling to the floor. Or perhaps Juan was doing a little myth making of his own.

But Mishima was also a genius, and it wasn't just because of his craftsmanship with the pen. It was because, in his own way, he faced the conflict between the word and reality, and when it came to it, he didn't back down. It was an unyielding, obsessive commitment to the narrative he had built, which eventually guided the blade that killed him.

The comedy in this tragedy was that it meant nothing. He killed himself after the soldiers, who were meant to be roused by the speech he made after barricading himself in with the Tatenokai, merely laughed at him. Their laughter must have rung in his ears like the jests of the schoolboys, who snidely called him 'poet', who teased him so mercilessly that he had to hide his aspirations as a writer. Later in life, nominated to be a Nobel Laureate, and still the punch line of a joke. He spent years weight training, focusing on his body. Sun and Steel. Still he was just the poet. There was nothing to do but die honorably, and that too was a failure. His second could not perform his deed, and Koga had to step in and behead them both.

In a moment, death nullifies the meaning of time. From the vantage point of the end of history, it matters little if we die tomorrow or in one hundred years. From the vantage point of the present, it matters a great deal. From the outside, all that survives and bridges the gap between life and death is the myth. After the point of death, we are no more. The myth lives on, now freed of its tethers.

There's an oddly selfless element to a suicide like Mishima's. To die for the myth is to live on only for the Other. While living, we must live our myth and balance that with the unembodied interior life; a black hole, an aberration only known by the way it distorts all that wander too near to its event horizon. A singularity, not so much very small as not taking up any space at all. Of the interior life, and the zero point of death, we must by all necessity be stricken deaf and dumb.

Nothing can escape this paradox—a voice crying out that is only heard when we, its double, mimic that ephemeral gesture. We cannot feel what an actor feels, only what they show.

Some few might see the act of Seppuku as something beyond all moral consideration, an act of transcendence. It was the absolute fixation upon this internal narrative, which demanded its own head be cut off.

'Yukio Mishima' made himself into a symbol. That is a pen name, an implied double, an it. The name of the man was Kimitake Hiraoka. His double demanded that he die.

Are there ideas, which are so tightly wound into your myth that you are willing to die for them? If not, does that make you stronger for carrying out the story past the final chapter, or does it simply make you like the actor, who after the final curtain call, stands on the stage, and repeats his lines over and over in some delusional hope that the curtain will rise again?

At the end of the lifespan of a universe, a culture, a life, it is destroyed, and a new one born. But for it to be born, and for life to be renewed, a divine sacrifice must be made. On the other side is a new dawn, and a new world. If my myth holds true, I will someday return. If not, the doctors were right.

As I climb, I think of the Mayan maize God. Of Osiris. It is one of the oldest myths we have: a God shedding his blood to feed the crops. He is cloven in two, and redeemed in the underworld, by ascending the world tree into the stars, or pieced together at the bottom of the ocean. This story is older than the tales we have of brother slaying brother, older than the Garden of Eden. I too, will become a story. How long will it be told? Days? Weeks? A milennia? All the same instant, to the dead.

As I look down over the thirteen stories of open air beneath me, I remind myself of this. There is no such thing as death. Only dying. Death? Death is a single heartbeat that lasts forever. A grain of sand awash in the ocean. It is nothing at all.

One more step to eternity. The world stands on its head, or I was born upside down. I have always been afraid of falling—

I look out over fields of white, and finally *see*. Maybe, in a manner of speaking, the snowfall has already buried me. Maybe it has always been burying me.

—But I am not afraid now.

XVIII. Gabriel's Epilogue

2022

A line of young intellectuals ran the full length of the campus book store like a snake. (That is, if snakes could pay thirty grand a year for college and wear Birkenstocks). And there I sit, at the snakes mouth, pleasantly swallowed a piece at a time.

The academy was once respite enough. But the ivory tower is a mirage on the horizon, an arcane incantation that turns obscurity into privilege. I recognize it's all a desperate, final cash grab, much like anything else in this second decade of the 21st century. And, in my own way, I'm just getting in on the action. Most of my life I lived like a hermit and treated the Order with the utmost seriousness. One day I reread Faust, looked at my thinning hairline, and said Fuck This Shit.

A strange and improbable series of events followed, and in another sense preceded this fall from grace, but the heft of it is, that former students, in short order, escaped a mental asylum, and went full-on Antichrist superstar before disappearing in clouds of dust and mortar fire.

It's been ten years since they vanished. Their falling star only flickered in the firmament for a moment, and it was only once it went dark that their myth was truly manifest. As the lot of them had taken the names of demigods and demons, how much easier to strike out any sense of the mundane? (An irony just occurs to me, now. The day I met Alexi, I told him we are all palimpsests. And how true that is, on so many levels).

I kept my head low, carved out a decent niche in that post-psychedelic psychedelic Yoga New Age hipster mish-mosh which continued throughout the decline. So, sure, be a shaman. Take ayahuasca in the jungle for $2k a head. Wear those sacred masks and eagle feathers. Most importantly, read my books and attend my seminars, they will teach you how to "Awaken the Inner You," using the same occult methods I taught Babylon. Namaste.

Their success was my proof. Gabriel De Leon, last line to their fallen heroes. Still alive, and telling all. I'm not guilty, but in a sense, this is a confession.

The story you just heard is about how I'd tell it. I'm not saying it's all made up, because it's not. That's what's come to bother me. Lying is easy, if you have the knack for it.

But I'm not saying it went down exactly that way, either, because we never know how much we're living in a fiction. That's how life is, though most people don't admit it to themselves.

Still, you're going to wonder about my motive. "He just did it for the money," "He was only in it for the sex," right? I'm cynical now too, the world is fucked, how can you not be—but I'm also a realist. U.S. dollars won't spend, soon enough. And the sex? The doddering professor does Debby schtick must get old eventually. As St. Augustine said, "give me chastity and continence Lord... but not yet." Most importantly, Babylon didn't get successful *because* of me. They became the myth because people believed in them. Simple as that. Why? I have no clue.

And so I've hidden the Order's secrets in plain view. There really are Fallen, eternal souls clothed in ever-changing flesh. And if the Fallen are real, then the face of eternity is a single cracked mirror. The real secret, an endless story hiding under the sleepy shroud of time.

I'm thinking all this as I sign the umpteenth book, give my pleasant nod to the umpteenth expectant, ubiquitous face, when my pen freezes mid-stroke. Halfway across the room, near the Romantic Fiction section, stands a blue-black figure, wearing a mask ringed with horns and teeth. Spikes rise from behind the mask, curved like bull horns. A vulture shifts uncomfortably on one of his shoulders.

Like everyone else in line, he is holding one of my books under his arm, patiently waiting his turn to get a signature from the author. Unlike the rest, he clutches an obsidian-tipped spear in his other claw-like hand. Severed heads bob from matted tufts of hair. He breathes menace in deep, rasping bellows.

I recognized him, if you want to call it that, as a Tovag. But here at a book signing? What can I say? At least he's waiting in line politely enough. I didn't know they were a fan of my work.

I'm not sure if you've ever seen something like this in the light of day. It takes a certain sensibility—or madness—to see these dream beings when they break through to the waking side. I have a bit of experience at it. You learn to hold your gorge, or your hysterical, "oh-sweet-Jesus, I'm-losing-my-mind" guffaws. You sign the damn books and move on.

And give a deep sigh of relief when you see that he has dematerialized upon your next hasty scan of the room.

The girl standing in front of me leans a little closer as my hand completes the stroke that passed as my signature these days. She didn't turn to leave, instead biting her lip and then blurting out, "They were really demigods, weren't they?"

I find myself adjusting my glasses for no particular reason. "What do you mean by 'real'?"

Her hand rests on mine for a moment. Warm. Real.

"If you're asking me if I write about internal experience, well yes... Mary," I say, looking down at the name I had just written on the inside of the book. "The freakish contents of your dreams, those half-glimpsed scampering beings in the woods, and the cog and wheel world of the physical are all equally real. Just in different ways."

She cocked her head in a curious way, like a parakeet contemplating if it wants to vomit in your mouth. "I've wanted to get into one of your classes for a while, but I'd have to transfer. Because when I was in high school I had a lot of experiences like that, a friend of mine, she was a Wiccan, and we did this thing with these candles and..."

Here it comes, I think. Let me guess, you were dancing around skyclad and some curtains rustled. Maybe some of the shadows didn't line up quite right. Yeah, yeah.

You didn't hear me. None of you are hearing me.

"When any being dies, it is... in a sense recycled," I said, after a momentary pause.

"You mean like reincarnation?"

"Not exactly, no. Have you read my book yet?"

"The first, but not the others."

"Well, I don't want to give anything away. To be properly recycled, a soul, if you like that word, needs to be wiped clean. Let go or be dragged, is the Zen saying. Memories all erased. But nothing is ever scraped *entirely* clean. And after many times through the twilit lands, the residue builds. Some refuse to let go. They build up so much gravity, you might say, that they become permanent residents of the Underworld, that deep dark nestled beneath the roots of the Feyn. Make no mistake. They are real."

The girl's eyes widened slightly as I spoke.

I trail off. She laughs uncomfortably and asks if she can have my number.

The people behind her were doing some rustling of their own. Finally, I manage to hurry her off after accepting a slip of paper with a phone number on it. I promise to call her. We could talk about the time she played spin-the-bottle with Lucifer.

I look back at the line. It seems even longer than before.

Haven't I played this game long enough? I don't even care about selling books; trying to put a spark into a youth who I doubt will grow to see adulthood. I'm fooling myself. This world makes no sense and no amount of blow jobs will set that right.

I stand and walk out of the room. I've told their story; it's laid out before you like an exquisite corpse.

As for me, I just want to go home. But where is that?

—

Long trips do funny things to time. I don't just mean because they're long, though certainly staring out the window for hours is tedious. The miles of track fly by, flinging clay from the spinning pottery wheel of Mind. And the rocking on a train, I've been told, somehow induces us into some sort of hypnagogic trance. There's something magical, and a little scary about it: you get on at one location, get off at another and move on with your life, but in that time in the middle you have nothing but your past and the scenery outside whipping by, if you travel by day. On a night like tonight, the windows are just blank portals leading to nothing, which is some sort of metaphor in and of itself, I'm sure. If I was prone to think about it.

A friend of mine had died. He wasn't a particularly close friend, but he was a friend of friends, if you know what I mean. College. I hadn't seen any of them in years. Three decades now! Life gets away from all of us, or it had from me, anyway. "Hey, it's been years. Let's catch up now that he's in his coffin." No, it's not quite like that, but it feels a little strange.

Yet, here I am. I bought my ticket without a seconds thought. The truth is, I'm halfway to the destination, and for some crazy reason, it has occurred to me to give you this completely inappropriate letter—which is about time, and life, and nothing at all—both as a greeting to you who were once my close friends, and who I think of from time to time, and also for my friend, who is dead now and could honestly give a damn whether I am at his funeral at all.

I am going to share these secrets about myself. The void provided by the timeless-time on this gently rocking trip to nowhere, is making me feel very odd. I suddenly don't give a damn what you think, I mean, I feel free to be honest with all of you. Will we even meet each other again? Probably not, and maybe that's why.

I can only imagine I'll share more with you now than I would in person. It is better this way. Funerals are awkward and unnatural. No one knows what to say, except for those who are so torn apart by their grief, they can't actually get anything out. Everyone else stands around, there's a lot of hand wringing and shuffling. There's a little fortune-cookie box of clichés that gets passed around before the ceremony begins, just in case anyone is caught without something cheap to say.

I don't even know what he died from, though I heard it was very sudden. Some freak thing.

What did I really know about this person? What could I possibly say to his red-eyed relatives? Would it be for the better or the worse if I started drinking early? The funeral was being held at a high altitude, and as some of you know, drinking at high altitudes when you aren't used to it can lead to unpredictable results.

I hadn't planned to come, and he hadn't planned to die. Nothing important in life is planned.

A very attractive attendant wandered down the aisle, offering some kind of refreshments. I didn't know they did that on trains.

I was parched, but couldn't stammer out a request because I was so taken by the shape of her face, and felt a strange recollection stirred by its features, though I couldn't quite place it.

I was just another passenger of hundreds on a train, and she probably did this every day. I was, well, really nothing more than an obstacle for her, a barrier between obligation and the sweet release of kicking off her shoes at home. Maybe she had a lover waiting for her there already, or maybe she lived alone. Either possibility was frustrating to me, in some completely pointless way: if she had a lover, clearly I had no chance, and what made him or her so special? Maybe they had met on a train, just like this one. But they had said something witty, or they shared some mishap or adventure together, and what do you know? Years later, they are sharing a home and she's privately hoping he doesn't leave the toilet seat up again. If they were a he, of course. And if she was going to return home alone, maybe to a yowling cat or just an empty space filled with nothing but the steam of ramen and some trendy, irrelevant band, well, that was an even deeper insult. Because that nothingness was still far superior to whatever I had to offer.

By now, she was already several rows behind me, asking the same question in the same cheery tone.

This was getting me off the trail of something, though. Distracting me, I felt, from... from what? I couldn't say. An enormous revelation. Stripped naked in the unblinking gaze of oblivion, but I'm not looking at that. I'm wondering why robots have such beautiful thighs.

There's a great shame that keeps us from facing the judgement of a mirror. I wondered if death was like that: the unveiling, the unraveling of all that we kept hidden. Staring at ourselves finally, without distraction, and thinking what? Feeling what?

I wonder if, instead, the moment before oblivion is a massive brain dump of all the things we kept hidden from ourselves. Maybe we hid behind thighs, or martinis, or guilt, or anger, but if you're dying, there's nothing to be ashamed of. WHAM! A trainload full of shameful memories, full-speed, head-on. Truth.

One bubbled up at that moment. There was a girl I once had in my class, Lola, this redhead with alabaster skin—I know that's a cliché but she really seemed constructed out of calcite, except when she smiled—but she wasn't cold. Her aloofness was in the indeterminacy of intimacy. You felt you had a private relationship, but if you were smart, you'd realize its how she engaged with everyone. One day, she gave me an invitation to a party she was having. At the bottom of the invitation, which was clearly printed out the same for everyone, she had written her phone number, in all caps no less, 'CALL ME'. She even underlined it.

Can you guess what I did? Nothing of the sort. I can't, for the life of me, remember how I rationalized it, but I didn't go to her party. I didn't call her.

You know what's really strange though? I still have that invitation, stuffed in a box along with all of the other memories I can't seem to let go of, as if one day I will get the nerve to call the number and she will be on the other end, still twenty, smart and rebellious, and God knows what trouble we'd get up to together.

Man. This is what I'm talking about with long rides. Some people pass out, others read magazines with disinterest, thumbing through with drooping eyes, looking like there isn't a thing in the world that could possibly make them smile or care about anything. Not me.

I still feel weird going to the funeral. All I knew of him was that outer shell, the very most outer layer of what we show one another. I'll be honest. I can't even remember what his face looked like.

Now that I think of it, and I beg your pardon, that's probably how it is with most of you as well. My friends. We thought we knew each other but what we know is already dead skin stretched taut over cardboard cut-outs. If we met up, would we be happy to see one another? Would we remember all those collective memories, communal stories, which we previously forgot? I honestly don't know. But the very thought of it makes me feel kind of nauseated.

I hope that doesn't offend any of you. It isn't personal.

Through the windows, factories gradually gave way to a twilight forest. I regretted I hadn't overcome my little fixation and ordered a drink when dim lights finally flickered to life throughout the cabin.

There is some muted announcement that I am fairly certain no one can understand. Hopefully it isn't something dire, like 'Pull on the lever beneath your chair if you want to live!' Because, if so, there are going to be a lot of dead people in a few moments.

No? Nothing. We continue to rock in place, the lights flicker ever so subtly, and I find myself wondering about Lola again, thinking about how strange it was seeing her on TV all those years later. Pretty soon, I'm drifting even further back in time, as if the story of my life is some sort of walkway and all I need to do is fall half-asleep and I can stroll through it.

In the process, I wondered, could I somehow find myself? Not that outer shell, the face like my dead friend who I couldn't remember. But some inner self.

Who knows. As we get older, these stories get longer and more twisted and tangled until no one, and I mean no one, has the patience to sit and listen to how all the events of your life interconnect and fix on whatever moment you happen to be lodged in. As time speeds up, and it does as you get older, you can feel this approaching: the end of the line, we call it.

On some level, it's probably the same with everyone—you have close friends, you feel what you think are unbreakable bonds, whisper secrets to one another at night, enjoy a beer together after work, however it is that you share life together. Then you notice the crowd begins to thin. With all those who are left, all you have to talk about is the past. You see them at weddings, but you lose them that way, too, and to their jobs, to lymphoma, to simple apathy.

In the time spent sharing space and life with another, a lexicon develops which no one outside that inner circle can penetrate. An almost magical, shared language ripens in the growth of a relationship. With the death or loss of a friend, you lose their company, but you also retain something. You retain the language that you developed with them, rich with nuance, inside jokes, and meanings which have become so layered and subtle, you need only feel them, for they have escaped the conscious sphere altogether.

But here's the kicker: it is a dead tongue, a language you can share with no one else. If you approach new faces with it, you risk alienation. If you never speak this language again, you do a disservice to your past, and find that—maybe not all at once, but eventually—you live in a world that no one cares about any longer. Their indifference isn't the result of callousness, though there is plenty of that to go around in the world. They don't react because they don't and can never really understand. All of those who could are now forever gone.

The world shrinks so slowly, you may barely notice this process, until you find yourself sucking oxygen through a tube like my mother, bless her soul, a liability to the few who stuck around. Maybe it's because we construct our lives in our minds as straight lines, something not unlike this train ride. You get on board, and it takes you on a fixed track from point A to point B. Of course, point A and B are never remembered. Life is always *in medias res*.

We get the messy middle, and it's only in that tangle that we can glimpse ourselves, if such a thing even exists, just for a moment. Like the reflection you see of yourself as you squint out the window, late at night. You see through yourself out into the world beyond, but in the unfocused horizon, you might make out your own face.

I only make out darkness, and a halo surrounding a blurry form. I can see everyone else clearly in the reflection but for some reason I am distorted, and hardly look human.

As my eyes half-close, I have no choice but to continue wandering.

I remember a very embarrassing moment, when I had—and it was completely innocent in its way, I swear—undressed a girl in her sleep. We were both children. And I was dreaming at the time, though I didn't realize that.

Bodies in photographs aren't bodies at all, they are ink and paper, no matter how much you might be able to fool yourself otherwise. A living body has a silent mystery to it that goes beyond artifice, and beyond explanation. When she rolled on her side, I could see two strange objects protruding from her shoulders. Closer inspection revealed that they were a part of her scapula, growing out, covered in clusters of feathers—a vestigial wing, stuck halfway between an eagle and a dragon.

Then I felt my own back, and I could feel the stumps of bone, preparing to burst forth and flower.

—

Hours passed, and even the cabin itself was dark. I was finally drifting off into a dreamless sleep, and for some reason, only at that point glanced at the ticket I had been clutching in my hand all the while. The usher lumbered by, faceless and nearly formless, a shroud of black with an outstretched hand of bone.

He nodded and moved on.

The name on that ticket seemed like it should be significant to me, though it was just my name. Gabriel. And then it hit me. The funeral I was going to was my own.

—

My mother died a few years back. The chemo, the pain, all those things only reaffirmed her faith. Yet for all her faith and struggle, she succumbed as we all do. For her, it was natural to bless the grace of God until the sucking sound of the tube in her mouth sufficed as her final prayer. For me, I had to doubt and put anger in the pouch where the believers store something else. Better there be no God than one that does this to his best Servants.

She was a good woman, though we were alien to one another. I may as well have come from Saturn. And I was across the country when the end came, which made last goodbyes impossible. I don't know what I would have said. Certainly not all of this.

We probably shared little more than genes and a host of forgotten memories. Some might return, little Kodak moments tumbling from between the folds of musty notebooks in the attic. But they will disappear again. Her faith was no choice, and as if to maintain some kind of cosmic balance, I had to be created the opposite. "We are made in his image," clay formed by our maker. But it is always in relief.

When she died, I learned many things about faith, which had been out of reach before. I saw inside it. Faith always re-affirms itself. Lack of faith does the same.

Yet she had named me Gabriel. The archangel who bears the message of God to Man, and who eventually blows the trumpet, signaling the end of the world. I wanted nothing to do with the myth. But maybe she was acting on some divine wisdom, in that moment. Sure enough, I bore the Word.

Trust, faith, they make nothing better, but life is less terrifying if you believe someone responsible is in the pilot seat. When I held her nearly transparent hand in mine the last time we were together, I lied to her for the first time. I told her God was waiting.

"What's his rush?" she joked. I could see in her eyes that she was afraid. Not of the pain, I don't think. The worst of that was over. But something else lingered in her mind, made its way to her mouth, forming that 'O' that begins a question. But it never came.

We sat in silence, the midday sun creating puppet-show patterns as it passed through the fake plants in her room. She had fallen asleep. I wonder what she wanted to ask.

Every time my mother took me to church when I was younger, I had an experience that you might say has colored my feelings for Christianity. Something very odd happened. Or maybe it wasn't so odd? Who can really tell? The odd thing is that anything should be at all. In the face of that, cir-cus freaks seem commonplace.

I remember the creak of the pews, the arcane and incoherent songs we were made to sing in praise of an inchoate saviour. Sex symbol for the soul. I was standing when I noticed the first line of choir girls, singing with such sincerity.

I had to hide my erection behind '1 Corinthians 13' and it refused to go away the entire time I was in the church. I couldn't walk into a church without being beset with elaborate daydreams—one might even call them visions—each class of angels are identical clones, all inflamed with passion, curly hair framing blushing cheeks, their upturned breasts swelling like immortal adolescents, but their crotches were like Barbie dolls.

There was simply nothing down there, as if God had forgotten, or per-haps, being the asshole patriarch that he was, he had designed the angels purely for the sake of bringing pleasure by singing his praise alone—which they did with amazing zeal, again and again, as the preacher would con-tinue some uninspired sermon about who gives a damn. The angels would wiggle, sing, and suck, driven by an insatiable hunger for divine seed. Logos. They were without self, and had no need for any pleasure, save that which comes from pleasing.

But Lucifer looked me eye-to-eye as the lesser angels continued to writhe around us; their mouths all open in endless expectation for the Holy Ghost. He knew what I was thinking about, what I had been thinking about my entire lifetime, of course. He was just like that.

In one of the many, long, imaginary chats I had with him, he told me that being genuine is only a problem for those who are genuine. It is merely fashion for everyone else. He was locked away for no greater sin than being true to his nature. For Polonius, "To thine own self be true" was sophistry. The Genuine demands a Self, something that reaches beyond each moment or act in time.

Lucifer is always himself. That is his curse. And it is mine, for we are as one.

Before you judge the Morning Star, think about this for a moment: he holds out two hands, two futures for you.

In one hand, the deal with the devil: you are rewarded for being false, fake. Nothing more than the mask given to you. The world is a Game that merely demands you hold true to nothing but the rules of that Game. Have no fixed self, and you are capable of anything.

In the other, the path of the Fallen.

You will be persecuted by society. You will be punished, perhaps even killed, for holding fast to what you are. And you can become immortal, sustained by the force of their dreams.

Jesus was brave enough to choose door number two, but how many Christians today would listen to what comes from within and accept death at the hands of their peers?

As a result of rebelling against God, Lucifer was exiled.

As a result of rebelling against man, Christ was crucified.

My mother's example showed me the emptiness of faith. And so Lucifer and I both turned out rebellious, bored. Same thing, if you're stuck being yourself.

How much better to be a series of empty masks, clattering around in the dark? I knew the answer then. I didn't need to ask. The game is rigged. We have been cast into our roles, just like archangels designed to rebel, angels to sing, or men to crave apples. Babies are wise to scream.

"In the end, there are no choices," Lucifer said to me then, in answer to my thoughts. In answer to my life.

And at times like these, yeah, the crazy thought might cross my mind, what if I *was* the Archangel Gabriel, but I had simply lost my faith? It would certainly explain what happened every time I walked into a church. (Though Botticelli hadn't dreamt of what an orgy Heaven is, if so. There really is no slut like an angel).

Anyway, this gave me some pretty ambivalent feelings about going to church. I had to hide my reaction, and though it might fly in a Baptist church, screaming "OH GOD YES!" in the middle of a sermon about capital punishment is just damn awkward. It also wasn't lost on me that invariably, my mother's funeral would be held in a chapel and I really didn't want to think about how that was going to play out.

I'm sorry. I had planned on ending this admittedly strange kind of letter before talking about angels and their genitals, but here we are.

What I'm trying to tell you is this. All my life I've hid from my true nature. I've hid amongst mankind. But maybe I really am the harbinger of the fall. If so, I had no choice. That's really the crux of what I've been getting at here.

Mankind's messenger was born without his faith. No warning blast for you. Least, not one that you will ever hear.

—

Figures seemed to emerge from the mists around me, like the shadows of weary travelers round a campfire. For a moment, I heard all their stories, all of these people born under different names but somehow, beneath it all, I was always Gabriel, always the Heirophant revealing the storm to come. The message always misunderstood. Here are all these lost souls, sharing their tales so they might be written in light by Chatillian scribes.

I shut my eyes and stamp closed my mouth. I just can't. I can't tell my tale any more than I have. It must be scratched out, blotted of meaning. The Order promises eternal life, but I don't want to remember anything anymore.

The voices of the fallen lingered, no longer than frosty breath might grasp the air. I could still hear the train singing its monotone lullaby, and the travelers were forgotten, along with their stories, which I'd so long clutched, an invisible tattoo wrapped round my heart like the letters of my name. G A B R I... So tired. I was so tired I couldn't remember.

—

There were still many miles to travel, an expanse which stretched out before us sleepers like the depths of the Mariana Trench: dark, silent and heavy.

THE SUMMER TREE
BOOK 2: THE FALLEN CYCLE

A GRAPHIC NOVEL

A battle between the light of remembrance and dark of forgetting, a war waged with stories and books as well as swords, guns, and magic. This chronicle is conveyed through the eyes of a girl named Ayta, and the voice of her Gran. A shaman from Siberia, Gran's stories transport young Ayta out of the isolation of her youth and into Alterran, a land of the distant future, facing its own apocalypse.

Ayta is forever an outsider, living half in her Grandmother's world, and the other growing up in the early 00s.

Many of the themes and characters established in the first Fallen Cycle novel are explored from a new angle in this lushly illustrated 4 part series, to be released separately and then together as a single volume.

About The Author

Photo: Jeff Cohn

James Curcio is a bewildered madman with a sledgehammer made of words. That's a bit long to put on a business card, so usually it's said "editor", "creative director", "designer," "professional dilettante" or "cat-wrangler."

This checkered career began around 2001 when he graduated Bard college with the world's most lucrative degree (Philosophy), and co-founded a media collective. Next stop was LA, where he played in the first of several bands, and released "JOIN MY CULT!" with New Falcon press. This was a Burroughs-esque satire about 90s counterculture groups that no one seemed to recognize as satire.

The following decade of "fast life and dissipation" on the Con / Fest circuit gave birth to albums, books, graphic novels, web media series, and essays. That at the least paid dividends in counterculture street cred and free mochas.

Many books and startups later, he's still keeping it irreverent, but has since developed a keener appreciation for fact. He lives with a harem of feral lesbians and lions somewhere in the mountains, probably.

www.JamesCurcio.com

JAMES CURCIO

Made in the USA
Middletown, DE
17 October 2016